"Trevor," she whispered.

The gentle sound of his name made him momentarily forget his troubles, and he went to the bed. The woman lying there wore no makeup. Her pale blond lashes rested lightly against the creamy smoothness of her skin, and her eyes flickered beneath nearly translucent eyelids. Silently he thanked the moon for shining through the window to reveal the loveliness of the woman in his bed.

Was she a guardian angel come to rescue him? He'd often prayed for help, prayed for someone to take away his demons. No one had come.

Last night, right before he'd stepped into the water, he'd asked for forgiveness. He could have prayed for a miracle. He could have begged for help. But all he'd wanted was an end to this agony and absolution for all his wicked ways. Maybe this time his request had been granted.

Maybe this woman was the answer to a lifetime of prayers.

Other Contemporary Romances by
Patti Berg
from Avon Books

TILL THE END OF TIME
WISHES COME TRUE

If I Can't Have You

PATTI BERG

AVON BOOKS  NEW YORK

AVON BOOKS
A division of
The Hearst Corporation
1350 Avenue of the Americas
New York, New York 10019

Copyright © 1998 by Patti Berg
Published by arrangement with the author
Visit our website at **http://www.AvonBooks.com**
Library of Congress Catalog Card Number: 97-94323
ISBN: 0-380-79554-X

First Avon Books Printing: April 1998

AVON TRADEMARK REG. U.S. PAT. OFF. AND IN OTHER COUNTRIES, MARCA
REGISTRADA. HECHO EN U.S.A.

Printed in the U.S.A.

WCD   10 9 8 7 6 5 4 3 2 1

For Bob

Acknowledgments

Many thanks to Ann McKay Thoroman, editor and friend, for loving this book nearly as much as I did, and for giving me unending guidance and support. You're the greatest!

Special thanks to Carrie Feron for her faith in me from the very beginning; Robin Rue, agent extraordinaire, for her enthusiasm and boundless wisdom; and Jen and Lu for Tuesday nights and all the other times in between.

My deepest gratitude to the movie legends of the '30s whose films have given me so much enjoyment over the years, and who provided me with the inspiration for this book. Special thanks to my two favorite stars: Cary Grant—for the smiles, the laughter, and the romance. Errol Flynn—for an infectious laugh, for being a dashing and daring hero, and for having wicked ways. May your memory last forever.

✑ Prologue

July 4, 1938

What a grand night for dying.

Trevor Montgomery gazed at the fireworks exploding over the swaying palms and the magnificent columns of Sparta, lighting the midnight sky with a profusion of sparkling colors. Off in the distance he could hear laughter and loud voices ringing out as partygoers gathered on one of the crowded terraces of Harrison Stafford's palatial seaside estate, eating his food, drinking his liquor, and celebrating Independence Day in the grand fashion people expected from the self-made tycoon.

Trevor had laughed with Harrison earlier in the evening. He'd let his closest friend beat him at a game of chess, and he'd strolled among the other guests with a picture-perfect smile on his face as if he hadn't a care in the world. Inside though, deep down where no one could see, he felt scared, and alone; happiness, he realized, was part of his past. As if in a movie, Trevor had put his keen skills to work this night and deceived everyone. He was an actor, after all. A great actor.

The only one he hadn't fooled tonight was himself.

When the mixture of too many sounds grew loud and oppressive, he'd walked away from the party, wandering through gardens fragrant with roses and honeysuckle and down a meandering path that led to one of the lower terraces and a pool where he'd swum just a few weeks before.

Now, he stood on the marble steps of the Grecian temple Harrison had spared no expense in building, one hand tucked in the pocket of his crisply pleated trousers, the other pressed against a marble column for support. Instead of looking up at the rain of firelight, he cast his eyes downward and studied the reflection of a million sparkles on the calm surface of the pool.

Slowly, he smiled. He couldn't have picked a more glorious night or a more perfect place for his final performance.

Casually, he unbuttoned his white dinner jacket and knelt to retrieve the nearly empty bottle of Chivas Regal that rested by his shoes. One glass of the potent liquor hadn't been enough to satisfy his thirst, so he'd taken the bottle from the bar, surprising no one by his actions. It wasn't the first time Trevor had been seen with a bottle of booze in his grasp, but it would definitely be the last. He tilted the bottle and swigged the few remaining drops of whiskey, no longer feeling the burn in his throat, feeling only the thrum of noise reverberating in his head. He'd consumed a fifth of liquor, maybe more, in the past twelve hours. It was amazing he felt anything at all when his sole purpose had been to completely numb his body and paralyze his mind.

It was no use though. He couldn't rid himself of the horror. Not the blood, not the knife, not the smell of death.

The bottle slipped from his fingers, but he couldn't

hear the shatter of glass on cold hard marble, not when it competed with the crash, crackle, and bang of the fireworks exploding in the sky.

As he had done a thousand times before, he ran his fingers through thick ebony hair, combing back the lock that insisted on falling over his forehead when caught in the cool night breeze. He'd perfected that gesture in front of the camera. Always the tall, good-looking, stalwart hero. Tonight, though, he played the coward.

"Not one of your better endings, Trev," he whispered to himself, then laughed one last time. "There won't be any applause. Not tonight."

Taking a deep breath, he sucked in the scents of star jasmine, closely clipped grass, the obtrusive smoke and gunpowder from the Fourth of July festivities, and, from a distance, the salt air of the Pacific Ocean that he loved and would never see again.

The time had finally come. He closed his eyes, asking forgiveness from the God he'd nearly forgotten, and casually walked down the steps and into the pool. He'd heard of people drowning while in a drunken stupor. Those were accidents, of course, and, with any luck, his friends would believe his death had been accidental, too. Suicide wasn't his style. It was something he'd never even contemplated—until today.

He took one last deep breath as water seeped through the silk of his tuxedo, into his shoes. He willed himself to remain calm, to relax. He let his arms go limp at his sides. His legs and body floated easily to the surface, and he pillowed his face comfortably in the water. His thoughts drifted from his fear of not being able to breathe, to his first screen test, to planting his hands in wet cement at Grauman's, to the friends he would miss.

And he thought about dying, and not having to remember the nightmare.

Water lapped against his ears, a hollow, drumming sound. He heard the faint reverberation of a woman's scream.

A dark void filled him then, he felt tired, he wanted to sleep, and . . .

❧ One

July 5, 1998

"Just a little farther to the left. A little farther. There, right there. Now, put one foot on the running board. Perfect."

Adriana Howard stood in the shadow of a twisted Monterey pine and listened to the clicking of the camera as she watched the photographer dart about shooting left angles, right angles, highs, and lows. Through dark glasses she observed the model being photographed. He stood perfectly still, one hand in his pants pocket, the other resting on the edge of the car as the Pacific Ocean breeze wafted through his hair, blowing a dark black lock over his forehead.

The photographer said he'd found the perfect Trevor Montgomery—but he was wrong. This man didn't have the same broad shoulders, the same slim waist and hips. The cleft in his chin wasn't as pronounced. His eyes didn't sparkle or brood with as much intensity. And he didn't look nearly as good in black tie and tails.

The similarity was remarkable, though, and she could easily see other people mistaking this man for the long-ago film idol. But other people didn't know as much about Trevor; other people no longer idolized the star of the thirties, not the way Adriana did. For her he was larger than life—he was perfect.

No one else could ever live up to the man of her dreams.

Sunlight glinted off the chrome of the Duesenberg, drawing her attention away from the model to the car that had once belonged to Trevor. It looked just as it had that day in the thirties when the Hollywood star had driven it off the showroom floor. It was still painted primrose yellow, the color Trevor had specially ordered. The leather, cared for weekly to keep it soft and supple, was still the same pale green as the fenders. The only difference was that the vehicle now belonged to Adriana—just like most everything else that had once been Trevor Montgomery's.

"Move to the front so I can get a better shot of the hood ornament and grille," the photographer instructed, and the model trailed his fingers over the shiny paint as he moved. Once again Adriana noticed the differences. Trevor had walked with authority, with style. He had been more handsome than Tyrone Power, even Cary Grant, or so the biographies proclaimed; more dashing and daring than Errol Flynn; he was a man every woman desired and all men envied.

He was a man who had enthralled millions—then disappeared, leaving the world to wonder why.

"That should do it, Ms. Howard." The photographer walked toward the car and Adriana met him there, pulling her scarf closer to her face before she reluctantly shook his hand. "I'll get these developed within the week and let you take a look. This Duesey with that model of mine ought to look pretty good on the cover of your catalog."

Mr. Paxton capped the lens of his camera and slung it over his shoulder. "I was wondering, Ms. Howard, what are the chances of you letting me snap a few photos inside Mr. Montgomery's house in Santa Barbara? Anyone can shoot photos here at Sparta, but Montgomery's home is a complete mystery—to me and everyone else. I hear you've kept it just like it was sixty years ago when he dropped off the face of the earth."

Adriana shook her head at his request. Sparta, this majestic estate, had been her home once. Now it was a tourist attraction, and the intrusion of photographers didn't matter. But Trevor Montgomery's house—the unpretentious adobe she now called home—was completely off-limits to prying eyes. Her privacy was too sacred to admit outsiders.

"I'm sorry, Mr. Paxton. I don't allow anyone to take pictures of the rancho."

Paxton shrugged as if being turned down was nothing new. "Well, it never hurts to ask."

He rubbed a speck of dust from the hood of the car, then turned and looked pointedly at Adriana. "Just one more thing, Ms. Howard. Do you think he did it?"

That question again. Oh, how she hated that question. "Did who do what?"

A broad grin crossed Mr. Paxton's face. "The murder, of course. Do you think Trevor Montgomery killed Carole Sinclair? Surely you have an opinion."

"I believe in facts, Mr. Paxton. Not opinions."

Adriana looked at her watch as she walked toward Mr. Paxton's van. It was early afternoon, the photo shoot was over, and she didn't want to talk, especially to a photographer. "The grounds will be closing soon. Thank you for coming all the way out here."

Adriana looked from the photographer to his van, a subtle hint that his services and his conversation were no longer needed or wanted today. The model had already climbed into the passenger seat. His tie was loosened and he was blowing cigarette smoke out the window, obviously uninterested in the history and beauty of Sparta, or the mysterious death of Carole Sinclair.

To her dismay, Mr. Paxton didn't seem in any hurry to leave. Instead, he uncapped his camera and shot a few more frames of the mansion that resembled the Parthenon in size and detail, then, without warning, twisted and began snapping photos of Adriana.

Her hands flew up to block her face. "What do you think you're doing?"

"It's just a few photos, Ms. Howard. People never see you in public. Now I've got a few souvenirs to prove you really do exist," Paxton quipped before opening the driver's door and putting his camera inside.

She hated having her photo taken, hated having her picture in papers and magazines so people could gossip once again about Harrison Stafford's heiress.

She moved closer to the van and faced Paxton head-on. "I didn't pay you to take photos of me, Mr. Paxton. What I did pay for was this shoot, and every piece of film you've used. Unless you want to forgo payment, I'll expect those negatives of me to be returned with the other negatives and the developed photos."

He grinned, undaunted by her remarks. "I suppose that could be arranged."

Reaching into his shirt pocket, Paxton pulled out a cigarette and lit it. She wished he would leave, but he casually leaned against the van and stared at Adriana. "I've heard rumors that you know the truth about the murder and about Trevor Montgomery's disappearance."

"You shouldn't listen to rumors," she said coolly. She had dodged questions like that for years. Just because she now owned Trevor Montgomery's home, his cars, and nearly all his other belongings, just because she was reputed to be an expert on his life, didn't mean she knew the truth about that night.

Again she looked at her watch. "I have an appointment, Mr. Paxton. You have my business address. Please send the photos—and the negatives—when they're ready."

"Why don't I deliver them personally—to your home. Santa Barbara's not too long a drive from L.A."

Adriana shook her head. "Send them to my store in Hollywood. Please."

Mr. Paxton sucked on his cigarette, blew out a puff of smoke, and saluted her with two fingers before he climbed into his vehicle and drove away.

Adriana watched the silver van cruise slowly down the winding cobblestone road, hoping that was the last she'd see of Mr. Paxton.

"You're deep in thought."

Adriana spun around at the sound of the familiar voice. "Just another nosy photographer," she said, smiling softly at the elderly gentleman. "Hello, Elliott." She wrapped her fingers lightly around his wrinkled hands and leaned close, briefly touching her cheek to his.

The old butler pulled away in his ever-so-proper manner, yet the smile he offered was warm and comforting. "I should have come outside earlier. From the look on your face it appears that man's upset you dreadfully."

"No more than any other photographer," Adriana answered, brushing off the incident as if it didn't matter. "Actually, my mind was wandering. That's all."

"Back to the past, I suppose," Elliott said, standing formally in his conservative black suit and tie, looking just as dignified as he had when she'd come to Sparta twenty-three years ago, at the age of six.

"You do realize, Miss Adriana, that you're becoming more like Mr. Stafford every day."

"I can't think of better footsteps to follow in," Adriana responded, fondly remembering Harrison Stafford, her guardian and mentor, who'd given her everything a person could ever wish for, except the privacy she craved.

Pulling the black silk scarf from her head, she dropped it on the passenger seat in the Duesenberg, and took Elliott's arm in spite of his half-hearted attempt to draw away again. She didn't have to hide from Elliott, only from curiosity seekers.

Walking up the steps leading to the mansion, she snapped a yellow rose from a bush blooming in a marble urn, and tucked the fragrant flower into Elliott's lapel. He was nearly eighty and much more a father figure than a servant. Over the years he'd lectured her about proper etiquette and perfect posture. He'd told her it wasn't polite to swear. And he'd stood at her side and cried right along with her when Harrison Stafford had been buried.

She missed Elliott DeLancey more than she missed living at Sparta. Fortunately she could still come and go as she pleased, and Elliott would always be there, as a special reminder of the life she'd once known.

When they reached the massive carved entryway, Elliott opened the door and stepped aside for Adriana to enter the foyer. She set her black-velvet handbag and sunglasses on a marble-topped table underneath a six-foot oval mirror framed in 14-carat gold leaf. Adriana had grown up in these rooms filled with treasures collected from around the world. The bed she had slept in as a teenager came from the Palace of Versailles, and as a child she'd romped around marble statues of the gods that had been salvaged from Greek and Roman ruins. She'd played hide-and-seek in rooms where intricately painted mummy cases and suits of armor stood at attention. She'd eaten off gold-plated dishes that were a gift from a king, and played with dolls that had once belonged to a queen.

She wasn't the least bit in awe of this place. After all, at one time Sparta had belonged to her. That was a long time ago, though. Even so, each time she walked through the doors she felt at ease, comforted. This was once her home. She'd been loved here, cared for by one of the greatest men who'd ever lived, and his memory filled every room.

"Will you be staying for dinner?" Elliott asked, interrupting her thoughts of the past.

"Thank you for the offer, Elliott, but I can't stay long. I'm going upstairs for a while, then go down to the gardens and pool."

"Perhaps you can come another time. This big old place isn't the same without you."

"I'll be here for Thanksgiving. Christmas, too."

"That's a long way off. Come before . . . if you can."

Adriana brushed a quick kiss across Elliott's wrinkled skin. "I'll do my best."

She watched Elliott cross the room, his highly-polished black shoes clicking on the floor, his tall, gentlemanly figure reflecting in the black and white squares of marble tile until he disappeared into another room, and she remembered the most important reason she'd come to Sparta today.

It was the fifth of July—eight years and one day since Harrison Stafford died; sixty years and one day since Trevor Montgomery disappeared. She'd come every year on the Fourth to pay her respects . . . to remember. She'd never been late before, but this time work had interfered. Harrison would definitely have understood her need to take care of business first.

She ran up the circular staircase, the high heels of her black-velvet sandals clicking on the marble.

Slowly she opened the door to Harrison's rooms and stepped inside. This part of the house was off-limits to the public. This part of the house still belonged to her. She'd bequeathed all of the land to the state, from the top of the hill to the valley on one side and to the ocean on the other. She'd given them the magnificent mansion, too. But not all of it. This wing of the third floor she'd kept. Besides her, only Elliott, her closest friends, and the housekeepers were allowed inside.

There was a fifty-seat screening room where she'd sat with Harrison and watched old movies. There was a small indoor pool where she'd helped him exercise after the first of his three strokes. The library was filled with his favorite books, and framed photos of friends, acquaintances, and a huge assortment of pictures of Adriana—from age six to age twenty-one.

He'd been the best of friends, and she missed him terribly, especially when she remembered their days together.

"Come in. Come in," Harrison had encouraged her the first time she'd sneaked into his suite. In the dead of night, after her father, the curator at Sparta, had drunk himself to sleep, she'd explored other rooms in the mansion, but it had taken months before she'd found the nerve to check out Harrison Stafford's inner sanctum.

"I didn't think you'd be awake," she'd said, walking slowly across the room and standing close to his chair.

"I never was much of one for sleeping at night." He'd folded his paper in his lap, closed his eyes, and leaned his head back into the soft, burgundy leather. "In the old days we had parties here till the wee hours of morning. When everyone was gone, then I'd sleep."

"I've never been to a party," Adriana whispered,

fearing the old man might be falling asleep.

His eyelids jerked open. "Never? Surely you've had a birthday party or two?"

"No, sir. My father doesn't like parties." Adriana backed away. "He wouldn't like me being here, either. I'd better go."

She remembered the deep frown on Harrison's face, and the way he brought one index finger to his lips. "I can keep a secret. Can you?"

Adriana nodded. She'd never tell her father she'd been talking to his employer, that she'd been wandering around the mansion. He'd told her not to, and he didn't appreciate disobedience.

"Good. I get tired of sitting around this place at night with no one to talk to but Elliott. Besides, he doesn't like the movies the way I do." He leaned close to Adriana. "Do you like watching old movies?"

"My father doesn't like . . ."

Harrison interrupted her with his laughter. "Does your father like anything?"

"Gin," Adriana answered innocently.

Harrison's laughter died just as Elliott, mussed hair, disheveled robe, and bare feet, pushed through the main door of Harrison's suite.

"I heard noises in here. Is something wrong, Mr. Stafford?"

"Of course not. Do you think you could sneak downstairs and find us some cookies and milk. We're going to have a party."

"We?" Elliott questioned.

"We," Harrison stated flatly. "All three of us."

There were many such parties over the years, the only fun she was able to steal under her father's watchful gaze.

Ten years later, Harrison stood by her side at her father's funeral.

"What do you plan to do now?"

"I don't know," she'd said. "I have no family, no one else to stay with."

Harrison had reached for her hand and squeezed her fingers. "Then it's settled," he said, wiping a tear from his cheek and clearing his throat. "You'll stay at Sparta as you've always done. You've been like a daughter to me, so if you have no objections, we'll make it all nice and legal."

The unshed tears she'd wanted to cry for her father emptied from her eyes. Her throat tightened, and she pulled her hand from Harrison's and threw both arms around his neck. "I love you," she'd said, for the first time in her life.

"I love you, too," he'd repeated. It was the first time anyone had ever said the words to her, and she tucked the moment deep in her heart.

She crossed the sitting room and went down a hallway to the theater, the place where she and Harrison had spent a great amount of their time, where Harrison had recounted so much of his past. Adriana thumbed through the library of home movies and took out a favorite of his taken in 1936. It was one of many films shot at Fourth of July parties over the years.

She slipped the reel onto the projector, wound the film through all the proper twists and turns, then sat down in Harrison's chair and flipped the switch built into the arm.

The room darkened and the projector light flicked on.

The screen seemed to glow the moment Trevor Montgomery stepped in front of the camera, flashing that picture-perfect movie-idol smile, and warmth spread through Adriana's chest.

He tossed down a glass of champagne, then swept a beautiful woman across the floor, weaving elegantly around statues, up and down stairs, around marble planters overflowing with flowers, and amongst other couples. Trevor was so graceful—so perfect—and he smiled and laughed at every turn.

Harrison had been too big, too clumsy to be much of a dancer, so he hadn't even tried. He preferred watching his friends. Adriana knew the feeling well. She'd been too tall and felt too awkward to dance, and she avoided every opportunity to learn that social grace. She'd had the desire, but she'd been too self-conscious.

Being a mystery woman and rarely going out into public had been such an easy role to assume.

Trevor Montgomery, however, loved being in the public eye. He was everything Adriana wasn't, and he didn't appear to have a worry in the world. For him, dancing, smiling, laughing, and having fun in life was as much a part of him as acting—and he did all of it effortlessly.

If Trevor Montgomery had been around when she was growing up, Adriana thought that she might have forgotten her fears and learned to dance.

She'd idolized Trevor Montgomery the first time she'd seen one of his swashbucklers. At six, she'd wanted to be a pirate, and Harrison had given her a sword, an eye patch, and a bandanna to tie up her hair. With rubber swords he'd fenced with her in the library and around the pool, and when they were quiet again, Harrison would talk about his friend for hours.

In her teens she'd fallen in love with Trevor. While others her age fell for rock stars, she was mesmerized by the gentleman who had looked debonair in either buccaneer breeches or black tie and tails. The man she saw on the screen was suave, worldly, and handsome. He was everything she'd wanted, and she'd constantly begged Harrison to relate more tales of their friendship. She felt she knew Trevor intimately, but she'd always longed to know more.

Where had he disappeared to, and why?

But no one could tell her. No one knew. There were only the rumors, stories Adriana refused to believe.

All she knew was that she'd been born in the wrong decade. She belonged in the thirties. She belonged to a time when women were graceful and elegant, and men were sophisticated and gracious. If she'd been alive back then, she might have found a man to marry. No one today suited her. She wanted the life that Harrison had introduced her to, a life that consisted of friends like Trevor Montgomery.

Sadly, that life no longer existed, except in her dreams.

When the last of the film flicked through the projector and clacked again and again, she flipped off the switch and stared at the blank screen. The movie was over—but the desire for a life she couldn't have stayed with her.

She left Harrison's suite, quietly went down the stairs, and out to the gardens. She wandered the paths around manicured lawns, beds of red and pink roses, fragrant white gardenia, and geraniums of many hues. She pictured the place as it had been sixty years before, bustling with stars and politicians, the rich, the famous and the infamous, and wished she could step back in time to meet the people who had become so familiar to her.

If she could, her life might be fuller.

In the distance, she heard voices, and knew she'd have to hurry if she wanted time alone before the next tour group arrived at her favorite spot. She stole a red rosebud from one of the many bushes as she traversed the paths and terraces. Trevor Montgomery had stolen a rosebud once in one of his earlier movies. He'd kissed the velvety petals and tossed it on top of the coffin of the woman he loved. He'd prayed for her to return, and Adriana had wept, just as she did every time she watched that scene. If Trevor Montgomery had a grave, she'd toss a rose and make a wish. . . .

She let the notion wither away, and laughed at her thoughts. She had a life many could only dream about. She had no business feeling sorry for herself, or wanting something that could never be.

She swept her hand over marble statuary of water nymphs and mermaids, sea horses and dolphins, and stopped momentarily when she came in sight of the Poseidon Pool, with the sky and the mountains a backdrop to its beauty. She never tired of this spot. She'd been drawn to its splendor since she was a child. Back then she thought the pool was magical; she still saw it that way today.

She wrapped her arm around a column, placing her cheek against the cold, hard marble, and looked wistfully at the pool, the last place Trevor Montgomery had been seen. Sixty years ago a woman had claimed that she'd seen Trevor's body lying facedown in the water. No one else saw it. No one else believed. Sixty years ago Trevor Montgomery had disappeared—and he was never seen or heard from again.

It was a long time ago, Adriana thought. She closed her eyes, knowing the vision of Trevor Montgomery's body floating on the surface of the pool would come to her as it had over and over again, year after year. She'd never told anyone about the vision, not Harrison, or Elliott. Definitely not Stewart, her attorney. Not even Maggie, his wife, who would have believed. She'd never told anyone how vivid Trevor seemed when she saw him in her dreams—the ones she had when she was awake during the day and the ones she had asleep at night. They'd think she'd gone mad.

Secretly she enjoyed having him come to her this way. She'd lost Harrison, the only man she'd ever loved. If she didn't have the dreams, she'd lose Trevor, too.

And dreams of Trevor were so much better than being with or loving anyone else. She'd dated a few men, but they'd been interested in her money, not in her, and they had no interest at all in her passion for the glamour days of Hollywood.

Life was so much better alone with her dreams.

She let go of the column and walked to the edge of the pool, looking down at the surface that glittered with sunlight. She closed her eyes to shut out the glare. "Why did you go away?" she asked. "My life might have been normal if you hadn't." She laughed at those words. Nothing had been normal about her life. How could she possibly think Trevor Montgomery might have made a difference?

She kissed the red rose she'd picked, tossed it into the pool, and watched it drift on the surface. It was a lot like Trevor dropping a rose onto a casket. Of course, he couldn't wish his lover back any more than she could wish for Trevor's return, but it didn't matter. She liked to dream, she liked the movies, and that scene had been one of her favorites, especially Trevor's words and the loving way he'd whispered them.

She closed her eyes and softly repeated Trevor's lines. "Come back to me. Please. Come to me."

ℒ❧ *Two*

Trevor Montgomery shot out of the water, arms flail-
ing, his chest tight, as if he were being pressed in a
vise. His heart beat rapidly and he sucked in great
gasps of air, fighting for breath, for control, for life.

The blessed darkness that had engulfed him had
thrust him out of its grasp, into the bright light of
day. What was happening? He'd wanted to end his
life. He'd wanted all the horror and fear to disappear, so why was he trying to breathe? Had he been
frightened of death and changed his mind at the last
moment? Was self-imposed drowning impossible?

Oh, God! He didn't want to live, yet his body was
battling with his mind, and winning.

He swam, and when he reached the edge of the
pool, he flattened his hands against his temples. The
pain was unbearable. The alcohol he'd consumed
made his head spin, and the sunlight glinting off the
water and shining into his eyes caused even more
pain. He couldn't even think.

Sunlight? Why? How? It should be dark, he
thought. Except for the sun in the sky, everything
was the same, but where was the shattered bottle of
whiskey?

A red rosebud floated in front of him, and he

grasped it tightly in his hand. He put it to his nose, smelling its sweet fragrance. He thought he might be in heaven, or hell, or maybe even purgatory. He thought his attempt to blot out all memories might have worked, but the scent of the rose made him face reality.

He'd failed.

He tucked the rose into his pants pocket and climbed out of the pool, his shoes sodden, his dinner jacket and trousers clinging to his body. Water dripped from his clothes, his fingertips, his hair, even the end of his nose, leaving a puddle at his feet.

From somewhere near the pool he heard voices and wondered if his friends were coming to look for him. He couldn't and wouldn't let anyone see him this way. They'd seen him drunk before, but never disoriented and disheveled. He had to get away quickly so he ran, hiding behind a statue of Poseidon surrounded by half a dozen mermaids.

He peered around the sea god's muscular back and watched a group of men, women and children heading toward the pool. People on tour, he assumed, snapping photos of the statuary, the ornately tiled pool, the magnificent temple. He'd never known Harrison to allow strangers on the grounds, but maybe they were friends, people Trevor didn't know. Still, it seemed so odd.

The woman at the head of the group cleared her throat and the twittering among the others hushed. "I'm sure you've all heard the rumors about Trevor Montgomery."

She was speaking about him. *Him?* But why? Her words came out in a hushed but dramatic tone, and he listened intently. "This is the spot where he was supposedly seen floating. Of course, no one ever found his body, and no one's seen him since. That, as some of you might recall, happened sixty years ago."

Trevor frowned at the woman's preposterous words. What had she said? Sixty years ago? He must not have heard her correctly. It was only last night.

He plowed his fingers through his hair, digging them into his scalp. Pain pulsated in his head, the whiskey grabbing hold of his senses. There was no logical reason for anything that was happening. God, he'd wanted to die. Had he gone insane instead?

Finally, the woman ceased talking about him, about the pool, and through blurry eyes he watched the group file away to a different part of the estate.

He sat down on the cold, hard marble and rested his head against the wall behind him. He thought about the woman's words. *Trevor Montgomery disappeared. Sixty years ago.* He had to be dreaming, that was the only explanation, and he wished he had a bottle of whiskey so he could try to drown out one more nightmare. He'd never had hallucinations, never created people in his mind who spoke of crazy, insane things. This was a first.

But it was the first time he'd tried killing himself, too.

What on earth had happened?

Pulling himself to a standing position, he tightly grasped the curving fin of a mermaid for balance.

Maybe it was for the best that his friends and acquaintances weren't around. He could find his car, drive home, clean up, and no one would ever know what had occurred, what he had attempted to do. And then he wondered if the police would be waiting at his home when he returned. Would they take him to jail? Would he stand trial for murder?

"Dear God," he prayed, even though he wasn't sure he believed in God. "Let me remember what happened."

Releasing the fin, he tested his balance by putting weight on his legs. He felt steady enough, although the nausea hadn't subsided, or the throbbing in his head. In spite of how he felt, he had to get away. He had to.

He started out slowly, edging his way around the pool, then willed himself to go faster before anyone saw him. He took the stairs two and three at a time, ran across terraces, down rose-lined paths. Things seemed so different, lush, overgrown, not like they'd looked yesterday. But he'd consumed too much whiskey. Things were bound to look different.

When his breath came in short gasps, when he thought he could run no more, he found his car. At least he remembered where he'd left it. Thank God one thing in this crazy nightmare he was living through seemed familiar.

Reaching into his pockets for the key, he found a handful of loose change, his money clip with a dozen or so folded bills, and his cherished gold doubloon from Jack Warner. What had he done with the keys? He checked the ignition, hoping he'd left them in the car. But it was empty.

He had to get home. He could think better there, figure out what was going on.

He went to the other side of the vehicle and searched the glove box. An eyeglass case. A white handkerchief edged in lace. Things that did not belong to him. And no keys. Gripping the edge of the windshield, he pressed his forehead against the warm metal frame. He rested there for a moment, trying to think of something else to do, some other way of starting the car. But it was useless. All he could think of was the pain in his head and his desperation.

The sweet scent of a woman's perfume wafted up from the car's interior. He thought he might have found the wrong vehicle, but he tilted his head to the left and through blurry eyes he saw the gold nameplate in the middle of the Duesenberg SJ's dash: *Custom built for Trevor Montgomery—1932.* At last, something familiar, something that was his.

A woman's scarf lay on the passenger seat. He lifted it, running the long length of black silk through his fingers. The perfume's fragrance was stronger now. It permeated the scarf. Had a woman been with him on the drive north, a woman he couldn't even remember? Was there anything else in the car he didn't remember?

A yellow-and-green plaid blanket rested next to a tan leather briefcase on the backseat. Just like the scarf, they didn't belong to him and didn't look familiar. He'd brought nothing with him on this trip except the tuxedo he was wearing. There'd been no need for anything else—he hadn't planned to stay . . . or to leave.

A wave of nausea wove from his stomach to his throat to his temples. He rested his head on the side of the car, telling himself if he got through this, he'd never drink again.

That was a lie, though. It would take more than this god-awful feeling to make him stop. He'd tried before, and failed. This time he had good reason to drink, and he wanted a bottle—now.

He wanted his keys, too, and suddenly he remembered that he'd kept a spare hidden under the rubber floor mat in the back.

Climbing into the car, he sat on the edge of the seat and the heavy door swung shut behind him. He searched but found nothing. Kneeling on the floor, he looked further, running his fingers over and around each crack and crevice. Water still dripped about him. His head ached and his stomach lurched from looking down and being in a tight, confining space.

And then he heard voices and footsteps.

He was going to be seen. There might even be a photographer around who would relish catching him this way. Louella claimed to be a friend, but she'd be in seventh heaven if she could catch the always-perfect Trevor Montgomery in such a vulnerable spot.

He wasn't about to let that happen. Louella's gossip column normally didn't bother him, but today it did. His image could easily be ruined.

He crouched low on the floor and pulled the blanket he'd seen on the seat over his head and body. The driver's door opened. He heard the distinct creak of leather as someone sat on the seat, heard a key grinding in the ignition and the roar of the engine. *His engine.* The engine of the car he'd driven yesterday from Santa Barbara to Sparta at well over eighty miles an hour on the winding coastal road. Why was someone else driving his car? Why did someone else have his key?

"I'm sorry I can't stay, Elliott."

It was a woman's voice he heard. A soft, sweet, very feminine voice.

"Perhaps you could drive up one evening just for dinner."

"I'd love to, but I'm so busy with work right now. Maybe I can make it in a few weeks."

He heard a light sigh of frustration before the man spoke again. "That's all I can hope for."

They were quiet, too quiet, until Trevor heard the kiss and their good-byes. They weren't lovers. He could tell the difference. He'd kissed many lovers, many friends, and many young stars who'd been both.

What the hell was he thinking about? He was hiding under a blanket on the floor of his very own car, strange things were going on around him, yet he was wondering if the woman sitting in the front seat might be worth kissing. The melodic lilt of her voice mesmerized him. The hint of her perfume filled his senses. Had she dabbed it just behind her ears, or behind her knees and on the soft bend of her elbows, too? The fragrance he'd noticed on her scarf wafted throughout the car, drowning out the scent of tobacco he remembered from yesterday. Now there was only the sweetness of a woman. God, he must be crazy. He must be a lunatic. Instead of thinking about making love, he should be climbing out of the car and asking for an explanation, finding out what the hell was going on. But he didn't want to be seen—not like this.

The car jolted to a start, and he felt the rumbling of the wheels as the Duesenberg moved over the cobblestones. He had no idea where he was going, no idea who was driving, no idea why queer things were happening, but none of that mattered. Not at the moment. His eyelids had grown heavy, and the warmth and darkness under the blanket, along with the gentle rock and sway of the car and too much whiskey were lulling him to sleep. Maybe when he woke he'd be at home again. Maybe the nightmare would have ended.

He prayed for both those things. And slowly, with the sweetness of her perfume and the soft music on the radio easing the pain in his head, he slept.

Trevor woke when the engine stopped. He heard the driver's door open and the sound of a woman's high heels clipping on pavement, moving away from the car. He waited until the footsteps silenced, then shoved aside the blanket and cautiously peered over the door of the convertible.

Thank God! He was parked in his own driveway, right next to the small, Spanish-style ranch house he'd bought in 1931. Two bedrooms, two baths, nestled in the middle of one acre overlooking the Pacific. Just big enough for one person, maybe two, if he'd ever cared enough to find someone to share it.

He'd probably never share it with anyone now.

Once the police showed up, he'd be locked away for good.

That didn't matter now, though. He was at home, and an odd, clenching sensation caught in his throat. His eyes burned. In spite of what had happened with Carole, in spite of all the crazy things he'd heard around the Poseidon Pool, in spite of some stranger driving his car, and the fact that he might soon be in prison, he was home, and once again on familiar ground.

In the moon's glow, he could easily make out the features of the tall, willowy woman who'd been driving his car and now stood at his kitchen door. Her hair was the color of corn silk. Parted at the side, it waved softly about her face and caressed the tops of her shoulders. She wore black high heels and a jumpsuit that looked like a sleeveless black-and-white tuxedo, the pant legs billowing slightly in the evening breeze. The black scarf he'd touched earlier trailed from her fingers. She was absolutely beautiful. Everything about her matched the sweet, feminine warmth of her voice.

Was she some starlet he'd picked up? Had he drunk so much that he couldn't remember her?

She stepped into the house, turned on the light, and disappeared from view. Trevor hopped over the side of the convertible and hid behind the hedges, watching, listening, waiting for a chance to get into the house.

He laughed at himself. Hell, this was his home. He should walk right in. But the stranger might see him. He'd rather wait until he could clean up, make himself presentable, and look like the Trevor Montgomery the world was used to seeing.

He peered around the edge of the open door. The woman was nowhere in sight, but just as he started to step inside, he heard her footsteps on the red terra-cotta tile. Again, he crouched between a hedge and the white adobe wall, and watched her walk to the car.

Tall, leggy, and blond. Three of his favorite things in a woman. Of course, he liked them short, too. Plump hadn't mattered either, and he'd never been averse to redheads or brunettes. He liked the way this one walked, with a little sway to her hips, a slight swing to her arms. She climbed into the car once again, started the engine, and he watched in amazement as the garage door opened of its own free will and she drove the Duesey inside, right next to his cherry red '32 Auburn Speedster. The cars were in the right places, but how had she opened the door?

And who did that strange-looking green vehicle belong to that was parked alongside the garage?

He couldn't think about those things now, though. He had to get into the house while she was still in the car.

Except for the kitchen, all was dark inside. He longed to get to his closet, to get out of the tuxedo that had shrunk on his body and now felt tight, confining, and damp. Quietly, he maneuvered through darkened rooms, bumping into a living-room sofa that had been moved since yesterday morning. He didn't want to think about who had moved it or why. Instead, he rushed down the hallway and into his bedroom.

He tried to ignore the fluffy white bedspread and ruffled pillows he could see in the moonlight shining through the window. They weren't the least bit masculine. They weren't anything close to what he'd had on the bed the last time he slept there. Had his housekeeper decided to make changes without consulting him first? He had so many questions, but none of them mattered. Not now.

He opened the closet, pulled the string to turn on the overhead bulb inside, and gripped the edge of the door, feeling the nausea once again. There wasn't anything masculine in sight. No tuxedos, no top hat. He rummaged through the garments hanging on the rod. Long silk and satin gowns. Colorful blouses and skirts. High-heeled shoes, low heels, sandals. An assortment of purses on a vertical shelf next to the shoe rack.

Where were his things? The handmade loafers he'd bought in Italy? The leather jacket he'd bought in Spain? Where were the cashmere suits, the starched white shirts, the dozens of silk ties?

His breathing grew deep and rapid. What was happening?

Again he heard her distinctive footsteps on the tiles.

Quickly he grabbed the ring at the end of the pull string, accidentally ripping it from the short chain near the bulb. He balled up the string in his hand, pulled the chain to rid the closet of light, and closed the door. Without making a sound, he pushed to the back of the tightly stuffed closet. Hidden in the dark, he saw nothing, and smelled only the sweet perfume that had filled his senses since he'd entered his car.

He stayed out of sight while the woman moved around his bedroom. When it appeared she wasn't going to open the door, he pushed aside the hanging garments just enough so he could peer through the louvers.

Light shone from an overhead fixture and from a small Tiffany lamp next to the bed. The slats in the door made it difficult to see her clearly, but he watched her step out of her heels and unbutton the collar that fastened at the back of her neck. He thought he should close his eyes, that voyeurism wasn't right, but he couldn't take his eyes off of her. Her arms were long, her back slender. She unfastened the button at the back of her waist and let the outfit slip to the floor. She was wearing the skimpiest panties he'd ever seen, nothing more than a few little straps across the back. He couldn't see the front of her, but his imagination ran wild. She bent over the bed, picked up a silky white negligee, and slid it over her head before she turned around.

He ran his fingers through his hair, frustration more than evident in the depth of his breathing, in the way his body was reacting of its own accord.

He could see the slight roundness of her breasts through the white satin—small, much less than a handful. The fabric molded to her body, and he could see every curve, her slender waist, her narrow hips, the line of those almost nonexistent panties underneath.

A thick lump caught in his throat, and he nearly gasped when she reached under the shimmering satin. Her fingers slipped around the straps at her hips and she pulled the panties away, sliding them slowly down her legs, stepping out of the small scrap of fabric one foot at a time.

Life wasn't the least bit fair, he decided. She'd put on a strip show, teasing him with just a hint of what was yet to come, then covered up the best before he got a peek. Maybe he had died and gone to heaven, or maybe, just maybe, he was in hell, having to watch naked women for all eternity without being able to touch. Was that to be his punishment for a life that had been less than perfect?

She lifted the black-and-white garment from the floor, slipped it onto a hanger, and moved toward him. He crouched at the back of the closet, hoping the clothes would quit swaying before she opened the door.

All he could see when she stepped in front of him were her slender ankles, her feet and toes, all tanned a nice shade of golden brown, and he wondered if the rest of her body would be tanned as nicely if he

saw it in bright light without the hindrance of louvers.

When she closed the door, he moved through the
clothing again and watched her shove something
black and rectangular into a metal box on top the
dresser. She climbed under the frilly white covers,
fluffed the pillows, and wiggled until she got comfortable.

She picked up another black object, pointed it at
the dresser, and he saw snow and heard static in the
glass-fronted box. Words flashed across the screen.
He could just make out the beginning, something
about it being illegal to make copies. He tried to
make sense of the words, but they disappeared and
something familiar met his eyes. The Warner Bros.
emblem blazed across the screen in black-and-white,
and in big letters, *Trevor Montgomery in Captain Caribe*. He smiled, not at his name, but at the thought
that she had a movie theater right here in the bedroom. He liked the concept, liked the idea of lying
in bed and watching gorgeous young starlets, maybe
a bevy of Busby Berkeley beauties, parading before
him as he fell asleep. He'd heard talk of an invention
like this, but he didn't think it had been developed
to this extent. The woman must be rich to afford
such a thing.

He watched her resting against the pillows, finding the lady in his bed much more interesting than
his own small image. She cried during the love
scenes, wiping her eyes again and again. She smiled
when he climbed the mast and swung from one ship
to another, pulling out his sword and fighting the
soldiers who'd soon be hanging from the yardarm.
And close to the end, her head gently dropped to
one side, and Trevor knew she'd gone to sleep. The
movie played on, the credits rolled, and once again
snow and static appeared on the screen.

The noise didn't disturb her sleep and he hoped

his movements wouldn't either as he retied the string below the light bulb, crept out of the closet, and started for the door. Maybe somewhere in the house was an explanation for what was going on. As far as he knew, it was July 5, 1938. Two days ago he might have murdered a woman; last night he'd tried to commit suicide and failed. Today someone strange—but beautiful—was living in his house, driving his car, and even worse, he'd heard all that talk about his disappearance—sixty years ago.

It didn't make any sense at all.

He headed for the door, then stopped when he heard a soft sigh from the bed.

"Trevor," she whispered.

The gentle sound of his name made him momentarily forget his troubles, and he went to the bed. The woman lying there wore no makeup. Her pale blond lashes rested lightly against the creamy smoothness of her skin, and her eyes flickered beneath nearly translucent eyelids. Silently he thanked the moon for shining through the window to reveal the loveliness of the woman in his bed.

Was she a guardian angel come to rescue him? He wasn't sure if he believed in God, but he'd often prayed for help, prayed for someone to take away his demons. No one had come. Maybe things hadn't been bad enough.

Now they were. His life seemed to be crashing in around him. Nothing made sense anymore.

Last night, right before he'd stepped into the water, he'd asked for forgiveness. He could have prayed for a miracle. He could have begged for help. But all he'd wanted was an end to the agony and absolution for all his wicked ways. Maybe this time his request had been granted.

Maybe this woman was the answer to a lifetime of prayers.

*   *   *

Adriana jolted awake. Somewhere in the house someone or something was rummaging, and for the first time since moving into Trevor Montgomery's home, she felt a tremor of fright.

Maybe the neighbor's cat had sneaked inside when she'd come home. That had happened before, but in daylight. The cat had gotten into a pile of papers set aside to be recycled and had pushed and pawed and made a bed. Perhaps the curious, mischievous feline was at it again.

Sliding out of bed, Adriana tiptoed across the cold tile floor, careful not to make any sound. Down the hallway she moved, silently, slowly, more than halfway afraid it might not be a cat disturbing her belongings. She reached the doorway to the living room but stayed hidden, listening to the definite rustle of paper.

Peeking around the edge, she saw a man sitting on the sofa, hunched over looking at the books on her coffee table about Trevor Montgomery.

She jerked back, cowering behind the cover of the wall. Holding her breath, she prayed that he hadn't seen or heard her. *Get out of here now,* she told herself. *Run to the neighbors. Run to your bedroom and try to get out a window before he finds you.*

No, she couldn't run away. She couldn't risk him taking her precious belongings.

Oh, God! Her heart beat heavily. A lump had formed in her throat, and her legs and arms tingled with fear.

Stay calm. Don't panic. He's in the living room looking at books. He didn't sneak into your bedroom. He isn't rummaging through drawers or hastily throwing silver and crystal into a bag.

He's not here to hurt you. Just tell him to leave.

Forcing herself to breathe slow and easy, she again peered into the living room. The man hadn't moved.

Her gaze darted to the front door. Locked, and he

was directly in its path. There was no easy way to escape if her foolishly brave plan didn't work.

For the first time in her life, she wished she had a gun for protection. She settled for the tall, sleek, but heavy bronze sculpture of a man in top hat and tails sitting on the table just inside the room. The carving would make the perfect lethal weapon, unless the intruder had something better, like a gun or a knife. That thought horrified her.

She kept her eyes on the stranger and stepped quietly into the room.

The man lifted his head and looked toward the bar. He hadn't heard her or seen her . . . not yet anyway. She raised the statue to her shoulder, just in case she had to use it. Call the police, she told herself. Let them get rid of him.

She grabbed the phone.

The intruder's head jerked around and, even though his face was cloaked in shadow, she could see the intensity of his eyes as a thin beam of moonlight slashed across his face.

Oh, God.

The phone slipped from her fingers and fell to the floor, its dial tone ringing annoyingly in the stark silence of the room.

Run for help. Don't try to be brave. She knew she shouldn't be standing there, but she felt completely hypnotized by his eyes.

"Who are you?" she asked, her voice wavering in fear. "What are you doing here?"

He didn't answer her question. He just stared.

Her chest rose hard and fell even harder as she tried to breathe, tried to calm her fear. She should run, but, as if in a dream, she couldn't move.

The intruder rose from the couch, and in the dim light of the reading lamp, she could see the unkempt nature of his clothes. His jacket sleeves and pants were far too short, and it looked as if he'd been swimming in his shoes. Was he a vagrant dressed in a salvaged tuxedo, a homeless person who'd selected her house for a night's lodging?

"I asked you a question," she said, attempting to sound in control of the situation. "Who are you?"

"Put down the sculpture. I won't hurt you."

His voice sounded familiar. Deep, resonant, refined. She didn't know this person; she didn't know anyone who lived on the streets, and it didn't matter that she knew that voice. She didn't want him here.

"You don't belong in my house. Get out . . . now." An icy chill raced up her spine when he didn't move. "Please," she begged.

"It's you who doesn't belong," he stated flatly.

She wished she could see more than just his eyes, see who was uttering such nonsense.

"This is my house," he continued. "I'm the one who should be asking *you* to leave."

"You're crazy. This is my home. Mine. Do you understand?"

"I'm not crazy," he said emphatically, his voice deepening. "You're in my home; you've been sleeping in my bed. I don't know who you are, I don't know what's going on, but I want things back to normal again."

Adriana backed against the wall. He was mad; totally and completely insane. Who was he to make such strange accusations?

"Who are you? Tell me. Please," she repeated.

Slowly he bent down and picked up one of the books about Trevor Montgomery that sat on her coffee table. He held it in front of himself and she could see Trevor's beloved face on the front.

The man glared at her again.

"According to these books of yours," he said with an old familiar laugh, "I'm a man who disappeared in 1938."

Three

The woman reached behind her, flipped a switch, and the room filled with light.

She stared at him for the longest time, and a flicker of recognition crossed her face. Her eyes narrowed slowly in question, then widened again as she drew in a deep, quick breath. She backed away, bumping into the wall, but she continued to watch him as if she didn't want him out of her sight.

Her lips began to tremble, and the white silk of her flimsy gown shimmered as her body shook.

All of Trevor's earlier thoughts about her being an angel had diminished. His doubts arose when he began reading the books about himself, about all the drinking and carousing and womanizing, about his involvement in Carole's murder, and about his disappearance. God! He hadn't disappeared. He'd been yanked out of one decade and thrown into another. If this woman had been sent to him by some heavenly being, why was he trapped in hell?

He watched her raise the statue to her shoulder like a ballplayer would a bat. Did she plan on swinging it, or throwing it across the room directly at his head?

Her fingers tightened around the bronze. Her gaze

shifted from Trevor's eyes to the book he held, then back again to his face. "Who are you?" she asked again.

How could she ask such a question? Everyone knew him. He was one of the most photographed and well-known movie stars in the world, whether he looked it or not. Had the events of the day before changed him so much?

Somehow he managed a short, brisk laugh, and pointed to the cover of the book. "I'm surprised you don't recognize me. You've got half a dozen books about my life."

She didn't laugh. Instead, her voice quivered when she spoke. "I'm not in the mood for jokes."

"I'm not either," he blurted out. "But let me tell you, lady, either I've gone totally insane in the past twenty-four hours, or someone's playing the joke of the century on me."

"You must be insane. Why else would you break into someone else's home?"

"This is my home," he protested again. Wasn't she listening? "I bought it in 1931."

Her frown deepened and she shook her head. "You're crazy. Get out. Now!"

She swept the oddly shaped telephone from the floor with one hand, and somehow managed to keep the heavy statue balanced on her shoulder with the other. She stabbed her finger three times against the receiver and Trevor heard three awkward beeps.

What was she doing? If she was calling the police, he had to stop her.

He ran the short distance across the room, jerked the phone from her hand, and slammed it back down on the table.

From the corner of his eye he saw the statue swing toward him and he pivoted. She missed his head, clipping his shoulder instead. Pain shot through his arm. His fingers tingled, but somehow he managed to wrench the sculpture from her and toss it across the floor. When she tried to run, he grabbed her wrists and pushed her against the wall.

"Don't try that again. And don't call anyone." He couldn't believe the sound of his voice—the anger, the fear, making him sound like a lunatic on the run from the law.

"Don't hurt me," she begged, as she attempted to tug her hands free from his grasp. "Please."

Dear God! What was he doing? Had he truly gone mad?

He stared into her frightened blue eyes and saw the reflection of his own. He looked just as frightened as she. Maybe more so. He should let her go. She didn't deserve to suffer because of his rage, his frustration.

He loosened his hold and in less than a second she struck out with her foot, landing a blow to his shin. A dull ache ricocheted up his leg, but the pain wasn't strong enough to slow his actions. She was a hellcat, a woman who had taken over his home. He wasn't about to let her get the upper hand.

His fingers tightened around her wrists again and he wedged her between him and the wall. He could feel the tremors in her body as he pressed against her—thighs against thighs, chest against breast. He didn't want to hurt her, he just didn't want her to move. What he was doing wasn't right, but at least now she couldn't call the police or hurt him again.

Tears slid from her eyes. He didn't want to see them. He didn't want to know her fear. He rested his beard-roughened cheek against her soft one, holding her head to the wall so she couldn't lash out at him with her teeth. He closed his eyes for just one moment, trying to think of what he should do next, but the only thoughts that came to him were visions of those nightmarish photos of Carole Sinclair he'd seen in the books he'd been looking through: platinum blond hair matted with blood; white-satin sheets; and a naked body, slashed and gouged and streaked with something dark and horrible.

The photos were black-and-white, but Trevor remembered the color quite vividly—dark reddish brown.

He remembered the slit across her throat, the wounds in her chest, the gashes on her arms and legs, and he remembered the warm, sticky feel of her blood on his hands, his arms, his face, and on the mattress where he lay beside the dead woman.

His eyes flashed open. He didn't want to see the horror anymore.

The woman twisted and he was suddenly confronted by a pair of terrified blue eyes, eyes that bothered him just as much as the sight of Carole's battered body.

"Please let me go," she whispered.

"Promise you won't run? Promise you won't call the police?"

She nodded slowly, but he didn't believe her. Looking into her eyes, he could tell she was lying. The minute he dropped her hands, the second he moved away, she'd bolt, or she'd grab that statue again and try to kill him.

He'd never hurt a woman before, but he was hurting this one now, and he hated the fact that he had no other choice.

He could feel her heavy breathing as her chest rose and fell against his. He could feel her blood pumping rapidly through the veins in her wrists. He stood so close he could smell the sweetness of her perfume, the scent masking the vile metallic odor of blood that had permeated his senses since he woke in Carole's bed of death.

Another tear slid down her cheek. "Please," she begged.

He eased his hold on her wrists and saw the redness where his fingers had dug into her skin.

The horrid realization of what he was doing settled in. He'd hurt her. A woman who didn't deserve any of this.

Anger and frustration swept through him as he stumbled backward, getting as far away from her as he could. He stopped when he reached the bar. He needed a drink. He needed to figure out what was going on. He needed to know who the woman was and why she was in his house.

She hadn't moved away from the wall, she hadn't run, she hadn't picked up the phone again to call the police. She just stood there rubbing the red marks on her arms, breathing heavily as she stared at him.

"Who are you?" he asked.

"It doesn't matter," she told him, her gaze darting to the phone then back again to his eyes. "The police should be here soon. Why don't you leave and we can pretend none of this ever happened."

"I'm not leaving," he stated flatly. This was his home. He wasn't leaving unless he was carted away.

"They'll arrest you."

He laughed at her words. "It doesn't matter. Not anymore."

Trevor pulled the stopper from one of the decanters and filled a glass with whiskey. He ignored the bucket of ice, preferring his liquor neat instead of watered down. This way he could enjoy the slow burn as it hit his mouth and throat.

He tossed down a healthy swallow of liquor and stared at the woman over the top of the glass. "You're free to leave if you want. I won't come after you."

She didn't move, but her hands clenched into fists at her side. Her pretty blue eyes narrowed in anger. "This is my house," she shouted. "Mine! I'm not going anywhere till you get the hell out."

He downed another gulp of whiskey, thinking

that she must be just as crazy as he, and shrugged. "Then we're at an impasse."

"I'm sure the police will see things differently."

"Then, I'll wait around."

He heard the deepness of her sigh. Beautiful—but gutsy. He wondered how long it would be before she came at him again.

Absently, he turned his attention from the woman to the things around him. Everything sat on the bar just as he remembered it. Glasses. Decanters. Ice bucket. Even a white terry cloth towel embroidered with an elegant gold *TM* hung from a gold-plated ring. The bar hadn't changed. The living room hadn't changed either, except for the way the furniture was arranged. So much was the same; so much was different.

Why couldn't he remember what had happened? Why didn't anything make sense? How could sixty years of his life have gone by without him knowing?

The woman by the pool had said he'd disappeared sixty years ago. The newspapers in the house said it was 1998. Nothing made sense.

He'd vanished. That's what the books had said. No one knew why. No one knew where, but each author had a theory. Each author told a different story about his life before his Hollywood years and during.

He drained his glass, again studying the woman across the room as he drank. She was cold, shivering. Her arms were clasped over her chest, over that flimsy silk nightie, and she just stood there staring at him as if he were mad. Hell! Maybe he was.

Or maybe this was some kind of nightmare. Maybe he'd wake up and life would be normal again. That's what he'd hoped when he'd awakened in bed with Carole. But that was no nightmare. That was death—horrible and brutal.

Damn! He just wished everything would go away.

Ignoring the woman, ignoring the blue of her eyes that glared at him, he again filled his glass with whiskey.

He thought about the clippings he'd seen in the books. He'd seen them all before—when they'd first appeared in the papers. Now, though, his Hollywood years had been wrapped up neatly on glossy paper and bound in leather. He'd reread columns by Hedda and Louella, and stared at photos taken at the Brown Derby and some of his other haunts, places where he'd eaten and drunk and danced with friends. Page after page he'd turned until he'd reached the photos taken the night before his "disappearance." In one, he and Carole Sinclair were locked in a tight embrace next to his Duesenberg following a premiere party at the Trocadero. In another, Carole was blowing a kiss to the photographer as they sped away to their own entertainment.

Then he'd seen those photos of Carole.

He remembered the blood so vividly. And the knife.

He plowed his fingers through his hair and tossed down another swig of whiskey. He'd forgotten so much, why did he have to go on remembering the nightmare?

A scraping noise from across the room startled him. The woman. He'd nearly forgotten about her.

Was she a fool? Why hadn't she run away? Why hadn't she called for help? Why was she picking up that statue and putting it back on the table, as though straightening the house really mattered right now?

A sudden pounding on the door made him jerk around. Through the window he saw headlights in the driveway. He heard static and voices—a police radio.

Muscles tensed in his neck and shoulders. How

did they know he was here? She hadn't spoken to anyone.

He twisted around to face the woman, but she'd already moved across the room. Her fingers fumbled as she unlatched the chain, turned the lock, and yanked open the door.

A uniformed officer stepped over the threshold, and Trevor knew his freedom was coming to an end.

"We received a 9-1-1 call from this address," the officer said, quickly scanning the room before he turned his attention back to Adriana.

"Did you make the call?" he asked.

Adriana nodded as the officer quickly inspected her face, which she knew was streaked with tears. His investigative eyes glanced over her silk night-gown, her bare arms, and hesitated at the red skin circling her wrists. His gaze darted across the room to the man standing at the bar, and just as he'd inspected her, he did a quick appraisal of the stranger before looking back in her eyes. "Did you make the call?"

All semblance of speech froze in her throat, and she hugged her body, for the first time feeling the chill of night. Or was she feeling the shock of what was happening?

She tilted her head and looked at the man in the shrunken tuxedo, at the books on her table, and again at the intense brown eyes that continued to watch her.

He couldn't be Trevor Montgomery. He was insane, and she wanted him out of her house.

Looking back at the policeman, she swallowed deeply. "Yes, sir," she finally answered. "I made the call."

"Do you mind telling me what the problem is?" the officer asked, scanning the neatly kept living room.

There was no broken glass. No objects thrown on

the floor. How could he possibly believe there was a problem?

The stranger didn't look threatening—just drunk and disheveled. He looked like he might belong in the house, especially the way he swigged down his whiskey, walked over to the sofa, sat down, and picked up her favorite book, *Trevor Montgomery— The Man and The Mystery*.

From the corner of her eye she could see the officer turn his attention back to her, but she couldn't turn her gaze away from the stranger. He lifted the book, holding it so she could see the cover—see the face. Slowly, he smiled at her—the same smile that was on the cover.

Another shiver raced through her body and goose bumps rose on her arms.

The officer cleared his throat. "Excuse me, ma'am. Do you mind telling me why you called for help?"

"I was afraid."

"Of him?"

"Yes," she hesitantly told the officer. "He . . ." She touched the tender skin around her wrists and took one more look at the stranger. His smile had disappeared. His shoulders slumped, and the book fell to the floor.

But he hadn't stopped looking at her. *Please, help me*, his eyes seemed to beg. *I'm telling the truth, you must believe me.*

She looked down at the floor, hating to see the despair in his eyes, frightened of the words he'd uttered earlier about being Trevor Montgomery. She couldn't let those things sway her from turning him in.

She bit her lip and turned toward the officer. "I heard noises," she began, ready to tell her story. "I thought someone might have broken in."

The policeman took a pen from his pocket, absently clicking the end again and again, and Adriana was suddenly reminded of today's photo shoot and the photographer who'd tried snapping pictures of her.

An overwhelming knot caught in her throat as she thought of other photographers, the ones that had refused to leave her alone, the ones that had sold pictures of her to the gossip rags.

The same thing could happen again.

Oh, God! She'd tried so hard to stay out of the public's eye, to keep her picture out of the papers. If she turned this man in, the press would have a field day at her expense.

If she turned this man in, she might be locking away the man of her dreams.

No. How could she think such a thing? He was a stranger. She had to believe that. He was a stranger whose sudden appearance could thrust her into turmoil if the press learned of this incident.

She'd get rid of him herself. She'd get rid of the officer, too.

"Are you all right, ma'am?" the officer asked.

She was staring across the room but seeing nothing as she rubbed her arms, trying to rid herself of the cold and her fear. She sighed deeply, trying to regain her composure. "I'm sorry, Officer. I should have called back when I realized I'd made a mistake."

"Mistake?"

She laughed lightly, taking a brief moment to think of a story to tell. "I heard noises. I thought a burglar might have been in the house, but I hung up as soon as I realized who it was." She nodded toward the stranger, then leaned close to the officer, and whispered, "He drinks too much. I've tried to tell him to stop, but he won't."

She smiled sweetly, trying her hardest to make the officer believe. She'd seen so many movies, surely she could draw on the acting talents of hundreds of stars to make her story sound believable.

For one brief moment she wondered if she was doing the right thing, but she glanced at the stranger again, at his hauntingly familiar brown eyes, and knew she couldn't turn him in.

"I know I shouldn't indulge him," she continued, "but when he's in this condition he's afraid to go home to face his wife. It's not the first time this has happened. The last time I wasn't home, so I gave him a key, just in case it happened again."

She was talking too fast. *Slow down*, she told herself, *or the officer will sense your lie*.

"He says he knocked, but all I heard was someone wandering around out here. When I thought there might be an intruder, I called 9-1-1."

"You don't mind having a drunk in the house?" the officer asked, frowning as he looked at the stranger.

"I mind, but he's a friend."

The officer raised a skeptical eyebrow. "You're sure?"

She nodded, hoping she'd put on a good enough show.

He looked at her arms again, his gaze trailing all the way down to her hands. "What about your wrists? Did he do that?"

He had, and he might do it again. *No*, she told herself. *He won't do it again*. She'd seen the horror in his eyes when he'd pushed her against the wall. He'd been frightened, just as she was frightened.

"I was wrestling with a friend," she answered, trying to laugh it off. "We got a little carried away."

The officer grunted out a laugh and shook his head in frustration. He poised his pen over his clipboard. "I need a few details for the record."

"This information isn't given to the newspapers, is it?"

"They've got access to it."

"Names, too?"

"It's just a log of incidents. No names at all, but I suggest you and your friend here play a little less rough in the future. Then you don't need to worry about calling for help or having people you don't want to know find out."

Trevor quietly watched the scene playing out across the room. Warner Bros. would pay a mint to have someone with that woman's acting skills on contract. She was doing a damn fine job deceiving the officer but, hell, couldn't he see the fear deep in her eyes?

Trevor saw it plain and clear, and couldn't help but wonder why she was making up stories about what had happened when she seemed so frightened. Why didn't she have him arrested? He deserved it, considering the way he'd pushed her against the wall.

He looked across the room, watching her gently massage the redness around her wrists. They'd be black-and-blue tomorrow. God, she didn't deserve what he'd done to her any more than he deserved her help.

He finished his whiskey, keeping his head tilted toward his glass, hoping no questions would be directed at him, but his concentration and gaze remained fixed on the woman and the policeman.

Too many minutes dragged by as she answered questions. He suffered the brutal looks from the officer, and, finally, the woman closed the door when the policeman departed.

Silence stood between them for long moments until the headlights backed away and disappeared.

"I've helped you all I can," the woman said, her hand still wrapped around the door knob. "Leave. Please."

"And where do you propose I go?" Trevor walked to the bar and leaned against the polished wood to steady himself. "This is the only home I have."

"It's my home," she corrected.

"Of course. I'd almost forgotten," he said sarcastically. Hell, why didn't he just apologize to her and leave?

He filled his glass again and raised it to his lips. This time his fingers trembled on their own. He tried to steady his hand. He'd never shaken before; not like this.

The tremors were bad, but even worse was the way the woman stared at him. He wasn't a drunk. This wasn't delirium. Some hellish thing was happening.

He slammed the glass on the bar, and it shattered, spraying shards of glass and amber liquid over his hand, the shrunken length of his sleeve, his unbuttoned jacket, and wrinkled shirt.

He felt the sting and stared at the trickle of blood on his fingers, grabbed the towel from the bar, and gripped it tightly to stop the flow.

Looking up, he saw the woman's frightened eyes. He wanted to grab her, hold her, tell her he wasn't a madman. He wanted her to believe him because maybe, if she believed, he might believe he was sane, too.

He plowed his fingers through his hair, then turned around and looked at his own bloodshot eyes in the mirror over the bar. His cheeks were hollow, his chin and jaw coated in heavy black whiskers. The circle of skin below each eye was dark and swollen, his face red and blotchy.

Dear, God! What had happened to the Trevor Montgomery he normally saw in the mirror?

Turning slowly, he looked at the woman at the door and took a deep breath. "I have no memories of your time, your present," he said in a low, hesitant voice. "Apparently I have no home any longer, and if the things I read in that book are true, I doubt I have any friends."

She opened the door wider. "I think you'd better go."

He had no energy to argue. It wouldn't do any good, anyway. She'd already formed an opinion about him, and she wasn't about to change her mind.

He grabbed a full decanter of whiskey and walked toward the woman, hoping she would offer some sympathy, a helping hand, or at least ask him to stay. He needed someone to talk to, someone to help make sense of this lunacy happening around him. He needed to stay in his own home, the only place that still seemed sane.

But she did nothing but step back and give him plenty of room to walk through the door.

Trevor stopped at the threshold. "I wanted to die," he said, looking into her eyes that held many emotions, especially contempt. "I would have, too, but something went wrong. I don't know how. I don't know why." He looked past her to the inside of his house one last time. "Thank you for not telling the officer about me."

"I didn't do it for you. I did it for me," she said. "What was I supposed to do, tell him you're Trevor Montgomery?" She laughed lightly. "He would have thought I was crazy."

Trevor smiled, shaking his head. "I'm the one who's crazy. Not you."

"Please leave," she repeated.

He owed her his freedom. The least he could do was grant her request, although he had no idea where he'd go.

"I'm sorry for what happened," he said as he stood in the doorway.

She didn't acknowledge him, though, she just looked over his shoulder and out at the night sky.

He smiled softly and stepped through the door. She closed it tightly, and he could hear the sounds of bolts and chains locking him out of the only place where he had thought he might be safe.

Leaning against the door, Adriana stared across the room to the bar where the intruder had stood, drinking her whiskey, gazing at her with bloodshot eyes that looked vaguely familiar.

He'd implied that he was Trevor Montgomery. She didn't believe it. It wasn't possible, but the stranger had sounded like someone she knew.

Was it the fear of photographers and having her picture in the papers that had kept her from turning him in, or was it the familiar voice and eyes?

Any other man—or a man who'd had a so-so smile and dull, boring eyes—who had broken into her house, shoved her against a wall, bruised her wrists, or made her think she was going to die would have been on the way to jail by now.

She supposed her intruder should have been on his way there, too.

How could she have let her fear of gossip and those piercing brown eyes that begged for help keep her from telling the truth?

She pressed her fingers to her temples, confusion making her head ache.

It wasn't just the fear of photographers, or his eyes or voice that had made her lie. It was the disheveled hair and that one single lock that hung over his forehead in spite of the many times he'd brushed it back with his fingers. She'd seen Trevor Montgomery practice that gesture again and again in the movies.

What was she thinking of? The intruder didn't look like Trevor—not at all like the man she'd idolized, the man whose flawless features had graced the movie screen.

Trevor Montgomery would never have worn a

rumpled white dinner jacket, or been attired in clothing at least a size too small.

Trevor Montgomery would never have hurt her,
either.

She should have turned him in. If he came back,
if he touched her again, she'd call Stewart and let
him deal with the intruder. There had to be some
way to keep him away from her and keep her safe
from the press, too.

She crossed the room, sweeping the bloodstained
towel and broken pieces of glass from the bar into a
wicker trash basket, taking the decanter he'd emptied into the kitchen.

Flipping on the light over the sink, she turned on
the hot water and shoved her icy hands under the
stream. But not even the heat could take away the
trembling in her fingers.

She meticulously scrubbed the crystal with dish
soap, took a linen towel from a drawer and dried it
till it sparkled. She wiped away all traces of the man,
wanting to forget he'd ever been in her house.

She turned off the light, and through the window
she saw him standing near the garage. He held the
decanter he'd taken with him in one hand. His other
hand was tucked into his pants pocket. He was gazing toward the window. Had he been watching
while the light was on? He couldn't see her now, not
in the dark, but she could see him clearly. His familiar stance. A well-known profile when he turned
from the window and looked toward the ocean.

She watched as he tilted the decanter to his lips
and took a drink. How could he continue to drink
that way? How could he possibly stand? That container had been full when he'd left the house, and
he'd downed part of another while he'd been inside.

Rumor had it that Trevor Montgomery drank hard
liquor every night—all night. Rumor had it, too, that
no one had ever seen him pass out, and that he'd

always been the first to show up on the movie set in the morning. He may have had a drinking problem, but it hadn't interfered with his work.

He was a consummate professional. Every book, every old friend had said the same thing.

The man standing outside couldn't possibly be Trevor Montgomery. Yet, beneath the whiskers, behind the bloodshot eyes, was a familiar face. He'd spoken few words, but his tone had the same resonant qualities as Trevor's—part British, part upper-crust Chicago with a touch of bad-boy charm thrown in when he laughed.

And that smile. How could she possibly turn him in after she'd seen that smile? She'd seen it so many times in the movies. It was Trevor's smile.

But there was no way Trevor Montgomery could disappear on July 4, 1938, and turn up in her living room on July 5, 1998—without aging a day.

She set the decanter on the counter instead of returning it to its rightful place at the bar, and watched the man for just a few more moments.

The Trevor Montgomery she'd imagined, heard about, and studied in pictures had been more self-assured. He'd stood a little straighter, laughed and smiled more.

Adriana touched her reddened wrists. They'd be bruised tomorrow. She'd seen dozens of movies starring Trevor Montgomery, and never, not even once, had he ever hurt a woman.

But that was in the movies, where life went according to script. Maybe she didn't know as much about his real life as she'd always imagined.

The man outside might bear some resemblance to Trevor Montgomery—like the model she'd seen at Sparta—but they definitely weren't one and the same. Besides, if Trevor Montgomery were still alive, he'd be over ninety years old. The man standing outside couldn't be much more than forty.

The man outside was a stranger, an intruder, and Adriana planned to put him out of her mind.

But she couldn't, not with him staring at the window where she stood.

She continued to watch as he took another swig of liquor, ran his fingers through his hair, and walked across the lawn toward the sea. He could walk for miles once he got to the beach. Maybe an early-morning fisherman would find him and take him in. Maybe the police would find him, think he was a vagrant, and arrest him for being drunk in public.

It didn't really matter anymore what happened to him. He was gone. Let him be someone else's problem. Adriana didn't want to be tortured by her nagging thoughts about him any longer.

She went to her bedroom and climbed back into bed, but the stranger didn't leave her thoughts. She leaned into the pillows, and looked at the videotapes on the shelf next to her TV. *The Scarlet Coast* and *Treasure By Night*, two of the pirate movies that had made Trevor Montgomery a star, the dashing, daring hero who stole the hearts of millions. The man outside couldn't possibly be the man she'd watched so many times.

Scanning other titles, she stopped at *One More Tomorrow*, the movie Trevor had won an Oscar for, the film glorified by the critics, and shunned by moviegoers because they didn't like the image portrayed by their favorite star.

Adriana climbed from bed, removed *Captain Caribe* from the VCR and replaced it with *One More Tomorrow*. Sitting on the edge of the bed, she fast-forwarded to the scene where an alcoholic Trevor begged forgiveness from the woman he loved. His eyes were bloodshot following a week-long binge, his hair disheveled, his clothing rumpled. His face was darkened with a stubble of beard and swollen circles surrounded his reddened eyes.

She froze the frame on her screen and studied the man who'd been glamorous in every other film.

There was nothing glamorous at all about a drunken Trevor. He looked totally different. He looked like a man in pain, in distress. He looked like a man who needed help.

He looked like the intruder.

She didn't want to believe it. She couldn't. But in spite of her fears, something about the man made her feel compassion.

Stopping the tape, Adriana stepped into a pair of shorts and tennis shoes, and pulled a baggy sweater over her head. She didn't believe the man outside was Trevor Montgomery. She didn't know what she believed, but she knew if she ignored him, she'd always wonder about the truth.

The man could be a liar. He could be a fake, a look-alike wanting to capitalize on the mystery surrounding Trevor Montgomery.

At the moment, she'd rather believe either of those things than to believe that Trevor Montgomery might have traveled through time.

$\mathscr{L}$♥ *Four*

Adriana stood at the top of the twisting wooden stairs, searching the beach below for the man who'd invaded her home and her thoughts. She tried to push aside the fact that he'd hurt her; instead, she remembered how incredibly lonesome he'd looked when he'd walked out the door. He'd looked lost. He'd looked like a man who had no reason to live. He'd even told her he wanted to die. She'd never felt compelled to take in strays or interfere in other people's lives, but if his body washed up on the shore the next morning, she'd feel guilty for not attempting to help.

When the moon peeked out from behind a cloud, she saw him standing where the waves gently lapped on the shore. His arms were hanging limp at his sides, one hand still gripping the decanter. He frightened her, but she couldn't let him stay down there alone. Maybe she could get him to a hospital, to a psychiatrist, to someone who could help.

She also wanted another opportunity to look at his face, to see his smile. As much as she didn't want to believe it, there were some startling similarities between this man and Trevor Montgomery. The ebony color of his hair; the lock that fell over his brow.

There was that distinctive cleft in his chin. And that smile. Trevor Montgomery's smile had warmed many of her lonely nights; the intruder's smile—she hated to think it—could easily do the same.

If he hadn't smiled at her, if she hadn't seen his eyes or heard his voice, he might be locked up now, and she'd be safe in bed.

Instead, she was thinking of doing the craziest thing she'd ever done in her life—helping a madman.

A cool breeze teased her hair as she climbed down the steps leading from the edge of her lawn to the beach below. With each step she asked herself why she was letting herself get involved. She liked her solitude; she didn't like getting mixed up in other people's business; she despised drunks.

The man walking into the water was different, though—she didn't know how or why, but he seemed to need her. He obviously didn't have anyone else.

She stopped at the bottom of the stairs and looked at the man who now stood knee-deep in water. She looked at the whiskey decanter in his hand, at his disheveled clothes. He was a drunk; possibly a vagrant or someone poor and down on his luck.

He was everything her father had told her to hate.

But this man needed her, and she wanted to be needed.

Stars twinkled overhead and the bright moon cast a glow across the sea. Adriana walked to where the tide left a trail of foam on the beach and rubbed her arms for warmth while she watched the stranger.

He tilted the bottle to his mouth and drank. When he was done, his arm dropped lifelessly to his side, and the crystal container slipped from his fingers into the water. It bobbed up and down a time or two, then drifted off with an outgoing wave.

He was a picture of desolation with his shoulders

sagging, his head bent. She knew he was suffering; knew he was confused.

He stepped farther into the sea, and the water lapped at his thighs. Adriana froze in place. She should go to him; stop him from trying to end his life—if that's what he planned.

A wave splashed over her feet, trying to pull her with it as it rolled back out to the sea, urging her toward the stranger.

He walked farther into the ocean. Water splashed against his hips and his coat floated on the surface, twisting about him as each wave rolled in and out.

Slowly his face turned heavenward.

Was he praying for help?

She had to go to him. She had to.

She took a step into the water, then another and another, but the surf fought every one of her movements. Her tennis shoes were being sucked up by the murky sand. Cold water bit at her skin, slapped at her shorts.

She stroked the water away with her hands and arms and pushed herself deeper into the ocean. She was waist-deep. She was chilled to the bone. But she had to get to him.

Water splashed about her as she neared him. She heard nothing but the sound of the waves and her heart beating hard and fast.

She gripped his arm and his head jerked around. Dark brown eyes pierced hers. Swollen, bloodshot eyes—just like Trevor Montgomery's in *One More Tomorrow*.

She pushed her thoughts away, telling herself she'd help the man simply because he needed her; she wasn't doing it because he bore such a strong resemblance to the man she'd idolized most of her life. No, she wasn't that superficial. Or was she?

Wind and water slapped at her face, and an unexpected wave knocked her off-balance. She slid below the surface as the undertow pulled at her feet and legs. She struggled against the current, but it was too strong. She choked on a mouthful of salt water; her sweater weighted her down.

She couldn't breathe. She couldn't get back to the surface. Oh, God. Was she going to die in her attempt to help a stranger?

Fear pulsed through her veins until she felt strong hands around her waist. The same strong hands she'd felt hurting her wrists. Was he going to help her? Or hold her down?

Suddenly she felt air against her cheeks. She was able to breathe, and she spit out water and gasped for oxygen as he pulled her against him. Once more their chests met, their eyes. Once more she struggled to free herself, but he held on tight.

Salt water streaked his face; it slicked back his hair. His dark eyes bore into hers with more intensity than she'd ever seen in a man. She wanted to look away, but she couldn't.

She knew those eyes. They'd stared at her from a movie screen, from her television, from books. They were Trevor Montgomery's eyes.

And those lips. She'd seen close-ups of them just before Trevor had kissed his leading lady.

Trevor Montgomery's lips and eyes had made millions of women swoon, and right now they were making it difficult for her to breathe.

She wanted to look into those eyes forever. She wanted to be kissed by those lips.

No! She wanted to be kissed by Trevor—not this stranger.

She struggled again, but he wrapped one arm about her waist and pulled her even closer. His free hand smoothed wet strands of hair from her cheeks, and he kissed her. Softly, oh so softly.

She didn't want to like it—but she did, even though he tasted of salt water and whiskey. She liked the way his body pressed against hers, the hardness of his chest, the strength of his arms, the touch of his fingers on her neck. She liked. . . .

My God! What was she doing? This kiss was wrong. Her thoughts were wrong. The man was unbalanced, mad.

Suddenly the softness of his kiss turned to passion. His lips were hard against hers, his whiskers scratched at her face. He was holding her tight, tighter.

She wanted to get away.

This was wrong. So very wrong.

She pressed her hands against his chest, trying to push him away, but the kiss intensified. This had to stop. It had to.

Without another thought, she slapped the side of his head.

He jerked back. His breathing was short and raspy. His eyes were redder than before, full of fear, sadness.

He didn't look at all like Trevor Montgomery.

She had to get away. She'd made a big mistake coming out here, thinking she could help. How could she forget that he was mad, that he'd tried to hurt her?

Her father had been right about men. Why did she continually forget?

Pushing away, she struggled for shore, her heavy, water-laden sweater dragging against her as the waves battered her back and forth.

It seemed an eternity before she reached the beach. She'd lost one shoe in the surf, the other slogged as she ran toward the stairs. Had she escaped? Was she free of the man she never should have gone to?

She screamed when a hand clutched her arm and spun her around. Dark brown eyes pierced hers.

He was gasping for breath, his brow was furrowed with pain and too many other emotions she didn't want to see.

"I'm sorry," he said, his chest rising and falling heavily as he spoke. "I don't know what came over me."

Adriana pulled out of his grasp and stepped back a few feet. "Don't touch me. Don't ever touch me."

He shoved his hands into his pockets. "Why did you come out here?"

Adriana looked away. She couldn't bear looking into his tortured eyes. She took a few steadying breaths, trying to remember why she'd wanted to help when it was such an insane idea. "Maybe I'm just as crazy as you are," she muttered, more to herself than in answer to his question.

"I'm not crazy," he whispered, "but everything around me is." He stepped into her line of vision and looked at her once more with eyes that yearned for understanding. "My life, even the world as I knew it, is gone."

Maybe he'd been hurt. Maybe he had amnesia. There had to be some logical explanation for his actions. She tried to stay calm, tried to think and talk rationally. "Were you in an accident? You could have a concussion," she stated, looking for any signs of injury.

Slowly he shook his head. "When I woke up yesterday it was 1938. Suddenly it's 1998 and I haven't aged a day. Ask me any questions you want about the twenties and thirties and I can answer them. Ask me something about the forties, even this decade, and I can't tell you a thing." He turned away from Adriana and looked toward the ocean. "I'm not mixed up. I've just somehow skipped the last sixty years of my life."

Adriana moved to his side. She started to put a comforting hand on his arm, then drew away. "I know a good psychiatrist . . ."

"No doctor in his right mind would believe what I have to say. How could they, when *you* don't even believe me."

"Why should *I* believe your story? You broke into my house—"

"You drove me here from Sparta," he interrupted. "I was in the backseat of the Duesenberg."

"That's not possible. I would have seen you."

"I hid under a yellow-and-green blanket in the backseat. You kissed a man good-bye. When you went to bed, you watched *Captain Caribe*."

How could he possibly know about that, unless he'd been in her room? She backed away slowly, wondering if he'd been watching her all evening?

"Don't be frightened of me, please," he begged. "I'm not going to hurt you. I told you that before."

Adriana rubbed her wrists lightly. "You've already hurt me."

"I didn't mean to."

"You could do it again."

"I won't. Please. Believe me."

Adriana did believe him, but she didn't understand why. Still, she wanted him safely away from her. "Isn't there somewhere you could go? Family? Friends?"

"I left them all behind more than half a century ago."

Adriana frowned at his words. Was he going to keep up that story forever? "What do you want from me?"

He smiled softly. "Let me stay with you."

"No!"

"Just a few days. That's all. I won't hurt you. I won't even touch you. Just give me a chance to make you believe."

"I can't," Adriana said, shaking her head. "You frighten me."

The smile disappeared from his face, and that

haunted, lonely look returned. "I frighten myself, too."

He reached out as if he was going to caress her cheek, then shoved his fingers through his hair instead. "You came into the water to help me. Help me, again. Please?"

Adriana turned away. She couldn't stand to look at his smile. She couldn't stand to see his fear. He claimed to be Trevor Montgomery, which was the most insane story she'd ever heard.

He couldn't be Trevor Montgomery. He couldn't. He was a crazy man begging for aid.

She, unfortunately, was the crazy woman who was going to help.

Through her partially opened bedroom door Adriana watched the stranger in the room across the hall. He sat on the edge of the bed in the guest room with his elbows balanced on his knees. His chin rested on the backs of his knuckles. Pain, uncertainty, and maybe a touch of fright radiated around him. Adriana wished she could help, but tonight her thoughts were too mixed up. All she'd been able to do was make him coffee and a sandwich, which she'd left unceremoniously on top of the dresser. They hadn't even talked when they walked up from the beach, she at least twenty paces ahead of him.

He hadn't touched the sandwich. He'd ignored the coffee.

He'd asked for more whiskey when Adriana had taken the tray to the guest room, but she'd ignored his request.

He needed to sober up. He needed to remember his name. And she needed to help him find somewhere else to stay. One night in her house was all she'd give him. Tomorrow he'd have to go.

Slowly he tilted his head and looked at her with those swollen red eyes. "Thank you," he whispered, and she saw the trace of a smile touch his lips.

She should go in and talk to him. She should make him eat the sandwich and drink the coffee. Instead, she closed her door and leaned against it, listening for movement in the guest room, any sounds in the hall. For several long minutes she heard nothing. Finally she heard the slight creak of bedsprings and silence again.

She hoped he'd go to sleep.

She hoped he'd be gone in the morning.

She hoped she'd be able to sleep herself, but how could she with that tormented stranger in her house?

She must be mad to have allowed him to stay.

Locking her bedroom door, she slipped out of her still-wet shorts and sweater and into a nightgown. The sheets were warm and inviting when she slid into bed, but sleep wouldn't come when she turned off the light.

She thought of the stranger. She saw his familiar profile, the cleft in his chin, the strong jaw, and the radiant black hair with a strand that continually fell over his brow.

Trevor Montgomery's profile. Trevor's cleft, and jaw, and hair. How many movies had she seen where Trevor Montgomery brushed a strand of hair from his brow? Every one. It was one of his trademarks.

But it wasn't possible. Trevor Montgomery would be much, much older.

Trevor Montgomery was probably dead.

She drowsed in and out of sleep, tossing and turning. Dreams came in bits and pieces, and suddenly she was fifteen again and inside the toolshed, hidden so well behind tall rhododendrons. Robbie, the young gardener she'd had a crush on, was with her, brushing grass clippings from his jeans, pulling his T-shirt over his head. He kissed her nose, then pressed her against the wall.

"*Your father won't find us in here, I promise.*"

"*You're sure?*"

"*I won't let anyone hurt you, Adriana, especially your father.*"

"*You make him sound so horrid. He's not, Robbie. He just wants me to do what's right.*"

Robbie smiled as he gently touched her cheeks. "*I want you to do what's right, too.*"

He kissed her. So sweet. So tender. His fingers brushed over her white cotton blouse, nimbly unfastening one button and then another. He touched the warm skin of her stomach, and slowly found his way to her bra.

The door burst open and slammed against the wall. "*What's going on in here?*"

"*Nothing, Daddy.*"

Her father's long, slender fingers captured her wrist, and he jerked her away from Robbie. "*Didn't I tell you to stay away from that boy?*"

Adriana jolted awake, but the dream was too vivid, her father's words and her own still filling her mind.

"It was only a kiss, Daddy."

He'd laughed, and even now her memory held the smell of gin on his breath. "Why should I believe you, girl? Why should I trust you? You've disobeyed and dishonored me your entire life."

"I won't do it again. I promise."

A tear slid down her cheek and she wiped it away. She didn't want to think about that promise that she'd failed to keep. She didn't want to think about crazy intruders, or nosy photographers, or gossip. All she wanted to do was slide back into her make-believe world, where life was so much sweeter.

She wanted pleasant dreams of a pirate swinging from a yardarm, or a man in a tux plucking a rose for his love.

Turning on to her side, she nestled into her pillow

and hoped those blissful thoughts would lull her
back to sleep.

The coffee was cold, but it was strong and sober-
ing, and with any luck it would keep him awake.
He didn't want to go back to sleep and relive the
nightmare. The sight of Carole's bludgeoned body,
the pain of knowing she'd died so violently, was far
worse than the horror he was living through now.

Trevor breathed in the scent of cool ocean breeze
whispering through the open kitchen window, and
thought instead about the woman in his bed, about
the fact that it was 1998 even though his brain
screamed out to him that that couldn't be true.

He wished he was back in 1938. He wished that
he'd done everything differently on the Fourth of
July—like spending the evening with Janet Julian instead of going home with Carole Sinclair. If only he
could go back. He'd do things differently.

He took another deep breath and set the empty
cup on the kitchen counter. Absently, he opened one
of the cabinets and took out the spare bedroom key
from the rack he'd installed a few months back.

Suddenly he laughed. The woman in his house
hadn't moved the rack, hadn't taken out the keys,
had changed hardly a thing in sixty years. He didn't
understand her any more than he understood what
was happening to him.

But he wanted to see her again, and the only thing
that kept them apart was that she'd locked him out
of her room.

Leaving the kitchen, he walked down the hallway
and leaned close to her door. He listened for sound,
for any movement within. When he heard nothing,
he quietly turned the key in the lock and stepped
just a foot inside and watched her sleep. Her blond
hair feathered over her pillow, surrounding her head
like a halo. She was the most beautiful creature he'd

ever seen, and he'd seen a hell of a lot of beautiful creatures.

At one time tonight he'd thought she was an angel. Later he decided she was the devil in disguise, taunting him at the gates to hell. Now, sober again, he realized she *was* an angel. God knows only an angel would take him in and give him shelter.

He didn't deserve it. He was a drunk, although he'd admit it to no one but himself. He'd shoved her against a wall. He'd bruised her wrists. He'd tried to make love to her in the middle of the ocean, wanting to know how good she felt, wanting something sweet to distract him, to help him escape his pain.

Instead, he'd agonized over what he'd done, and now he felt like hell.

It was nothing new. He'd felt that way quite a few times in the past twenty years. He'd never admit that to anyone, either.

He walked softly toward the bed and in the first light of morning he could see her eyes fluttering rapidly beneath tightly closed eyelids. She frowned, a deep crease furrowing her brow. Were her dreams haunted, too? he wondered.

She rolled onto her side and a lock of straight blond hair fell over her eyes. As if by instinct, Trevor slid a finger under the strands and curled it around her ear.

So soft. So very, very soft.

She'd made up a story and saved his worthless hide when she should have had him arrested. She'd rushed into the ocean to save him. He hadn't planned on committing suicide that time, he only wanted to cool off. But she'd come for him all the same. She'd made him coffee, a sandwich, and she'd stood just inside her bedroom and watched him as if she cared.

She was special, not like the women he'd known before. Caring rather than self-indulgent. Vulnerable instead of tough. Fragile, where too many others had been hard and hadn't given a damn—any more than he had. He'd never known anyone like her, and he hoped he knew how to treat her the way she deserved.

Daylight beamed through the curtains, slashing across Adriana's face. She rubbed her eyes, yawned deeply, and stretched. Morning had come far too soon.

Cracking open one eyelid, she peered at the clock. Eight o'clock. Maybe she'd just go back to sleep and try to have pleasanter dreams. Last night's sleep had been fraught with too many nightmares, like intruders in the house, and the police coming in the middle of the night.

She rubbed her eyes again and saw the bruises on her wrists. Suddenly she remembered. Last night hadn't been a dream at all.

"Good morning."

Bolting up in the bed, she saw the stranger standing in the open doorway with a tray in his hands.

Adriana dragged the sheet over her chest, feeling terribly naked in his presence even though she'd worn a more revealing gown last night.

"How did you get in here?" she asked. "I locked the door."

He smiled. The same smile she'd seen in peaceful dreams, in books, on her TV screen.

"I keep a spare key in the kitchen cupboard . . . right behind the coffee mugs. You never moved it. You haven't changed much else since I went away, either."

Since he went away! He hadn't been gone sixty years, she tried convincing herself. He'd just drunk too much and lost his mind.

He was right, though. She hadn't changed what had once been Trevor Montgomery's. She'd had no reason to believe Trevor would ever return, but each thing was a part of him, and it seemed an easy way to help keep his memory fresh and alive.

But no one else knew about that camouflaged key holder. She'd found it by accident. How could this stranger have known? Easy, she told herself. He'd stumbled across it when he took out the coffee mugs.

There was an explanation for everything.

"You shouldn't have come in here," she told him. "I locked the door to keep you out."

"I realize that."

He moved toward her. He was wearing his shrunken slacks and a sleeveless ribbed undershirt, the kind her father had worn when she was a child. His beard was thicker. Dark circles had formed under his eyes. He looked exhausted, but he also looked sober—the first good sign.

"Did you sleep?" she asked.

"No. I drank the coffee you made instead, and once I figured out how to operate your percolator, I drank even more." He set the black-lacquered tray beside her on the bed.

Coffee steamed from the cup next to a glass of orange juice. A white linen napkin was folded in a neat triangle, and a pink rose from her garden lay on top.

"You shouldn't go into the garden. Someone might see you."

"I bought this place because it's private. It sits far off the road, and the adobe wall keeps out intruders."

Adriana frowned. He'd been nosing around again. It made her uncomfortable. She liked her privacy. That's what made this place so perfect.

Just as he'd said.

She lifted the orange juice from the tray and took a sip, trying to ignore his piercing gaze.

"You didn't sleep much better than I did," he said,

sitting finally in the chair next to the bed. "I could hear you from the guest room."

"I'm sorry if I disturbed you."

"You didn't disturb me."

He leaned back in the chair, his eyes never leaving hers. He smoothed his index finger over the pencil-thin mustache above his lips. With his growth of whiskers she hadn't noticed the mustache before, but it was definitely there.

Just like Trevor's.

"I still frighten you, don't I?" he asked.

"Yes."

"I admit my appearance could give anyone a start."

"It's not that," Adriana interrupted. "No one's ever broken into my home before, and if someone had, they wouldn't be serving me coffee in bed."

"That's not what's frightening you. It's the fact that I'm Trevor Montgomery, and you think I'm a madman."

"If Trevor Montgomery were alive, he'd be in his nineties."

"Ninety-four."

You don't look much more than forty."

"Thirty-four. Stress has a way of aging a man."

"Too much liquor can do that, too."

"So I've been told."

The intruder got up from the chair and walked around the room. He touched the videos beside the TV, picked up one after another and read the titles. "Which is your favorite?"

"*Captain Caribe.*"

Shaking his head, he laughed lightly. "Just like every other woman. They like those dashing, daring heroes." The stranger leaned against the dresser and stared absently at the videocassette. "I sprained my ankle swinging from the yardarm," he told her. He seemed to be reminiscing, but Adriana knew he was telling a lie. She'd never heard this story before, and she knew everything there was to know about Trevor Montgomery.

"We had only two more days of shooting," he said. "I was young, and that was my first starring role. I didn't want anything to jeopardize the film or my career, so I wrapped the ankle myself, borrowed a few painkillers from a friend, and pretended nothing was wrong. That night I took a little whiskey along with the pills."

He looked up at Adriana, a deep sadness, maybe a little regret in his eyes. "I didn't feel a thing after that. The ankle healed eventually. I didn't need the liquor anymore, but . . . whiskey dulls many kinds of pain."

"You drank enough to kill yourself last night."

He laughed and shook his head. "And the night before, too. I've come to the conclusion that I'm indestructible."

"You're not. You've been in an accident, hit over the head or something. That's why you can't remember."

"You're wrong. I walked into a swimming pool and, quite by choice, floated facedown until I couldn't breathe any longer. The next thing I remember, I popped out of the pool—and now I'm here—sixty years later. I remember all of that quite vividly. I just don't remember what happened in between."

He put down the videotape and leaned against the wall, arms folded across his chest. "Of course, there's always the possibility that I'm a ghost."

"You're insane."

"You've told me that before. In fact, I'm starting to believe it myself."

Adriana stared at him. She wanted to run away, but she was mesmerized by everything he said. His voice was deep, and in spite of his words, he was extremely calm.

He sounded just like Trevor Montgomery, a man who had laughed in the face of death.

She wished she could laugh at everything, but she found no humor in what was going on, especially when she thought that she might be the one who'd lost her mind.

"I should call a psychiatrist," she blurted out. "You need help."

"You're all the help I need."

Adriana pulled the covers closer to her neck when he reached over the bed. She thought he was going to touch her again. Instead, he took the cup of coffee from the tray he'd brought into the room.

"If you're not going to drink this, do you mind if I do?"

Slowly Adriana shook her head, finding speech too difficult.

He sat back in the chair next to her bed and sipped at the coffee. "I read your paper this morning. There's a President Clinton in the White House now." A faraway glare clouded his eyes. "President Roosevelt was living there a few days ago. There is page after page of theaters with a dozen movies playing at each, and I didn't recognize the names of any of the stars. No Shirley Temple, no Spencer Tracy, Clark Gable, or Errol Flynn. There's nothing in the paper about Hitler or the fighting in Europe, but there are wars going on in countries I've never heard of."

He rested his head against the back of the chair. "Maybe I am mad," he said, trying to stifle a yawn. "This was my house yesterday. I slept in this room. I was the one who decided who could stay. Now, suddenly, I'm a guest." He laughed lightly. "You say the house belongs to you, yet I don't even know your name."

"Adriana Howard," she said quite easily, as if they were going to be the best of friends.

He smiled and closed his eyes. "Adriana," he whispered. "It's a nice name."

And he had a nice voice, in spite of all his faults.

She climbed from the bed when he looked as though he might drift off to sleep. She took the cup from his loosened fingers before it could fall to the floor. "You're tired. Why don't you sleep a while."

She pulled a blanket from the end of her bed and draped it over the stranger. He looked peaceful and unthreatening with his eyes closed. She saw what could be a very handsome man beneath the puffiness, under the beard. Without thinking, she reached out to caress his cheek, then stopped when her fingers were less than an inch away.

What was she doing? Why would she want to touch this man who had intruded on her life?

"I'm going to go out for a while," she whispered, hoping he might already be asleep.

He grabbed her arm, instantly awake. "Don't leave me."

Adriana pulled away. "I'm not going far. You need some clothes. I need some groceries."

"You need to get away from me."

"That, too."

"At least you're honest."

He reached out and stroked her cheek with his thumb and Adriana flinched. "Don't touch me."

He smiled and closed his eyes.

"Don't be long. Please."

♥ Five

The home in Encino was tucked away behind old magnolias and tall spreading cedars, with manicured grounds so magnificent Adriana hardly noticed the eight-foot-high black wrought-iron fencing that surrounded the two-acre parcel.

But she knew it was there, and why. Magnolia Acres was the kind of place where they kept people who acted like the stranger in her house, people who didn't have a total grasp on reality.

Perhaps I should be locked away here, too, she thought, laughing at herself as she drove her Mercedes through the gates that were immediately closed and locked behind her. If she told anyone what had happened last night, if she even hinted that she was close to believing the man in her house was Trevor Montgomery, she'd probably be tranquilized, put in a small, silent room, and observed by a dozen psychiatrists.

She didn't plan to tell a soul, though. Stewart Rosenblum, her attorney and friend, would laugh, just as he always had when the subject of Trevor Montgomery came up. She could tell Stewart's wife, Maggie, though. A man traveling through time was something she'd relish. It would be a kick. She'd probably ask him to go out dancing, to tell her stories about the past.

Maggie, however, would probably tell the entire world what had happened, and Adriana's name would be back in the papers. She couldn't let that happen. Not again.

She planned to keep the man's presence a secret. She planned to find out if he was a fraud, or if he was telling the truth, as difficult as that was to believe.

So she sought out Janet Julian, a woman who'd lived within the protective confines of Magnolia Acres for sixty years, a woman whose mind wasn't any more well balanced than the intruder's.

Adriana hoped that Janet might be able to offer some insight on Trevor Montgomery. Of course, everything depended on Janet's frame of mind.

Adriana had visited the lady several times before. She was a connection to the past that Adriana had always wanted to know more about, and when she was lucid, Janet told wonderful stories about Hollywood and days gone by. Adriana rarely learned anything new, but she'd enjoyed listening, she'd laughed at the stories, and she'd kept the sweet old lady company. Occasionally Janet would venture to talk of her infatuation with Trevor Montgomery, but that's when the tears would come. When she remembered the last time she'd seen him, lying facedown in the pool at Sparta, she'd begin to cry. There'd be no more stories after that.

Today, Adriana hoped to keep the conversation away from that moment. She wanted to know more about Janet's earlier days with Trevor. She wanted to know if there was anything about the man that no one else would know.

Somehow she had to find some way to prove that the man in her home was not Trevor Montgomery.

Her mind would be at ease then, and she could readily tell him to leave.

Adriana climbed from the metallic green Mercedes and was halfway to the front steps when Charlie Beck came from around the corner. The gray-haired gentleman in baggy charcoal trousers and a tweed jacket walked toward her with the aid of a cane. His shoulders were stooped, but his clear brown eyes sparkled.

"Good afternoon, Miss Howard," he said, balancing on the cane as he stopped in front of her and held out a hand in greeting.

"Hello, Mr. Beck. Dr. Andrews told me you were with Janet today. I hope you don't mind the intrusion."

"We never mind having you drop by. You're the only company she has besides me. She gets lonely, you know."

His brown eyes misted, and Adriana could easily see Charlie's love for Janet. He'd been her constant companion for sixty years.

"How is Janet today?" Adriana asked.

"Quiet."

Not a good sign. Still she'd try to strike up a conversation.

Charlie looped his arm through Adriana's and led her toward the gravel path that meandered through rose gardens and beds of camellias and azaleas until it reached the back of the house. The outside was lovely with the fragrance of abundant flowers and the sweet sounds of birds chirping, bees buzzing, and the whisper of wind through the deodora pines. The outside charm was a total contradiction to the antiseptic odors that permeated the old wood inside the house. It masked the pain of men and women who'd lost touch with reality.

Adriana sensed a lightness in Charlie's step as they rounded the back of the house. There was a faint twinkle in his eye and his lips turned up in smile. A moment later, Adriana saw the reason for his happiness.

Janet was seated in a white wicker armchair on the back verandah, a lacy pink afghan over her lap. She stared across the rose gardens, past a bubbling fountain, and off into nowhere.

Charlie placed a gentle kiss on Janet's forehead.

"You have a visitor, dearest," he said. "Your friend Adriana."

Janet didn't move. Her eyes didn't flutter, not even when Charlie caressed her cheek. He looked at Adriana, worry showing clearly on his face as he stood by the side of the woman he so obviously loved.

Adriana scooted a chair close to Janet and squeezed the old lady's hand. "I've brought you something special, Janet. Your favorite Godiva chocolates."

Janet's cloudy gray eyes continued to stare out across the yard.

Adriana tried to imagine the pretty young woman she'd seen in pictures, a petite brunette who was always laughing and gay. But that young lady had been replaced by a vacant shell, a woman with snowy white hair cropped close to her head for easy care, although someone—Charlie, more than likely—had been kind enough to fluff wispy curls about her face to soften the harshness of the cut. Her skin was smattered with dark red and brown blotches, and wrinkles made the skin sag at her eyes, her cheeks, her neck. She looked far older than eighty-two. She looked close to death.

It had been sixty years since she'd claimed to have seen Trevor Montgomery's body floating in the pool at Sparta, sixty years since she'd had the breakdown, and sixty years since she'd been declared insane.

A promising future for a young Hollywood starlet

had been destroyed the same night Trevor Montgomery had vanished. And it saddened Adriana terribly.

There must be thousands of wonderful memories hidden deep in Janet's mind. She'd made only seven films in her career, and her name had never burned bright on a theater marquee, but she'd graced all the best Hollywood parties, including the one at Sparta the night Trevor Montgomery made his last public appearance. She'd lived a glamorous life full of rich and intoxicating fun. She'd known everyone who was anyone, but best of all, she'd been one of Trevor's dearest friends.

Considering the life she'd lived since his disappearance, Adriana thought that Janet might have had a more fulfilling existence if she'd never known Trevor Montgomery.

It seemed odd that she should think that, though. She'd always believed that her own life would have been richer if Trevor had been a part of it.

Adriana watched Janet patiently, and slowly a frail, lace-gloved hand reached out from under the afghan to steal a piece of chocolate. Janet daintily bit the edge, turned to Adriana, and smiled. "You always bring me the nicest things."

"And you always tell me wonderful stories."

"Not always," Janet said, in a delicate, whispery voice. She took another bite of the chocolate. "Sometimes I can't remember my name." Her eyes clouded with tears. "Sometimes my head hurts terribly if I try to remember too much."

Maybe this was the wrong time to talk to Janet, Adriana thought. Did her questions really cause Janet pain?

She turned to Charlie, and, as if sensing her concern, he whispered. "It's all right. It's good for her to talk."

Adriana leaned close to Janet, and spoke soft and

slow. "What about old friends, Janet? Does thinking about them make you hurt?"

Janet frowned, put the half-eaten candy back in the box, and fidgeted with her lace-covered fingers. "I only have one friend now. Charlie comes to visit every day. Charlie takes care of me. He always has."

"Charlie's a very nice man," Adriana said, glancing at Charlie. He winked; then, with great effort, bent over and kissed the top of Janet's head.

"I can see you have enough to talk about without me getting in the way," he said. "If you'll excuse me, I think I'll walk in the gardens a bit."

"Are you going to pick me some roses?" Janet asked, smiling coquettishly.

"An armful."

Charlie's simple words made Adriana's heart flutter. How wonderful to be loved so long and so well by an affectionate man.

"Charlie's very sweet to me," Janet said. "I know I'm a burden to him, but he tells me that isn't true. He's loved me for a long time. When I was a star, he used to take pictures of me."

"They're beautiful pictures, too," Adriana told her, thinking of the hundreds of photos she'd seen of Janet with this star and that star, at premieres, out on the town, on the beach, next to some other star's backyard pool. She might not have been a star, but Charlie had memorialized her in numerous books and had made her a legend.

"I have Charlie's books scattered all around my house," Adriana continued. "He captured the Hollywood of the thirties and forties better than any other photographer."

Janet smiled wistfully. "He was just a cub reporter when I met him. Such a dear boy. He wanted to marry me." Janet took a new piece of chocolate. "Trevor Montgomery wanted to marry me, too."

This is what Adriana had really wanted to hear.

As much as she cared for Charlie, it was Janet's life with Trevor that intrigued her.

"Tell me more about Trevor," Adriana asked, resting her elbows on her knees, leaning close so she could hear Janet's faint, whispery voice.

Janet giggled softly. "He was a very wicked man, but I'm sure you know all about that. He drank far too much; of course, most of our friends did, too. We went from one party to another, dancing and singing."

Hesitating, Janet nibbled on her chocolate.

"Trevor loved women. Every night there was someone new on his arm . . . and in his bed, too, I'm afraid."

Janet looked directly into Adriana's eyes, leaned forward, and whispered. "He asked me to marry him once, but I turned him down."

"Why didn't you marry him? I thought you loved him."

"I did." She hesitated, staring at the candy in her trembling fingers. "He left me, though."

Janet sighed deeply, closing her eyes. "Trevor didn't love me, not the way Charlie does. Trevor loved me and left me. He liked other women too much." She opened her eyes, and Adriana could see a red tinge of sorrow. "I knew he could never be happy with just one woman. Not even me."

She shouldn't pry further, Adriana realized, but she had questions to ask, things she needed to know. In spite of the tear sliding down Janet's face, she kept the conversation going.

"I'm sure Trevor loved you, Janet. You knew him better than anyone."

"He was my best friend." For a moment Janet seemed lost in her memories, and then she looked about her and whispered, as if she didn't want anyone to hear. "He was my lover. We kept that a secret though. We didn't want the public to know."

What an odd comment, Adriana thought. They were two very public people. Surely a touch of scandal—if it could be considered that—wouldn't have hurt them.

"Why didn't you want the fans to know you were lovers?" Adriana asked, pushing Janet's mind back to the past.

Janet frowned. "I don't remember if that was Trevor's idea or mine. The studio usually told us what to do." Her gaze seemed far away as she bit into another piece of candy. "I remember now. They wanted Trevor to love Carole, not me. If Jack Warner had found out, he'd be upset with us, and no one wanted Jack to get upset—about anything."

"Was there anything else about Trevor that the public didn't know? Did he have any birthmarks? Any scars?"

Janet shook her head. "I don't know. I can't remember."

She was fading. She was beginning to take deep breaths, frowning as if her head had started to hurt.

Adriana had to hurry.

"Janet?" she said, regaining the old lady's attention. "May I ask something that might bring back bad memories?"

Janet looked away. She pulled off her gloves and stared at her trembling fingers. "I'm very old now. The doctors tried to make me forget the bad things because they make my head hurt, but I still remember some things."

"What do you remember about Carole Sinclair?"

"She was my friend." Janet clenched her fists, and her eyes widened when she looked at Adriana. "She was murdered. They said Trevor killed her."

"Do you believe those stories?"

Janet smiled wistfully. "Trevor made love to women. He drank a lot and took them to bed, but he never argued with anyone, he just did what was expected."

Adriana knew all that. She wanted to know more. "But could he have killed Carole?"

"Carole was my friend."

"Yes, Janet," Adriana said softly, wanting to learn more but knowing she was losing Janet's attention. "I realize Carole was your friend, but was she afraid of Trevor? Had he ever tried to hurt her, or you?"

Janet pressed her hands to her temples. "Trevor loved women. He would never hurt one, not even if she provoked him. I wanted Trevor to be tough— like Cagney—but that wasn't his style."

Slowly she lowered her hands and smiled directly at Adriana. "One time I wanted him to play rough. I did everything I could to make him mad. I even scratched his back until it bled. But he wouldn't play my game. He just left me."

Janet stared for a few moments at her fingers. She slipped on her gloves, studying her hands. Slowly, she looked at Adriana, and frowned. "Are you a new nurse here?" she asked, and Adriana was saddened to realize that their conversation had come to an end.

"Have you met Charlie?" Janet smiled. "He comes every day."

Adriana didn't know anything new—not really. There was book after book about Trevor's amorous escapades. Many a woman had offered to tell all after Trevor disappeared. Most stories seemed contrived. Most were nothing more than fiction.

But Janet Julian's story was probably true—most of it anyway. There was documented evidence that she and Trevor had spent time together. Press clippings, gossip columns, photographs of the two out and about. Party after party after party.

Trevor always had a woman on his arm and a drink in his hand, and he went through the ladies just as fast as he went through the booze.

Adriana smoothed a hand over Janet's cheek and kissed the old lady's brow. Janet was staring off across the garden again with those cloudy gray eyes, her memories buried deep inside. There'd be no more revelations today.

Leaving the verandah, Adriana stopped in the gardens to say good-bye to Charlie, who was gathering a huge bouquet of flowers for his lady, then went to her car and drove away from the beauty and sadness of Magnolia Acres.

Did she really want to learn the truth? Did she want to find out that the man in her home was a fraud?

She drove mechanically, the road stretching out before her nothing but a blur as she remembered the stranger's smile, the rose he'd brought to her on the breakfast tray that morning, and the little-boy-lost look in his eyes.

She shook her head to rid herself of the thoughts.

The man was an impostor. There was no other explanation. Instead of smiles and roses she should be remembering the way he'd bruised her wrists, the way he'd forced his kisses on her.

It didn't matter how nice that kiss had been at first, or how her body had tingled when her cold, wet breasts had been crushed against his chest, or his tenderness when he'd gently pushed dripping hair from her face.

She slammed on her brakes when she suddenly noticed that traffic had come to a dead stop on the freeway.

She had to get her emotions under control. She had to get her life back to normal.

She'd never allowed a man to get under her skin before, but this one was burrowing in deep, and that wasn't a good sign. Somehow she had to fight this insane attraction before he intruded on her dream.

♣ Six

Trevor sat on the patio and absently rolled his gold doubloon between his thumb and index finger as he stared out the wrought-iron gates he'd had installed for privacy's sake when he'd first moved into the rancho. He studied the silver van that had been parked across the street most of the day, and the occasional car whizzing past his home while he waited for Adriana to return.

Where could she be? he wondered, checking his watch for at least the tenth time in the past few hours, forgetting that the solid gold timepiece had quit working after his botched and unsound venture into the Poseidon Pool at Sparta. She'd lied to him. She'd said she'd be back shortly, but she'd left the house at 9:00 A.M. and it was now half past six. The longer she was gone, the more frustrated he became.

He needed a drink—or at least a cigarette. God, he hadn't had either in well over eighteen hours. He'd searched the bar, and found nothing. He'd haphazardly searched some of the kitchen cabinets, even the guest room where she'd told him he could stay.

The guest room! He wanted to sleep in his own room, in his own bed. He wanted to go there now and look for a bottle of whiskey and a pack of cigarettes but, hell, it didn't seem right. That was her room now. Her private place.

The place where she'd probably hidden the things he needed the most.

She'd hidden herself away, too, and right now he needed her as much as he needed the whiskey and cigarettes.

He didn't want to be alone.

And he didn't want to worry about her any longer. Had she been in an automobile accident? Had she been mugged? Was she lying hurt in a ditch?

Or had she decided to stay away?

He wouldn't blame her if she had. He'd thought about running away a time or two himself because too many things in this world he'd been thrown into didn't make sense.

But he'd run away once before, and when he'd wanted to go back he found out he was no longer wanted.

He pressed his fingers against the pulsing nerves in his temple, trying to ward off the headache and the memories he felt coming on. It was no use though. He couldn't push either away.

It was too easy to remember that Christmas Eve in 1920. Even now he could feel the tightness he'd had in his throat when he'd tried to talk, the way tears had welled up behind his eyes when he heard his father's words.

"I'm sorry, but you're mistaken. My wife and I have no son."

"How can you say that, Father? I'm your son," he'd said frantically into the telephone.

"No. I'm afraid you're wrong. If we'd been blessed with an obedient child, he'd be following in my footsteps. Surely I would remember such a son," his father had said in a cool, contemptuous voice.

"Please, Father. I've told you how much being an actor means to me. I don't want to be a lawyer. Surely you can understand."

"It's Christmas Eve, and I'm a very busy man."

"I know it's Christmas Eve. That's why I called."

"I don't give handouts to beggars."

"I don't want anything. I just wanted you and Mother to know that I love you."

"Then perhaps you should call your own mother and father. As I've said before, we don't have a son. Now, if you'll excuse me, I have company to entertain."

He'd never felt as empty and alone as he had the moment their connection had been cut off. He was sixteen years old, and the parents he had loved no longer wanted him. The money he'd spent on that phone call would have been better spent filling his empty stomach. That hadn't mattered, though. His appetite had disappeared as rapidly as his parents had forgotten his existence.

In the dim light of the backlots, he'd found his way to his makeshift home, one of the castle interiors Douglas Fairbanks was using in *The Three Musketeers*. The three-walled set provided little warmth and comfort, but it was the only home he'd had.

He'd found a nearly empty bottle of Jack Daniel's that one of the film crew must have hidden, curled up in his forlorn pile of rags that he called a bed, and had his first taste of whiskey.

Then he cried himself to sleep.

The next morning, when Christmas dawned bright and beautiful, and he realized that a big portion of the world's population was happily spending the day with family, he promised himself he'd never be lonely again. He'd never allow himself to love again, either. Rejection was too painful.

Trevor laughed darkly at the memory. History was repeating itself. He'd run from Carole's body, from his friends, from life itself, and he'd been thrust into a new and different world, one he more than likely couldn't escape.

Not only that, he was being rejected again, by a heaven-sent beauty who called herself Adriana.

And he was lonely.

God, he was lonely.

He looked at his watch again. *Where could she be?*

Before frustration and worry had sent him outside to watch for her, he'd spent a good part of the morning reading those crazy books about himself and looking at newspapers to learn more about current events. He'd figured out how to work the television and the black instrument that controlled it. He'd watched women romping around beaches dressed in next to nothing; men drinking beer and belching; and children sassing their parents.

This new world was all rather strange. There was nothing refined or dignified in people's mannerisms, morals, or style. He might like the beautiful bodies on those women cavorting on the beach, but he didn't think they should be parading around in public for everyone to see. Naked women belonged in the bedroom—preferably his bedroom.

He laughed to himself. He didn't have a bedroom any longer. Not only that, he'd lost sixty years of his life and, for some odd reason, the thought had just crept into his mind that the loss might not be all that bad.

He'd escaped a possible murder conviction and a life in prison or death in the electric chair.

Then again, he had no job, no income. He'd found the money he'd stashed away sixty years before—when banks were the last thing he'd trust—but that wasn't about to last forever, and the only home he had now belonged to someone else.

Someone who might have disappeared or run away.

Someone whose kisses tasted finer than the best

of wines and the richest desserts. He remembered those kisses more vividly than he remembered wanting to die. He couldn't think of a sweeter replacement for bitter thoughts.

But where was she?

What would he do without her? The angel who'd been sleeping in his bed was the only sane thing in his life. She might be frightened of him, she might not understand him, but for God knows what reason, she'd taken him in and, if he played his cards right, she just might offer more help.

Adriana Howard, as surprising as it seemed, might be the answer to a lifetime of unanswered prayers.

He was so caught up in his thoughts that he didn't hear the gates open. He wouldn't have known she was home if the sun hadn't glinted off that flashy green paint on her car.

Suddenly the darkness of his world began to brighten. Adriana had come back to him, and he was going to shut out his fear, mask it with a well-practiced charm—and give her reason never to leave him again.

He hadn't disappeared. Part of Adriana sighed with relief, part of her was disappointed that he hadn't gone.

He walked toward her, cheeks covered in whiskers, eyes red, still as disheveled as he'd been this morning. What had made her think this unkempt and unbalanced stranger could be her dream come to life?

Well, she'd bought him clothes, toiletries, all the other things he'd need. Once he was cleaned up, she'd send him packing. She'd be rid of him.

And she wouldn't have to face his eyes or his smile ever again.

She reached for the handle, but the intruder was faster.

"Where have you been?" he asked, pulling open the door.

It was none of his business, so she ignored him.

When she swung her legs from the car, he gripped her fingers and pulled her close. "I've been worried half out of my mind wondering if something had happened to you."

She twisted out of his grasp, hating the warmth of his hands on hers, despising herself for feeling a shock of desire. "I told you not to touch me," she snapped.

He threw up his hands as if surrendering to her words, and winked as he backed away. "I'm sorry. Somehow it slipped my mind."

"That and everything else," she threw back. In spite of his wink and his irrepressible smile, she refused to let him lighten her mood. "There's one thing you need to get firmly embedded in your brain. I'm not in the habit of people keeping tabs on me. I said you could stay here for a day or two, but don't go thinking you can interfere in my life."

She grabbed the bags from the passenger seat and when she turned, several bags firmly gathered in front of her, a twinge of embarrassment rushed through her. He stood, hands tucked casually in the pockets of his shrunken trousers, and quite brazenly, studied her body. Maybe she shouldn't have worn such a short, form-fitting sundress, but it was scorching in L.A. What did it matter, though? Let him stare. In fact, she'd stare right back.

She studied the pronounced muscles beneath the tight ribbed undershirt he wore, the rich bronze tone of his skin. Slowly she allowed her gaze to inspect his face. The smile. The dimple.

An infectious grin.

That was enough!

She stormed toward the house, upset with herself for letting him get to her, and mumbled under her breath. "The least you could have done was gotten cleaned up while I was gone. You look like a derelict."

"I've played that role before," he stated, marching at her side, hands clasped behind his back. "Would you prefer another look? Riverboat gambler? Playboy?" He took a quick step in front of her and stopped, facing her head on. "Perhaps you'd like a swashbuckler? When you were watching *Captain Caribe* last night I got the distinct impression you liked watching me swing from the yardarm. I could tie ropes from the trees around here and swing for you."

A smile teased her lips when she tried to scowl.

"What do you think?" he asked, when she didn't comment on his suggestion. "Would you like me better with a patch over my eye? How about . . ."

"What I'd prefer is someone who doesn't reek of booze and salt water."

The intruder laughed easily. "Your wish is my command, fair lady." He nearly swept the ground with his hand as he offered her a courtly bow. His gesture couldn't have been more effective at easing her tension if he'd had a musketeer's hat with a feather sticking from its brim.

Still, she rolled her eyes and tried to walk away, but he zigzagged in front of her, thwarting all her efforts to get to the house.

He plucked one of the bags from her hands and peeked inside. "For me?" he asked, cocking one dark brow.

"Obviously. I don't often wear aftershave, although it doesn't appear you indulge in such things, either."

"I take it that you'd prefer I wear what's in these bags rather than these trousers that smell like seaweed and brine?" he asked, teasing her as he tugged on the bags still in her hands.

"I have no preference at all in what you wear," she said, handing him a black bag and a white one with gold letters. The pretty pink bag she kept for herself.

"If you had no preference, you could have walked into any department store and grabbed the first things you saw." He peeked inside the bags again. "Looks to me like you went to more trouble than that."

"I like nice clothes."

"Yes, I can see that," he said, looking at her belly.

She drew the pink bag in front of her stomach and whipped around him.

"Do me a favor," she said, looking back at the stranger before she rushed through the door. "Take a shower before you get dressed."

"You might want to consider washing the sheets and everything else I've touched, too. There's no telling what I've contaminated around here."

She hadn't thought of anything but his body—big mistake. "Thanks for the suggestion."

"You know, Adriana, if you'll give me half a chance, you might find I'm not such a bad sort," he said before she crossed the threshold.

"Take a bath. Clean up. I'll make my judgment then." She skirted past him, through the living room, the dining room, and into the kitchen. She dumped her bag and purse on the table, dropped her sunglasses there, too, and unwrapped the scarf from her head.

Without looking back to see if he'd followed or gone to the guest room to clean up, she busied herself by looking into the refrigerator, anything to take her mind off the man who agitated her. But he didn't leave her thoughts, or her side.

He leaned against the counter next to the icebox,

folding his arms over his chest. "I've already looked," he said, staring down at her as she studied the spare glass shelves. "There's nothing much to eat in there. I was hoping for bacon and eggs. A steak maybe." He glanced at her belly, then back at her eyes. "It's easy to see why you stay so thin."

She slammed the refrigerator and backed across the room. "I don't need to be interrogated on my comings and goings, and my eating habits are no one's business but my own."

He didn't flinch at her words, just continued to smile, casually studying her body as she opened and slammed more cabinets.

"Don't you have something better to do than stare at me?" she asked.

"Better? No, I can't think of anything."

She slammed another cabinet. "Just take a shower, okay?"

He grinned, obviously delighted by her discomfort and rapidly building anger. "Since I'm going to be staying a while—"

"You're not," she tossed back quickly.

"Just on the off chance you decide to change your mind, perhaps you would consent to purchasing some real food."

Adriana turned away from his insufferable grin, and stared out the kitchen window. "I'll think about it."

"Some cigarettes maybe?"

"Anything else?" Exasperation rang out in her words, and she wished with all her heart that he'd leave the room so her nerves would calm.

"No. Not right this moment."

"Good. Then take a shower."

Laughter filled his voice as he spoke. "Your wish is my command, fair lady."

In the window she could see his reflection, his courtly bow, and his back as he walked out the door.

She took a deep breath, willing some sense of normalcy to return. Instead, the room felt empty, and loneliness overwhelmed her.

Adriana stared out the kitchen window for the longest time, thinking about the intruder's winks, his grins, his smiles. Why did he have to be so charming?

She pushed those thoughts aside and remembered the lecture she'd given herself on the drive home from Encino. *Don't let him pull the wool over your eyes. Don't fall for his smile. Don't fall for his game. Get him help and get him out of your house.* It seemed the only way she could do any of those things was to be rude and disagreeable. Unfortunately, he'd seen through her little charade. Why had he made her smile? Her smile, her laughter, slight though it was, had spoiled everything she'd tried to accomplish.

She heard the bedroom door open at the end of the hall and the intruder whistling some old tune as he walked toward the kitchen. She prepared herself not to smile, not to fall into his seductive trap, but her breath caught in her throat when he stepped through the door wearing nothing but the black Levi's she'd bought him, guessing at his size, and a fluffy white towel draped over one shoulder.

His chest and arms were bronzed from hours in the sun, his shoulders broad, his arms lean and muscular as though they'd been made to carry women in distress. She had to fight her raging desire to reach out and touch the flat, smooth planes of his stomach and the contours of his chest to see if they were as hard and strong as they appeared.

Instead, she put her hands behind her and braced herself by gripping the edge of the counter and forcing herself to look from his beautiful body to his beautiful eyes. Doing so didn't give her much reprieve from the uncommon longing she felt.

"You look . . . clean," she said. It was the most noncommittal and unwitty thing she could think of, and she hoped it would wipe the silly grin from his face, the one he'd been wearing the entire time she'd stared at his body.

"I also look and feel extremely uncomfortable," he said, tugging on the waistband of the jeans. "Is this your idea of a joke? I can't breathe."

"That's the idea," she said, forcing back a grin of her own as she turned again to the counter and the salad she'd been making.

"What am I supposed to do, walk around with the top two buttons unfastened?"

She hoped not. Then, again . . . She pushed her indecent thought away. "They'll stretch."

"And I'll have to eat nothing but rabbit food until they do."

He leaned over her shoulder and plucked a cherry tomato from the cutting board, popped it into his mouth, then leaned on the cabinet and watched her work.

"Anyone ever tell you you're pretty?" he asked after he licked his fingers.

Adriana's gaze darted to his smile for just a moment, then she hacked at a cucumber and concentrated on her resolve to ignore him. But she couldn't ignore the fresh scent of the shaving cream or the muskiness of the cologne she'd bought him. Nor could she disregard the warmth emanating from the close proximity of his body.

Get away from him, she told herself. *Far away*.

She threw the cucumbers into a bowl, right on top of the lettuce, the tomatoes, and celery, tossed it a time or two with wooden tongs, and carried it to the table.

Sitting down, she unceremoniously spooned salad onto his plate and some onto hers, then dug in. She was bound and determined to keep her eyes off his half-naked body.

"Do I bother you?" he asked, when he sat down across from her.

Adriana's gaze flickered up to his face, and once more she nearly lost her breath. He was cleanly shaved, except for the trace of a pencil-thin mustache. Ebony hair that had gone every which way earlier had been slicked back and parted neatly on the left. Of course, that one unruly strand still hung over his brow.

He was much too handsome for anyone's good, especially hers.

Yes, he bothered her. Much, much too much.

She stabbed a slice of cucumber and tried to avoid his stare, but he was leaning over the table, watching her instead of eating his food.

"I do bother you, don't I?"

"Yes!"

She stood and paced the floor, sneaking glimpses of the man at her table every time she turned. The redness had dimmed in his eyes; the circles below them weren't nearly as dark.

As much as she hated to think it, he looked exactly like Trevor Montgomery. He had that same dark, smoldering glare that had set millions of hearts aflame, the same cleft in his chin, the same dimple just to the right of his lips when he smiled.

"If you'd bought me a shirt, I wouldn't have had to come to the table half-naked" he said, interrupting her thoughts. "Maybe then the sight of me wouldn't be bothering you so much."

"But I did buy you a shirt," she stammered. How could he possibly think she wanted to see him naked? "Maybe I left it in the car?"

"Maybe you did that on purpose because, just maybe, you *did* want to see me half-naked?"

Adriana sighed as she shook her head. "I have no

desire whatsoever to see you naked. Stay here. I'll go look."

He captured her hand before she could leave the room. "Eat your dinner, Adriana. You were kind enough to buy the clothes, the least I can do is find them and wear them."

"You don't have to wear them . . ." she blurted out before she realized what she was saying.

Trevor laughed softly. "We'll never have a decent conversation if I don't."

He slid his chair back and pulled the towel from his shoulder as he walked out the kitchen door.

Once more Adriana's breath caught in her throat. She couldn't take her gaze off his strong, bronzed back, for racing over his shoulder blade were five very distinct, very red claw marks. What had Janet Julian said? *I wanted him to be tough like Cagney, so I scratched him.*

Absently she moved from the table and stood at the door, watching him walk toward the car. The scratches could have been made by a cat. No! They were much too wide. They could have been made by any lover. Surely this man had women in his life. He was too handsome, too charming, too . . . too perfect not to have a woman—plenty of them, in fact.

Surely the scratches hadn't been made by Janet Julian sixty years ago.

He smiled at her as he walked back to the house. The dimple to the right of his lips was there as clear as day. His brown eyes smoldered. Just like . . .

No, he couldn't possibly be Trevor Montgomery.

He stood next to her in the doorway, so close she could hear him breathing, could sense the rapid beat of his heart. Or was it her own breathing? Her own heart? Both were totally out of control.

"You're not eating," he said.

"I lost my appetite."

"We can't let that happen too often. Eating's one

of the finer things in life. Maybe I can teach you how to enjoy it."

"No one else ever has."

"I can teach you many things, Adriana, if you'll give me half a chance."

"You won't be here long enough," she said abruptly, and saw a touch of apprehension mar his smile.

"No matter." He tightened his fingers around the bag and headed down the hall. "Won't take me a minute to finish dressing. Save a bite of that salad for me. It's not much, but I'm starving."

Crossing to the refrigerator, she absentmindedly opened the door, searching for some nonexistent thing she could add to the stranger's meal. She didn't want to think about salad, or food, or the thought that he might be Trevor Montgomery.

She took out a slab of nonfat cheese, unwrapped the plastic, and sliced a few hunks. She found an apple, a breadstick, placed everything on a plate and set it next to his salad.

She seemed to be moving as if she had no will of her own. All she could think of were those marks on his back and Janet Julian's words. "I scratched him."

The stranger walked back into the room with a white oxford shirt tucked neatly into his trousers and the cuffs rolled halfway up his forearms. He was still barefoot, he was still smiling, his eyes still smoldered. He was a picture of perfection.

Could he really be Trevor Montgomery?

"I have something for you," he said, and pulled a hand out from behind his back.

Oh, God! Adriana's heart raced. The man was holding a rose, a red rose like the one she'd kissed just before she'd wished that Trevor would come back. She didn't have roses like that in her yard.

"I found this floating in the Poseidon Pool at

Sparta," he said. "I have the feeling someone might have thrown it in." One dark eyebrow raised in question. "I was wondering if it might have been you?"

She felt weak. A cold chill swept through her body. Her head spun.

She felt dizzy.

And suddenly everything around her faded to black.

♥ Seven

The darkness lasted for only a moment. Adriana remembered the weakness that had flashed through her body and turned her muscles and bones to mush. She remembered the shiver of shock that raced up her spine as lights twinkled before her eyes, and she remembered everything turning black. She didn't remember falling, though, or Trevor Montgomery—*the* Trevor Montgomery—kneeling on the floor to cradle her head in his lap.

"Feeling any better?" he asked in that deep, warm voice she knew so well. It was a voice she'd heard so many times in the movies he'd made a long time before she was born.

Taking a deep breath, she struggled to sit up, but he held her close, smoothing warm fingers over her cool cheeks and brow.

"Did I faint?"

He nodded, and the smile she remembered from those very same films touched his lips. "I've had women pass out on me half a dozen times, but only in the movies. I didn't think it happened in real life."

"I guess shock can do it to a person."

He cocked one dark, well-defined brow. "Have I shocked you?"

Adriana laughed nervously. "You're Trevor Montgomery."

"I've told you that at least a dozen different ways."

"You should be an old man."

"I should be dead . . . but I'm not."

Again Adriana pushed away, and this time Trevor let her go, but his long, sensuous fingers trailed over her arm and down the length of her hands as she stood, sending a different kind of shock through her body, one she rather enjoyed, even though she knew she shouldn't.

She went to the sink, filled a glass with water, and took a sip, staring out the window, trying to make sense of her feelings and of what was going on.

"Is it the rose that made you believe me?" he asked, standing now at her side with the bedraggled flower in his hand.

It was the rose; it was the scratches, too, but those she didn't want to think about. The thought of Trevor Montgomery and all his romantic escapades angered her. How could a man of his charm, his class, hop into bed without thinking of anything but a moment's fun? His sexual appetite hadn't bothered her much before—it was all part of his mystique. But now, with him standing near, that was all she could think of. It had cheapened all those charming things he'd said to her because he probably said them to all the women he met.

Her father would have despised this man. He would have chastised her for allowing him into her home.

Why, then, did she find him so appealing?

She took the rose from his fingers. The red petals were crushed, some had fallen away, but a trace of the fragrance remained and she held it to her nose. "Never in my wildest dreams did I think I could pull a man through time simply by tossing a rose into a pool and making a crazy wish."

"So, that's how you dragged me sixty years through time."

His voice was filled with laughter, but Adriana could only frown.

"It doesn't sound possible, but I can't think of any other explanation."

"What did you wish for?"

Adriana gazed at Trevor for a moment, then turned away, afraid of what he would think.

"Tell me," he implored, lightly touching her chin with an index finger and tilting her face toward him. "Please."

"It was silly, really."

"Tell me," he repeated in that spellbinding voice that made her want to divulge all her secrets, things she'd never told a soul.

She walked away from his touch and sat down at the table. Lifting her fork, she picked at the now wilted salad on her plate. "I was standing at the pool," she said, trying to remember that moment. "I'd closed my eyes and seen a vision of you lying facedown on the water. It wasn't the first time. It seemed to happen every year on the Fourth of July, and always when I was standing beside the pool."

Adriana looked up at him. She feared she'd see a grin on his face, but instead, he had the softest of smiles. "I remembered the movie where you threw a rose on your lover's casket."

"*Desperate Hours*," he added, supplying the name of the film that most people rarely remembered when they thought about Trevor Montgomery's roles. It was too obscure, but it was one of her favorites, a movie that showed the depth of his emotions, the strength of his talent.

He sat across from her, rested his elbows on the table, and leaned forward. "What happened then?"

"I kissed the rose." Again she looked at her plate, knowing he'd laugh when she told him what she'd said. "I didn't say much. Just . . ." She sighed deeply. "Come back to me. Please. Come to me."

All she saw was a trace of a smile on Trevor's face when she raised her eyes. He wasn't laughing, not in the least.

"Why did you want me to come back?"

She couldn't tell him the truth. He'd laugh for sure if she told him she'd been in love with him—with Trevor Montgomery—since she was six years old.

"It doesn't matter . . ."

"It does to me," Trevor interrupted softly.

Adriana shook her head. "The important thing right now is to figure out what we're going to do."

"You mean figure out how to send me back to 1938?"

Send him away? That was something she hadn't even considered. But he'd been pulled away from friends and family. Maybe he wanted to go home. "Do you want me to try to send you back?"

He shrugged, and his brow furrowed into a frown. "I don't belong here," he said, shaking his head. "I don't know anything about your time. I want to live the life I was supposed to live. But I've read those books of yours. They don't paint a very pretty picture of me. If I could go back and change things, then yes, I'd want to go back. Unfortunately, the only things waiting for me in my own decade are prison bars and the scorn of old friends. I don't know if that's what I want. Then again, what if . . . what if I wake up tomorrow and I'm old and wrinkled and looking like I'm ninety-four years old? What kind of life is that?"

"I don't know."

She left the table, but Trevor grasped her fingers before she could walk out of the room.

"Don't leave me, Adriana," he said, not only his

words but his dark brown eyes imploring her to stay.

She tried pulling her hand away, but he held on tight.

"I need to be alone for a while," she told him, wanting to get away to digest this craziness about a man traveling through time, about Trevor Montgomery being in her home, in her life. "I need to think."

"About what?"

"Things."

"Like whether or not I'm a murderer?"

"Are you?"

His eyes flashed briefly with anger, then he looked away. He pushed up from the table and crossed the kitchen, staring out the window. His deep sigh filled the room. "I don't know."

Adriana gripped the edge of the door. Those weren't the words she wanted to hear. Why hadn't he said *no*?

"I'm going for a walk," she said, expecting him to turn around, expecting him to want to go with her. But he remained silent, staring into the dark.

A light, cool mist had rolled in from the Pacific, but when she crossed the lawn she could feel the heat of his eyes watching her from the kitchen. Even as she walked down the stairs and along the beach she could sense him thinking of her, just as she was thinking of him, as if there was some odd connection between them, something that had drawn them together.

Trevor Montgomery was a womanizer. Trevor Montgomery was a drunk. Trevor Montgomery might have brutally murdered a woman, stabbing and slashing her again and again.

Trevor Montgomery was in her home.

Trevor Montgomery could easily murder her, too.

She slumped down to the sand, drew her knees to

her chest, and wrapped her arms around them as she watched the fog-shrouded sun sink into the ocean.

She thought about Captain Caribe romancing his lady love, wrapping her in pearls and rubies and chains of gold that he'd pulled from a long-buried chest. She thought of the riverboat gambler who'd lost thousands of dollars but laughed in the face of defeat. She thought of the sheik riding across the blazing sands on a midnight stallion while kissing the woman he held in his arms.

Those were the things she remembered when she thought of Trevor Montgomery. His laughter, his smile. His smoldering eyes when he looked at his woman.

Too many other people thought of those horrid photos of Carole Sinclair's body and the way Trevor Montgomery, a suspected murderer, had disappeared. Too many other people had forgotten the happiness he'd brought to millions in his swashbucklers, his romantic comedies, his emotion-packed dramas. They wanted to remember the bad. They'd sensationalized his name, his life. The good was long-forgotten.

But she remembered his laughter, his passion, and his tenderness when he kissed his lover.

Lightly she touched her mouth, remembering the heat of his kiss, remembering how wonderful his lips had felt.

His caress wasn't the touch of a killer.

She wanted to believe.

She needed to believe.

Trevor lay in bed with his arms folded under his head and stared into the dark, wondering when Adriana would return. He hadn't heard her come up from the beach. He hadn't heard her drive away, but several hours before, he noticed that her car was gone. He wondered if she planned to stay away the rest of the night, or come back and erase the loneliness he felt in her absence.

And he wondered if she thought of him, just as he thought constantly about her.

She didn't like to eat. She rarely laughed, and she definitely didn't like to be touched, but she'd responded to his kiss when they'd been in the water. She'd kept that sweet mouth of hers closed, but he'd sensed her wanting to open up and let him taste her completely. He'd never forced a woman; he'd rarely had to try. Most women came to him easily, begging for more and more. Only a fool would have said no.

And he hadn't been a fool.

Until now.

Did Adriana have any idea what she was doing to him? Did she know that her warm blue eyes were melting his frozen heart? Did she know that her innocence scared the hell out of him? He hadn't been around sweetness since he was a child. Hell, he doubted he'd been around it then. His childhood was a memory he tried to forget, and when he couldn't, he'd drown it with liquor; his recent past— Carole's death—was something he'd like to forget, too. And while he was at it, he'd like to forget what life would be like if he was whisked back through time. His past was over.

For the first time in a long time, he wanted to think of the future.

He wanted to think of Adriana. About the blond hair that fell soft and sleek over her cheeks, hiding too much of the slenderness and beauty of her face. About the fullness of her pale pink lips that didn't smile often enough. About her long, slim body and the fact that he wanted to strip off her clothes, taste those nearly nonexistent breasts and caress the nicest bottom he'd ever seen. He wanted to know why she backed away from his touch, why she hated his drinking, why she lived in his home, and why she'd called him across sixty years of time.

He'd never shared his secrets with anyone. He didn't plan to do it now, but he felt that the sheer power of her innocence could erase all his nightmares.

Closing his eyes, he willed himself to dream of Adriana's kiss, her eyes, the sweetness of her voice.

He still wasn't sure if he believed in God, but he thanked some higher power for sending him to Adriana, for giving him some reason to change his life.

❤ *Eight*

Adriana stood in the doorway of Trevor's bedroom, watching in horror as he thrashed around in the bed, unconsciously rubbing the sheets as if he were trying, in vain, to wipe something from his hands.

Was it Carole's blood he was trying to rid himself of? *Had* he murdered her? Oh, how she wished she knew the truth. She wondered if Trevor knew what had happened, or if not remembering was just an act, another role he played so well.

Hesitantly she neared the bed, her desire to run away hampered by her desire to help. He looked tormented and frightened. Damp strands of hair clung to his feverish face, and without thought for what was right or wrong, she stroked her cool hand over his brow.

"Carole!"

He seized her wrist and she attempted to struggle, but he held her tight.

"Carole!"

"Let go," she begged, trying to wrench free of his tightening grasp. "Please, Trevor. Let go. It's Adriana. Not Carole."

He jerked up in bed. Panic filled his eyes as he stared at his hand around her wrist.

105

Releasing his hold, he plowed his fingers into his hair and lowered his head as if he were trying to suppress a terrible ache. "I've hurt you again, haven't I?" he whispered.

"You didn't mean to," she said through trembling lips. She lightly touched her already-bruised wrists, hoping there was truth in her statement. "You thought I was Carole."

"You're nothing at all like Carole," he said, raising his head to gaze into her eyes. "You're not like any of the women I've known."

"You don't know me at all."

"I want to," he said softly, his mesmerizing voice almost enough to make her give him anything he wanted.

But she was too afraid to let him know her completely. She was afraid to have him in her house, afraid of his nightmares, afraid of his drinking. And she was afraid of his passion, his smoldering eyes, and his charming smile.

She backed toward the door, needing to get away from him, but Trevor might as well still be holding on to her wrists for all the power in his eyes.

"Stay with me," he pleaded. "Please."

"I can't."

"I won't hurt you."

"I don't know that for sure."

"I'm not a killer."

"You were calling out Carole's name. You were trying to wipe something—like blood—from your hands. I want to believe you're innocent, but . . ."

"I *am* innocent!"

Trevor tore off the covers and climbed from the bed, dressed only in a white undershirt and boxers. He crossed the room in just a few short strides, and when he reached out to touch her cheek, she backed into the hall.

He stood in the doorway, staring at her in the

dark. "I need you to believe that I didn't kill anyone. I couldn't have."

"But you don't know for sure."

"No, I don't."

"I know you don't want to see a doctor, but I think you should. You need help."

"What I need is you."

"I can't help you. I thought I could, but I've been wrong."

"I've been wrong about a lot of things in my life, too," he said, again pressing his fingers to his temples.

"God, I need a drink. Where did you hide the whiskey?"

"You don't need it."

"I'm not in the mood for any more lectures."

He brushed past her and stalked down the hallway toward the living room. She ran after him, watching him throw open cupboards.

"Where did you hide it?" he asked again.

Adriana refused to answer, and he glared at her, finally stalking from the living room, through the dining room, and into the kitchen.

Adriana followed, standing in the kitchen door as he searched for the liquor.

"Drinking won't solve your problems," she said calmly, even though her heart and mind were pounding with fear. He was acting like a madman, tearing open cabinet doors.

"Nothing's going to solve my problems, but at least I might be able to forget."

"Drinking's what made you forget everything in the first place."

"You don't know anything about that night."

"Do you? Do you remember what happened?"

"No. And I don't ever want to remember. I woke up covered with blood, holding a knife. It's highly possible I murdered a woman—someone I knew.

Someone who didn't deserve to die. Someone whose death haunts me every second of every day. Is that something you'd want to remember?"

Tears streamed down Adriana's cheeks. She hadn't wanted to hear those words. She didn't want to believe that he'd really been with Carole that night. She wanted to believe he was innocent. "Tell me you didn't do it. Please."

"Haven't you heard a word I've said? I don't remember that night. I don't remember anything at all." He stared at her, ignoring her tears, her fright. "Where's the whiskey?"

He was acting just as her father had each time she'd hidden his gin. She didn't want to go through that again. She couldn't.

With the back of her hand she wiped away the tears, and told him the same thing she'd told her father time and time again. "Getting drunk won't help."

"Don't preach."

"Please."

"Don't beg, either."

She glared at him, not caring that tears continued to stream down her face. Her father had yelled. Her father had ignored her. Why should Trevor Montgomery be any different?

She ran to her bedroom and pulled three bottles from the bottom of her lingerie drawer, then turned around and faced the crazy man she knew was standing in her doorway.

"Drink it. Drink all of it," she shouted. "Fall down flat on your face if that's what you want. Then get out of my house and don't come back."

Trevor stared at her as if giving her ultimatum some thought, then he crossed the room, grabbed one of the bottles and twisted off the cap. He swigged a long gulp, then another.

He braced a hand on the dresser, not once turning

around to look at her. "Do you really want me to leave?" he asked.

She didn't need to be involved with another alcoholic. Once in a lifetime was more than enough.

"I don't have time for a drunk."

Slowly he turned, his reddened eyes, the slight waver of his voice, the slump of his shoulders defining an overwhelming sadness. "You're sure?"

"Very sure."

"Then I'll get out of here in the morning. As soon as it's light."

"Just get out of my room now. Please."

He tilted the bottle and took another sip, but his gaze never left Adriana's tear-streaked cheeks.

"I'm sorry things had to turn out this way," he said

"But not sorry enough to do anything about it."

She'd hoped he'd be different, nothing at all like her father. She'd wanted to believe in Trevor. So many things were good and right about him, but too many other things were wrong.

Having him around brought back the unhappy memories of a father who hadn't cared, who believed most everything good in life was a sin, who thought liquor was more important than his only child.

"I never should have wished for your return," she said sadly.

"No, I suppose you shouldn't have."

Slowly he stepped into the hall. When she heard his footsteps at the opposite end, she closed and locked her bedroom door, afraid that he might return.

And then, again, she was afraid he wouldn't.

She didn't know how long she stood there crying. She'd thought she could help, but she knew the only one who could help Trevor Montgomery was himself.

She heard the front door open and close. She heard the garage door open.

Oh, God! Was he going to get in the car? She didn't want to help any longer, but she couldn't allow him to drive while he was drinking.

She rushed out of the house, stopping at the edge of the hedges when she saw him standing beside the Duesenberg, smoothing his fingers over the green-and-yellow paint. The opened bottle of whiskey was gripped in his tightened fist, as if he were holding on to a lifeline.

Turning slowly, he leaned against the automobile and looked toward the back of the house, toward Adriana's bedroom window.

She watched him raise the bottle to his lips then hesitate, as if giving serious thought to his actions. But the thinking didn't last long. He must have decided drinking was the most important thing at the moment. He tilted it again to his mouth.

Suddenly, he hurled the bottle across the drive. It crashed on the patio, and liquor and glass sprayed everywhere.

A dog barked somewhere down the street. Another began to howl.

And Trevor stood silent and still, staring off into the dark.

A cool wind breezed across the yard, shaking the palms, the rosebushes. Adriana rubbed her arms for warmth. She should go inside, leave him alone and let him work out his problems. But she couldn't leave, she couldn't stop watching. She was afraid he'd disappear if she let him out of her sight.

Where could he go, though? He had no other home, no one to take him in. Besides, he wasn't dressed for a drive around town or anywhere else.

She laughed to herself, wondering again why she even cared.

Finally he moved, climbing into the front seat of

the Duesenberg. He leaned back against the soft green leather, but he didn't start the car. More than likely he didn't have the keys.

She walked quietly to the patio, her bare feet cold on the terra-cotta tiles. She pulled a multicolored serape from one of the chairs, wrapped it around her shoulders, and sat down. Surely he wouldn't stay out all night. Surely he'd get tired and go inside to bed.

She yawned, thinking how crazy it was for her to be outside watching him, worrying about him. She should be inside, in her bed, where it was warm and comfortable.

Several hours must have gone by before the sun peeked over the hills to the east. Adriana's joints ached from the cool, damp air. She stretched and rubbed her eyes, looking across the lawn to the garage.

Trevor was still behind the wheel, his head still resting against the soft green leather.

Gathering the serape about her, she walked to the side of the car and looked down at the sleeping man. His cheeks and chin were rough with whiskers, the skin below his eyes was puffy and dark. He hadn't drunk that much, and for just a moment Adriana wondered if he might have been crying?

It didn't seem possible. He was Trevor Montgomery. *The* Trevor Montgomery, a man who knew no fear, who laughed in the face of danger. Could a man like that possibly cry?

Lightly, she touched his shoulder. "Wake up, Trevor. Come inside and have some coffee."

His eyelids twitched, opening slowly. A half-hearted smile touched his lips. "Do you plan to sober me up completely before you kick me out on the street?" he asked, the smile turning to a grin.

"Against my better judgment, I'm not kicking you out."

"You're sure you don't want to give it a little more thought?"

Adriana shook her head. She'd thought about it before she fell asleep. She'd thought about letting him stay the moment he'd thrown the bottle. He was a troubled man with a troubled past, and he was probably going to bring even more trouble into her life. But tossing the bottle was proof that he wanted to try and change. If he could try, she figured she could try to help him.

She opened the car door and he stepped out. They were the perfect fodder for gossip, he in his underwear, she in a short, flimsy silk gown. *This is how trouble begins*, she thought, and she wasn't just thinking about gossip, she was thinking about her feelings, about how good he looked fully dressed or nearly naked. And she thought about the way her heart was beating wildly within her chest.

Trevor Montgomery was definitely trouble, so she decided to do what she'd always done where men were involved. She'd back away.

"Thank you for not making me leave," he said, and doing what seemed so much a natural part of him, he reached out to touch her cheek.

Adriana avoided his touch, walking briskly toward the house. She would help, but she wouldn't get too close. That was the only way this would work. She'd help him establish a new life, a new identity. Once he was able to take care of himself, she'd back even farther away—if she could.

When they reached the house, she went straight to the shower and turned the water to hot, letting it pulsate over her body while she cursed herself for making another mistake. Why was she letting her emotions get involved. She was a businesswoman. She was smart. She was logical. But she hadn't used her brain or her logic where Trevor Montgomery was concerned. She'd just let him enter her house and disrupt her life.

And she had more emotions coursing through her right now than she'd ever had.

She felt happy.

Of course, she'd felt happy each time her father sobered up, but those times were few, the moments short. Then he'd drink again. Then he'd get mean.

She hadn't been able to change her father's ways. Could she change Trevor's?

She half expected Trevor to be leaning against her bedroom wall or stretched out on her bed when she came out of the bathroom. Instead, she smelled strong coffee emanating from the kitchen, a hint of cigarette smoke, and she heard his whistling.

The sound was such a treat in her usually quiet house.

She dressed in black-linen trousers with a high waistband that came nearly to her breasts. She wore a billowing white silk blouse, and avoided putting on shoes. They were definitely the bane of a woman's existence.

Slipping into the kitchen without him seeing her, she curled up in a chair and watched him chopping onions and bell pepper. He was dressed in the white shirt again and the black Levi's. She really should consider buying him a few more changes of clothes, although he looked rather handsome dressed in the jeans.

His feet were bare and he tapped his toes as he whistled. He reached for the cigarette resting on the edge of the sink and sucked the smoke and nicotine into his lungs. It looked so sexy, so glamorous in the movies, and it seemed so much a part of him that she didn't have the heart right now to ask him to stop.

He blew out a puff of smoke and slowly cocked his head to peer at her over his shoulder. "Are you going to stare at me all morning, or try some of my coffee?''

"You knew I was here?''

"I have very good hearing. I could almost hear you breathing when you watched me from the patio during the night.''

"You knew?''

He stubbed the cigarette out in one of the ashtrays that had once belonged to him, then took a long drink of coffee. "I'd hoped you'd come. I wouldn't have bet on it, though.''

Adriana crossed the room and poured the thick, strong brew into a cup. It didn't look the least bit appetizing, but Trevor was drinking it down as if it was water.

"Need any help?'' she asked, looking at half a dozen eggs resting on the counter along with a slab of cheddar cheese.

"I've got it well under control, but thanks. Thanks for shopping last night, too. You could have waited until today.''

"You were hungry, and I needed some time away.''

Trevor smiled and turned back to the counter.

"Your cooking skills surprise me,'' she said, curling up once again in the chair.

"I wasn't always rich and famous. I didn't always have a cook to prepare my meals, either.''

"What about the women in your life? Surely they would have cooked for you.''

"I rarely stayed in a woman's bed till morning, and the women I knew were interested in things other than making my breakfast.''

"You're awfully proud of your sexual encounters, aren't you?''

Trevor dropped half a cube of butter into a pan and tossed the wrapper into the trash. He wiped his hands on a towel and turned around. A slow grin crossed his face. "You seem to be an expert on my life. What do you think?"

"That you were lonely."

He laughed and went back to work on the onion, tossing it into the sizzling butter. "I didn't have time to be lonely. I'm surprised you're not aware of that."

"Well, there were rumors about a lot of women."

"And, naturally, the gossip columns don't lie. Let's see, supposedly I was with a different woman every night of the week. Women came into my dressing room in the afternoons, and I indulged my carnal appetite in a very expedient manner."

"Is it true?"

"Not the expedient part." He winked. "I like taking my time and enjoying myself."

"You don't deny the rest?"

"I like women, Adriana. I've never denied that to anyone. I won't deny it to you, either."

Adriana swirled the coffee in her cup, watching it go around and around. It was a safer place to look than into Trevor's eyes. She could easily see why so many women had fallen for him, why they'd gone to his dressing room in the afternoons, and to his bed at night.

If she wasn't careful, she could end up there herself.

But she was always careful. She wasn't going to make an exception for Trevor Montgomery, no matter what he said or did.

"I've been thinking about all the things you need to start over," she said as she skirted around Trevor, attempting to open a cabinet without touching his clothes, his skin, or any part of that body that radiated so much heat and passion.

"I'm glad one of us is levelheaded," he said. "I haven't given any thought at all to the future. Instead, I've been thinking about you, about your smile, about the way you rarely laugh, and the fact that you're afraid to let me touch you."

"None of those things are important right now," Adriana tossed back, somewhat ignoring his words as she gathered plates, silver, and napkins to set the table.

"They'll matter sooner or later, especially if I'm going to be living with you."

Adriana glared at him, at his smile, at the lights glinting off his smoldering eyes. "Living here is only temporary," she reminded him, again concentrating on setting the table, trying not to think about how good his words made her feel. "Right now, we need to get you a Social Security card."

"I have one. Of course, I'm not too sure I like this new idea of giving the government money to take care of me in my old age, but the studio insisted everyone apply for one early last year."

Adriana smiled at his words, remembering that Social Security was a brand-new plan in 1938. "It's an old idea, Trevor. People have been giving money to the government for years. You'd be collecting it now if . . ."

"If I hadn't disappeared? If I was ninety-four years old and still alive?"

She found it difficult to picture Trevor as an old man. He was too virile, too attractive. Too, too perfect. She forced herself not to think of him, but of the subject at hand.

"You can't use your Social Security number. It's too old. People would question your identity."

"People on the street are going to question my identity."

Again she shook her head and smiled. "You've been gone for sixty years and, I'm sorry to say, you're not exactly a hot item in Hollywood anymore. I seriously doubt anyone will point at you when you walk down the street and say 'There's Trevor Montgomery.' "

"Ah, fame is so fleeting."

He said it jokingly, but she sensed the loss of his identity hurt him deeply.

"I never forgot you," she whispered.

"For which I'm extremely thankful."

He joined her at the table, placing a plate before her that contained an omelet rich with butter and cheese. It smelled like heaven. It had been a long time since she'd indulged in anything so decadent. It was just one more sinful thing to add to the list of things she'd given in to since Trevor had come into her life.

It was one more thing her father wouldn't have approved of. Sweets. Fats. Men. But she was able to forget her father and the fact that he found disfavor with anything unhealthy or fun when she noticed the way Trevor studied her mouth as she tasted a bite of egg and cheese.

"You have nice lips, Adriana."

"I'm sure you say that to all the girls, but that's beside the point."

"What is the point?" he asked, his eyes still concentrating on her lips.

She chewed the omelet and his intense scrutiny nearly made her choke as she tried to swallow. "Let's see, you need a new Social Security number, a driver's license, and a birth certificate. I suppose you'll need a new name, too."

Trevor's fork stopped midway to his mouth. "The name sticks. I wouldn't let the studio change my name, and I'm not going to let you change it, either."

"I can probably explain a mystery man showing up on my doorstep named Joe Jones, but I'll never be able to explain Trevor Montgomery. You look too much like him."

"I *am* him! I don't intend to be anyone else. You

can make up some cockeyed story about my history, but you're not changing my name." Trevor shoved the eggs into his mouth. "And while you're at it, do you mind explaining to me how you propose to get a birth certificate for me? I was born ninety-four years ago. Don't you think someone will question my birth year when they look at the certificate and look at me?"

"I'm not going to get a copy of your original birth certificate, I'm going to get a new one. Baby boy Montgomery, born in some month on some day in 1964."

"Do you propose to get this certificate illegally?"

Adriana nodded.

"Do you do illegal things often?"

"Never."

"And what makes you think you can do it now?"

"Connections. Money."

"You're not involved with the mob, are you?"

Adriana smiled and took a bite of the omelet. The thought of her doing something wrong and possibly being involved with the mob seemed to make him uncomfortable. It felt only right to let him squirm after the way he'd stared at her lips and made her absolutely miserable.

She chewed slowly. "This is delicious."

"Of course it is. I'm a good cook. But don't ignore my question. Are you involved with the mob?"

"Would that bother you?"

"Of course it would bother me. I've never done anything illegal in my life."

Except maybe kill someone, Adriana thought. Suddenly the omelet didn't taste so good, and her teasing was no longer fun.

"I'm not involved with the mob," she said, turning serious once again. "My attorney knows his way around the system. He can get all the I.D. you need. Then you're set."

"Does being set mean you'll be through with me? That you'll kick me out?"

"It simply means you'll be able to go on with your life."

Trevor leaned back in his chair. "But I'll always have the old life hanging over my head, all the fears, all the uncertainty."

Adriana wished those things had disappeared when he'd traveled through time. Of course, maybe that's why he'd come forward to 1998—to find out the truth, to rid himself of all the uncertainty.

"We'll work on the identification first," she said softly. "Later, I'll help you deal with the rest."

Trevor studied himself in the bathroom mirror, surprised by the image he saw. Gone was the slicked-back hair, the pencil-thin mustache. Gone was the man who'd graced movie screens and magazine covers around the world. This was a new role he was playing—the clean-cut all-American boy next door instead of the dashing, daring, devil-may-care hero.

He didn't know if he was up for the part. He didn't know if he could give up the liquor, the parties, the women . . .

No, with Adriana in his life, having other women around didn't matter. She piqued his curiosity. She was using every ounce of her will to fight him, but what she didn't realize was that it was having just the opposite effect.

No woman had ever fought him before. The conflict between them roused his passion, the challenge stirred his desire. Winning her over slowly would be the greatest triumph of his life.

Losing her was something he'd never accept.

He wiped the last speck of shaving cream from his jaw, folded the towel neatly, and laid it next to the sink.

Again he looked at the new man in the mirror and hoped he could be all that Adriana needed.

He found her in the living room, scribbling away at her desk.

"Well, what do you think?"

She turned around and he saw her eyes narrow into a frown. It wasn't a very good beginning.

"You look so different," she said.

"Good or bad?"

"Do you want an honest answer?"

He nodded, although it appeared she was going to deliver some ego-shattering words.

"I liked the other you," she told him. He watched the way her eyes focused on his hair, on the strand that still hung over his forehead, at his clean-shaven upper lip. "It doesn't seem right that you're having to make so many changes."

"I'm an actor, and this is just one more role to play. It doesn't bother me nearly as much as it seems to bother you."

"It's just that . . . well, I liked your mustache, I liked the way you wore your hair. I was used to you the other way."

"You've just met me. All you knew before was some man on a movie screen."

Adriana looked away, absently doodling on a piece of paper. When she spoke, her words were soft and reflective. "I fell in love with the man on that movie screen."

Trevor leaned over her desk, inhaling a hint of sweet perfume. "What was it you loved about Trevor Montgomery?" he asked. "His looks? His playboy image?"

"You're laughing at me."

"I just want to know how you could have loved a figment of some studio mogul's imagination."

"The Trevor Montgomery I saw on that screen was everything good. He was handsome and carefree. He was gentle but strong. He loved hard and he loved forever. Any woman in her right mind would have fallen in love with him."

"The women on screen fell in love with a character in a script. Other women fell in love with who they thought was Trevor Montgomery. But no woman ever got close enough to him to know what he was really like." He swept her soft blond hair behind her ear so he could see her pretty face, see the expression in her eyes. "Are you interested in knowing the real me?"

"Do you think I can separate fact from fiction?"

"Only if you want to. That decision's entirely up to you."

He listened to her sigh. He wanted to kiss her. But not right now. Not until she wanted it just as badly as he did.

She looked at the slim gold watch on her wrist, a watch that didn't come close to hiding the bruises he'd put there.

How could she possibly want him after what he'd done? He had to make up for it. He had to.

She straightened the already-neat papers on her desk, obviously doing anything she could to avoid him. "We have an appointment with my attorney at one o'clock," she said. "He's an old friend. I'm sure he'll help us out."

"I'll be on my best behavior."

"Just don't forget who you're supposed to be."

"I'm a quick study, Adriana. I've never flubbed my lines before."

"This isn't just any role, Trevor. It's your life we're dealing with."

"I'll play the role perfectly. Everyone will believe I am who I say."

Slowly, very, very slowly, he caressed her cheek.

"Only you will know the real me, Adriana. Only you."

✍ *Nine*

"Let me get this straight," Stewart Rosenblum said as he leaned into his black-leather executive chair. "You're Trevor Montgomery's son?"

Trevor nodded, smiling his long-ago famous Trevor Montgomery smile, the one the columnists said made his brown eyes sparkle, the cleft in his chin deepen. He might have shaved off the pencil-thin mustache that appeared in all his movies, he might have softened the style of his hair and modernized his clothes, but no one could mistake his smile for anyone's but Trevor's.

"You know, son, a million people would pay you top dollar to see your dad, to talk to him and find out if he killed Carole Sinclair."

"He didn't kill her," Trevor said adamantly. "And I'd pay top dollar if I could see my dad again, too. Unfortunately . . . he's dead."

Trevor couldn't help but notice the way the attorney studied his face, obviously looking for signs that he was lying, but Trevor had long been able to fool the public. His acting was too real, too true to form.

Still, Stewart continued the interrogation.

"Why did he disappear? Why didn't he turn himself in to the police and explain what happened?"

"Because he didn't know what happened," Trevor said, easily remembering the events of that morning in 1938 and the night before, but nothing in between. "He was with Carole. Everyone knew it. They'd driven away from a party together and gone to Carole's home in Santa Monica. He drank too much." Trevor looked at Adriana, at the concern in her eyes as he related the story. "My father always drank too much, but that night it was more than normal."

"Why?" Stewart asked, and Trevor rested his forearms on Stewart's desk.

"He didn't want to be with Carole," Trevor said, "but she was his costar, and the studio wanted him to play up the romance, make the filmgoers think they were just as much an item in real life as they were on the screen. Good gossip brought a lot more people to the theaters back then."

Stewart grinned, his look somewhat skeptical. "Your father told you an awful lot, didn't he?"

Trevor leaned back, absently stroking the mustache that was no longer there. "He had no one else to talk to."

"So what did he tell you about running away? Why did he disappear?"

The worry in Adriana's eyes had heightened, and he knew she was afraid that he'd say the wrong thing, that Stewart wouldn't believe him, that someone would learn that he'd traveled through time. What would happen then? he wondered. Would he be hauled off to some laboratory for study?

Would Adriana care? That was the only thing that really mattered to him now. That he wouldn't disappoint Adriana. That he'd look good in her eyes.

He'd always wanted to look good in people's eyes. The hell of it was, he'd never succeeded with the people who'd mattered the most—his parents.

Adriana was giving him more of a chance than they ever had. Maybe she was an angel after all.

"If I tell you what happened," Trevor said, "I'd appreciate it if you wouldn't talk about it with anyone but us."

"Stewart's a friend. And he's your attorney now, too," Adriana said. "He'll keep everything you tell him confidential."

She reached over, and Trevor thought for sure she was going to squeeze his hand, but she drew away. It didn't matter. Her smile gave him reassurance enough.

Trevor looked back at Stewart, ignoring the way he was staring at Adriana, at him, probably wondering what kind of relationship they shared. He couldn't let the man's scrutiny bother him. Right now he was forced to think of the all-too-real events of that evening and relate them to Stewart, substituting *my father* for *I*.

"My father told me that the last thing he remembered was climbing into bed with Carole and passing out. When he woke, he was covered with her blood, and he had a knife in his hand."

"Then he did murder her," Stewart stated, already assuming the worst.

"I don't think so. Trouble is, he couldn't remember."

"Then why didn't he stick around? Why didn't he call for help?"

"She was dead, and he was frightened. Everything pointed to him as the killer. Would you have stuck around to tell the police you were innocent?"

"I wouldn't have gotten myself into that situation in the first place."

"No, I doubt you would have," Trevor said, wishing he could wipe out a lifetime of making wrong decisions—but he couldn't. All he could do was start over. This was his chance to have a new life.

"My father was a coward," Trevor said.

"He wasn't," Adriana protested.

But Trevor nodded his head, remembering that morning in Carole's room. "He didn't want to suffer through bad press. He didn't want his image smeared. Those things and acting were what mattered the most in his life."

Trevor hoped Adriana would forgive him for destroying the perception of the man she'd idolized. "My father thought about committing suicide, but he disappeared instead. He didn't want to face anyone or anything. He just wanted to run away. That's what cowards do."

Adriana had turned away, staring out the window. Trevor didn't want her loving a myth, he wanted her to get to know him, the real, living, breathing Trevor Montgomery. The man who wasn't as heroic off-screen as he was on. The man who had demons that haunted him. The man who'd never been in love because he'd never learned how to love.

The man who thought he might have finally found the woman to teach him.

"So," he said, turning back to Stewart, "that's why my father disappeared. What else do you want to know?"

Stewart picked up a pen and hastily scratched on a yellow pad of paper. "Where did he go?"

Trevor hesitated, not to think up a reason, because he and Adriana had already dreamed up a story, but to pause, as if remembering the events of his father's past. "He went to Mexico. He'd gone there quite often with friends. It was easy to get across the border and even easier to hide. He lived by himself for nearly thirty years, in a village where no one knew him, where no one had ever heard the name Trevor Montgomery."

Stewart kept his eyes down, his pen poised over the paper. "What's the name of the village?"

The man was testing him, but Trevor felt ready for anything Stewart might throw out.

"Santa Elena. It's not on many maps."

Stewart glanced at Trevor over his glasses. "How very convenient."

"It was for my father."

Trevor looked out the window, reciting his story as if he'd expertly memorized lines from a script. He gave each word the proper inflection, his tone was low and reflective, his gaze distant, anguished. His acting was perfect.

"He was close to sixty when he met my mother. Not long after I was born she decided she didn't like the quiet, rural life, so she left him to raise me on his own."

"Was he a good father?"

"I have nothing else to compare him to," Trevor said, which was a lie. He knew that, in spite of his own less-than-perfect ways, he'd be a damn sight better father than his real one had been.

"I'm sure he did the best he could," Trevor continued, dreaming up words to say as he went along. "He passed away ten years ago . . . when he was eighty-four. He refused to see doctors—no matter how much I begged—because he was afraid someone might figure out who he was."

Stewart looked up from his paper and rubbed the bridge of his nose. A frown marred his face. He was a good lawyer, Trevor imagined. Skeptical of everyone—especially the man talking to him now.

"How did he die?" Stewart asked.

"Old age, I imagine. I never really knew, except that I went into his room one morning and he wouldn't wake up."

"Where's he buried?"

Trevor shook his head, already prepared for the question. "He wanted to be cremated. I don't have any records. I don't have anything that belonged to him before he went to Mexico, and he didn't have much of anything the last fifty years of his life."

Stewart rested his elbows on the desk, his hands steepled. He tapped his index fingers together, obviously deep in thought.

Trevor just wanted to get the meeting over with and get out of there. He'd never liked attorneys—good or bad. They reminded him too much of his father. Stern, skeptical, and cold. Stewart was no exception, even if he was Adriana's friend.

Stewart took off his glasses and set them on top his yellow pad. "It all sounds very interesting—and quite contrived. Why should I believe you're Trevor Montgomery's son?"

"Because I look exactly like him. I have his eyes, his nose, his mouth, his hair. We have the same voice."

"There's an impostor for just about every famous person."

"I'm not an impostor," Trevor said calmly, thinking that Stewart might be looking for a reaction. "I'm the son of a famous person."

"What do you think, Adriana?" Stewart asked. "Is he telling the truth?"

Adriana nodded, nervously twisting the black silk scarf in her lap. "I didn't believe it at first, but it's true. He knows things only Harrison and I knew about Trevor."

"So what is it you want, Mr. Montgomery? Your father's property back? Your father's money?"

"Citizenship," Trevor said. "I want to live in this country, but I have no records at all of my birth."

"How did you get across the border?"

"I gave a sob story to a very American-looking family about my girlfriend running off and ditching me on the streets of Tijuana. They believed me. I climbed into the backseat of their car, and we crossed the border."

"Do you have any money?"

"Some."

"Do you have any way of supporting yourself?"

"I can act."

"That's not very lucrative—unless you're a star. Do you have any experience."

"Some."

"Is that what you did in Mexico?"

"That's enough!" Adriana blurted out. "You're my friend, Stewart. I believe him, and I need for you to believe in him, too. He needs a birth certificate, a Social Security card, and a driver's license. That's all. As for money, I told him I'd support him until he gets on his feet."

"Do you think that's wise?"

"He told me he didn't need any support. He wanted to do everything on his own, but I insisted we come and see you. If anything I'm doing is un-wise, it's sitting here telling you everything. I've al-ways trusted you, but you're making this more difficult than it needs to be. Please, get us the iden-tification. July 4, 1964, is his birth date. His father was Trevor Montgomery. His mother was . . ."

"Gabrielle Montgomery," Trevor interrupted. "Her maiden name was Ramon."

Rosenblum leaned back in his chair, studying Tre-vor, studying Adriana, then slowly leaned forward and scribbled on his pad. "I'll need dates of birth."

Trevor nodded, gave Stewart the necessary infor-mation, and hoped his composure would keep Stew-art from digging up information that didn't exist.

"How long before we can get the I.D.?" Adriana asked.

"A few days," Stewart told her. "A week maybe. I'll get in touch with you when it's ready."

Trevor reached across the desk and shook Stew-art's hand. "Thank you for your help."

Stewart laughed. "Thank Adriana, not me. She pays me very good money to be a very good attor-ney. What you're asking of me isn't legal, and I could lose my license if I get caught. But Adriana's not only a client, she's a friend, and I'll do whatever she asks. I'll tell you one thing, though, Mr. Montgomery. You hurt her in any way, and I'll come after you. I'll find a way to expose you as a fraud."

"Hurting Adriana isn't in my game plan," he assured the attorney. No, he had no intention of hurting her at all.

☙ Ten

They stood across from each other in the crowded elevator and not once did Adriana seek Trevor's eyes. Even through her dark sunglasses he could see her staring at the floor, at the wall, at the back of an old lady's head.

What could possibly be going through her mind? Trevor wondered. Was she worried that he might be an impostor? Lord, he hoped those words of Stewart's hadn't made her doubt him all over again.

He lit up a cigarette when they walked out of the building, relieved to be away from Stewart's interrogation, out of the confining elevator, and in the fresh, coastal air.

"Do you have to do that?" Adriana asked, frowning at the cigarette in his mouth.

"Does it bother you?"

"Yes," she said flatly, then turned, headed toward the parking garage.

Trevor stubbed the Chesterfield out in a sand-filled ashtray at the edge of the office building, then rushed to catch up with Adriana.

"What's bothering you?" he called out before she could climb into the Mercedes.

She turned around slowly, then leaned against the

car door. "I feel like I've been sitting in a courtroom for the past two hours, waiting for someone to find me guilty of perjury."

"It wasn't all that bad," he said, taking a place at her side. "I thought things were going well, right up to the end, that is. You realize he didn't believe a word of it."

Adriana's head snapped toward him. "Why do you say that?"

"He's too smart, and all he saw was a good friend being suckered by a con artist."

"But you're not."

"No, I'm not a con artist, Adriana, but Stewart's going to prove that I am, and we have no way of proving I'm not, unless we tell him the truth. Of course, he won't believe that, either."

Adriana rubbed her arms as if a sudden chill had rushed through her.

"I should have gotten a birth certificate some other way, from someone who wouldn't ask any questions," she stated.

"And then you'd open both of us up to God knows what. Getting the certificate from Stewart won't be legal, but it's better to deal with someone you trust than with some back-alley thug."

"You've watched too many old movies."

"Maybe I've just made too many."

That brought a smile to Adriana's lips. "You didn't make enough."

"I have a new life, Adriana. Maybe I'll make some more."

"Is that what you want? To act again."

"I've always wanted to act. But not right now." All he wanted was to spend time watching her smile, enjoying her occasional laugh. His life had been consumed with making movies, with being a star. He'd never taken the time to have a life that wasn't orchestrated by the studio. He'd never wanted anything more—until now.

"Show me around Santa Barbara," he said. "Let me see how things have changed."

"Someone might see you."

Her words made him laugh. "Do I look like a freak, Adriana? A man from outer space?"

She shook her head slowly. "You look . . . perfect, and everyone's going to stare."

"Jealous?"

"Of course not."

"Good. I saw an advertisement on your television about a place called McDonald's. I want to try a Big Mac and french fries."

"Absolutely not. Fast food isn't the least bit healthy."

He smiled at the persnickety woman standing in front of him. "I've indulged all my fantasies and all my cravings for years." He reached out and stroked her cheek, knowing full well that she'd pull away—which she did. "I think I look pretty good for a ninety-four-year-old man."

"You're terribly vain, do you know that?"

"I know it, you know it, and half the world knew it in the thirties. I'm proud and stubborn, too. I don't have many sterling qualities, Adriana, but do you mind if we discuss my lack of character some other time? I'm hungry, and that Big Mac looked awfully good."

Adriana shook her head in disgust. "Don't blame me if you get fat."

They walked briskly through the parking lot and out onto State Street, lined on either side by Spanish- and Moorish-style buildings with tiled roofs that glistened in the sun.

Trevor captured Adriana's arm and slowed her down. "Take a moment to enjoy it all, Adriana Life's too short to rush."

"I thought you were hungry."

"I am, but I want to enjoy the sights, too."

Slowly he pulled the black silk scarf from her hair. "You don't need to hide behind this, you know. You're one of the prettiest sights in town."

"I'm not hiding."

"That's the way it appears to me." He tucked the scarf into his pocket, ignoring her attempts to take it back. Instead he took her hand and pulled her into the sunlight.

"Well, what do you know." He pointed to the building just across the street. "The Granada Theatre's still standing. I bet you didn't know that I appeared on stage there once."

"With Helen Hayes, as I recall."

She did know a lot of details. But no one knew the real truth about Trevor Montgomery, those things he'd never told a soul. Still, he said, "Your knowledge is impressive."

"I know everything there is to know about you."

"I doubt that seriously. There are many things only I'm aware of, many things I just might share with you—if you're good."

They turned into a courtyard of winding paths, fountains, and tiled pools. Hanging baskets and red clay pots decorated their way, each filled with red and white geraniums, bright orange marigolds, sweet alyssum, and other colorful flowers he couldn't begin to name.

He'd seen many of these buildings before, but the atmosphere had changed. There were more shops now, more people. Wide windows displayed artwork, women's clothing, and elaborate gold and silver jewelry. He stopped in front of a window and admired a man's three-piece wool suit, then dragged Adriana inside for a fitting, groaned at the staggering price, but peeled numerous bills from his clip.

"Where does all this money keep coming from?"

Adriana asked when they left the store.

"A secret stash. I'm surprised you've never found it."

"It's in the house?"

"You can't get into banks twenty-four hours a day. I never knew when I might need it."

"We have automated bank tellers now. You just go up to a machine, punch in a number, and withdraw money out of your account."

"Interesting concept. I'll let you show me one of those machines, and maybe someday I'll show you the secret panel in . . . your home."

"It's *your* home, Trevor. I don't feel right claiming it's mine. Not any longer."

"Then we'll share. For now."

She looked uncomfortable but intrigued with the thought. Trevor was just as intrigued. Sharing the house, the cars, the food . . . the bed.

It sounded so good, but he had to slow down. He was more than ready. She wasn't even close.

Strolling along the walks, they passed women and men sitting at intimate tables for two, sipping coffee and other drinks. No one seemed to be staring at him. In the thirties when he'd walked down State Street at least one or two people would ask for his autograph, and he'd gladly obliged. He rather missed the notoriety.

Finally they reached a place with golden arches painted on the windows. "McDonald's?" he asked, clutching Adriana's arm and pulling her to a stop.

She smiled indulgently. "You know, there's a lovely little restaurant not far from here. They have salads and herb teas."

Trevor shook his head. "Big Mac and fries. My treat."

He wove his fingers through hers and didn't let go when she tried to pull away. She was the most uptight woman he'd ever met, and he was bound and determined to loosen her up.

They stood side by side at the counter and Trevor started to order. A Big Mac, a large fries, a hot apple turnover, and a Coke. "What would you like?" he asked Adriana.

"I thought you'd ordered enough that we could share."

Sharing food with Adriana wasn't a bad idea. Sharing her home wasn't a bad idea, either. Both had endless possibilities.

Carrying the tray, Trevor found a table that looked out onto the courtyard, sat down, and immediately peeled off wrappers. "Let's see if this is as good as they say."

The first bite was all and more than he'd hoped for. He loved the sauce and cheese that oozed over the bun and dripped onto the table. He liked the way the sandwich slid apart, the bread going one direction, the meat another.

He peeked over the top of his burger and watched Adriana pick at a french fry, then delicately lick the salt from her fingers. He didn't say a word, just watched her enjoying the tastes she was putting into her mouth.

"Try this," he said, holding the sloppy burger out to her.

"I can't. It's much too fattening."

"I might not be around forever, Adriana, but while I'm here, I have every intention of showing you how to live." He moved the burger a little closer. "Try it."

Some of the pinkish sauce stuck to the corner of her lip after she bit into the burger, and before she could wipe it off with her napkin, Trevor stroked it away and licked it from his thumb.

"What do you think?" he asked with a wicked wink.

"That you're a little too hedonistic for me."

"I doubt that seriously. But I was talking about the burger, not about me."

"I think I should stick with salads."

"I think you should stick with me. When was the last time you did something just for fun?"

She didn't answer immediately, which wasn't a good sign. Hell, Trevor made a point of having a good time, at least once a day.

"I went to the theater with Stewart and Maggie a month or so ago," she said. "Going out isn't my style."

"Hiding behind silk scarves, dark sunglasses, and adobe walls is?"

"I like my privacy. Besides, it's good for business. It gives me a certain mystique that makes people curious. That curiosity makes my shop and my work more intriguing. People seek me out because of it."

"Work isn't the only thing in life."

"I enjoy reading and watching old movies."

"Ever swim naked in the ocean?"

"Of course not."

"Will you do it with me?"

"No."

Trevor sipped his Coke, watching the pretty lady over the top of the plastic lid. She didn't know it yet, but Adriana Howard was going to go into the Pacific naked as a baby, and she was going to do it with Trevor Montgomery. It might take a day or two, maybe a week, but she was definitely going to give it a try.

"Where are we going now?" she asked, when he took her hand and led her out into the courtyard.

"Ice cream."

Adriana pulled back. "I don't want ice cream."

"I do. If you don't want to indulge, you can watch while I do."

They went into the ice-cream shop and Trevor

stared at a room full of flavors. He'd thought about strawberry or chocolate, but suddenly he was faced with dozens of choices and he wanted to try them all.

"Which one?" he asked Adriana. He needed her advice, but she just leaned against the counter and smiled at him. She probably didn't even know she was smiling, and he was sure she didn't know how good it looked on her.

"You're like a little boy," she said, pulling napkins from a chrome container.

He couldn't help but reach out and gently palm her cheek. "It's all so new. I want to try everything."

She pulled his fingers away, but he felt her absentmindedly stroke his knuckles with her thumb. "You'll have plenty of time," she told him.

"What if I don't?"

She looked down at the black-and-white-tiled floor. "I don't want to think about that."

She cared. She was trying not to show it—but she did.

He settled on a sugar cone with a scoop of chocolate macadamia nut and one of black walnut and headed back out into the fragrant courtyard and down a walkway. Finding a small, grassy lawn, he pulled Adriana down beside him and leaned against a palm.

"Have you ever stomped grapes with your bare feet?" he asked her, delighted by her sudden laugh.

"Of course I haven't. Why would I want to do that?"

"It feels good. So do a whole lot of other things." He slowly licked the ice cream cone, watching the way her eyes studied his tongue, his lips. "What makes you feel good, Adriana?"

She slipped her shoes off and wiggled her toes as the sun hit them. "Finding a rare piece of memorabilia, getting it for a good price, and selling it much higher."

"Making money's good, but I was thinking of something more along the lines of going to parties with friends, playing croquet on a Sunday afternoon, dancing on a Saturday night."

She shook her head slowly. "I don't dance ... much."

He took one last bite of the cone and tossed the remains in the trash can not more than ten feet away, then stretched out on the grass, folding his arms under his head like a pillow. "Y'know, Adriana, I can't imagine going more than a few days without dancing. Sometimes I used to hit two or three clubs in a week—the Trocadero, the Cocoanut Grove, the Palomar. One night we'd go to hear Benny Goodman, another Phil Harris or Jimmy Dorsey."

"None of those places are around any longer. We don't have big bands," she said. "Hollywood's different now, and all those nightclubs are just a part of history."

"Memories don't die, Adriana. For me, they just happened yesterday. I know the feel of Ginger Rogers' waist and I remember Betty Grable's legs. I remember Jackie Cooper sitting in with one of the bands and playing the drums. I remember sharing drinks with Cary Grant, trying to beat Fred Astaire in a dance contest, and getting drunk with Errol Flynn." He opened his eyes. "Those were the good times."

"Were there any that were bad?"

Too many bad times. Being locked away in his bedroom for weeks at a time just because he'd been caught going to see a movie. The switch his tutor took to his backside when he spoke of Valentino, Mary Pickford, or Douglas Fairbanks, rather than reciting Latin or key phrases from his father's legal texts. His mother pushing him away when he'd wanted a hug. But Adriana didn't need to know those things.

"Life was always good," he told her instead. "What's been good for you—besides making money?"

"Walks on the beach, reading."

"What about friends? People you go out with?"

"Stewart and his wife, Maggie. I have business acquaintances over for cocktails, Stewart and Maggie come for dinner occasionally. That's all."

"Boyfriends? Ever been married?"

Adriana shook her head. "I like being alone."

"You don't like men?"

"No one's ever interested me."

"Do I interest you?"

"You've always interested me."

"What about the me who's here right now? The real Trevor Montgomery—not the one on the screen."

She hesitated, and when she turned away, he sat up and tilted her face toward him. "What about me, Adriana?"

"Yes, you interest me."

His fingers lingered a moment on her cheek, then he drew his hand away. Take it slow and easy, he told himself. Don't frighten her.

There were so many things he wanted to teach her, so many interesting things he wanted to experience with her.

Someday.

Across the table sat the most beautiful woman Trevor had ever seen, but Adriana didn't appear to have any idea how her blue eyes radiated or how her lips curved into a sweet smile even when she tried to look detached.

She picked at leaves of green lettuce while he devoured steak and lobster and a baked potato loaded with butter, sour cream, and chives. She'd wanted to go home and work, but he'd insisted the evening was too young to call it a night. Besides, there was so much to see and do in this new world he'd been thrown into, and he wanted to share every exciting thing with her.

He wanted to know everything about her, too.

"Why do you live in my old house?" he asked, taking a sip of the wine she hadn't wanted him to buy. "Why do you have so many of my belongings?"

She wiped her mouth with the linen napkin, folded it neatly in fourths, and laid it beside her plate. He thought he'd been neat in his lifetime, but she had him beat. Slowly her gaze flickered from his eyes down to the glass of ice water which she took in her hands, holding it in front of her mouth as if it were a shield. Lord, he hoped one of these days she would relax in his presence and not feel the need to hide.

"I inherited everything," she finally answered, looking terribly uncomfortable when she spoke.

Trevor frowned at her words. "I didn't leave a will. I had no family that I knew of."

"After you disappeared, when it looked like you'd never return, the state wanted to confiscate everything."

That didn't make sense. Not at all. "But I had money in the bank. I had a business manager. Surely he looked after things."

Adriana shook her head, and suddenly the full depth of what had happened sank in. He had nothing any longer.

"Your business manager hired detectives to look for you, or so I was told, then he disappeared, along with your money. Apparently he didn't want to bother getting rid of the house and your cars."

"That was generous." Trevor downed the remains

of his wine, ignoring Adriana's frown. "Remind me to fire him if I ever get back to 1938."

"Do you want to go back?"

"To a murder charge? No. To the life I was leading the day before Carole died? I'm not sure."

He saw the look of nagging fear cross her pretty face. She lifted the dessert menu from the table and attempted to hide by looking for something sweet, which he knew she didn't want to eat.

Putting an index finger on top of the menu, he pushed it down slightly so he could see her eyes. "I'd like something chocolate, and I'd like you to tell me how you inherited all my things."

A moment later the waiter took the order for chocolate Grand Marnier, and Adriana rested her arms on the table, leaning closer to Trevor as if she didn't want anyone else to hear.

"Harrison Stafford gave it to me."

"Harry?"

She nodded. "His attorneys found a way to claim every tangible item that belonged to you at the time of your disappearance. He couldn't recover the money, but he did get the cars, the house, your furniture. He was sure you'd come back someday, so he kept everything just as it was."

"Good old Harry. The two of us go way back. Is he still living at Sparta?"

Adriana shook her head. "No."

Trevor saw the sadness in her eyes and suddenly he knew. He'd been gone sixty years—things were bound to have changed.

He looked away, not wanting Adriana to see the grief that was making his lips tremble.

"Is he dead?" he asked, although he was sure of the answer.

"Eight years ago."

Death. It was something he hadn't considered.

How many of his other friends were gone? He hated to think about it.

"Mind if we go home?" He was no longer interested in the food or atmosphere of the restaurant, no longer wanted to enjoy the night. He wanted to be alone, to think.

In less than half an hour he climbed from the Mercedes and headed toward the stairs leading to the beach, not giving any thought at all to Adriana until he sensed her standing at the kitchen door watching him. He turned around, saw her face in the moonlight, and he held out his hand.

Slowly she came to him. She didn't take his hand, but she slipped off her shoes and left them at the top of the stairs before she walked at his side down to the beach.

He sat in the sand with her beside him, and together they watched the gentle waves rolling back and forth.

"Was Harry your father?" he asked finally, trying to understand her connection with a man who, he imagined, would have been a hundred years old if he were still alive.

"My legal guardian," Adriana said softly. "My father was curator at Sparta, and when he died, Harrison took care of me."

"That wife of his must have loved that," Trevor said sarcastically.

"Not exactly. She fought it every step of the way. She even tried to have the courts declare him incompetent."

"Harry incompetent? Never! But I can understand that wife of his trying to prove it. She refused to live anywhere but New York. Refused to let him see his own children. The only mistake Harry ever made in his life was marrying that woman. What about her? Is she still around?"

Adriana nodded. "Bitterness seems to keep her

alive. She had one goal, and that was to have everything that ever belonged to Harrison. She figured if she outlived him, she'd have it all. Of course, Harrison's attorneys put together an ironclad will, and he managed to stay alive until I was legally old enough to inherit it all."

"Everything?"

"Almost. He left a sizable fortune to each of his children, even to his wife, but he left Sparta to me, along with all the property, the businesses, most of the money, your house, your cars."

"All of that, yet you choose to live here instead of Sparta."

"Sparta doesn't belong to me any longer. Not all of it anyway."

Suddenly she rose from the sand. "It's getting late."

"It's early—and I want to hear more."

"It's not something I like talking about."

Reaching out, Trevor took hold of her fingers and kept her from walking away. "Tell me, Adriana. Please."

She sat beside him again, wrapping her arms around her knees, and stared out at the ocean.

"You told Stewart today that you'd been a coward, that you didn't want to face the press. Well, that's the same reason I no longer own Sparta."

She was silent a moment, reflective.

"Harrison became my legal guardian when I was sixteen. What should have been a simple proceeding got dragged through the press because his wife accused him of having more than a fatherly interest in me."

"That's impossible. Not Harry."

"You know it, I know it, but the press had a field day. Every time I turned around there'd be a photographer shoving a camera in my face. If I picked up a paper, I'd see my picture on the front and some despicable headline. They called me a gold digger, a seducer of older men. Harrison laughed it off, but he was used to the press. Not me. The notoriety died down after a while, but it all started again when Harrison died. More pictures, more gossip. I rarely went out in public before he died, but after, well, I didn't want to go anywhere. I just wanted it all to stop."

"Did it?"

"No. It only got worse."

"Let me guess. His wife contested the will."

"She did more than that. Where she got them, I don't know, but she had photos of me sitting on Harrison's lap, of the two of us walking hand in hand on the beach, and she intended to give them to the tabloids."

"They sound innocent enough to me."

"Not when you put a different spin on the pictures, like *Harrison Stafford and his child paramour*."

"Would she really have stooped that low?"

"I didn't want to find out. I didn't want anything bad to end up in the papers about me or about Harrison. He was like a father to me. I'd grown up at Sparta. I loved him, and he loved me. There was nothing more to it than that."

"So, you made a deal with her."

Adriana nodded. "Stewart didn't want me to, but it was the only thing I could do."

She told him about giving most of Sparta to the state, about ensuring that Harrison's butler and cook were allowed to stay on. "Harrison's wife didn't care about his Hollywood memorabilia or your things in Santa Barbara. She didn't even care if I kept Harrison's suite of rooms at Sparta. All she wanted were his businesses and his money."

"You gave all of that to her?"

"Stewart knew what I wouldn't give up. The rest of the negotiation I left up to him. When he was through, I had what I wanted plus a sizable chunk of money in the bank and custody of all the pictures she had had taken of Harrison and me."

"In other words, she got away with blackmail."

"It doesn't matter. Not anymore. Besides, I have wonderful memories; all she has is money and hate."

"Share a good memory with me."

Her smile made him feel warm inside.

"Watching old movies with Harrison, listening to his stories of the past. Watching him walk again after he had his first stroke. Sitting at his bedside and reading to him when he lost his sight."

A tear slid down Adriana's cheek, and Trevor caressed it away with his thumb.

"I have good memories of Harry, too. Would you like to hear one?"

She nodded as he stroked away another one of her tears.

"I was riding in an empty boxcar, taking my first cross-country trip from Chicago to Hollywood. I was sixteen. I was cold, broke, hungry, and I thought for sure I'd get kicked off the train when we stopped in Kansas City. I huddled in a dark corner, hoping the train would pull out before I got caught. This big, burly fellow swung up into the car just as the train jerked out of the station, and he just stood there, staring out the open door.

"I didn't make a sound, afraid the man might be a guard. I was sure he hadn't seen me, but then he took off his heavy coat and threw it toward me.

"'Not such a bright idea to be riding the rails in wintertime,' he said. 'Especially without a coat. Suppose you don't have any food, either.' He pulled a loaf of bread from the bag he was carrying and tossed it to me along with a hunk of cheese. I didn't expect kindness from a stranger. Took me totally by surprise.

"That was the best trip I ever took. Harry Stafford hunkered down beside me in that boxcar and talked all the way to California. He was twenty-two, he'd made big bucks in oil, and he planned to build a castle on the Pacific. But first, he wanted to see how guys like me saw the world. I told him it wasn't a very pretty sight. All he did was laugh, and go on talking about his dreams.

"We parted company at the train station in Hollywood. I gave him back his coat and he gave me ten bucks and told me I could pay him back when I made my own first million. Took ten years for that to happen, but I paid him back.

"Guess I can honestly say there's only one person I've ever loved in this world, and that was Harry Stafford."

"He never told me that story," Adriana said. "I thought I'd heard them all."

"I could tell you hundreds more, if you feel like listening."

"Harrison said that's one of the things I did best."

Her smile touched his heart, warming that spot that had been cold for so many years.

He captured a strand of breeze-tossed hair and curled it behind her ear. For the first time, he realized that she hadn't flinched or moved away from his touch. He wanted to lean forward and kiss her, he wanted to tell her how happy she made him.

But she wasn't quite ready.

Not yet.

❧ *Eleven*

Trevor paced the living room while Adriana sat serenely at her desk with the phone pressed to her ear. For almost four hours she'd been in nearly the same position. "I have business to take care of," she'd told him, and nothing turned her away from her task, not even the yellow roses he'd clipped in the garden or the plate of fruit he'd sliced and slid in front of the phone.

He could understand the obsessive desire to work hard at something you loved, but not at the expense of enjoying the other things in life, like dancing, stealing kisses in public, or making love. He had to wonder if Adriana had ever taken part in any of life's special delights. If she hadn't, he planned to introduce her to those things and many more.

"Of course I'm interested," she told the person at the other end of the line, "but I need to have the signature authenticated before I can give you a bid." She flipped through a leather-bound calendar. "Two-thirty tomorrow's fine . . . At the airport." She scribbled a name on the page. "I'm also interested in seeing the script you have from *Magnificent Obsession*, the one with Rock Hudson's notes."

That movie title roused Trevor's curiosity, as did the name she'd mentioned.

"Who's Rock Hudson?" he asked, leaning over her shoulder.

"The star of the movie," she whispered in irritation.

"No, no, I wasn't talking to you," she said into the phone.

"Robert Taylor was the star," Trevor whispered back. "It should have been my movie—me and Irene Dunne, but . . ."

Adriana frowned, cutting off his words with her glare and her attempt to brush him away, but he didn't move. How could she possibly buy and sell Hollywood memorabilia when she had her facts all wrong?

"I look forward to seeing you, too." She hung up the phone and swiveled around in her chair.

"This is my business, Trevor. I can't make money if you bother me while I'm trying to negotiate."

"How can you possibly make money when your information's all wrong?"

Adriana smiled indulgently, shaking her head as if he was the one who was wrong—which he wasn't.

"Robert Taylor was in the *first* version of *Magnificent Obsession*," she said. "Rock Hudson starred in it in 1954."

"Never heard of him."

"The rest of the world has. I think we're going to have to bring you up to date on what's happened in the past sixty years."

"And maybe we should bring you up to date on what happened in the thirties."

"I know all about the movies of the thirties."

Turning back to her desk, Adriana scribbled a few notes on a tablet, then tilted her head and looked back at Trevor.

"I didn't know that you auditioned for the Robert Taylor role."

Trevor leaned against her desk and shrugged slightly. "I didn't actually audition, but I let everyone, including Irene Dunne, know I wanted the part. Unfortunately, Jack Warner wouldn't loan me to Universal."

Smiling, Adriana closed her notebook and rested back in her chair. "I suppose there are some things I could learn from you—about the movies."

"Thousands, more than likely. But not today."

"Why?"

"Because I want to teach you that Saturdays were made for fun, not for staying cooped up in the house, and definitely not for working."

"My business doesn't operate just on weekdays."

"I suppose I could go out by myself."

"That's not such a good idea."

"Why? Do you think I'll get into trouble?"

"Of course not. But someone might see you."

"You're the one who doesn't like to be seen. Not me."

He pulled her from the chair and moved in close. He could smell the sweetness of her perfume, could feel her muscles tense as he trailed his palms lightly over her arms.

Still, she didn't pull away.

"Since you're so worried about how I'll handle myself in public, go out with me. Let me show you how to enjoy yourself."

"I enjoy making money, which I won't be able to do if you keep dragging me from my work."

"You seemed a somewhat willing accomplice yesterday."

"Did I have a choice?"

"You could have said no to me." A slow grin crossed his face as he brushed his knuckles over her cheek. "Of course, very few women have ever said no to me."

"So I've heard," she mumbled, backing out of his arms.

The number of women in his life seemed to bother her tremendously. Of course, not one of them had interested him the way Adriana did.

"I suppose I could take you shopping," she said as she straightened the papers on her desk.

"I had more than that in mind." He took a step toward her, backing her against her desk. "I want to go dancing."

"I don't go dancing."

"Yes, I know. You work ... but not tonight. I'm taking you out on the town."

"I need to work. I have a client flying in tomorrow."

"That's tomorrow." Trevor touched her shoulders and lightly trailed his fingers down to her hands. "Tonight I'm taking you dancing," he whispered. "First, though, I want you to show me that shop of yours that occupies so much of your time."

"You might find it boring."

"Nothing you do is boring. I want to learn everything about you." He drew her hands to his lips and kissed them lightly. "There are so many places I want to take you."

A tinge of fear mixed with excitement filled Adriana's eyes. "Maybe I've been there already."

He shook his head slowly. "Never with me."

Trevor leaned against the Mercedes parked at the curb and contemplated the front window of Adriana's shop. A nearly perfect likeness of Clark Gable dressed as a Southern gentleman stood before a mural of an antebellum mansion. Next to him was a beautiful, dark-haired Southern belle, and he hadn't a clue what the scene was supposed to represent.

"I recognize Clark Gable," Trevor said, "but who's the woman?"

"Vivian Leigh," Adriana told him. "*Gone With the Wind* came out late in 1939. It was just in the planning stages when you disappeared."

"*Gone With the Wind*," he repeated. "I've never heard of it."

"It's one of the biggest money makers of all time."

"That's no surprise. Gable had a unique way of picking the winners."

Trevor pushed away from the car. "So, what's inside?"

"A world full of wonderful things."

It was dark and quiet when they stepped into the shop, but when Adriana turned on the lights, the glamour Trevor remembered came into view.

Mannequins in the likenesses of Ginger Rogers, Fred Astaire, Ronald Colman, Rudolph Valentino, and Errol Flynn graced the floor, dressed in roles Trevor remembered so well: Ginger in flowing white, Fred in a tux, dancing together in *Flying Down to Rio*. That was the kind of elegance he longed for; Colman as the stand-in prince in *Prisoner of Zenda*; Errol as a pirate in *Captain Blood*; and Valentino as *The Sheik*.

"Pretty impressive," Trevor said, walking about the shop, his hands crossed behind his back as he inspected one costume after another. "I don't see any mannequins of me. I would have thought since I was your favorite that you'd have my likeness every-where."

"I'm only a collector where you're concerned. I don't sell anything that belonged to you."

He sat down in a high, flare-back wicker chair and rested his hands on the rounded arms. "Why?"

"You've asked that same question half a dozen times."

"I want to know, Adriana. Why this fixation for a

man old enough to be your grandfather?"

"You weren't old in the movies. You were handsome and fun and daring. You never got sick, or mean, or old, and you never died. When I was little, I wished my father was like you. When I got older, I quit seeing you as a father figure."

"I'm glad to hear that."

Adriana pulled a long white gown from one of the racks and held it up in front of her. "Do you like this?" she asked.

Trevor nodded. It looked sinful and seductive, and it would look much better on Adriana than on a hanger.

"It's a 1931 Molyneux. I used to imagine myself dressed up in a gown like this, dancing with someone like you."

"Your father never danced with you?"

Adriana shook her head. "My father didn't approve of dancing. He didn't approve of much of anything, actually. That's why I fantasized about you. If he didn't know what I was dreaming about, he had no reason to get mad."

Adriana shoved the dress back on the rack. "My father died, I got older, but the fantasies didn't go away. They just got stronger. Pretty soon I decided the fantasies were better than real life."

He understood that feeling full well. He felt best on a soundstage, acting out the roles of men who weren't anything at all like him, men who lived completely different lives.

Trevor got up from the chair and pulled the white crepe gown back off the rack. "I want to go dancing, Adriana. I know the ballrooms are gone now, but there must be someplace around where the music is nice and slow and the atmosphere's elegant and refined."

She shook her head, but he wasn't going to accept no for an answer. He held the gown in front of her.

"Dress up for me, Adriana. My world's gone away, but you can make it come back again—for tonight anyway."

A soft smile curved her lips. "Will you wear a tux?"

"If you have something you think might fit."

"I have an entire wardrobe full of things that should fit you like a glove."

"Let me guess. They're mine."

Adriana nodded. "Harrison always hoped you'd come back. I hoped you would, too, but never in my wildest dreams did I actually think it would happen."

"I'm here, Adriana. I'm not a dream, and I don't plan on going away."

It was well past 10 P.M. when they arrived at the Regal Biltmore. The valet helped Adriana from the car, and she and Trevor walked into a world nearly as opulent and majestic as the one she'd grown up in at Sparta. Marble floors, high-vaulted ceilings carved and painted by master craftsmen. It was warm, inviting, and beautiful, and Adriana felt more elegant than ever before as she climbed the stairs on the arm of a dream.

All eyes were on them as they strolled through the Main Galleria toward the Crystal Ballroom. The Molyneux gown dipped much too low in the front and even lower in the back, and it hugged every non-existent curve she owned before it swirled at her feet and trailed behind her on the floor. Trevor had draped a rope of pearls around her neck and insisted she wear silver three-inch heels when she was opting for white. He'd made the wiser choice, just as he had when he'd suggested black tails and tie for himself rather than the white dinner jacket she had wanted him to wear. He looked debonair. He looked like a fantasy come true.

It was a stroke of luck that she remembered the announcement she'd received that the hotel was re-creating the flavor of the twenties, thirties and forties as part of their seventy-fifth anniversary celebration, and ballroom dancing was just a portion of the festivities. The evening couldn't be any more perfect.

Trevor's eyes glistened in the light of the chandeliers as they stepped into the ballroom. All about them were glittering mirrors, ornate ceilings, and beautiful men and women dancing to the strains of music from another era.

"Is this familiar at all?" she asked Trevor, as they were led to a table not far from the dance floor.

"I received my Oscar here. Some of the best bands in the country used to play in this room, and we'd all come to listen and dance. I hardly ever sat down."

He ordered champagne as soon as they were seated, then moved his chair closer to Adriana's and listened intently to the orchestra.

He was going to be terribly disappointed when he asked her to dance. Why hadn't she practiced when she watched those old home movies? Why had she been too afraid to ask Harrison for dancing lessons?

All Trevor wanted this evening was to dance, and she didn't know how. Would he leave her and find a beautiful woman in the room, someone willing to spin around the floor in his arms?

"Dance with me," he said when the music slowed.

"Couldn't we just sit this one out?"

He shook his head. "I've been thinking about how you'd feel in my arms. I don't want to think about it any longer."

Adriana felt the heat of embarrassment rush into her cheeks. "I'm afraid you're never going to know how I feel dancing in your arms because ... well ... I don't know how to dance."

The cleft in Trevor's chin deepened, as did the

dimple to the right of his lips. "That's easily reme-
died."

He pushed from the table and pulled her chair
back. With his hands resting lightly on her shoulders, he bent over and whispered into her ear. "All
you have to do is hold me tight, Adriana, and let
me lead the way."

ℒ❤ *Twelve*

Dancing, in Trevor's mind, was the closest thing to making love. Holding a woman was heaven. Guiding a woman, moving rhythmically together to the gentle strains of soft, sweet music or the passionate crescendos that came hard and fast took his breath away. Just pulling Adriana close and leading her to the dance floor was like lifting her in his arms and carrying her to his bed. Her fingers trembled, she was hesitant, she looked at him with confusion, a mixture of want and desire and just a hint of wonder.

Slowly he guided one of her hands to his shoulder, the other he tucked close to his chest. Only twice before had they stood just inches apart, and both times she'd looked at him with frightened eyes, like a lamb facing a lion, wondering when it would be devoured.

Those times he'd been crazed. He'd acted like a madman.

But not this time. This time he wanted her. This time he needed her, and he knew it showed in the depth of his eyes.

"This isn't so bad," he whispered. "Is it?"

She shook her head. "I'll probably step on your feet."

"It doesn't matter. Just hold me tight and don't take your eyes off mine."

Her back felt soft and smooth and cool under his hand, and he guided her closer, gently gathering her against his body. He could feel the slow rise and fall of her breasts as they lightly grazed his chest. The warmth of her breath against his neck sent a slow burning desire through his body, inflaming his heart and his soul.

He might miss many of the things about the life he'd lived before, but he realized that his life would mean nothing—no matter what decade he was in—if Adriana wasn't beside him.

Sliding his hand farther around her waist, he swayed with her in his arms, not even bothering to move his feet.

"You're not dancing," she said, her blue eyes twinkling with just a touch of mirth. "Isn't the object to move around the dance floor?"

"One step at a time, Adriana, and this is the first one."

"Do we have to move on to the second?"

He teased her ear lightly with his lips, and whispered, "Each step is just a little nicer. But let's not rush. I'm in no hurry—no hurry at all."

He inhaled the sweet fragrance of her perfume, marveling at the feel of soft skin against his rougher face. He'd held women close before, women just as soft, just as sweet-smelling, but he'd never ached with want the way he did right now. His heart had never thundered in his chest. His mind had never thought beyond the moment, but right now he was thinking of how it would be to grow old with this woman, teaching her something new every day of their lives.

Slowly he pressed his right leg against her left one,

and just as slowly she moved with his lead. Left foot forward, right foot back. A slight turn to the right. A little sway. Right foot back, and she followed him. With each movement he held her closer, with each step she relaxed a little more, until they were dancing cheek to cheek, breast to chest, hip to hip, perfectly in sync as if they'd been designed to be two parts of a whole.

He hummed softly to the tune the band was playing, vaguely remembering the way Fred Astaire had sung the song to Ginger Rogers in *Swing Time*. He couldn't quite remember the words, but he gave them a shot, singing them softly in Adriana's ear. "When the world is cold and I'm awfully low, I will feel a glow just thinking of you . . ."

"I didn't know you could sing," Adriana whispered when Trevor went back to humming.

"I can't, and no one ever asked me to."

"I liked it," she said with a faraway smile.

He pressed his hand against her back again, at the same time his right leg pressed her left, and hummed more of "The Way You Look Tonight," thinking how perfect the words he had remembered were. He did feel a glow while thinking of Adriana, and dancing had never felt so wonderful, even though she'd stepped on his toes a time or two.

"I'm beginning to think you lied to me, Adriana."

"About what?"

"The fact that you've never danced."

"But I haven't. This is the first time."

"No one would ever know." He tilted his head to see her face. "It's a shame you've never tried before. I think you were made to dance."

She smiled softly. "Do you think so?"

"It's either that, or you were made to be in my arms."

She laughed lightly. "And how many women have you fed that line to?"

It wasn't a line—not this time. How could she ever believe that, though, when all anyone had ever known about him was his playboy image. He'd hidden behind that facade for a long time, using it to mask the anguish of not knowing how to love.

He didn't want to hide anymore.

"I deserve that, but I want you to know, Adriana, that everything I say to you is true. No one else ever felt the way you do. I never felt this way, either, like I could hold you forever."

Under his fingers he could feel her muscles tense. He felt her pulling away, but he pressed his hand against the small of her back and held her close. "Believe in me, Adriana. Please believe in me."

He swept her around the floor, holding her tight, his gaze locked on hers. Around and around the room, in and out, between other couples, until the music slowed again and he just stood with her in the middle of the dance floor and swayed.

"Why do you find it so hard to believe that I could care for you?"

She attempted to turn away, but he captured her cheek with the gentle touch of his hand.

"Tell me."

"I read somewhere that you'd seduced a thousand women."

Trevor grinned at her words. "Oh, at least that many." He winked. "Maybe more."

Once again he kept her from pulling away. He'd meant to tease, but apparently she hadn't understood. Damn! He was making a mess of everything.

"A lot of things have been written about me. A lot of truths. A lot of half-truths. I can't justify anything I did back then."

"Just tell me the truth now, Trevor. Are you trying to seduce me, too?" she asked.

"Yes. I won't lie about that. I want you, Adriana.

But you're not the least bit ready, and I'm not in any rush."

She sighed and closed her eyes, and he rested his cheek against hers.

"Don't worry," he whispered. "Just like dancing, we'll take everything one step at a time."

He held her close, losing himself in the music, the softness of her body, his thoughts about his past, about the future, and where Adriana fit into his life.

They were so much alike, both afraid to commit to a relationship. Just like him, she'd never been in love. Could he change all that? God, he hoped so.

But how could she possibly fall in love with a self-centered man whose parents had disowned him, a man who'd never been taught the first thing about loving, a man who'd found liquor to be the best companion and something that would never turn him away or leave him lonely?

He gathered her closer, and she tilted her head and smiled with trusting eyes before resting her cheek once more against his.

He could change his ways. He could try, at least. He'd do just about anything for this soft, love-starved woman who'd crawled into his heart and made it swell to the point he thought his chest might burst.

He swept his hands over the curve of her spine, swirled with her around the room, and hoped she'd bear with him while he tried to mend his ways.

Softly, he kissed her temple, and when the beat turned Latin and the rhythm of the dance suddenly changed, he led her back to the table, her hand gripped tightly in his.

"Why didn't you ever marry?" she asked, taking him completely by surprise as he poured champagne into his glass and hers. "Weren't you ever in love?"

"I was always in love." He ignored the look of

shock on her face. She'd asked the question, and he intended to answer.

"There were too many women around to fall in love with only one. Some liked to dance, some liked to swim, some liked to go to bullfights in Mexico. I was in love with whoever matched my mood at the moment, and no one ever seemed to care that when my disposition changed I'd move on to someone else."

"I don't believe any of it. I don't understand why no one ever fell in love with you."

If she'd been around in the thirties, she would have known why no one had fallen in love with him. He intended to tell her, and then he planned to show her that he was different now, that she was the turning point in his life.

"I went to Hollywood to become a star, and I didn't let anything interfere with that goal. At times I worked seven days a week, maybe eighteen hours a day. I didn't want a wife sitting at home waiting for me when I might never show up. I didn't want children that I'd probably ignore. Most of the actors and actresses I knew felt the same way."

"A lot of them married."

"And got divorced, too. That's not my style. Getting married means you stay married, for better or worse. If I'd gotten married, I'm afraid the 'worse' part of the vow would have been at the forefront, and that's not fair to anybody."

"What about now? You have a whole new life ahead of you."

"Do I?" he asked, suddenly realizing that as much as he wanted Adriana, he could be ripped away from her without warning. He could be lonely again.

"Of course you do. You're the best actor who ever lived—"

"Don't stretch the truth. I was a good actor, not the best."

"In my eyes no one ever compared with you. A talent like yours is something you never lose. You could start again. Get an agent, some acting jobs."

God, he didn't want to start over again. He'd been a star. He'd spent eighteen years climbing from errand boy to Oscar winner.

He took a sip of champagne, wishing he'd substituted the sweet, bubbly stuff with bourbon or scotch, anything to drown out the thought of being a nobody once more.

She reached across the table and placed a warm hand on his. "You told me to believe in you. I do, Trevor, but you have to believe in yourself. You can have everything if you want it."

"I do want everything. I want the best parts of my old life and the best parts of this new one, but what if there's no future for me? I've been ripped out of one decade and forced into another. It could happen again at any time. Hell, Adriana, I don't even know if I'll have another tomorrow with you."

He poured more champagne, drinking it down just as fast as he could pour it out, then called to the waiter and ordered another bottle. Adriana frowned, and he realized immediately that changing his life wasn't as easy as making a wish and having it all come true.

"Adriana, darlin'!"

A petite, flame-haired beauty swept up behind Adriana and wrapped her in feathered arms.

"What a surprise," the woman gushed. "Never in my wildest dreams did I expect to run into you here."

Adriana's eyes brightened when she hugged the woman. The lady was wrapped tightly in glimmering yellow cloth that stretched over vivacious curves, and with the amount of feathers covering her arms and bosom Trevor thought for sure she could take off and fly. She looked a lot like Big Bird, the strange-looking creature he'd seen when he'd spent two hours playing with that contraption that controlled Adriana's television set.

Behind the woman stood the somber gentleman Trevor remembered too well: Stewart Rosenblum.

"Good evening." Trevor pushed up from the table and extended his hand to Stewart.

The woman was fascinating and gay; Stewart was dour, his gaze analyzing Trevor's attire, Adriana's, and the bottle of champagne on the table. *Charming gentleman*, Trevor thought sarcastically.

"You haven't met my wife," Stewart said, giving Trevor a quick, polite handshake. "Trevor Montgomery, may I introduce you to Maggie Rosenblum."

"Oh, my," Maggie chortled, gazing from Trevor to Adriana, then back again. "You've landed yourself an absolutely heavenly creature, Adriana."

Adriana rolled her eyes, and Maggie winked at Trevor, continuing her rapid chatter. "He's gorgeous, and I do mean just about the most handsome thing I've ever seen. Don't you agree, Stewart?"

"I see him in quite a different light, my dear."

"Oh, you would, wouldn't you?" Maggie stood on tiptoes and pecked her husband's cheek.

"You don't mind if we join you, do you, Adriana?" Maggie asked.

"Of course not."

Lively companions and partying till all hours of the night had been at the heart of Trevor's existence, but right now he didn't want to be sharing the table or his evening with anyone other than Adriana. Even so, he pulled a chair out for Maggie and once again took his seat.

"Do you come here often?" Trevor asked, directing his words to Stewart.

"Not to this particular place," Stewart answered.

"Oh, Stewart, must you be so precise?" Maggie

chastised her husband, but her bright, loving smile never dimmed. "We go dancing once a month," Maggie stated. "I just love ballroom dancing, and Stewart is absolutely divine on the dance floor. I imagine you're divine on the dance floor also, Mr. Montgomery. You have that look about you."

"You'll have to excuse my friend," Adriana interrupted. "She has a nasty habit of saying exactly what's on her mind."

"It drives Adriana absolutely mad," Maggie continued, not the least put off by Adriana's words. "But she's a dear, and we're the best of friends. Have you known each other long, Mr. Montgomery?"

"It's Trevor. And it's been just a few days. We're still learning each other's secrets."

"That's lovely. Stewart and I learn something new at least once a week. Keeps things exciting, doesn't it, sweetie?"

Stewart grinned, shaking his head as he leaned over and kissed his wife. Their attraction amazed Trevor. Stewart appeared to be the type of man who'd show disdain toward a woman like Maggie, but he seemed utterly and completely enthralled. Maybe the man had a few redeeming qualities after all.

Catching the waiter's attention, Trevor asked that more glasses be delivered to his table.

"You will join us for a drink or two?" he asked.

"Oh, I'd love to," Maggie gushed, then looked at her husband, her crimson fingernails trailing down his arm. "You don't mind, do you, sweetie? Just one, maybe two little ones?"

"I'm the one with the problem, my dear. Not you."

"Thank you." She kissed Stewart's mouth, leaving a trace of red lipstick behind. "Stewart's a recovered alcoholic," she whispered to Trevor. "He hasn't had a drink in eight years. Isn't that right, sweetie?"

Stewart smiled indulgently. "Eight years, three months, and . . ." Stewart shrugged. "I'm sure Mr. Montgomery doesn't want to hear this story, and Adriana knows it by heart."

Trevor poured champagne into Maggie's glass when it was placed in front of her. Adriana's was still full—she hadn't touched a drop. He refilled his own, then leaned back and sipped the bubbly liquid, once again ignoring Adriana's frown. He planned to change his ways, but he'd take it one step at a time. He'd deal with the self-absorbed part of his character first, then he'd concentrate on the drinking.

Suddenly, a hand clamped down on his shoulder and he jerked his head up, staring into the face of a middle-aged stranger. "Hello, Mr. Dean," the man said, a scowl marring his face.

Trevor caught Stewart's dubious stare out of the corner of his eye. The last thing Trevor needed was to be mistaken for someone else.

"Mr. Dean?" Trevor questioned. "I'm sorry. You must have me confused with someone else."

The stranger laughed. "Trying to pull a fast one again?"

"I honestly don't know what you're talking about," Trevor said.

"You look exactly like someone my mother used to know, but . . ." The man shook his head and shrugged. "Maybe I'm wrong. Sorry to disturb you."

Adriana studied Trevor with frowning eyes as the stranger walked away, but Maggie lightened the moment by turning the attention to herself.

"Isn't that the funniest thing? I can't tell you the number of times I've been mistaken for someone else. They say we all have a twin roaming around somewhere. I do think it would be terribly interesting to meet mine."

"There couldn't possibly be two women just like

you," Stewart said. "I believe I was lucky enough to find the one and only."

"Oh, you're such a sweetie."

Maggie sipped her champagne and watched the dancers, her index finger bouncing through the air in time with the music.

"You know, Trevor," Maggie continued, "I've tried to coerce Adriana into going out on the town at least half a million times, but she constantly turns me down. It's delightful to see that someone's finally charmed her into loosening up."

"He hasn't charmed me, Maggie."

"But he has, darlin'. Why, you're absolutely dazzling tonight. I see those little sparkles in your eyes light up every time you look at this gorgeous creature you're with."

Maggie leaned toward Trevor. "She doesn't care much for men, you know. Doesn't care much for drinking, or dancing, or anything of that sort, either."

"Maggie, dear." Stewart put a hand on his wife's, but she brushed him off with just a glance.

"She's much too uptight. Dressing like Greta Garbo and acting out the life of a recluse has gotten completely out of hand. Isn't that right, darlin'?"

Adriana's cheeks pinkened. "I rather like being a recluse."

"No you don't. It started out as a way to hide from those nasty photographers, and then you figured out how to make it help in your work. Just like Stewart. Work, work, work!"

"If it wasn't for all that work, work, work," Stewart said, "you wouldn't be wearing those feathers, you wouldn't be dancing here, and you wouldn't have two homes and three sports cars."

Maggie appeared contrite for a moment, but the humbled look melted away in an instant. "I compensate for all the hours he's away from home by doing extra special things when he's around. It's the way of the world, I imagine. For better, for worse. That was the vow—I just learned how to turn the 'worse' part into something nice."

Maggie wove her fingers through her husband's. "I feel such a need to dance, sweetie. Indulge me?"

Stewart laughed and let his wife tug him from the table.

"How about you?" Trevor said to the beautiful lady sitting across from him. "Care to indulge me a bit?"

Adriana hesitated, then smiled slowly.

Trevor slipped his hand around her waist as they walked out to the floor, and as if she'd done it a thousand times before, she moved into his arms and let him lead her to the music.

"Maggie's a jewel," Trevor said, as he waltzed Adriana through the crowd.

"She has a heart of gold. Of course, she rarely thinks before she speaks, but I suppose that's one of the things I love about her."

"I take it you've been friends a long time."

"Since she met Stewart. Thirteen years ago—right about the time my father died."

"She must be half his age."

"Twenty-four years younger, but does age really matter?"

"To some people, but not to me."

"She was accused of being a gold digger, out for Stewart's money. It wasn't true, though. They love each other."

"It's amazing what prying busybodies will say without knowing the truth. You know, things like how a man's seduced a thousand women."

"It isn't the truth?"

Shaking his head, he smiled into her questioning eyes. "I'd be dead, Adriana. Suffice it to say, there have been more than a few, far fewer than a thousand, and"—he lightly caressed her cheek—"I only plan to seduce one more."

The fear popped into her eyes again, but it flickered away into something close to desire. Lord, when Adriana decided it was time, he was going to be much more than ready.

The song was too short, and Trevor would have kept on holding Adriana tight, but Stewart tapped him on the shoulder.

"Mind if we switch partners for a moment?"

"Yes, please," Maggie pleaded. "I told Stewart I just *had* to dance with you."

How could he possibly turn Maggie down?

One moment Adriana was warm and innocent and perfect in his arms, the next a dynamo was clutching his hand and leading him into the crowd.

"Stewart tells me he's not too certain you're a proper acquaintance for my Adriana. Is it true?"

"You don't pull any punches, do you, Maggie?"

"Not where Adriana's concerned. My husband's a very cautious man who checks out anything and everything. In spite of all my efforts, I'm afraid he's going to be putting you and your life under a very intense microscope."

"That doesn't surprise me."

"He does have an air about him, doesn't he. Grand Inquisitor and executioner rolled into one," Maggie quipped. "Underneath the exterior, though, is a man who cares deeply about certain people. Adriana's one of them."

"I can understand the feeling."

She studied his eyes and smiled slowly. "I like you, Trevor. I'm a good judge of character, and you seem rather nice. I must tell you though, you're a little worldly-wise for my Adriana. She's not used to men like you. Actually, she's not used to men at all."

"I get the feeling she's been shut away from the world most of her life."

"More like she's found more comfort in a make-believe world than the real one. Go easy, Mr. Montgomery. You're not a dream, and she's been hurt more than enough by the real thing."

ℒ❧ Thirteen

"Just one more dance?" Trevor urged, looking down at Adriana with those smoldering brown eyes that had burned into hers most of the night.

"It's late. We really should go," Adriana protested, as she scanned the ballroom and noticed that most of the tables had emptied.

"It's not quite two," Trevor said. "For me, that's early."

"It's a long drive home. I have to work tomorrow."

Trevor shook his head and pulled Adriana up and into his arms. "One more dance. That's all."

How could she possibly turn him down, especially when it felt wonderful being held so close?

They moved together slowly and rhythmically, a warm hand against the bare skin of her back, the other holding her fingers so snug against his chest that she could feel the steady beat of his heart.

"The music sounds familiar to me," he whispered. "I've been in this hotel dozens of times before, still, everything's changed. Sixty years ago I could dance like this every night of the week, not just on weekends or special occasions."

Adriana felt his hand pressing her closer, holding

her as if he was afraid she'd disappear the same way
his old life had.

"I don't know if I can get used to all the changes,"
he said. "I miss the elegance of the thirties."

"But it's not gone completely. You were able to
recapture some of it tonight."

"It's not the same. I didn't know a soul, except
you. I wonder if my old friends found the change as
difficult."

"They probably didn't notice. Things changed
gradually, not overnight, like they did for you."

"I doubt my old friends would even recognize me
if I paid them a visit. Who knows, they might not
even remember me."

"I'm sure they would. But . . ." Adriana hesitated,
knowing her next words were ones he wouldn't
want to hear. "There aren't many left to visit."

Trevor stopped in the middle of the dance floor.
She could see the hurt in his eyes as he understood
the full impact of what she'd said. He sighed, resting
his forehead against hers.

"Is Tyrone Power still alive?" he asked, his words
little more than a whisper.

He could feel the shake of her head. He didn't
have to hear her words to know his old friend was
gone.

"What about Janet Julian?"

He looked at her this time, but instead of seeing
Adriana, he saw Janet's pretty blue eyes, her innocence, her sweetness.

"She's in a rest home," Adriana told him.

"I imagine she doesn't have brunette hair any
longer, either," he remarked dryly, then attempted
a halfhearted laugh.

"I went sailing with Errol Flynn not too long ago,"
he said. "Please don't tell me that someone strong
and healthy like Errol—"

"You've been gone a long time," she interrupted. "People aged, got sick . . ."

"Died," he said bluntly. "Hell, Errol was a good five years younger than me. What about Gary Cooper? Cary Grant?"

She shook her head slowly.

Trevor plowed his fingers through his hair. "I was laughing and drinking with them just a few days ago."

"Sixty years, Trevor, not just a few days. The nightclubs you loved are gone. Most all of the people you knew are gone. All that's left are memories."

Sighing deeply, he held her close, dancing slow and easy, and when the orchestra played its final note, he looked into her eyes again. "Maybe if I say good-bye to that old life of mine, I can get on with the new one."

"Is that what you want?"

"I'm an old hand at starting new lives. I've done it before, I suppose I can do it again."

The gates were locked outside Hollywood Memorial Park, the place where so many of Trevor's friends had been buried. In the darkness of night, they sat in the parked Mercedes and Trevor told Adriana tales about the parties they'd attended and the pranks they'd played. He opened her eyes to life on the studio lot, and to what Hollywood had really been like in the thirties.

As morning dawned, they drove through towns that had been nothing but orange groves in Trevor's day, on freeways jammed with traffic the likes of which Trevor had never seen, and gazed at the dismal gray skies that had been a pristine blue when he'd first arrived in Hollywood.

They stopped at Mann's, the elaborate Chinese Theater that had been called Grauman's on the day Trevor pressed his hands in wet cement. They strolled past concrete squares that bore the names of others he'd known, like Shirley Temple and Norma Talmadge, until they reached the two-by-two square dated June 12, 1938.

Trevor knelt down and put his hands into the imprints, then tilted his head and smiled. "It's still a perfect fit."

And at eight in the morning, when the gates were scheduled to open, they returned to the cemetery so Trevor could pay his respects.

He said good-bye to Tyrone Power. They'd had so many good times together, attended dozens of parties in the company of beautiful women. How could he possibly have died so young?

They strolled past the reflection pool that was part of Douglas Fairbanks, Sr.'s grave, and Trevor remembered the way the man had scaled the walls of castles, fought with a sword, and swung from the masts of ships. He'd been Trevor's idol, he'd given Trevor his very first acting job, and he'd died just a year after Trevor's disappearance.

It didn't seem possible that someone so virile could be gone.

It was nearly 10:00 A.M. when they walked across the grass at Forest Lawn in Glendale. Just the year before he'd come here for Jean Harlow's funeral, and now Adriana was leading him past the markers of so many other old friends—Clark Gable and his beloved Carole Lombard, Robert Taylor, who'd won the movie role Trevor had craved, and his drinking and carousing partner, Errol Flynn.

"God, he was only fifty when he died," Trevor said, kneeling down to trace the numbers on the simple stone embedded in the lawn. "Not too long ago I watched him filming a few scenes from *Dodge City*. He was laughing and carrying on as if he hadn't a care in the world."

Trevor looked up at Adriana and saw the sadness in her eyes. "We were a lot alike."

He brushed a few wilted flower petals from the stone and read the inscription aloud. " 'In memory of our father from his loving children.' " Trevor shook his head slowly. "I never thought either one of us would have kids. There wasn't enough time for something important like that."

Again he touched the stone, as if doing so would bring him closer to an old and cherished friend. *Children*. He could picture Errol out on his boat, teaching sons and daughters how to sail.

Would he, himself, ever be blessed that way?

Hell, he didn't know the first thing about raising children, but he was sure he could do a better job than his parents had done with him.

If he was ever given the chance.

He sighed deeply, for the life he wanted, for the friend he'd lost.

"What happened to him?" he asked.

"Drugs. A scandal." Trevor felt Adriana's fingers slide over his shoulder, an attempt, he supposed, to comfort him. "He drank too much and lived too hard," she added.

"So did I," Trevor stated, remembering the way he'd often partied till dawn and showed up on the set with a hangover. He remembered the taste of scalding coffee the makeup and wardrobe girls would bring him. He remembered the way the directors would sigh with relief when he walked onto the set and showed them he could remember his lines and play his part perfectly in spite of the liquor he'd consumed. He'd never been late. He'd rarely needed prompting on his lines. But how much longer would he have been able to go on like that?

Errol Flynn had died at fifty. Trevor was thirty-four. Would his career have hit the skids in a year, maybe two?

He lowered his head and closed his eyes, remembering, again, the horror of Carole's slashed body lying beside him.

If he hadn't been torn away from 1938, he, too, would have been involved in a scandal, and surely his life and career would have collapsed.

Looking up at Adriana, he said the words he was sure she must be thinking: "That could be me lying there, couldn't it?"

She nodded. "My father drank too much, and he died at forty-four. It happens all too often."

"Is that why you didn't touch your champagne?"

"I don't like the taste," she admitted. "And I don't like seeing what too much drinking can do to someone."

"Like me?"

"You. My father. Stewart nearly lost his practice because he missed too many court appearances and his clients got tired of his irresponsibility. He tried to stop for the longest time and couldn't. Finally he had to get help. My father, unfortunately, didn't feel he needed any help."

"I can stop anytime I want," Trevor said. "I've done it before."

"And started again."

"It's never impaired my thinking. I've never missed a day of work." He'd thrown up in his dressing room. He'd had excruciating headaches. Again and again he'd told himself to stop, but then he'd go to another party—or he'd remember his childhood—and he'd pick up another glass of bourbon or scotch and forget everything that was wrong in the world.

That was the only reason he drank . . . to forget. He wasn't addicted to anything, except the pretty blue eyes that were watching him.

He caressed the softness of her cheek. "I could

quit right this moment and never touch another drop."

"Then do it," Adriana asked. "Go home with me and get rid of all the liquor in the house."

"I don't see where that's necessary."

"That's what my father said, too. The temptation was always there in front of him, and it was too easy to reach in a moment of weakness."

"Look, Adriana. If you want me to stop, I'll stop. I promise."

"I've heard those words before, too. After a while it's one lie after another until you get to the point where you don't even know what promises you made, what things you said, or what you've done."

"That's not going to happen to me."

"It's not?"

"Of course not. I've always been in total control."

"You haven't. You lost all control once. I'll show you the proof."

She grabbed his hand and rushed across the lawns, skirting around stones, elaborate crypts, vases of flowers and beautiful statuary. Finally she stopped beside a tall, marble angel, its wings stretching toward heaven. "This is what happens when you drink too much," she blurted out.

Trevor's gaze flashed to the name *Carole Sinclair* blazing across the base of the monument. His stomach roiled once again at the memory of Carole that continually haunted him.

"I didn't do it," he murmured. "I couldn't have."

"But you don't know for sure," she said softly, although he could hear the condemning tone in her voice. "Do you know why?"

Trevor turned on her, anger building inside. "Of course I know why. I was drunk."

"But you can handle it. Right?" she blurted out, then bit her trembling lips. She took a deep breath and swallowed hard. "You can stop anytime you want. Right?"

"Stop it, Adriana."

He grabbed her arms and attempted to pull her close, but she struggled free.

"I've lived with a drunk once. I lived with a father who valued his liquor more than he valued me, and when he got drunk he got mean. You do the same thing."

"I don't."

She held out her arms, shoving the evidence—the bruises on her wrists—in his face. "You did this when you were drunk. Maybe you were upset. Maybe you thought you were going crazy. But that's no excuse for hurting someone."

"I'd never do it again."

"How do I know? What happens the next time you get drunk? Will you hit me? What if you totally forget what you're doing, get a knife, and stab me over and over again. And what if you don't even remember?"

Tears burst from her eyes and she clasped a hand over her mouth. "Oh, God, Trevor. I didn't mean that. I'm sorry."

Silence permeated the morning. A silver vehicle drove by and stopped a short distance up the road. And a wave of fear ripped through Trevor's soul.

"I'm not a murderer," he told her. "But I have no way of proving it to you—or to me. I wish I did."

He took a good long breath, trying to build his courage. "I can't erase what happened that night, but I can change things now. If you want me to quit drinking, I will. If you want me to throw out every bottle in the house, I will. I've tried proving to you that in spite of all those stories you've heard about me, I have a few good qualities. They've been buried for a long time, and you're the only one who's ever had the power to bring them out. But, if you can't trust me, Adriana, if you think you never will trust me, then we have nothing."

She tried to wipe the tears from her face, but they kept on falling as she spoke. "In spite of all the horrible things my father said to me, I loved him. If he hadn't died, I'd still be trying to sober him up. I don't give up easily on the things I want—and I want to believe in you."

"Then you don't want me out of your life?"

Slowly she shook her head. "I don't want you to leave . . . ever."

Those were the most blessed words he'd ever heard. They were the words he'd wanted his parents to say—but they hadn't, and he'd run away from love ever since.

He held out his hands to Adriana and she hesitantly touched his fingers.

"Come here," he beckoned, wanting her to make the first move into his arms.

She slid her hands over his shirtsleeves, his shoulders, and wove them around his neck.

She was trembling, and when he pulled her close he could feel the rapid beat of her heart as her breasts touched lightly against his chest.

"I'll never hurt you, Adriana. Never."

The morning was unusually cool, but his body warmed the moment he kissed her. A gentle sigh escaped her lips when he caressed her slender back and the slight flare of her bottom.

He trailed kisses from her mouth to her cheek and to the delicate hollow beneath her ear.

His body was reacting to her touch, to the warmth of her breath, to the softness of her sighs. But he had to slow down.

"Until you believe in me, without any doubts at all, this thing we have between us won't mean a thing. Not to you. Not to me, either."

"Make me believe in you, then. Take away all my doubts."

If only he could, Trevor thought, but how could he, when he wasn't sure if he believed in himself?

An unexpected noise jerked Trevor away from Adriana.

The click of a camera.

Another click. Still another.

Before he could move, the photographer ran up the road, jumped into a silver van, and sped away, tires screeching.

Adriana was trembling when Trevor turned around. Her eyes had glazed over, and he gathered her into his arms.

"Why can't they leave me alone?"

"Because they get paid too well. Because the public wants to know all about the lives of famous people."

"I'm not famous."

"You've lived with one of the richest men in the world. You inherited his wealth. It's only natural that people would want to know more about your life." He kissed the top of her head, comforting her as he would a child. "Thank God it was just a few harmless pictures. You and me kissing, that's all."

She drew back and glared at him. "All it takes is an insane caption printed beneath the picture to turn it from something innocent into the makings of a scandal. I've avoided all of that for nearly eight years."

"You've run away from it, that's all. But you've run away from life at the same time. You can't run away forever."

"Why not?"

"Because running away doesn't solve anything. Just ask me. I know all about it."

She stared at him for the longest time, then rested her head on his shoulder.

"You taught me how to dance tonight," she whispered into his ear. "Can you teach me not to be afraid?"

"I'm afraid of things, too, Adriana. I need your help just as much as you need mine. We can't change things overnight."

"One step at a time, right?" she asked, tilting her head to look at him once more.

He kissed her forehead, her nose, then tenderly kissed her lips.

"And we'll take each step slow and easy. There's no need to rush, Adriana. No need to rush."

♣ Fourteen

Adriana touched her lips, lightly smoothing her fingers over the tender flesh, remembering the kisses she'd shared with Trevor in the cemetery, in the car during the long drive home, and when they'd parted company at her bedroom door just an hour ago. So many times she'd dreamed of his kiss, but her dreams couldn't compare with the warmth she'd felt in his arms. Never before had she felt such gentleness, such passion.

The man she'd dreamed of had traveled sixty years through time to show her there was nothing wrong, nothing sinful about enjoying a kiss and the touch of a man. For only a moment she let her father's anger cloud her memories. She remembered the last time he'd caught her with one of the young gardeners who worked at Sparta. It was the second time he'd caught her with Robbie, it was the second time he'd yelled and screamed, but it was the only time he'd had a stroke.

This time no one told her what she'd done was wrong. This time she hadn't questioned herself or even thought of her father. For once in her adult life, she wasn't going to question the right or wrong of something. She was just going to cherish the memory and pray there would be many more to come.

She stifled a yawn as she slipped her feet into black patent sandals. She'd slept briefly during the trip home, giving in to Trevor's pleas to let him drive. But sleep was far from her mind now. She wished she could ignore the meeting she had to rush off to and spend the day with Trevor, allowing him to teach her new and wonderful things. Fortunately, there was always tonight.

The scents of frying bacon and strong French roast coffee wafted down the hallway when she opened her bedroom door. He'd said he'd fix her breakfast, even though it was well past noon. She wasn't hungry for anything more than his kisses, but he'd insisted on preparing her a meal she'd never forget. Cooking was a trait she hadn't expected from him. Golf, maybe. Polo. Betting at the track. Those were the hobbies men like Trevor indulged in—not cooking or clipping roses. He was so much different from the man she'd idolized, so much better than the man she'd dreamed of.

She found him standing over the stove turning slices of crispy bacon in a pan full of hot grease. She leaned against the doorjamb and contemplated his body. Strong, long legs encased in slim black jeans. His legs had looked good in tights when he'd played a knight of the realm and a devil-may-care pirate— they looked even better when he acted out the all-American boy next door. The white cotton shirt, its cuffs rolled up two complete folds, stretched across his shoulders and back, and she could see the flex of his muscles under the sleeves. He looked like a piece of heaven fallen down into her home.

A piece of heaven with many earthly faults.

Maybe it was all of those faults that made her care so much.

"Smells good," she said, wanting to capture his attention.

He turned, and when she saw that movie-idol smile shining across his face she felt a tug at her heart and a quiver racing through her chest.

He switched off the flame on the stove and perused her body slowly, from the tip of her head, over the white silk T-shirt she wore with a lacy camisole beneath, down the entire length of her black pin-striped trousers, to the toes of her shoes, then back again. Slowly he beckoned her toward him with a wiggle of his finger, and she floated into his open arms.

Tilting her face toward him, he captured her lips.

Gentle, so very, very gentle. How could anyone find fault with a feeling like this? There was no sin involved, just pure, heavenly bliss.

"You've been sampling the bacon," she whispered.

"I was hungry," he murmured, "and you weren't around."

She tensed when his fingers brushed over her bottom, when he trailed tender warm kisses from her lips, over her chin, and down to the hollow of her throat. "You smell of strawberries."

"Raspberries."

"I could have smelled like raspberries, too, if you'd let me shower with you."

"I believe you said something about taking things slow and easy."

"Maybe I lied."

She felt his fingers slide through her hair as he pulled her close, his kisses turning hot and hard. She opened her mouth to him and shivered with excitement when his tongue danced with hers.

The hand he held against her back tugged at her blouse, pulling it from the waistband of her trousers, and suddenly she felt the warmth of his palm against her bare skin, felt the strength of his chest, the hardness of his desire.

What little experience she'd had with men hadn't prepared her for the intensity of his passion, but an instinct as old as time seemed to take over. Like Trevor had done with her blouse, she pulled his shirt from his jeans and slid her fingers over his back. His skin was smooth and warm, and . . .

She felt the five welts on his shoulder blade, welts made by another woman at another time in another heat of passion.

This wasn't right. It wasn't right at all.

She drew away, and his eyes narrowed in question.

"What's wrong?" he asked.

She shook her head, unable to tell him. "Nothing." She tucked her shirt back under her waistband. "I have an appointment I need to get to."

"Don't run away from me, Adriana."

"I have a meeting. You know I have to go."

"I'm not interested in your meeting. I'm interested in knowing why you're running away from the feelings you have for me."

"Things are going too fast."

"You're making excuses. Dammit, Adriana, I thought we were beyond all this. I thought you'd finally stopped pulling away from me."

"I made a mistake, that's all. I got wrapped up in the dancing and the music and . . . and I made a mistake."

"You think kissing me was a mistake?"

"Yes! Letting you into my life was a mistake, too."

"Why?"

"Because you're trying to seduce me."

He laughed darkly. "And I've failed at every attempt because you get scared and run away."

"I have good reason to be scared of you."

"Give me a reason."

"I could give you plenty."

"Let's start with just one."

"Okay. That's easy. I don't like drunks."

"What you like is making excuses rather than facing things head-on."

"That's not true."

Trevor shook his head, then ripped open a cabinet above the sink. He pulled down the only bottle of whiskey remaining in the house, twisted off the cap, and poured the amber liquid down the sink.

"You wanted to see me get rid of the whiskey, well I have. What's the next reason you have for being afraid of me? My well-documented womanizing? Do you want me to wear blinders, so I'll never look at another woman?"

"You're being ridiculous."

"I can stop drinking for you, Adriana. I can easily forget other women because I'm not interested in anyone other than you. But I can't do the one thing that you really want. I can't prove to you or to me that I didn't murder Carole Sinclair. Either you believe in me or you don't."

She looked away from his eyes and walked to the window, staring out at the bright blue sky but seeing nothing. "I want to believe."

"Wanting to believe and actually believing are two different things."

"What do you want me to do, forget sixty years of speculation about that murder? Do you want me to forget the fact that you woke up in bed with a dead woman? Forget that you were holding the knife and that you were covered with blood?"

"That's exactly what I want you to forget."

She spun around. "Then you forget it first. You're the one who brings it up constantly. You're the one who lies in bed at night tossing and turning, then drowns out the fear with a bottle of whiskey."

"I'm not the only one trying to hide."

Adriana sighed deeply. They were getting nowhere. The morning had been ruined, all because of those scratches on his back and a reputation and murder he could never live down.

For the first time in days she wished he'd never stepped foot into her life. She wished that she was lonely again.

She wished she'd quit lying to herself. She wasn't afraid of Trevor's past, she was afraid of herself. She was afraid of falling any deeper in love—then losing him.

She looked at her watch, knowing she had to get away before they said even more things they might regret. "I've got a meeting to go to."

"Go ahead. Run again, but nothing will have changed while you're gone."

"I'm not running. I'm taking care of business."

Turning, Adriana walked out of the kitchen, but she couldn't miss his parting words.

"I've come sixty years through time to find you, Adriana. You can run from me, push me away, even tell me to leave, but I'm not going to give you up without a fight."

What the hell was he doing? For nearly a week he'd done nothing but cook, eat, clip flowers, and feel sorry for his lot in life. But not any longer. He was bored with others telling him what he should or shouldn't do. Tired of sitting around with nothing fulfilling to occupy his time, with the exception of the glorious moments he spent with Adriana.

Hell, how could he possibly fight for her or make her love him when he had nothing to offer?

All of that was going to change, though. He was taking charge of his life. He had to find a job, preferably one in Hollywood. He had to make some money to replace the stash he'd hidden away in 1938 and nearly depleted in 1998. And he had to get that new I.D. He had very little money, no job, and an identity he could never prove. He had to start a new life, and he wasn't going to sit around and wait for Stewart Rosenblum to call Adriana about the identification. This was one issue he had to take into his own hands.

Half an hour later Trevor was seated in Stewart's office. "Any luck obtaining a birth certificate?"

Rosenblum leaned back in his chair, his hands steepled in front of his face. "Why the hurry? I told Adriana I'd call her when the paperwork was ready."

"I need to find a job. It's difficult getting one without some form of identification."

"You could always lie."

"I could, but I've never been good at it."

Rosenblum raised a doubting brow. "My sources tell me otherwise."

Stewart reached into a desk drawer and pulled out a file of papers. "I sent someone to that little village in Mexico. Funny thing. No one had ever seen you."

"We lived in the mountains," Trevor lied, keeping calm as he attempted to patch the holes Stewart had uncovered in his story.

"There are no mountains nearby."

"Then your spy must have gone to the wrong Santa Elena."

"I don't think so," Stewart said. He thumbed through the papers and ran his fingers down a typewritten page of notes.

"The only Gabrielle Ramon Montgomery we could trace was born in 1872. She was a socialite, the wife of a well-respected Chicago lawyer in the early part of this century. His name, by the way, was Trevor Montgomery."

"My grandparents."

"You've done your homework well, haven't you?"

"Actually, I'm quite familiar with my family history."

Stewart leaned forward, resting his arms on his desk. "This is quite a little charade you've got going. Obviously you've done a lot of research trying to find out everything you could about the real Trevor Montgomery. But when you couldn't figure out what had happened to him after he disappeared, you made up a story to explain your birth. You made a big mistake, though, using the name Gabrielle Ramon."

Trevor didn't let the calm, cool look leave his eyes, in spite of his anger over his mistake. He should have known better than to use that name. In all his years in Hollywood, no one had ever known the truth about his parents. He didn't want anyone knowing. Not then. Not now.

"Who are you?" Stewart asked.

Trevor met Stewart's glare eye to eye. He couldn't back down now. "I'm Trevor Montgomery. Perhaps you haven't been listening."

"Want to make up another story?"

"I can't."

"I could have you take a lie detector test."

"Go right ahead."

"The prospect of being proved a liar doesn't bother you?"

"Not in the least. Hypnotize me. Give me a lie detector test. Stick me in an office with a psychiatrist for a month and my story won't change. I am and always have been Trevor Montgomery."

Stewart shook his head. "I *will* prove you're a fraud."

"How? By sending more investigators to Mexico? By sending more photographers to spy on Adriana and me?"

"Photographers?"

"The man who's been watching us. Last night. The day before. He's not very shrewd. That silver van of his is as inconspicuous as Mae West in a nunnery."

Stewart frowned. "Someone else must be investigating you. If I'd hired a photographer, you never would have seen him."

"I can't think of any reason I'd be followed. Maybe it's Adriana he's interested in."

"Adriana's name's been dragged through the papers enough in her lifetime. Why don't you get out of her life so it doesn't happen again."

"What makes you so sure I'm bad for her?"

"You're a fraud."

Trevor pushed out of the chair and paced the room. "Tried and convicted without a trial, right? Is that your usual style?"

"I'm known for making good character judgments. I've doubted your claim to be Trevor Montgomery's son from the moment you threw that insane story at me."

"I don't care what you think about me. Investigate me all you want, you're not going to find a thing. But I'll clear up one thing in your mind right now. I have no intention of hurting Adriana. I care for her. I'd get out of her life if I thought being with her was going to cause her any harm."

"I could almost believe you're sincere."

Trevor braced his hands on the desk and glared at Stewart. "I've never been more sincere about anything in my life."

Stewart pulled an envelope from the file he'd compiled on Trevor's made-up past and slowly pushed it across the table. "That's the identification you want. It doesn't matter much to me who you say you are, but maybe you'll take that and get out of Adriana's life."

Trevor took the envelope, not bothering to look inside. He didn't care much for Stewart Rosenblum, but he trusted him to do what Adriana had asked.

"It's been a very interesting conversation, Stewart.

I'd hoped we could be friends, for Adriana's sake. But that doesn't seem possible."

"I'm sure she'll be wanting you out of her life as soon as she hears this news about you. Then we won't have to bother becoming friends."

Trevor grinned. "She knows that story already. In fact, she's the one who made it up."

"Why would she do that?"

"Why don't you ask her, since you find what I say difficult to believe."

"Perhaps I will, as soon as my investigator gets back to me with a few other pieces of information."

"It's going to take a hell of a lot better information than what you've already come up with to make her change her mind about me."

"Then I'll keep digging."

Stewart pushed up from his desk, walked across the room and opened the door. "I'm a busy man, Mr. . . . Montgomery."

He'd been branded a murderer, a womanizer, an alcoholic, and now a fraud. Maybe sticking around in 1938 would have been easier.

But Adriana was in 1998. She made all the accusations easier to bear. Besides, he said he'd fight for her. He meant it, too.

He held out his hand when he got to the door, but Stewart ignored his gesture. Hell! He was getting awfully tired of people backing away from him.

"I'll be watching you," Rosenblum said. "And I'll be keeping an eye on Adriana, too. Make sure you don't hurt her."

Hurt Adriana? That wasn't his plan at all. He was going to seduce her, and he wasn't going to wait another night. She'd pulled away one too many times, but she wasn't going to back away from him again.

When he looked into Adriana's eyes he could see the want and need. It was mixed in with a hell of a

lot of fear, but that was something they could over-
come. She had to give in to her own feelings.

He walked out of Stewart's office knowing exactly
what he had to do. Something completely unexpected. Something wicked. He'd done a lot of
wicked things in the past, and he'd tried to be so
damn good since he'd stepped into the future. But
he was tired of being good.

✧ Fifteen

All afternoon Adriana had thought about Trevor's wish that she believe in him. If only she could snap her fingers and wish away the doubt, but she couldn't. As much as his touch set her on fire, as much as she wanted to spend an eternity in his arms, at the back of her mind was the fear.

He could be a murderer.

He's a drunk and might never change.

He's a seducer of women.

Those things haunted her, but in spite of her fear she was easily drawn in by the power of his smile, his charms, his enticing voice that rang with laughter or whispered with passion. He was everything she'd longed for in a man.

The man she was falling in love with wasn't a dream. He was real—flesh and blood. A man with faults. He'd held her, he'd kissed her, he'd made her laugh, made her angry. He'd made her feel when for so very long she'd felt nothing.

The man she was falling in love with was better than a dream. And she wanted so very much to believe in him.

The car's headlights flashed across the patio as she pulled into the driveway, and she could see Trevor relaxing in one of the chairs, legs crossed, a crystal wine goblet in his hand.

So much for belief.

Slamming the car door, she headed toward the patio. The sleeves were rolled up on his white cotton shirt. He was barefoot and wearing the black Levi's that had become as much a part of him as the wineglass in his hand. His eyes smoldered as they looked at her. He didn't smile. He didn't frown. He just watched intensely. Slowly he raised the glass and took a sip of the wine.

"What are you doing?" she asked angrily. "You promised not to drink anymore."

A slow grin crossed his face. "What I'm doing, Adriana, is making you angry. Has anyone ever told you how pretty you are when you get upset?"

"Don't change the subject."

He swirled the wine around in his glass. "I can't think of a better subject to discuss than you. Where should we begin? The brightness of your eyes? The way your cheeks are blushing right this moment?"

"You're ignoring me."

"Never. I'm just admiring the view."

Adriana turned away. "I don't want to be looked at."

She thought about going in the house. She thought about kissing the smugness off his face. Damn! Why did he have to infuriate her so? Why did he have to make her blood boil and her heart pound when she knew she should run away from him?

From the corner of her eye she could see him lift a bottle and refill his glass. "Care for some?"

Her head snapped around and she glared at him. "How can you ask me that?"

"Quite easily," he said, taking another sip. "Sparkling cider's not all that bad. Of course, if you're not thirsty . . ."

Her glare shot from Trevor's arrogant face to the

light green bottle that, indeed, said sparkling cider, then back again to his face.

What had gotten into him? She didn't like his idea of a joke. She didn't like the way he was trying to make her mad.

Turning, she took one step toward the house, but Trevor wrapped his fingers around her arm and held her back.

"I'm not through admiring the view."

Her chin jutted out. "I'm not here for your amusement."

He smiled wickedly. "It's pleasure I'm after, not amusement."

A quiver ran through her chest, her belly, her very soul.

He planned to seduce her.

She planned to let him.

She hoped.

His fingers loosened around her arm as he stood. Slowly, methodically, he set the glass on the table, then pulled the strap of her purse from her shoulder and discarded it next to the glass. Her briefcase was next.

He gently curled her hair behind her ears, trailing his fingers along her jaw and down to the hollow of her throat. She could hardly breathe or swallow; she was too mesmerized by his eyes, his touch, the seductive sound of his voice.

"Take off your shoes, Adriana."

"Why?"

He put a finger to her lips and silenced her. "Don't ask questions. Just trust me."

Was she making a mistake? Would she regret doing what he asked? It didn't seem to matter after she looked into his eyes. The intensity of his desire seemed to hypnotize her. Right now she'd do anything he wanted.

She stepped out of her sandals onto the terra-cotta

tile. It was warm, but it was his eyes that sent fingers of heat rippling through her body.

What would he ask her to do next?

"Kiss me."

"That's all?" she asked, a bit wary of what the kiss might lead to, a bit disappointed that he might not want more.

He grinned as he silenced her again.

"Don't talk. Just kiss me."

It seemed an easy enough request.

Standing on her tiptoes, she leaned forward and gently kissed his lips, then waited for his next request.

His eyes flickered to the silk of her T-shirt, to the lace concealing her breasts. She took a long, deep breath as he watched her chest rise and fall.

Suddenly, he swept her up in his arms, and carried her like a babe toward the stairs leading to the beach.

"What are you doing?"

"That kiss was just the beginning. Now I'm going to show you what pleasure's all about."

"I don't know if I want to find out."

"Hush, Adriana," he said softly. "Just put your arms around my neck and don't let go. When I want you to talk or do something else, I'll let you know."

He carried her as if carrying women was something he did every day. Of course, he'd held a woman while swinging from one ship to another. He'd cradled a woman in his arms as he rode across the desert's blazing sands. He'd carried a woman up a flight of curving stairs, taken her to his bed, and made love to her.

He'd been the brash and adventurous hero in so many movies. He was playing that role again right now, and it was so easy to let him.

Stars were shining overhead when Trevor stepped onto the beach. A light breeze wrapped around them, and a calm tide lapped back and forth.

The stretch of sand was deserted, as it usually was this time of night, and she was thankful for the solitude.

She wondered, again, what Trevor had planned to heighten the intense pleasure she was already experiencing. But she dared not ask. No, he'd only tell her to trust him. And she wanted so much to trust.

She wove her fingers into his hair as he walked toward the water. She could feel the strong beat of his heart, the warmth of his breath against her cheek as he carried her across the sand.

"This is where the pleasure begins," he said in that deep, bad-boy voice.

Was he going to take her into the ocean? Was he going to make love to her in the pounding waves?

Slowly he lowered her to the ground, her toes digging into the sand as he let her slide over every hard, muscular plane of his body.

Beside them sat half of an old wine barrel, and even in the darkness she could see the moonlight shining on the pale green grapes.

"What are the grapes for?" she asked, but he put an index finger to his lips and shook his head, silencing her question.

He leisurely caressed her arms, her hips, her thighs, then slowly, ever so slowly, he slid his fingers under the waistband of her trousers.

Adriana came to her senses. What was he doing? She didn't want to make love. She wasn't ready. Not yet. Maybe never.

She grabbed at his wrists, but he looked at her once more with those smoldering brown eyes and smiled. "Trust me, Adriana."

Trust him, she repeated to herself. Just give in to the feeling.

She gasped for air when his fingers skimmed over

her belly and expertly unfastened the button at her waist and slid open the zipper.

The trousers were baggy and the moment he let go of the band they fluttered to the ground in a pool around her feet.

The cool ocean breeze wrapped around her legs, but the look in his eyes as he perused her body warmed her completely. "Do you trust me?"

Somehow she nodded. She was standing before him in only the briefest black bikinis, a white silk tee with a lace camisole beneath. She shouldn't trust him at all, but she did.

In an instant he again scooped her up in his arms, his fingers sliding over the sensitive skin of her bottom, her thighs and under her knees as he adjusted his hold and stepped into the barrel.

Tenderly he kissed her ear, her cheek, the corner of her lips. "Close your eyes now."

Her eyelids felt heavy, her entire body felt, once more, as if she'd been hypnotized. He had her under a spell, and at the moment she hoped she'd never come out from under it.

For the longest time he held her, kissed her, teasing her tongue with his, then all too soon he released her, easing her ever so slowly over his hips, his thighs. Her toes slid along his legs until her feet touched the grapes.

They were standing in nearly a foot of cold, wet grapes that squished between her toes. If Trevor's strong hands weren't holding her waist, if her fingers weren't tightened about his neck, she was sure she would slip.

"Don't open your eyes, Adriana. Just crush the grapes nice and slow. Don't think about anything but what you're feeling right now."

His fingers lightly circled her hips as she cautiously moved her feet up and down. It was the most decadent thing she'd ever done. He was right. It did feel good. It took her mind off every worry and every care she'd ever had.

He kissed the tip of her nose and her eyelids. The sound of her heart pounding in her chest and the rush of blood through her veins nearly drowned out the sound of the grapes being smashed, the birds' wings fluttering overhead, the outgoing tide, and even Trevor's breathing.

He pulled her hips close to his. She could feel the strength of muscular thighs, the hardness of his need. It frightened her, but she didn't pull away. Again he stroked her waist, the small of her back, and the swell of her breasts beneath the silky blouse.

His eyes were open when she peeked.

"Close your eyes, Adriana. Just relax and enjoy all the sensations."

It was easy to give in, to let him show her so many new things.

His fingers brushed down her arms, capturing her wrists and gathering them together behind her back. He could bind her hands and feet and tie her to a stake, but she'd never be any more a prisoner to him than she was at this moment.

"Kiss me, Adriana. Don't open your eyes, don't use your hands, just kiss me."

Slowly, ever so slowly, she leaned forward and kissed the roughness of his cheek. She could sense him tilting his head and she nibbled on his earlobe, traced the edge of his ear with the tip of her tongue.

His fingers tightened around her wrists. A low moan sounded deep in his throat. She'd never known such power. She liked what she was able to do to him; she wanted to do even more.

She trailed a path of kisses across his jaw, feeling his muscles tighten as she kissed his dimple, the cleft in his chin, the base of his throat. Blindly, she found her way back to his lips.

She pulled away and opened her eyes to see his

blazing dark with passion. "Don't stop, Adriana. Don't ever stop."

Again she closed her eyes and captured his lips which opened easily and let her explore.

He released her wrists and his hands found her hair, weaving through the strands. He pulled her mouth even closer, as all the fire of his desire exploded in his kiss.

A sudden flash, like the one in the cemetery, jerked her back to awareness.

"What's going on?" she asked, when she saw the photographer she'd seen at Sparta and in the cemetery.

"You wouldn't give me access to the rancho, so I figured I'd come in the back way." The man lingeringly eyed her up and down. "Nice outfit, Miss Howard."

Trevor jumped from the barrel and grabbed the photographer by the collar. "You have no business here. Get out."

"There's a law against manhandling people," Paxton declared boldly. "I suggest you let go now."

Adriana rushed to Trevor's side, gripping his arm. "Let him go. Please."

Trevor stared at her. She heard him exhale a gasp of pent-up air as he shoved Mr. Paxton aside.

"I want you off this property, and I want you off now," he bellowed.

The photographer laughed. "I've got just as much right here as you do."

"This beach is private," Trevor insisted.

"Sue me, then."

Adriana shivered in the cold, embarrassed at being caught, upset with herself for having let down her guard and allowing a photographer to catch her half-dressed and in the arms of a man. The only saving grace was that the moon had gone behind a cloud, and the beach was darker now.

Still, she stood behind Trevor for cover and glared at the prying photographer. "We have no desire to sue you, we'd just like some privacy. Please, I'd appreciate it if you'd leave."

Mr. Paxton capped his camera and pulled a cigarette from his pocket. "I suppose I could. I've got all the pictures I need, anyway. Stomping grapes. Wandering around a cemetery. Pretty impressive stuff. The gossip ought to be buzzing around town any day now, Ms. Howard."

"Please. Don't print them," Adriana pleaded.

Paxton grinned. "It's the way I make my living."

"Then I'll pay you for them."

Mr. Paxton took a long puff on his cigarette. "That might be worth thinking about."

"We're not paying anything," Trevor informed Paxton before turning to Adriana. "You've been blackmailed before. Don't let it happen again."

A tear rolled down Adriana's cheek. She couldn't stand to be in the papers again. She couldn't bear living through the stares, the gossip. "A thousand dollars?" she asked.

Paxton only laughed. "I can get far more than that from half a dozen tabloids."

"Ten," Adriana stated flatly, but Mr. Paxton shook his head.

Trevor gripped her arm and made her face him. "You won't give him a penny. You have nothing to hide."

"I can't live through the gossip again. I told you that before."

Adriana looked at Mr. Paxton. "Twenty thousand."

Trevor shook his head. For a moment she thought he was going to walk away and let her deal with Paxton on her own, but suddenly he had Paxton by the shirt. He ripped the camera from the photographer's hands.

"You want money?" Trevor asked, as he flung the camera far out into the waves. "We'll send you a check for that, but nothing else. Now get out of here."

Paxton stumbled in the sand when Trevor jerked his hands away from the man's shirt. He stared toward the ocean as if the camera would float back to him on a wave, but it and the film were gone for good.

Paxton's eyes burned with anger when he faced Trevor and Adriana. "I have other pictures. Take my word for it, they'll show up on the newsstands in a day or two."

Trevor's eyes narrowed in controlled rage. "I'll haunt you from now until doomsday and make your life a living hell if they do show up."

"Go right ahead and threaten me. I'll just snap more photos, and the next time the price to keep them out of the papers will be even higher."

"Get out of here," Trevor shouted. "Next time I call the police."

"Yeah, we'll see about that."

Paxton gave Trevor a two-fingered salute and strolled nonchalantly down the beach.

Adriana stared after him. "He's going to cause trouble," she whispered through her tears.

Trevor shook his head. "He's not going to hurt you, Adriana. Neither are his pictures. You can't let people like him push you into hiding."

She wanted to believe him, but it was too difficult to forget the photos and words that had been printed about her in the past. She'd been branded a gold digger, a child paramour, and the press had had a field day with any and all pictures they could find, innocent or not. She hated scandal, but her life had been wracked with it. Now it was going to start all over again.

All because she'd allowed Trevor Montgomery

into her life. She should have known he'd bring her trouble. She should have remembered her father's lectures.

She jerked away at the sudden feel of Trevor's fingers near her cheek. She didn't want him touching her again. It was too easy to fall under his spell. Too easy to be seduced. It wasn't right to want him the way she did.

"Don't pull away from me," Trevor pleaded. "I'm not the one who's hurt you."

"You're wrong," she tossed back. "None of this would have happened if you hadn't come into my life."

She ran into the ocean, standing knee-deep in the water, and let the splash of the tide wash away her tears, wishing they could just as easily wash away the photographer's intrusion in her life and all her other fears.

She never should have allowed Trevor to stay with her. She never should have made that crazy wish.

He'd disrupted her life.

He was causing too much trouble.

A wave slapped at her, splashing its cold, salty spray over her face. And, like a much-needed slap, it brought her back to reality.

Trevor Montgomery had changed her life—for the better. He made her feel alive. He was the dream she'd always wanted.

And she needed him.

He was gone from the beach when she turned around. How could she have expected anything else? She'd pulled away from him one too many times, and he had every right to be angry, every right to leave.

Maybe she should just let him go.

That thought made her heart ache. In spite of his drinking, in spite of his womanizing, in spite of the agonizing thought that he could have murdered a woman, she wanted him.

And she needed him to want her just as much.

She ran from the water, scooped her trousers from the beach, and headed for the stairs.

He was in her bedroom, throwing clothes into a suitcase when she found him.

"What are you doing?"

"We're getting out of here," he stated, as he ripped a dress from her closet and draped it over the other clothes in the case.

"Why?"

"Because I'm tired of intrusions. I'm tired of Maggie, and Stewart, and photographers. Every time I think you trust me, something happens to make you pull away. I want to be alone with you. Just you and me and no interruptions."

"I have a business to run. I can't just pack up and leave."

Trevor glared at her, opened one of her drawers, tossed a handful of lingerie into the bag, closed the lid, and latched it.

"I'm going to take a shower. That gives you ten minutes at the most to get ready."

"I have to let people know where I'm going."

His eyes burned into hers, and in two long paces he was across the room. One hand shoved through her hair, the other grasped her waist, and he jerked her toward him.

"I don't want anyone knowing where we are. We're going to be alone, Adriana. No phones. No business. Just the two of us."

His mouth slanted over hers, hard and passionate. She didn't want to like it, but she did. The roughness of his face that needed a shave, the pressure of his kiss that she hoped would never stop.

But all too soon he drew away, leaving her limp, wanting and needing more.

"Ten minutes, Adriana," he said as he walked toward the bedroom door. "When we're alone, I'll seduce you all over again."

And Adriana realized as she watched him go, that that time couldn't come too soon.

ℐ◦ *Sixteen*

Trevor relaxed one hand on the Duesenberg's green steering wheel and let the cool sea breeze whip through his hair. The last time he'd driven north along the coast he'd contemplated ending his life. Now all he could think of was drawing Adriana into his arms.

His efforts to seduce her had been thwarted at every turn. It wasn't going to happen again, even though she'd sat silently throughout most of the drive, staring at the illuminated lines in the road.

"Good evening, Miss Howard," the uniformed guard said, looking over Trevor's head, when they reached the main gates at Sparta.

"It's nice to see you again, Kevin," Adriana said, breaking her silence. "This is a friend of mine, Mr. Montgomery."

"Nice to meet you, sir."

Trevor smiled at the gray-haired gentleman as Adriana continued.

"Elliott's expecting us, but I'd appreciate it if you wouldn't let anyone else know we're here."

"Is there some trouble I should be aware of?"

Adriana smiled, shaking her head. "A nosy photographer. I'd prefer that no one, not even the Rosenblums, be told that I'm here."

"Of course, Miss Howard." He opened the massive wrought-iron gates. "If there's anything I can assist you with, please let me know."

"Thank you, Kevin."

"Nice meeting you," Trevor said to the guard as he drove the Duesenberg through the gates and up the winding cobblestone drive.

He pulled the car to a stop near the garages where Harrison had kept his Bentley, his Rolls, and half a dozen other vehicles Trevor had admired. There were plenty of places to park the Duesenberg where it couldn't be seen. As soon as that was done, he planned to hide away with Adriana.

During the drive she'd told him about Elliott, who'd make sure they were left alone, about Juanita, the cook, who'd fix whatever they wanted, whenever they wanted it, put it in the dumb waiter, and send it up to Adriana's suite. They could easily hide away for months.

Right now that sounded like the perfect thing. He'd make love to Adriana good and proper and hold her tight for the next thirty days. But that would be just the beginning. After the month was up, he'd make love to her forever.

"It's astonishing! You're the very image of your father," Elliott told Trevor as he sipped a cup of steaming cocoa at the kitchen table. "He cut quite a figure here in the thirties, especially with the ladies. He had an eye for them. Of course, they had an eye for him, too—young, old, it didn't seem to matter. He was everyone's hero."

"You couldn't have been much more than a child," Trevor said, wrapping his hands around the pottery mug.

"In my teens, actually. The perfect age to learn a

few lessons from a master with women."

"Trevor Montgomery—my father—was a master?" Trevor questioned, trying to keep a straight face as he listened to tall tales about himself.

"I thought so at the time. I was very much in awe of his power over women. I even told him so."

The incident was fresh in Trevor's mind. It had happened just a few weeks before when the old man sitting across from him had been a gangly, pimple-faced boy Harrison Stafford had met at a soup kitchen in New York. Newly arrived from England, the boy had no money, no place to live, and a growling belly. Trevor had been in pretty much the same condition when Harrison had rescued him, too.

"Still telling stories, I see."

Trevor turned at the sound of Adriana's voice. She was wrapped in a robe, her hair was mussed, and she looked as if she'd attempted to sleep but couldn't. He'd asked her not to run off to her bedroom right after introducing him to Elliott, but she'd wanted to be alone for a while, and Trevor hadn't tried to stop her. She'd been nervous, on edge, and she had to work that out of her system before he could start his seduction all over again.

"Care to join us?" he asked, rising and pulling out a chair.

She took the seat Trevor offered, stifling a yawn.

"Would you care for some cocoa, Miss Howard? I told Mr. Montgomery it might aid his sleep. Perhaps it might do the same for you, too."

"Thank you, Elliott, but I'd rather you continue your tales about Mr. Montgomery. It's all very interesting."

"Yes, it was very interesting. Trevor gave me wonderful pointers with the ladies. Treat every woman—tall, skinny, fat, ugly—as if they were rare and delicate pieces of china," he told me.

"He said that?" Adriana grinned at Trevor when she asked.

"Yes, I believe those were his exact words. Of course, he had me hide behind one of the mummy cases in the Egyptian Room while he showed me the proper way to kiss. He said if I followed his example to a tee, I could have any woman I wanted."

"And who was he kissing?" Adriana asked.

"A hatcheck girl from the Trocadero," Elliott related.

Trevor remembered full well the kiss, but not much at all about the young woman.

Elliott cleared his throat and took a sip of his cocoa. "Her name was Lu, I believe."

Adriana stared at Trevor as if looking for confirmation, but he didn't say a word. All of that had happened sixty years ago. It wouldn't seem right to have knowledge of such an insignificant piece of trivia.

"Did you try out the kiss on anyone?" Trevor asked, instead.

"Of course I did. Mary Ellen, one of the maids here at Sparta, said it was the nicest kiss she'd ever had. I kissed her just the way Mr. Montgomery had shown me, and she didn't resist. We were married a year later. Needless to say, I've always held Mr. Montgomery in the highest esteem, no matter what was said about him after his disappearance."

"He was a wonderful man," Trevor said, winking at Adriana.

"Yes, he was," Elliott acknowledged. "And I consider it an honor having his son here with us. I do believe you've brought a glow to Miss Adriana's cheeks, just as your father would have done."

"Thank you, Elliott. I'll do my best to keep it there, although she has a tendency to push me away at times."

"My Mary Ellen pushed me away, too, but she

was rather powerless once I kissed her."

"I'll never be powerless," Adriana murmured, "to a kiss or anything else.

She shoved away from the table. "Have you shown Mr. Montgomery his room yet, Elliott?"

"No. I could do that now if you'd like."

"I'll take him. You really should get some sleep. It's well past two."

"I was enjoying my conversation with Mr. Montgomery. Perhaps we could have another discussion while you're here."

"I'd like that," Trevor said, shaking Elliott's hand and holding on to it tightly for just a moment. "My father talked a lot about his times here at Sparta. It's nice having a chance to re-create those days through your eyes."

"Miss Adriana can do that for you, too. She comes here often to watch the old family films. Maybe tomorrow, after you've had a good night's sleep, she'll show you some."

Trevor turned to Adriana. "I'd like that."

"As for your request," Elliott said, directing his words to Adriana, "if Mr. or Mrs. Rosenblum call, I'll let them know that I haven't seen you."

"Thank you, Elliott."

Adriana brushed a quick kiss across Elliott's cheek, and Trevor followed her from the kitchen.

They wound their way through a myriad of majestic and elegant rooms and up the grand marble staircase that Trevor remembered quite well. The last time he'd been here he could roam anywhere he liked. It seemed odd that so many strangers, people from all over the world, paid top dollar to tour the estate now.

"This wing still belongs to me," Adriana told him, when they passed through the ten-foot-tall carved-oak double doors. "Elliott makes sure there are always fresh flowers in the vases and that the linens are—"

"I don't want to hear about flowers or linens," Trevor interrupted, backing Adriana against the doors she'd just closed behind them.

He traced his fingers across her jaw and lightly brushed his thumb over her lips. "We're alone, Adriana. Just you and me."

"It's late," Adriana said, bracing her hands against his chest. "I'm tired."

"Why did you come down to the kitchen then? Why didn't you just stay in bed?"

"Elliott's old. I didn't want you keeping him up all night."

"That's not the real reason, and you know it. Admit it, Adriana. You wanted to be near me."

Adriana laughed. "Your ego's too big."

"And once again you're making up excuses to stay away from me."

"I'm tired," she repeated, skirting around him and marching across the sitting room, stopping at the first door off the hallway. "You can sleep here tonight."

"Where will you be?"

"In another room."

"Tell me which one," he urged, moving in close again and curling her hair behind her ear. "I might need to find you during the night."

She hesitated, then turned her gaze toward the double doors at the far end of the hall.

"Harrison's old room?" he asked, and slowly she nodded.

"It's awfully big for just one person."

"I suppose, but I've never found anyone I wanted to share it with."

"The perfect person could be standing fairly close."

Adriana looked away, but Trevor tilted her face toward him. "Kiss me, Adriana."

He could feel her sharp intake of breath, could almost hear the rapid beat of her heart as she looked into his eyes and raised up on tiptoes, leaning toward him as if in a daze. Her eyes fluttered closed. She was less than an inch away when her eyes opened and she jerked away.

Trevor grinned at her sudden movement. "See, you do have control over your thoughts. No matter what I do to persuade you, you're going to keep on backing away from me until you're good and ready to give in to what's in your heart."

Trevor pushed through the guest-room door. "Just don't make it too much longer. I'm only a man, Adriana. Not some idol up on a silver screen who acts according to a well-written script. I have feelings and needs. And right now I need you, more than I've ever needed anyone."

Drawing in a long, deep breath, he closed the door, separating himself from Adriana. He pressed his forehead against the wood.

"I don't know how much longer I can wait, Adriana," he whispered. "But, God knows, I will."

Trevor could smell the blood. He could taste it and feel it covering his face, his palms, his arms and chest. He rubbed his hands on the sheets, over and over and over again, but the blood wouldn't disappear.

He had to get rid of it. He had to.

He jerked up in bed, his eyes flashing open.

There was no blood. No body. Only a magnificent room that felt empty and alone.

Plowing his fingers through his hair, he tried to rid himself of the headache that came each night when he attempted to sleep. Somehow he had to make the nightmares stop. How could he possibly pull Adriana into his arms, make love to her, sleep with her, only to end up frightening her with his dreams?

Lying back in the pillows, he massaged his temples, but the pain continued to pulse through his head. All he needed was one small drink. Just one, and the headache would go away.

He'd seen a bottle when Elliott had taken cocoa from one of the cabinets. He'd told Adriana he could give it up, but that was easier said than done.

Quietly he closed the door to the guest room and walked down the hallway lined with ancient tapestries. Crossbows and swords hung on the walls, and suits of armor stood guard in carved out alcoves.

He walked down dozens of marble steps, wove through back rooms, and entered the kitchen. It was 6:00 A.M. and Elliott and Juanita were nowhere in sight. It was too early to drink, but that didn't matter now. The only thing that mattered was getting rid of the pain.

He retrieved the bottle from the cabinet and took it outside to one of the terraces. Sitting on a granite bench, listening to the faint rustle of wind through the palms, he twisted off the cap and tilted the bottle of bourbon to his lips.

Adriana didn't have to know. It was just one small drink. Just one.

But Adriana's words rang through his head.

After a while it's one lie after another until you get to the point where you don't even know what promises you've made, what things you said, or what you've done.

He'd promised her he wouldn't drink again, but he'd lied.

One lie after another.

He lowered his head and rested his brow against the top of the bottle.

He didn't need the whiskey. Not this time.

He needed Adriana.

She was the only intoxicant he wanted.

⚘ *Seventeen*

Dim morning light filtered through the stained-glass windows running the entire length of the inside pool. Adriana walked across the cool tile floor, mounted the diving board, and gripped the edge with her toes. The water looked inviting, cool and refreshing, something to give her the energy that a sleepless night had robbed her of.

Trevor had been on her mind since he'd closed his door on her. Trevor had been on her mind since he'd told her he needed her.

Did he know how much she needed him? Did he have any idea how torn she was inside? Her heart cried out for him, yet her head kept screaming that everything about him was wrong.

Listen to your heart, he'd told her.

Maggie had said the same thing.

She'd tried. God knows she'd tried. But those old fears were much too strong to fight.

She dived into the water and ticked off laps as she swam back and forth, back and forth, attempting to drive away her frustration.

Instead, she heard her father's voice and all those things he'd said to her over the years.

"You killed your mother. She'd be alive if you hadn't

been born." That was one of his favorite mantras when he was drunk.

"Sex is the root of all evil," he'd preached the first time he'd caught her with Robbie.

"Being with a man is a sin." She hadn't cared back then. She didn't know a thing about sex, she just knew that when Robbie kissed her she'd tingled inside.

She should have listened to her father, though. If she had, he wouldn't have gone into a rage, he wouldn't have called her a whore, and he might still be alive.

And he'd still hate her.

Adriana swam to the side of the pool, rested her head on the tile ledge, and wept.

"I'm sorry, Daddy," she whispered. "Please, believe me. I didn't think I was doing anything wrong."

She relaxed at the side of the pool for the longest time, then swam another ten laps as she pushed the ache to the back of her mind and heart.

Climbing from the pool, she tugged at her bikini bottoms and started to walk out of the pool room.

"Are you all right?"

She jumped at the sound of Trevor's voice, and in a dimly lit corner she saw him sitting in just a pair of swim trunks, his legs crossed casually, while his smoldering brown eyes gazed at her.

"Have you been there long?" she asked.

"I couldn't sleep and thought a few laps would help. I'd just sat down when I saw you walk in."

"Did you listen to the things I said?"

Trevor nodded. "I watched you swim. I listened to you cry. I heard you tell your father you were sorry. I don't know what happened between the two of you, but he was the drunk, Adriana. I imagine if anyone should be sorry, it's him, not you."

"I killed him."

Trevor came toward her.

She knew she should back away, but she couldn't. Not again.

He pulled her into his arms and held her close. "He had a stroke," he reminded her. "You had no control over that."

Adriana looked up and frowned. "How could you possibly know about that?"

"Elliott told me. He told me that your father had accused Harrison of having sex with you, that your father had threatened to leave and take you with him."

"Harrison never touched me, not that way."

"Of course he didn't. If your father had really believed that, if he'd been a good man, he would have taken you away. Instead, Harrison offered him money to keep you here, and he grabbed at it. A good and loving father wouldn't have done that."

"He needed the money."

Trevor laughed darkly. "Your father was a drunk. He was hateful. What else did he do to you?"

"Nothing."

He tenderly touched her chin. "Tell me, Adriana. Elliott said you refused to talk about your father with him or anyone else. You can't keep it inside forever. Tell me. Maybe I can help."

How could she tell him? He'd laugh at her for believing her father's words. No one in their right mind would have believed them, but he'd repeated the words so many times that they were firmly embedded in her mind.

"Tell me."

Adriana took a deep breath and turned away, not wanting to look at Trevor as she spoke. "He told me that being with a man is sinful. That sex is—"

Trevor's laugh interrupted her. How could he mock her?

He circled around her and tilted her chin so she'd look at him. "Kiss me, Adriana."

She shook her head in spite of the feelings she had inside, a yearning that said *give in to anything he asks*.

"Kiss me," he repeated.

Adriana touched his chest, easing her fingers over his shoulders and wove them through his hair. Standing on tiptoes, she kissed him, soft and gentle and warm, just as she'd done earlier on the beach, then backed away.

"Did that feel sinful?" he asked her.

"No."

Lightly, tenderly, he kissed her eyes, her nose, the hollow beneath her ear.

Her muscles tensed when his fingers slid over her shoulders and caressed her back, stopping at the clasp of her swimsuit top.

"Relax, Adriana. I'm not going to hurt you, I just want to show you that there's nothing sinful about making love."

He released the catch and drew the straps down her arms and, as if he knew how awkward she felt, he dropped the bra to the floor and pulled her into his arms.

She could hear him draw in a deep breath as her breasts grazed his chest. Lowering his head, he kissed her gently, and just as gently he smoothed a hand along her side and cupped her breast.

"Does this feel sinful, Adriana?"

She shook her head as tremors raced through her chest, her stomach, the very center of her being.

"Do you trust me?" he asked, and when she nodded, he kissed her again, sweeping her up in his arms.

What was she doing? she wondered again. She'd never been with a man. Not like this. She'd always stopped them after the first kiss, and they rarely came back again. But she'd let Trevor go far beyond a first kiss, and now she was frightened.

She drew away from his kiss and saw the heat of passion burning in his eyes. She had to tell him. He had to know before they went too far.

"What is it, Adriana?" he asked, his mind so completely in tune with her thoughts.

Tell him the truth, she told herself. The worst that can happen is that he'll go away and you can go back to your dreams—and an empty heart and empty arms. She took a deep breath, and prayed that he wouldn't leave when she shared with him another one of her secrets.

"I've never made love before."

His smile was just as warm and tender as his fingers, which waltzed over her skin. "Are you frightened?"

"A little. Mostly that I won't be able to please you."

"You've pleased me from the first moment I saw you," he whispered. "Right now, it's me that wants to please you."

He kissed her again, just a short prelude to what was still to come.

"I don't want you to be afraid, Adriana. I don't want you to worry about doing something right or something wrong."

He brushed a gentle kiss over her nose.

"Remember how frightened you were going out on the dance floor?"

She nodded. How could she forget even one moment of that night?

"But you enjoyed it?"

She nodded again.

"Making love's a lot like dancing," he said, pulling her even closer into his arms. "Just hold on tight, Adriana, and let me lead the way."

He carried her across the tile, down the hallway, and into the room that had once been Harrison's.

He laid her in the center of the unmade bed and kissed her slow and easy. It felt so right, so very, very right.

His thumbs lightly circled her nipples as he kissed a trail down to her breasts. His mouth and tongue lingered over each until a soft moan escaped her lips. Her skin tingled. Her heart pounded as he stretched over her and trailed even more warm, feathery kisses down to her stomach.

She felt his fingers slip under the tiny bikini and a tremor of desire rippled through her heart, but that was nothing compared to the jolt of electricity that ripped through her when his tongue swept over her belly.

Her first instinct was to push him away, but he captured her wrists in one hand. His hold wasn't the least bit tight, and she didn't bother to struggle. She was his prisoner, whether he held her tightly or not.

He slid the bikini down her legs and her body trembled as his mouth followed the same path. He kissed her knees, her ankles, the arches of her feet.

Her body had never tingled this way, had never been caught up in a torrent of emotions that ran the gamut from wicked to sweet. She wanted to cry, she wanted to laugh, she wanted to pull him into her so she would know what sin was truly like.

"Make love to me," she whispered.

He was ready, so very ready, but she needed more. She needed his tenderness, his patience, his touch, and he needed to know every inch of her, every hidden spot.

Trevor pulled his swim trunks away. He kissed her mouth again. God, he couldn't get enough of her lips, her tongue, or any other sweet place on her body. He'd never known desire like this, he'd never wanted to take his time, to explore, to let his need build and build until he couldn't take it anymore.

His breathing was ragged as he rose up to look into her warm blue eyes.

"Make love to me," she whispered again.

"That's what I'm doing, Adriana. Every kiss, every touch."

Again he tasted her lips, swirled his tongue over her nipples and felt them harden as he moved lower and lower, going back to the beginning so he could slowly enjoy getting to know her needs.

Adriana jerked when he kissed the arches of her feet. She wanted him desperately, but he stayed away, torturing—no, tantalizing her body with his lips, his tongue.

No part of her was safe from his touch, not her toes, not the balls of her feet, not her knees, not the inside of her thighs, or . . .

Oh, God! She moaned out loud and her hips rose from the bed to meet his mouth. Heat rushed through her along with wave after wave of desire as his fingers grasped her bottom and held her close.

Where was the sin in what they were doing? Her father had been wrong.

When she thought she would erupt with pleasure, Trevor rose above her. They were eye to eye now, and he looked at her, his brown eyes flaming embers. She felt something hard where his lips had been, felt him slide slowly into her, inch by inch by inch. He stopped, gasping for breath, then smiled slowly before he drove into her.

She'd heard about pain, but felt none at all. Only a fullness and a desire to keep him there forever.

He kissed her slow and tender, waiting for her body to adjust to his feel, then just as slowly, just as tenderly, he moved within her.

The first spasm hit, then the second, and she dug her fingers deep into the skin of his back. His kisses ceased, and he looked at her, fear in his eyes. "Did I hurt you?"

She shook her head. "I never thought..." She gasped for air. "Oh, God! Don't stop. Please, don't stop."

He smiled, took a deep breath, and filled her even deeper, until every nerve ending in his body screamed with pleasure, and his heart swelled with happiness.

With one last thrust, Trevor stilled, and slowly he rested atop her, cheek to cheek, breast to chest. Her legs were twined around him, binding them as closely together as the love they shared. He'd never known the true power of making love. Never known how much better it could be when the heart was just as involved as the body.

This wasn't instant gratification. This was love, pure and simple, and grander than he ever imagined.

Trevor yawned and stretched, sliding an arm under Adriana's just-waking body and pulling her on top of him. "Good afternoon."

She rested her head on his chest and sighed in frustration. "I didn't sleep the entire morning away, did I?"

"That and half the afternoon."

"But there were so many things I wanted to show you today."

"At one time or another this morning you showed me just about everything I ever wanted to see."

Adriana lifted her head and looked into his eyes. "You're very wicked, did you know that?"

"It's one of my claims to fame. Would you like me to change?"

"Actually, I'd like you to be wicked again. I rather enjoyed it."

Trevor rolled over and pinned Adriana beneath him. He held her arms at her sides and savored one small breast and then the other. "Is this what you had in mind?"

"For an appetizer."

"I take it you're aiming for a seven-course meal?"

"The more the better."

Trevor shook his head. "I've corrupted you in just one night."

"I think a touch of wickedness was just below the surface. All it needed was someone like you to bring it out of hiding."

Trevor gathered Adriana into his arms, cradling her head against his chest. He played with the silkiness of her hair, the soft curve of her ear, cherishing the warmth of her body so close to his. This was a part of lovemaking he'd never indulged in. In the past, sex was a sport. He'd played hard, and he'd always won, but he'd never basked in the glory. He'd just gone off in search of another game.

It wasn't a game any longer. What he had with Adriana wasn't a quick seduction and a night of extraordinary sex. It was slow, sweet enchantment. It was pure and passionate. It was something enduring, and he couldn't help but wonder what good thing he'd done in his wicked life to deserve someone so right, someone worth cherishing forever.

"Tell me about your childhood," she asked, swirling her fingers through the light coating of hair around his navel.

"You know everything there is to know about my past. You're an expert, remember?"

"You've already proved me wrong on more than one occasion. I have the feeling the stories I've read are nothing close to the real thing."

"They're not, but the truth isn't worth bringing up."

Adriana frowned and slid out of his arms.

"You wanted to know every minute detail about

my life. Isn't it time you divulged something about yours?"

Trevor shook his head, ignoring her plea. He didn't talk about his past. His memories and nightmares were enough.

He traced a finger over her chest and slipped his hand beneath the sheet, gently caressing one small breast with his palm. "Kiss me, Adriana."

She pulled away from his hand, but instead of fear in her eyes, this time he saw the sparkle of a smile. "I'm not going to be seduced again. Not now, anyway."

Climbing from the bed, she swept the sheet around her body and winked as she left him lying naked in the middle of the mattress. She sauntered across the room and stood beside the window, smiling back at him over her shoulder just one time before looking out across the estate.

It amazed him how that simple act of bravado made him want her all the more. She was teasing him, and she was going to tease until she got her way. Maybe he should tell her about his past. Maybe she could help him forget.

He crossed the room and stood at her back, wrapping his arms around her and pulling her close to his chest.

"I grew up in the middle of all this beauty," she said. "It's a lot different from where you grew up, isn't it?"

Night had rolled in, blanketing the coastline and hiding the view of the Pacific. Still, in the amber glow of lights that lit the estate, he could see the tall, majestic palms that dotted the grounds, the Grecian columns of the temple beside the Poseidon Pool, the marble terraces. Yes, Sparta was different from his Chicago home. Not just in size and beauty, but in atmosphere. Sparta had been a place of parties and good times; his home had had neither.

"The books talked about a crumbling shanty near the railroad yards and the noise of trains switching tracks all day and all night long," she said, breaking into his thoughts. "I can't imagine you living anywhere like that."

"I didn't. I lived in a penthouse, not a shanty. I had a view of Lake Michigan, not of railroad tracks."

Adriana twisted around in his arms and tilted her face to his. "But that's so much different from the stories in the books. Why?"

"I didn't want the studio knowing anything about my past, so they made up something they thought would get the most sympathy. It worked wonders. Son of a drunken switchman who slipped under the steel wheels of a locomotive. It looks impressive in print, and no other actor could lay claim to the same story."

"Why didn't you want them knowing the truth?"

"Because I'd worked too hard to forget the past. I was in Hollywood for nearly ten years before anyone was interested enough to put together a bio on me. My life had changed, and I had no connections with anyone in my old life."

"What about your parents?"

"All connections I had with them ceased the moment I got on that train headed for Hollywood."

Her soft hand caressed his cheek, offering him comfort he'd thought he no longer needed. He thought the pain of being disowned was gone, but it wasn't. It was buried deep in his heart. He'd kept it there for nearly twenty years, and every time it tried to come out of hiding, he'd take a drink and push it a little deeper inside.

Grasping her fingers, he drew them to his lips and kissed them. "I don't want to talk about the past anymore. I've got a new life . . . with you. What happened all those years ago doesn't matter."

"It does matter. You wouldn't let me run away

from my fears. Well, I've got news for you. I'm not going to let you do it, either."

"What happened to me has never interfered in my life."

"Maybe it did. Maybe it's the reason you drink."

God, why did she continually drone on this subject?

"I quit drinking. Remember?"

"That doesn't mean you won't start again. I know all about drinking. I watched it kill my father. He started drinking when my mother died. He thought he could drink away the pain, but he couldn't. He thought he could hide the pain, but he couldn't. You're trying to hide something, too."

"I'm not hiding a thing."

"But you are. Please tell me. Let me help."

"Stop harping, Adriana. That's the best way to help.

He stalked across the room and pulled on his jeans.

"I'm going for a walk."

"Fine. Go for a walk. Run if you want. You can go à hell of a long way, but you can't run away from whatever it is that's hurting you."

She didn't know what she was talking about. He'd walked away from the pain before. He could easily do it again.

He slammed out of the bedroom, through the sitting room, and took the marble stairs two and three at a time.

The house was quiet. The tourists, the guides, and the caretakers had left hours ago, while Trevor and Adriana slept and made love, and fed each other the food that had materialized in the dumb waiter.

He didn't see a soul as he breezed through the hallways, out one of the massive side doors, and down the paths leading to the Poseidon Pool.

The cool evening air beat against him, calming

some of his anger. Hell, all he'd wanted to do was make love to Adriana. He didn't want to solve his problems, he didn't want to dredge up the past, and he didn't want to dwell on his faults. Couldn't she just leave well enough alone?

Dim white lights shone on the temple when he reached the pool, and a few more cast a soft glow in the water. All else was dark, with the exception of the pale green lights that beamed into the tops of the palms.

There was no one around, and he did what he'd done early that morning to relieve his frustration. He stripped out of his jeans and dived into the Olympic-sized pool, swimming one lap after another. Back and forth, back and forth, until exhaustion grabbed hold of him.

He rested his head on the edge of the pool and closed his eyes. What was the matter with him? He'd long ago admitted to himself that he drank to drown out anything bad in his life. No one had ever cared before. He hadn't cared, either.

For the first time in his life someone gave a damn about his excesses, and he'd pushed her away. Just as she'd done to him.

God, they were two of a kind.

And he wanted her desperately.

Pushing himself from the water, he combed his fingers through wet hair, then struggled into his jeans. He had to get back to her, and he wasn't going to run away again.

He found her sitting in the front row of the theater, watching Captain Caribe laughing in the face of his captors as a noose was slipped around his neck.

"Pretty brave guy, huh?" Trevor asked, as he sat down beside her and wove his fingers through hers.

"I always thought so."

The sound quieted around them when Adriana adjusted the volume control on the edge of her seat.

Slowly she turned toward him. "He's still a hero to me."

"He laughed in the face of danger. I picked up a bottle."

"But someone always came to his rescue. Someone always wrote happy-ending scripts. No one did that for you."

"You're making excuses for me."

Adriana shook her head. "The man on that screen was a dream to me. I fantasized about him. I envisioned him holding me and making love to me, but it was only a dream. You're real, Trevor. You make me happy and angry, and at times you make me want to cry. I don't have to fantasize about you holding me because from the moment you stepped into my life you've been there for me. I didn't have to play one of your movies to feel good, you just seemed to know what I needed. You're the real hero, not Captain Caribe. You're the one I want to know. Every little detail."

"You're back to that again, huh?"

"I told you before I don't give up easily. I've been in love with a myth for a long time. Now I want to know the truth."

"I don't even know where to begin."

"How about the story of you sneaking in the back door of theaters so you could watch Mary Pickford? Truth, or fiction?"

It had been a long time since he'd thought about those early days, yet he recalled them quickly. "I had a nanny who took me to see Mary Pickford movies every chance she could get. We went at least once a month from the time I was six until I was nearly ten. When my parents found out, she got fired. They didn't exactly approve of actors or movies."

"Why?"

"I was supposed to study. My father was a lawyer, and my mother wanted the tradition to follow in the family. They were determined to have someone distinguished carry on the Montgomery name. Frivolous nonsense wasn't allowed in our home. Of course, I had other ideas. I wanted to be an actor, so I started sneaking away from the house. My first job was taking tickets in a movie house. I didn't get paid anything, but I did get to see the movies for free."

"And your parents never found out?"

"One of my tutors caught me." He drew Adriana's hands to his lips, kissing her knuckles, then held them close to his chest as he related the story. "They locked me in my room for a week. I was given food, and textbooks to read, but my mother and father refused to see me. Even the maid who brought my food was told not to speak to me."

Trevor laughed, a useless attempt to relieve some of his tension. "I was only ten. I was scared, and I didn't want my parents to hate me, so I read the books and studied and I planned to be the kind of son they wanted when they let me out of that room. But at night, when I tried to sleep, I thought about the movies, about being on the screen."

"I'm so sorry, Trevor."

"There's nothing to be sorry about. It's not like I was used to a lot of attention. My father was rarely home and when he was, I was confined to my room and my studies. 'Children shouldn't be seen and children shouldn't be heard,' that was his theory of fatherhood. My mother wasn't the affectionate type, either. They never yelled, they never called me names, they just ignored me. I thought if I made a success of my life, they'd love me then, but I stumbled at every turn. I was locked in that bedroom more than once. A week here. Two weeks there."

Trevor wiped a tear from Adriana's cheek. He thought he should end his tale, but he'd never told a soul, and it felt good getting it out in the open, sharing it with someone who'd understand.

"I spent a lot of years trying to be perfect, but at sixteen I decided the life they wanted me to have and the life I wanted were totally different. So I left. I thought they'd come around, that they'd miss me and want me back, but that didn't happen. I didn't give up hope, though. I was sure that when they saw me on the screen they'd be happy for me. But, no. The first time I tried calling home, my father told me he didn't have a son. He wouldn't listen to my arguments. God, I even begged. My letters came back after that. They didn't want anything at all to do with me."

He took a deep breath. "*That*, Adriana, is the story of my life before coming to Hollywood. That's the story no one else knows but you."

"Why didn't you tell Harrison?"

"Some things you just keep private."

"Maybe he could have helped."

Trevor shook his head. "Harry Stafford was the best friend I ever had. But Harry didn't like dealing with problems any more than I did. He just paid out lots of money to keep trouble from getting too close."

"Do you regret telling me?"

"Sometimes confession's good for the soul. You're the best thing that's ever happened to me. I think I can get through anything if you're by my side, even a sixty-year-old murder that I might have committed."

"You didn't. I know it."

"You might believe in me, but I need to believe in myself." Trevor leaned back in his seat and looked at the movie screen. "Captain Caribe might have escaped that noose, but I've still got one choking me."

Adriana climbed up from her seat and sat in his lap, wrapping her arms about his neck. He'd never been comforted that way, and he liked it.

"I'm the only noose I want you to have around your neck," she said. "We're going to have to get rid of the other one."

"It's been sixty years, Adriana. It's an old crime that's been investigated ad nauseum. What makes you think we can find out the truth?"

"Because you have more at stake than the people who investigated the crime. Because you know all the before-and-after details."

"I suppose I have to bare my soul about those things, too."

Adriana nodded her head. "But not right now. I want to hold you. I want to prove to both of us that we don't have to hide behind black scarves or whiskey. That if we're troubled, all the comfort we need is in each other's arms."

Trevor slid his beard-roughened cheek across Adriana's smooth one, and held her close. "I wish I'd known you over half a century ago."

"I always thought you did. I'd sit right here in this theater and I knew that every time you kissed a woman or said 'I love you' on screen that it was me you were kissing, that it was me you loved. I wished that you could step down from that screen and love me. Now you have, and every moment I pray that you'll never go away."

"I'm not going anywhere, Adriana."

"Promise?"

"Promise."

"Good." Adriana grinned, and drew a finger down the center of his bare chest and tugged at the tight waistband of his jeans.

"Have you ever made love in a theater?" she asked.

"Only on the movie screen. Pretty chaste, pretty calm stuff."

"I'm not chaste any longer," she whispered. "I'm not calm, either."

"Are you trying to seduce me?"

A slow smile crossed her lips. "Don't say another word. Just kiss me."

✐ *Eighteen*

They hid at Sparta for two entire days, watching old movies, skinny-dipping in the pool, walking through the gardens, playing chess, and making love morning, afternoon, and night.

And they tried to hide from Trevor's nightmare, but it found him whenever he drifted off to sleep.

"We need to go to Santa Monica," Adriana said. "You need to look at Carole's house and try to remember every detail of that night."

"Why? The nightmares bring it back all too clearly."

"There must be something you're forgetting, something I can help you figure out. Please. Let me try."

"It's bad enough that one of us should know. This is one thing in my life that I don't want to share with you."

Adriana slid cool fingers over his cheek and kissed him. "You're already sharing it with me. Every night when you break out in a cold sweat. When you scream Carole's name in your sleep. I can't shut this thing out of my life any more than you can."

"And you think reliving that night's going to make it go away?"

"No. Knowing that you weren't responsible is the only thing that's going to make it go away. I know you don't want to talk about it, but I think it's the only way to learn the truth."

Horrid memories of that morning in Santa Monica rushed through Trevor's mind, through his senses. The nightmarish sight of Carole's body and the vile odor of her blood tore at his stomach, tightened his throat. Not even the cool, salty ocean breeze or the light, sweet scent of Adriana's perfume could wipe it away.

"We shouldn't have come," Adriana said, squeezing his hand as they stood on the beach and faced the pastel pink exterior of Carole's old home. Once again she was reading his thoughts, and knew that this was the last place he wanted to be. "You don't have to tell me what happened, Trevor. Let's just forget about it, pretend it didn't happen."

"I'd pretend that in a moment, if I could," he said, drawing her down to sit beside him on the sand. "I'd like to wipe every disgusting detail from my mind, but I can't. They're all too vivid."

He stared at the house, at the redheaded woman and two young children building a sand castle at the base of the steps. Did they know a murder had been committed inside their home? Did Carole haunt the house the way she haunted his dreams? He hoped not. No one should have to live with such horrid nightmares.

He planned to get rid of them himself, and being in this place was the first step. He'd hidden his fears behind a bottle and a heroic facade for far too long. Not any longer though.

He'd told Adriana some of his secrets. Now was the time to bring everything else out into the open.

He turned toward Adriana when cool fingers touched his cheek. Her blue eyes radiated with warmth and understanding. God, how he loved her.

"Tell me the good things you remember about Carole," she said, as if she thought those memories could drown out the bad. "Try to remember the way she was before."

He smoothed a hand over one of Adriana's tanned, sun-baked legs, soaking up her softness, her gentleness.

There hadn't been anything soft or gentle about Carole. She'd been a gangster's mistress at seventeen and a bleached-blond sex goddess at twenty-six. He wished he could tell Adriana that Carole had had a heart of gold, but he'd never mastered the art of lying. Carole Sinclair was a cold, conniving bitch who'd slept her way into the movies and would stop at nothing to stay there.

"Trevor?" Once more Adriana brought his attention back to the present. "What's wrong? What are you thinking about?"

"Carole," he answered, laughing ruefully as he remembered the exaggerated swing of her hips each time she entered a room, and the way her luscious red lips puckered into a pout when she didn't get her way.

"She wasn't the best of actresses, but she sure as hell knew how to light up the screen. She had an infectious laugh—reserved only for the camera—and a body that . . ."

Trevor looked at Adriana out of the corner of his eye. "You don't want to hear about her body, do you?"

"No." Adriana shook her head slowly, but he could see the hint of a grin trying to tilt her lips. "I'm not interested in the other women you've known. Of course, thinking about her did make you smile. That's the first time since we got to the beach."

"I don't have a lot of fond memories of this place."

Few moments with Carole had been worth remembering, either. No one would have guessed that, though, considering all the pictures that had been taken of them together. The studios had loved the publicity. They didn't give a damn what went on behind closed doors, and they didn't much care that he didn't want to be hooked up with Carole.

It's for your career, he'd been told. *She's a knockout. The press will have a field day over the two of you together.*

The press did love it. The studio was right. But the only thing he'd had in common with Carole was an uncommonly strong desire to be with the opposite sex. Like alcohol, she was a quick and easy antidote for pain. She used him; he used her. They'd been the perfect match.

Thinking back on it, he should have told the studio he'd rather be paired up with Janet Julian. She'd been a friend, rather sweet and naive. A far cry from Carole Sinclair.

But Janet Julian didn't turn heads, and she didn't have her name up in lights.

Carole did—for two entire years—and then she was murdered.

Trevor pressed fingers to his temple. Would the pain of remembrance ever go away?

"Let me do that for you," Adriana said, kneeling behind him. With warm fingers she massaged the throbbing veins near his eyes and worked her way down to his neck. Her comforting hands slid over his ribs, grabbed the hem of his T-shirt, pulled it over his head, and worked at the taut muscles in his shoulders and back.

He took a long, deep breath, relishing her touch, and lowered his head and closed his eyes.

He could feel her lips softly brush his neck, felt the sun beating down on his skin, felt her love pouring into him.

He didn't deserve her.

But he'd never give her up.

"Tell me what happened before . . . before that morning," she said. "I know it isn't easy to talk about, but maybe there's a clue somewhere about what happened to Carole."

That night? Sixty years ago to Adriana, not much more than a week to him. It was easy to remember that night. It started out so well.

"I was at a party after the premiere of *Break the Night*," he began. "Reviews were pouring in already. People were saying I might get a second Oscar for the role, and I was drinking down champagne—one glass after another—to celebrate. Two Oscars. That's what I wanted."

A second Oscar. It seemed such a trivial thing to think about when he had so much else to deal with. It seemed inconsequential when he'd won Adriana's heart—the greatest prize he could ever attain. If he could win another Oscar, he'd just consider it icing on the cake.

"The Trocadero was packed," he continued. "Everyone was eating caviar and drinking champagne. I remember Jack Warner walking through the crowd, patting people on the back and making speeches. He wasn't always a nice guy, but he could be damned generous when the mood was right—and he was feeling good that night. He liked successful movies. We all did, and if everything went well, *Break the Night* had a chance of being the studio's biggest hit ever.

"We were having a gay old time, until Carole's ex showed up, jealous as hell. They'd been divorced a good year or so, but he wasn't ready to let her go—not to me or anyone else."

"I read that he beat her. Was that true?"

"I suppose. When we first started working together she'd show up on the set with a black eye or a swollen jaw. *'It was an accident,'* she'd tell everyone. One week she'd say she'd run into a door, the next she'd tripped and fallen down the steps. None of us believed her. She had a jerk of a husband, but Carole didn't let much bother her. She wasn't afraid of much, either, and for the longest time she refused to dump the guy. One day she got smart, went to Reno, and got him out of her life—legally, at least. That night at the party, though, he announced to everyone that he'd rather see Carole dead than to see her with anyone else—particularly me."

"I've seen the old police reports. They suspected him at first," Adriana said, telling him something he already knew from reading about the murder and subsequent investigations. "He had an alibi and pictures proving he was nowhere near Santa Monica that night."

"Maybe he hired someone?"

"That possibility was checked out, too, but the police never came up with a thing."

"What do you think? Did he have a hand in it?"

Adriana shook her head. "He was one of the few people who mourned at Carole's funeral. He put a rose on her grave every day, right up until the time he died."

"Maybe he should have shown some of that love for her while they were still married. Of course, we all should have done things differently. My entire life would have been different if I hadn't gone home with Carole that night."

He wrapped his arms around his knees and leaned forward as Adriana kneaded the tightness in his back.

"She was upset," he continued, "worried that her ex might try to hurt her. She asked me to take her home, to stay with her, just in case."

"Why didn't the studio hire a bodyguard? I thought they protected their stars."

"Carole had a unique way of getting what she wanted. She'd pout, she'd cry, and someone always gave in. But the studio was getting wise. She was difficult to work with. She was late half the time and driving up production costs. They weren't in any rush to spend money on a bodyguard, especially when they'd indulged her after too many other scenes with her ex."

"If she was so much trouble, why did they give her the part in *Break the Night?*"

"Because she made money for the studio, and because Jean Harlow died," Trevor said, a touch of sorrow filling his heart at the memory of a very dear friend. "The part was written for Jean. She would have been perfect for it, but . . . but life isn't always perfect."

He remembered the phone call he'd gotten from Carole the day after Jean's funeral. *"I got the part, Trev. God, what luck, Jean dying and all."*

Carole was a poor substitute for Jean—in life, and in the movies, Trevor remembered.

"Carole wasn't half the woman or half the actress Jean was," he said. "Unfortunately, the studio had commitments. It was either rewrite the script or hire someone who could somewhat handle the role. Carole was available, and she was more than ready to work. It seemed like the right thing to do at the time."

"So, the studio decided to strengthen Carole's image by pairing her up with you off-screen as well as on?"

"That was the idea. It worked, too, but it didn't make her a better or more cooperative actress. Press is press, though. All I ever wanted to be was a star. I liked having my name in the papers, and it didn't matter how it got there."

"Didn't you care at all?"

"I wasn't a saint, Adriana. I've told you that before."

He took her hand and pulled her around to his

side. He touched her cheeks and gently kissed her lips. "If I'd known you then, I wouldn't have gone along with the studio's games. I know I wouldn't have taken Carole home that night. My life would have been a hell of a lot different if you'd been a part of it then."

"You can't change history."

"If I could, I'd go back in a moment and set things right."

He curled a strand of wind-tossed hair behind her ear and cupped her cheek in the palm of his hand. "Would you go back with me . . . if you could?"

She nodded, and the warmth of her smile melted a little more of the ice surrounding his heart. "I wish we could change history," she said. "But I think all we can really do is learn the truth about the past and try to move on. Please. Tell me everything."

Trevor looked at the house again, and allowed his mind to drift to that night, to the interior of the Trocadero. He thought about the beautiful gowns the women were wearing, the champagne that flowed, and the pretty young starlet who'd been his friend. Hell, that's who he should have gone home with.

"Janet Julian had asked me to take her home from the party that night. God, she was a sweetheart—not a bad actress, either. A little mixed up at times, but she tried so hard to make people like her. There was this one young kid—a photographer—who'd lost his heart to Janet a few years before, when she'd first started at the studio. She liked him, but that was it. Crazy kid, she'd set her sights on me and no one else. I could have given her what she wanted, but I didn't like the idea of breaking her heart. She'd been through enough."

"Like what?"

"A year in a mental hospital. She kept losing touch with reality, actually becoming the people whose roles she was playing. I visited her in the hospital a few times. Charlie Beck, the photographer, was usually there, too. Nice guy."

"I've met him. He's still visiting Janet every day."

"She should have married him. She wasn't cut out for Hollywood, for someone like me. But that's what she wanted. The night of the party she told me she wanted to celebrate the success of our movie. She said she had champagne chilling at home. Like a fool, I decided to take her up on her offer. Then, when Carole needed a ride home, I backed out."

"How'd she react?"

"As she always did when things weren't going right. She slipped into one of her roles and fed me a line straight off a script. 'I knew you could never be true to just one woman.' She'd said those same words to me when she played my wife in *Break the Night*. I laughed at her in the movie, but I tried not to laugh at her then. I didn't want to hurt her, but Carole needed me more than Janet."

"So you and Carole took off?"

"We posed for a few photos, then headed for the beach. I remember the glaring lights as we drove down the highway, the cool wind blowing our hair, and Carole raving madly about her ex. She needed to get it off her chest, and I hoped she'd get over it by the time I got her home. I hadn't wanted to leave the party, but I figured we'd have one of our own once we got to her place."

"Did you?"

Trevor shook his head, still remembering Carole's anger, the way she'd stormed out of his Duesenberg and rushed into the beach house.

"She pushed me away when we got to the house. 'Leave me alone, will you!' she shouted. 'I'm tired of you and every other stinking man I've ever met.' I remember laughing as she slammed her bedroom door in my face. I knew she'd change her mind if I just gave her time to cool off. I found some glasses and a bottle of chilled champagne—"

"Chilled?" Adriana interrupted. "Who put a bottle of chilled champagne out for you?"

"I never gave it much thought. Maybe her housekeeper. Maybe she phoned someone before we left the party. Maybe she'd planned on bringing company home and put the bottle on ice before she left for the party."

"Then why did she go straight to bed?"

"She was upset. I don't know the why of any of this, Adriana. All I know is that there was a bottle of chilled champagne, it was hot that night, and I was thirsty. I stripped everything off but my trousers, grabbed the bottle, and walked out to the beach. I didn't even have to pop the cork. It was already out."

Trevor felt Adriana's hair brushing against his shoulder as she shook her head. "That doesn't make sense. Think about it. Why would someone open the bottle and leave it to go flat?"

"Like I said, she must have called someone."

"But who?"

"I don't know."

"Maybe one of her admirers brought the bottle and was waiting for her to come home."

"No one else was there. Just me and Carole."

"They could have been hiding."

"Maybe. I don't know. Like I said, I didn't give anything a thought. But if someone else was in the house, why would he hide?"

"Because he or she planned to kill her?" Adriana ventured.

"Then why bring champagne?"

Adriana sighed deeply. "I don't know. I'm just trying to explore all the angles."

She wrapped her arms around her knees and stared intently at the house, as if she herself were reliving the events of that night. Maybe she should have been the investigator on the case. He was sure she'd already asked more questions than the police had asked after Carole's body was found. He assumed the police had thought that they had an open-and-shut case: *Trevor Montgomery—guilty. Trevor Montgomery—disappeared. Case closed.*

He wanted to close it in his mind, too. He wanted to shut out the horror.

He was at the beach. The woman he'd give his life for was sitting beside him, and all he wanted to do was press her back into the sand and make love to her.

But she wasn't going to let him shut out the nightmare by hiding in her arms.

"Tell me what happened next," she prodded.

"I drank at least half the bottle while I watched the tide rolling in and out. It was hot. God, I don't remember it ever being that hot. My throat was dry. I remember feeling dizzy as I walked back to the house from the beach. I thought I might be getting sick. My head hurt, I felt nauseated. I'd planned on just going to bed, the hell with having a party with Carole.

"I remember turning off the lights. I remember Carole sneaking up behind me, throwing her arms around my neck and kissing my back. She'd picked a fine time to get amorous, and I'd picked a fine time to get sick."

Trevor attempted to swallow, but his throat felt tight, swollen, just as it had that night. His temples throbbed again, and he remembered the pain he'd felt. "My head hurt so bad I couldn't think," he told Adriana. "Everything was blurry. 'Not now, Carole,' I said, but she didn't listen. She wasn't about to give up. I stumbled toward the bathroom, but she was all over me."

Trevor lowered his head to his knees as the sickness churned in his stomach. He could still remember the nausea, the dizziness, the ringing in his ears, Carole's mouth on his neck, and her warm breath on his cheek. He reached over his shoulder and could feel the welts from the deep scratches she'd left on his back.

"She wouldn't leave me alone. I remember doubling over in pain, thinking I was going to die. 'Go to bed,' I told her. 'Can't you see I'm sick?' All she did was laugh at me. I tried getting away from her, but she grabbed my shoulder. I was in enough pain without her digging her claws into me."

Adriana gripped his arm, and he raised his head, shocked by the frown he saw on her face, the look of disbelief in her eyes.

"What's wrong?"

"Carole scratched you?" she asked.

"Five welts down my back. She liked to get rough, but she'd never drawn blood before. I had to get her away from me. I remember pushing her away, I remember hearing her start to cry. I didn't want to hurt her. I suppose I should have asked if she was okay. Maybe I should have comforted her, but I was sick. All I wanted to do was get to the bathroom and put my head down on something cool.

"I don't know how long I was in the bathroom, I don't even remember when I joined her in bed. I was so tired, so dizzy, and the room was completely dark. I thought I should apologize to her, but she was quiet. I figured she was asleep or still mad, and I just wanted to close my eyes.

"I must have been running a fever because my body was drenched in sweat. Even the sheets felt damp and uncomfortable. But none of that mattered. All I remember is putting my head on the pillow and falling to sleep."

"Did she speak to you at all?"

"No. Not in bed, not before, either. The last thing

she ever said to me was how tired she was of me and every other man."

Adriana shifted in the sand, kneeling in front of him, wrapping her arms around his knees. "When you woke up the next morning," she asked, "did you still feel sick?"

"Nauseated. Dizzy. I remember the sun beating down on me through the windows . . . feeling hot . . . wishing I had something cold to drink. There was this sickening odor in the room. Then I felt something sticky on my hands, and something cold clutched in my fingers. My eyelids were heavy, but somehow I managed to open them. I was holding a knife. Carole was beside me."

He looked away from Adriana, toward Carole's house, the bedroom where he'd woken up. He stared at the window and could picture the furniture inside. The big oval mirror over a French Provincial dresser. The gold brocade wing-backed chair that sat in the corner with a red silk robe thrown over the arm. The white-satin sheets that were stained a reddish brown. And even easier to see was Carole's body. The slash across her throat. Blond hair matted with dried blood.

He lowered his head to his knees, the nausea back again, and waited for the illness to subside.

"Let's not talk about this anymore," Adriana pleaded.

"I have to," Trevor said. "I have to remember everything."

He took a deep breath, looked again at the house, and into the bedroom. "Carole's eyes were wide open, staring up at the ceiling. Her arms were slashed, her stomach, her chest. The knife slipped from my fingers and I rolled away from her and onto the floor. Something shiny fell off the bed, maybe one of Carole's bracelets or something. I'm not sure, but I must have been sleeping on it. I ran to the bathroom and saw myself in the mirror. There was blood on my face, my hands, my back. I'd been so ill I didn't even know I'd been lying in Carole's blood all night.

"I remember getting sick, then forcing myself to take deep breaths. I tried to remember what had happened, but I couldn't."

He looked at Adriana, hoping to see understanding in her eyes, when he knew he should see revulsion and hatred.

Instead he saw warmth, concern, and understanding. And she was leaning toward him, not backing away.

God, he didn't deserve her.

"I'd never been so scared in my life," he said. "I remembered the knife that had slipped from my hand, and I wondered if I could have killed Carole. Everything in me screamed that I wasn't a murderer. But who would believe me? I thought about my career, my reputation. I pictured everything I'd worked for being destroyed in just one night. How could I possibly have thought about myself right then? I should have thought about Carole, her friends and family. But I thought about me!"

"It's all right, Trevor. You did what anyone in that situation would have done."

"But I imagine most other people would have called the police. Not me. I just wanted to get out of there. I took the knife, ran down to the beach, and dived into the waves. I stayed under for the longest time, hoping I'd drown in the tide, but I wasn't that lucky. I guess I came to my senses and threw the knife out as far as I could, then made sure the water had washed away all the blood. Finally I went back to the house. I found my shirt and the rest of my clothes and threw them in the car. Again, I went back inside and wiped my bloody footprints off the floors and my fingerprints from everything else. I even got rid of the footprints on the beach and around the house. When I was sure I'd left no traces of my being there, I got in the car and drove home. I figured if I had some time to think, I might remember what happened. I was worried, too, that if I couldn't come up with a logical explanation I'd be arrested. I just wanted to get away.

"There was a party at Sparta that weekend. It was the Fourth of July, and Harrison always threw a party to celebrate. I changed into a tux when I got home, got rid of the clothes I'd been wearing—I weighted them down and threw them into the ocean—and drove to Sparta."

"Harrison said you were acting strange when you arrived."

"Strange?" Trevor laughed. "I'd spent the night with a dead woman. I might have killed her, and I couldn't remember. Of course I was acting strange."

"You should have told Harrison. You should have told somebody what happened."

"I didn't want to drag anyone else into my problems. I'd already decided what I was going to do, so I just put on a good show for everyone, letting them think I was my normal self. I drank just as I always did. I ate and danced and played chess with Harry. Janet was there. I think she sensed something was wrong, but she didn't say anything. When the fireworks started I took a bottle from the bar and walked down to the pool. Nothing seemed right any longer. My life might as well have ended in that bed with Carole because I felt dead. I couldn't forget the sight of her body. I couldn't forget the smell of her blood or the feel of that knife in my hand. I drank the rest of the bottle and I remember it slipping from my fingers and shattering on the marble. I said a quick prayer, maybe asking for forgiveness or something crazy like that, and then I walked into the pool. I lay facedown in the water and tried to think of something other than death. Drowning seemed a pretty easy way to end everything. I was too big a coward to do it any other way."

"That must be when Janet saw you."

"I suppose. The last thing I remember was hearing someone scream, then everything went black, until I splashed out of the water and ended up here with you."

Adriana squeezed his fingers tightly, and he wondered how she could listen to that story and still want to touch him?

"I should have died," he said. "I didn't deserve this second chance at life." He looked into her warm blue eyes. "I'm sure I don't deserve you, either."

"Of course you do."

"I don't have many redeeming qualities."

"You're too hard on yourself," she told him, placing a gentle hand over his heart. "When I look in your eyes I see nothing but warmth and kindness. When you smile, I want to smile, too. I don't have to look too deeply to find the good, Trevor. It's right out in the open. I'm afraid you're the only one who hasn't seen it."

He leaned his forehead against hers and closed his eyes. "Maybe you bring out the good in me."

She shook her head. "It's always been there." She tilted her face and kissed him lightly.

"I could be a murderer."

"You're not," she said adamantly, shaking her head.

"What makes you so sure? Did I mention anyone else being in the house? Did I mention Carole having any enemies?"

"I think you've spent so much time wondering whether you killed her that you've failed to wonder who else could have done it."

"I was there. No one else was in the house."

"It was dark. Carole rushed off to her room. You

grabbed a bottle of chilled champagne that you can't explain and went outside for what, an hour? Two?"

"I wasn't keeping track of time."

Adriana knelt beside him again. "You were outside long enough for someone to kill Carole, someone who wanted to make love to you when you came inside."

"Who?"

"Janet."

Trevor laughed at Adriana's preposterous statement. "That's crazy. Janet wouldn't hurt anyone."

"I don't think she did it intentionally. I think she went crazy that night. I think your rejection at the party pushed her over the edge, and she didn't know what she was doing."

"Why would you think Janet did it?"

"That first day you were here, when I was gone all day, I went to see her."

"Why?"

"I was looking for some way to prove that you weren't really Trevor Montgomery."

"I'd almost forgotten that you didn't always believe me."

"I believe everything about you now. Everything—especially that you're not a murderer."

"If she told you that she murdered Carole, she must be reliving some movie she's seen."

"She didn't tell me that at all. She just wanted to talk about you. 'He was a very wicked man,' she told me. Of course, I already knew all that."

"You're stalling, Adriana. You're accusing Janet of murder. What did she say to make you think that?"

"She just kept telling me that you left her, that you didn't love her, that you liked other women too much."

"That was common knowledge."

"Let me finish. Please. She seemed so sad. She'd wanted you to love her the way she loved you."

"I already told you. I didn't want to get involved with her because I didn't want to hurt her. I never touched her. Not once."

"But that's not what she thought. She was sick, remember? She'd been in a mental hospital. 'He was my lover.' That's what she told me. She said that you had to keep it a secret from the public and from the studios."

"That's crazy."

"Of course it's crazy. But it's what she thought. She was in love with you. She hated the fact that the studio wanted you to be with Carole. She was jealous."

"Did she tell you that?"

"She didn't have to. If I'd been Janet, I would have hated what the studio was doing, too. I would have despised Carole."

"Enough to kill her?"

Adriana shook her head. "No, I couldn't do that. But if you'd seen the look in Janet's eyes, if you'd heard the way she told me that the doctors had made her forget all the bad things in her life, you'd believe that she was capable of killing someone."

"I still don't believe she did it. Where's the proof?"

"You're carrying it around with you."

"What?"

Adriana touched his shoulders, sweeping one hand down his shoulder blade, over the five welts on his back.

" 'I wanted him to play rough,' she told me. 'I did everything I could to make him mad. I even scratched his back until it bled. But he wouldn't play my game. He just left me.' That's what she told me, Trevor. I'm sure she was in the beach house that night. I'm sure she killed Carole. When you came up from the beach, and told her to leave you alone, she scratched you. She desperately wanted your attention."

"Do you think I wouldn't have known the difference between Carole and Janet?"

"You were drunk. It was dark. You were sicker than you'd ever been, and you said the woman who scratched you never spoke. You assumed it was Carole because it was her house. But I think it was Janet. That's the only thing I can think. Maybe those scratches on your back don't seem like convincing evidence to you, but they do to me."

Trevor took a deep breath, trying to remember what he had felt, trying to remember the kisses and the feel of the woman's hands on his body.

He closed his eyes, thinking about Janet and Carole. One tough, one sweet. One dead, the other possibly a murderer.

No, he could never believe that about Janet.

"It's too much of a stretch to think Janet could have killed Carole," he said. "A person would have to be mad to kill someone so brutally."

"You're forgetting something Trevor. Janet might be sweet, she might have been your friend, but she's been in a mental hospital for the last sixty years and, as much as you hate to believe it, she *is* mad."

✍ *Nineteen*

A breeze blew in from the ocean when Trevor and Adriana returned to Santa Barbara, cooling the unusually warm night air. They crawled into bed and made love, as if for the first time, as if for the last, and Adriana fell asleep in his arms, her soft breathing music in his ears.

He loved her. God how he loved her.

That blessed thought lured him to sleep, to dreams filled with Adriana.

There were no nightmares—at last.

The buzz at the front door startled Trevor from sleep.

"Ignore it," he begged as Adriana jumped up in bed. He rolled over and looked at the luminous numbers on the alarm. Nine o'clock. No sane person would ring unannounced at 9:00 A.M.

"I can't just ignore it," Adriana mumbled, climbing from bed and wrapping the body he knew so intimately in a white terry cloth robe. "What if it's something important?"

"What could be more important than staying here with me and making love again?"

She leaned over his naked body and kissed his

lips. "Nothing's more important than you, but I've given you my undivided attention for the past four days and nights. I have a job, responsibilities."

Another ring and a pounding knock silenced her.

"I've got to get that," she said, blowing him a kiss before she walked from the room.

Trevor slid from the bed and struggled into the tight black jeans Adriana had promised would loosen up. Man wasn't meant to wear tight clothes—he'd definitely have to go shopping again.

He was buttoning the top button on the trousers when he walked into the living room through one door, and Stewart barged in through the front with his wife right behind.

"Calm down, Stewart," Maggie mumbled as she followed her husband. "You're going to have a stroke, sweetie."

Stewart jerked around. Trevor couldn't see the look on the lawyer's face, but he assumed it was grim, considering the way Maggie instantly backed off and sat demurely on the love seat.

Stewart faced Trevor again, his face red with anger as he glared at Trevor's naked chest, his bare feet, and his mussed-up hair.

"You look a bit upset, Stewart," Adriana said, closing the door. "Would you like some coffee?"

"I'm not here for breakfast, I'm here for explanations," Stewart stated. "First off, where have you been for the past four days? I've called the shop, I've called your number here, I even called Sparta, and Elliott said he hadn't seen you."

"We were at Sparta." Adriana walked toward Trevor and slid her hand into his.

Stewart's brows knit together as his gaze darted quickly over Adriana's attire, then back to her eyes. "Why did Elliott lie?"

"I asked him to," Adriana said calmly. "I didn't want to be disturbed."

"Was that your idea, or his?" Stewart asked, turning his glare toward Trevor.

"Mine, originally," Trevor admitted. "I was tired of intrusions."

"Why? You needed to get Adriana alone so you could seduce her, make her fall under the same spell you've put on other women?"

Trevor frowned, not liking the vicious turn of the conversation, but he kept his tone light and a smile in his eyes. "I'm afraid I don't know what you're referring to."

"Neither do I," Adriana said. "Care to explain?"

"Why don't I begin here," Stewart said.

He threw one of the papers he was holding onto the coffee table.

"What the hell were the two of you doing wandering around Forest Lawn?"

"Looking at headstones," Adriana answered quickly. "Haven't you and Maggie done crazy, spur-of-the-moment things on occasion?"

"What my wife and I do or don't do isn't of the least importance at the moment."

"And what we do is absolutely none of your business, either," Adriana tossed back, standing her ground with Stewart.

"It *is* my business when you go gallivanting around in cemeteries. What I want to know is why the hell you had to check out Carole Sinclair's grave?"

Trevor grabbed the paper from the table and held it out so he and Adriana could see the photo. They were embracing in front of the massive marble memorial, and Carole's name blazed in the background.

" *Trevor Montgomery and Carole Sinclair—together again,*' " Trevor read. "Well, at least they've got my name correct."

"This isn't funny," Stewart bellowed. "Adriana's

in that photo, too. Maybe you should read a little further."

" 'He's the spitting image of Trevor Montgomery. Is he a ghost? Has he risen from the grave? Will Adriana Howard, the beautiful blond in his arms, be the next on his list of murder victims?' "

Adriana slumped down on the sofa, pain written clearly on her face as she stared at the article. "I knew this would happen," she whispered. "It's going to start all over again. The gossip. The nosy reporters."

"It's already started," Stewart stated. "I came by the house yesterday and got rid of a few. They were standing at the gate, waiting for you or . . . your friend to show your faces. They're not going to let up."

"They will," Trevor stated firmly, remembering how he'd dealt with the press on those few occasions when they'd annoyed him. "Laugh it off. Don't make a big deal out of it. You can't change people's minds, anyway. Trust me; if they want to believe trash, they're going to believe it no matter what rebuttals you fire back."

Stewart glared at him. "I would have thought you'd come up with some scheme to get even more press."

"I don't want any press, especially if Adriana's involved. She's been through enough of that in her lifetime."

"Let me get this straight," Stewart said. "You want to protect her?"

"Obviously you haven't been listening to me. All week long I've told you who I am and why I'm here."

Stewart laughed. "What you are is a fraud."

"Oh, Stewart, you're overreacting," Maggie said from her solitary spot on the love seat.

"We'll let Adriana decide if I'm overreacting

when I'm through giving her all the details."

"Please don't tell me there's more," Adriana pleaded, and Trevor wished he could take away the pain he knew she was feeling.

"Let me paint you a pretty picture." Stewart sat across from Adriana and Trevor, steepling his hands before his face. "A man shows up unexpectedly claiming he's Trevor Montgomery. He's mixed up. He doesn't know where he is or what's happened to him. Maybe he was frozen for sixty years, maybe he was caught in a time warp. Maybe he's been reincarnated—same body, same voice, same everything."

"We already told you, Stewart," Adriana interrupted. "He's Trevor Montgomery's son."

Stewart opened his briefcase and pulled out a stack of files, dropping one after the other on the table in front of him. "Trevor Montgomery showed up in this woman's life five years ago," he said, opening the manila folder. "He spent six months with her. She was sixty-two years old, quite wealthy, and had a fixation on the long-ago movie star."

Trevor frowned, lifting the paper to stare at the type-filled sheet. "I don't know where you got this information, but I never spent six months with any woman."

Stewart ignored his comment. "A year later you were with this lady," he said, flipping open the next folder and tapping the paper underneath. "That affair lasted nearly a year. She was a little younger, had just a little less money, but she was more than willing to buy you anything and everything you wanted."

From the corner of his eye Trevor saw the worry on Adriana's face as she pulled the file from under Stewart's hand and fingered through the papers. "There aren't any pictures here. What makes you think it was Trevor?"

Stewart dropped another file on the table. "My investigator found this photo in an old newspaper." Stewart thumped his middle finger on the picture. "It's not a good photo, but you can definitely see the resemblance. *This*, Adriana, is your Mr. Montgomery earlier this year with the woman he lived with for three months before he moved on to you."

"I don't believe it."

Stewart raised an eyebrow. "Believe it, Adriana."

"You're crazy," Trevor said. "I don't know any of those women. That man doesn't look a bit like me."

Adriana studied the photo, her eyes flickering back and forth from the paper to Trevor.

"Let me tell you about this guy," Stewart said. "His name's Paul Dean. Ring any bells?"

"No," Trevor said flatly.

"The man at the Regal Biltmore," Adriana recalled, looking at Trevor with concern in her eyes. "He called you Mr. Dean. He said something about you pulling a fast one again."

Trevor laughed. "I'd never seen that man before."

"Well, he'd seen you," Stewart snapped, "and he was more than willing to talk. The lady in that first photo is his mother. She fell head over heels for you. Took you into her home when you said you had no family, no friends. She thought you had amnesia. But you looked just like Trevor Montgomery, and she wanted to believe it was true."

"I'm sorry she got mixed up with some kind of gigolo," Trevor said, "but I can assure you, it wasn't me."

Adriana looked up from the papers, as if she'd just heard part of the conversation. "Did you say she thought he had amnesia?"

"That's what she thought. What else could she believe? He said he couldn't remember anything, and then he asked her to take him in."

Adriana's gaze bolted to Trevor, a mixture of fear, doubt, and anger radiating in her eyes.

He'd told Adriana the same thing, just before he'd asked her to take him in. How could she possibly believe his remarkable story was true after hearing this damning evidence against him?

"Her son had you investigated," Stewart continued. "Paul Dean was the name he came up with. He even tried having you arrested, but, unfortunately, you hadn't done anything against the law."

"I imagine he hasn't done anything against the law now, either, sweetie," Maggie said. She was the only one rising to his defense. "The only thing he's done, quite obviously, is steal Adriana's heart. You can't have him arrested for that."

"How about blackmail?" Stewart asked.

"Stop it, Stewart," Adriana implored. "I don't want to hear any of this."

"You might not want to listen, but I'm going to tell you anyway. Mr. Dean has a good friend named Bill Paxton."

"The photographer?" Adriana questioned.

"That's the one," Stewart threw in. "He's got a prison record for blackmail. Seems he takes pictures of wealthy women in compromising positions. When he says he's going to turn them in to the tabloids, the women always come through with money."

"He did the same thing with us," Trevor said. "I told him Adriana wouldn't give him a penny."

"He's used that ploy before, too. One photo shows up, like that one in the cemetery, then he comes back for more money."

Stewart turned to Adriana. "It's all a scam."

Trevor saw the tears running down Adriana's cheeks. *God, she believed it.* How could he possibly make her see it wasn't true?

He touched her shoulder, but he could feel her muscles tense.

"Your Mr. Dean, Adriana, is a part-time model and a wanna-be actor. Just last week he tried to capitalize on his looks by telling some producer at Warner Bros. that he's Trevor Montgomery's long-lost son. They're making a film about Montgomery's life, and Mr. Dean auditioned for the role."

Trevor paced the floor, trying to think of a way to make Stewart stop his incriminations and his investigations. He couldn't tell the truth. Stewart would never believe it. He wouldn't believe another lie, either.

Making matters even worse was the fact that Adriana was looking at him like he'd risen from the bowels of hell.

Stewart leaned forward in his seat and stared at Trevor. "You picked a real good candidate for your scheme this time, Mr. Dean. You even suckered her into getting you all that false identification to make your plan a little easier to pull off."

Turning to Adriana, putting a hand on her knee, Stewart said, "I can call the police if you want."

She shook her head. "What I want is for you to leave. I didn't ask you to investigate him. In fact, I specifically asked you not to interfere."

"It's what he does," Maggie interjected. She turned to Trevor. "He even investigated me and almost called it quits when he found out I'd been a stripper. I had to convince him to listen to his heart instead of his head. He was pretty stubborn, but finally he came around."

Adriana got up from the sofa and went to the window. Trevor could sense her despair, the agonizing torment in her heart and soul.

She wouldn't want him to touch her, to offer any comfort, not now, but he went to her anyway.

"I love you," he whispered into her ear, hoping

she'd believe him. "That's the only real proof I have
that I'm telling the truth."

"Paul Dean told a lot of women he loved them,"
Stewart stated. "Don't listen to him, Adriana."

She turned from the window and with tears
streaming down her cheeks she looked from Trevor
to Stewart. "I don't know what to believe."

"I've been your friend for a long time," Stewart
said. "You've trusted me before, you've got to trust
me again. He's an impostor, but you're too blind to
see. I've known for years about your fascination
with Trevor Montgomery. You've idolized him. You
live in his house, drive his cars, and you've spent
hundreds of thousands of dollars collecting everything he ever touched. It's easy to see how some
Trevor Montgomery look-alike could walk in here
and make you believe he's Trevor Montgomery's
son. He could have told you he was the reincarna-
tion of your hero, that he'd been frozen for sixty
years, or that he'd traveled through time and you
would have believed him."

Adriana spun around, her eyes flashing from
Stewart to Trevor, suspicion clearly written on her
face. "Please leave, Stewart. I'm a big girl, and I can
take care of myself."

"I'm not leaving you alone with him," Stewart
stated.

"Please," she implored, not bothering to wipe the
tears from her eyes. "I need to talk to Trevor.
Alone."

Maggie went to Adriana and wrapped her in an
embrace that wasn't returned. "Give your heart a
chance to think, Adriana. Don't just use your brain."

"I think my heart's overridden my brain too much
lately."

"For what it's worth," Maggie said so everyone
could hear, "I like your Mr. Montgomery. I don't
care if he's a fraud or not."

"That's enough, Maggie," Stewart said, taking his wife by the arm and drawing her toward the door.

"Don't do anything crazy, Adriana," Stewart said. "Don't let him sweet-talk you. Don't—"

"Please leave, Stewart," Adriana repeated. "You're my business advisor, my attorney, and you're my friend, but this is my personal life, not yours."

Trevor heard Stewart's sigh, heard his shoes and Maggie's walking across the terra-cotta outside, heard the start of the engine and the car pulling out of the drive, but he could not have cared less if they were still in the house or a million miles away. All that mattered now was Adriana, hoping the trust he'd built in her hadn't died.

"You have to believe in me," he said, going to her side. He didn't try to touch her, didn't attempt to make her look him directly in the eyes. He prayed his words and his tone of voice would let her know the truth. "I haven't lied to you. I *am* Trevor Montgomery. I was born in 1904. I was with Carole Sinclair the night she was murdered. Everything I've told you is true. The stories about my parents, about my childhood."

Adriana looked at him through tear-filled lashes. "Time travel makes no sense," she said. "It's impossible."

"I have a difficult time believing it, too, but you wished for me to come to you. You threw the rose into the pool and somehow I showed up. It doesn't make sense, but it happened."

"Stewart's story makes more sense," she said, fidgeting with the belt on her robe. "There was a model at Sparta the day you came into my life. Bill Paxton told me he could be Trevor Montgomery's double. I didn't believe him, of course. I thought for sure I knew what Trevor Montgomery looked like. I kept comparing the model with what I remembered of Trevor from movies and photos. I thought the model was too pretty."

Adriana walked across the room and sat down on the sofa, staring at the cover photo on one of the books. She looked from the book, to Trevor, then back to the book again. "You're too pretty, too."

"Those pictures were taken in the thirties. They're old. Maybe they don't do me justice."

"Maybe you're not Trevor Montgomery after all. Maybe you're a fraud. Maybe you're the model who was with Mr. Paxton and maybe the two of you didn't leave Sparta when I told him to. Maybe you came back, maybe you watched me toss the rose into the pool and say those words. Maybe you saw a lonely woman who needed to be loved."

"I did see a woman who needed love—and I loved her. I'll always love her."

"I wish I could believe you."

"I'm not Paul Dean," Trevor said, sitting on the coffee table next to the books. "Think about it, Adriana. My feet and hands matched the prints at Grauman's."

"Coincidence."

"I told you about spraining my ankle when I was filming *Captain Caribe*."

"A made-up story. I know everything about Trevor Montgomery, and I never heard that one before. You could easily concoct stories and say everything I knew was a lie."

"What about the scratches on my back? What about the things Janet Julian told you?"

"Everything's coincidence. You could have done your homework just like I've been doing."

"You're not going to believe me, are you?"

Slowly she shook her head and walked toward her bedroom. She grabbed a bag from the closet and went to the guest bedroom.

Trevor leaned against the doorjamb, watching her

neatly fold his suit and place it inside along with the shirts and ties, the underwear and shoes, everything they'd purchased. On top she placed the shrunken tux, closed the lid, and fastened the latches.

"I'd like you to leave," she said, her face devoid of expression except for the tears falling from her eyes.

"I'm not leaving. This is my home."

"It could have been if you'd just told me the truth. If you'd told me you were Paul Dean, if you'd said you were a struggling actor—"

She closed her eyes and sighed. "What does it matter. You lied to me. I don't want you here any longer, and if you don't leave now, I'll call the police and tell them you're an intruder and part of a blackmail scheme."

"You couldn't do it before. What makes you think you can do it now?"

"If necessary, I'll ask Stewart for help. I don't think he'll have any reservations about getting rid of you."

She walked toward the front door and held it open, just as she'd done that first night. "Please leave."

"What about last night? What about all our days at Sparta? What about everything we've shared?"

"You're a good actor, and I've been a fool."

"You're not a fool, Adriana. I've never known anyone like you."

"Unfortunately," she said, her lips beginning to tremble, "I've known too many men like you."

❧ *Twenty*

He felt like hell. He wanted a drink but no matter how bad things got, he wasn't going to touch a drop again. He'd made that promise to Adriana, and he wasn't going to break it, even though she'd kicked him out of her home and her life.

Adriana. Trevor thought of nothing else as he strolled along State Street, lugging the suitcase she'd thrust into his hands before she closed the door in his face. He thought of her smile, her laugh, and the tears cascading down her cheeks. He'd wanted to kiss them away; she wanted him gone.

He hadn't argued. He'd just walked out the door and hitched a ride into town.

He'd walked for hours, remembering each moment they'd spent together. The way she'd watched him dip lobster into drawn butter at a restaurant on the wharf. The way her eyes had studied his lips as he licked his fingers. He thought about the way her corn-silk hair breezed across her face as they walked on the beach. He thought of her warm blue eyes, her gentle smile. He thought of the tears of sorrow and concern she'd shed when he'd told her of his childhood, and how his heart had swelled when he realized that no one else had ever cried for him. He thought about all the hours they'd spent making love. In the beginning she'd been afraid of his touch. Last night she'd begged for it.

She wanted him still. He was sure of it.

And he planned to get her back.

He loved her. God, how he loved her. He'd do just about anything to win her love, but first he had to prove his worth.

How could he do that, though? He had no money, no car, no job. What he did have was a 24-carat gold, waterlogged watch. The movement no longer worked, but the pawnshop owner he'd shown it to seemed to recognize its value. It was worth a hell of a lot more than the ten dollars he'd been given, but that didn't matter. It was enough to get him to Hollywood and enough to make a phone call or two, if necessary. He could live on cheap hamburgers and coffee for a day or two. Then he'd be broke again.

But that wasn't going to happen. He'd survived Hollywood in the twenties when he'd had no money; he could easily do it again.

This time, at least he had Adriana at the forefront of his mind, and Adriana meant hope. He wasn't going to give up.

He didn't know how the studio system worked in the nineties, but he knew if he could get an audition with someone, anyone, he might stand a chance of getting a job. He'd begged before. Of course, he'd been only sixteen at the time and just about anyone could get a job at the studios. He didn't want to start out as a janitor this time, but even a job like that was better than nothing. He'd do just about anything to make a little money.

He'd rather act, though.

What was it Stewart had said? Paul Dean had auditioned for a part in a movie about Trevor Montgomery? Trevor smiled inwardly, realizing that the perfect opportunity for finding a job had just presented itself. Surely he'd stand a chance if he tried out for the role. All he had to do was get into the studio and be himself.

He thumbed a ride from a trucker and was deposited at a bus depot not far from the Warner Bros. lot. He changed clothes in the rest room, washing and shaving in a sink coated with dark gray grime, dressed up in the suit and shirt Adriana had so carefully folded, then deposited the rest of his belongings in a beat-up metal locker.

It wasn't exactly home, but he'd once lived in worse places.

Standing in front of the dingy mirror, he adjusted his navy-and-white silk tie, straightened the white handkerchief in his pocket, and buttoned the double-breasted navy pin-striped suit. He combed his hair, wetting it down and hoping it would stay put, just the way it had in the thirties. He wished he still had the mustache. That one added detail would probably clinch the role. It didn't matter that he was the genuine thing—he had to look the part.

With all the preliminary work out of the way, he walked toward the studio and stood outside the gate, hands in his pants pockets, waiting for just the right person.

She was pretty, blond, and young. She had on an obscenely short skirt, heels that looked like lethal weapons, and breasts that Mae West would have envied. She was perfect, and she was walking toward him and the gates as if she belonged inside.

"Good afternoon," he said, smiling his movie-idol smile.

She seemed a bit hesitant as she passed, and Trevor thought for sure she'd keep on walking, but he noticed her steps slow, and when she was at least ten feet away, she turned around and frowned. "Do I know you?" she asked.

Trevor shook his head. "No, and I'm not going to feed you a line about being someone famous. I'm a nobody who needs to get past those gates." He smiled again. His smile had won him favors before, he hoped it would do it again. "Think you can help me out?"

"What, no offer to buy me lunch or dinner? No twenty-dollar bribe?"

"I'm broke." He winked. "You get a smile and a thank-you."

"At least you're honest."

"I try."

Her name was Jen and she worked as a secretary to one of the producers who had offices at the studio. The guards at the gate knew her and didn't blink an eye at seeing her bring in a guest.

"You wouldn't by any chance know who's producing the picture about the life of Trevor Montgomery, would you?"

She stopped and gazed at him, from head to toe and back again. "I knew you looked familiar. At least ten men have auditioned for that part already."

"So you know about it?"

"A friend of mine, Andy Howell, auditioned yesterday. He wasn't right, though. Seems the producer's picky."

"You know the producer?" he asked.

"Not well, but I'd be happy to show you his offices."

She swung her purse as they walked. There wasn't as much activity on the lot as there'd been when he was one of the studio's biggest stars. He'd been here just a few weeks before, checking out the filming of *Dodge City*. Errol Flynn had been wearing a cowboy hat and a six-gun strapped to his hip. Alan Hale was riding a horse and Olivia de Havilland was playing Errol's lady love. A year before the same group were sporting tights and hats with feathers, filming *Robin Hood*.

Trevor had had lunch with David Niven and, using invisible swords, fenced with Basil Rathbone. He'd never shared the screen with either man, but he'd admired their work and found it an honor to be their friend.

But he knew no one on the lot today. He felt just as vulnerable as he had as a teen when he'd sneaked into the studio in much the same way. His smile had gotten him through many locked doors; he hoped it would do the same today.

He parted company with Jen and entered a bungalow with an unfamiliar production company name on the door. In the thirties he could walk straight into Jack Warner's office, sit down and chat. Of course, he'd been a star back then, and as he'd told Jen earlier, now he was a nobody.

Getting into the producer's office wasn't going to be as easy.

Trevor knocked lightly on the door and smiled at the red-headed secretary as he peered around the edge. "Excuse me . . ." He peeked at the nameplate on her desk. "Miss Erickson. I was hoping to see the producer."

Miss Erickson rolled her eyes when he closed the door and stepped in front of her desk.

"What do you want, Mr. Dean? I thought Mr. Castle asked you not to come back again."

Trevor smiled. He had the right place. Paul Dean had already left his mark, but the pretty young redhead was too savvy to succumb to his devious charm.

"I'm afraid you have me mixed up with someone else."

Miss Erickson raised a doubting brow. "You can change your voice, Mr. Dean, but that doesn't fool me."

"We've never spoken before. How could you possibly know my voice?"

"Stop teasing. Why are you here?"

"I've come to audition for the role of Trevor Montgomery."

"You've done that before, and, I'm glad to say, the part's already been filled."

"With the wrong person, I'm sure. If you'd tell your boss . . ." What was the name she'd used? "If you'd tell Mr. Castle that Trevor Montgomery's son is here, perhaps he'll give me a moment."

"You've tried that already, Mr. Dean. Mr. Castle's a busy man."

"Too busy to talk to the perfect actor for his movie?"

"Too busy for you."

Her phone rang and Trevor leaned against the corner of her desk, smiling while she talked, her gaze flicking from him to Mr. Castle's door and back again. She continued to frown. He continued to smile, but she wasn't falling for it.

Maybe he should just walk through that door and make his own grand entrance. No, that wouldn't work. He'd learned a long time ago it was better to humor the secretary, get on her good side, before trying to speak with the boss. Trevor knew who ran the show.

"You know, Mr. Dean, I could call security," she said, frowning at Trevor when she hung up the phone. "They'd be happy to escort you out of here, especially since you don't have an appointment."

"Yes, I suppose you could. But then you might feel guilty for sending me away when Mr. Castle hasn't had a chance to see me act. Would you like me to act for you?"

The woman shook her head, but Trevor ignored her, took a deep breath, and removed all expression from his face. He loosened his tie, mussed his hair, and rubbed his eyes until they reddened and teared at the corners. He slumped down in the chair next to Miss Erickson's desk and buried his head in his hands, letting his Oscar-winning lines from *One More Tomorrow* enter his mind.

"I have nothing left to offer you. I've squandered everything on too much booze, too much gambling, and, God forbid, too many women," he said, his voice filled with anguish.

Slowly he raised his head and looked into the secretary's mesmerized green eyes. "I have no right to ask your forgiveness, no right to ask for your help." He reached across the table and took the secretary's now-trembling hand. "You loved me once. I'm begging you to love me again."

"Quite impressive."

Trevor jerked around at the sudden applause behind him. A man in blue jeans and a T-shirt stood just outside Mr. Castle's door, eyeing him up and down, just as Miss Erickson had done earlier. Trevor swept his hair back and straightened his tie, then stuck his hand out.

"I'm Trevor Montgomery. You must be William Castle."

"Trevor Montgomery, huh?" The producer's eyes narrowed, creases formed in his brow as he studied Trevor's face. "I don't know if I buy that line, but I know you're not Paul Dean. Although, I must say, the resemblance is extraordinary."

"That's what people keep telling me. I understand, though, that he's not much of an actor."

Mr. Castle grinned. "Let's just say he won't be appearing in any of my productions."

"I'd like to appear in one, although Miss Erickson informs me the role of Trevor Montgomery is already filled."

"I'm always open to discussion, Mr. . . . . Montgomery."

"And I'm always willing to listen."

Mr. Castle peeked around Trevor and addressed his secretary. "Clear my calendar for the next hour or so. I have some negotiating to do."

Trevor stood just outside Adriana's memorabilia shop, fingering the gold doubloon he'd carried in his pocket since the premiere of *Captain Caribe*. He had three dollars left, he needed a place to stay, and he needed to find an agent. Shooting of *Shattered Dreams* was scheduled to start in another week. William Castle had offered him the role of Trevor Montgomery, but he knew full well that he needed an expert to handle all the contractual ins and outs. He hadn't accepted—not yet.

He'd located Jen hard at work in her office, taken her out for a cup of coffee, and got the names of several agents she said she couldn't recommend strongly enough, and then he'd found a phone booth and started making calls.

The first two weren't looking for newcomers. The third, Ron Epstein, was interested and wanted to meet for dinner. Trevor planned to treat, but he needed money first.

Tomorrow, in the light of day, he planned to check out Paul Dean, the impostor and the cause of all his misery. He'd sweet-talked Dean's address out of pretty Miss Erickson, and he planned to give the man a piece of his mind. But first he needed money.

He hated parting with his doubloon; he didn't even know if it would bring much cash, but considering some of the staggering prices Adriana had paid for old Hollywood props, like two hundred dollars for the insignificant patch he'd worn over his eye in *Captain Caribe*, or ten thousand for an original theater poster from Douglas Fairbanks's *Robin Hood*, he thought he might stand a chance of being on easy street for a while.

Looking at the memento one more time, he stepped into the memorabilia shop.

A flood of memories came rushing back. The way Adriana had lovingly touched one of his tuxedos when she'd shown him the locked cabinet where she kept what she'd called her most precious belongings. The way she'd stood in front of him and expertly tied his black-silk tie, while the sweet scent of her perfume wafted about him. The way she'd stepped out of her office in that long, shimmering white gown, and how her eyes sparkled when he draped ropes of pearls about her neck. She'd looked young, innocent, and completely beguiling.

She'd mesmerized him the first time he'd seen her, when he thought she was an angel. He'd fallen hopelessly in love with her when he'd held her in his arms and taught her to dance.

He loved her. He had to get her back.

"May I help you?" a woman asked, stepping out of the back room, her arms laden with a stack of what looked like old photo albums.

"I hope so," Trevor said, and watched the woman's eyes flick upward when she heard his voice.

She stared at him for the longest time, her eyes narrowed. Suddenly, they widened. "Oh, my!"

"Is there a problem?" he asked, taking hold of the woman's arm when she dumped the albums and gripped the counter.

"It's the most amazing thing, but you look exactly like Trevor Montgomery," she muttered. "When you work in a store like this, your mind has a tendency to step back in time. I thought I might have done it for real."

"I assure you, you haven't gone anywhere."

She took a deep breath, one hand to her chest, as she attempted to regain her composure. "Now," she said, exhaling, "what is it I can do for you?"

"I understand the owner of this store is highly interested in Trevor Montgomery memorabilia."

"Most shops are. Of course, it depends on the item."

Trevor held his palm out and the gold doubloon twinkled in the late afternoon sun shining through the window. "Jack Warner gave this to Trevor Montgomery at the premiere of *Captain Caribe*."

She laughed lightly. "Yes, I've seen a few just like it over the years. Fakes, every single one."

That was something he hadn't expected to hear. "I assure you, this one's real."

"I suppose you're the real thing, too. Trevor Montgomery come back to life?"

Trevor shook his head slowly. "Close. I'm Trevor Montgomery's son," he told her, sticking with the story he'd used with Stewart and then again with Mr. Castle, Miss Erickson, and with Jen. "My father carried this doubloon around with him everywhere."

She looked at him skeptically. Slowly her expression softened into a smile. "May I take a look?" she asked.

Trevor took the coin between his index finger and thumb, held it up to the light until it sparkled, then deposited it in her hand.

"The profile on the front is of my father in his most famous role," he told her. "*Captain Caribe* is inscribed at the top, the premiere date is at the bottom, and if you'll turn it over, you'll see Jack Warner's thank-you to Trevor Montgomery."

"It's a very interesting piece. May I ask where you got it?"

"From my father, as I already told you. It was in the pocket of a pair of tuxedo trousers."

"I believe we might want to purchase this from you, but I'll have to discuss it with the owner. Is there any possibility of my holding on to it for a day or two?"

A day or two? He needed the money now.

She must have sensed his thoughts. "I could give you a deposit of, say, five hundred until we can determine its value and whether or not we want to make the purchase."

"I believe five hundred will be fine."

"Let me just fill out some paperwork, sir." She set the doubloon on the counter and pulled a form from underneath. "Now, what did you say your name is?"

"Trevor Montgomery."

She shook her head, obviously still not believing his story, but wrote the name on a sheet of paper.

"And your address?"

"The bus depot. Locker number 372."

Her brows furrowed together in a much deeper frown than before.

Trevor winked at her. "I'm a little short of funds at the moment, but this advance should change my circumstances a bit."

She lowered her pencil. "Maybe I'm being too hasty."

"It's the genuine thing," Trevor insisted. "I'm sure another dealer would be happy to buy it."

"Well," she sighed in frustration, tapping her finger on the counter next to the doubloon. Her eyes flickered up to Trevor, back to the doubloon, then toward Trevor again. "I'm sure Ms. Howard will be interested in seeing this. Since you don't have an address . . ."

"I'll be back day after tomorrow to see how much your boss is willing to give me for the piece."

"I'll be sure to tell her."

"Would you give her a message, too?"

"And what's that, Mr. Montgomery?"

"Tell her if she'll watch *Captain Caribe* very closely,

there's a scene where he's taking off his boots. Ask her to take a look at his ankles and see if she notices anything odd."

Adriana flipped through book after book, studying the photos of Trevor Montgomery. She touched the cleft in his chin, the dimple to the right of his mouth, and remembered how a real cleft and a real dimple felt.

Did it matter that he wasn't really Trevor Montgomery? She'd fallen in love with the man who'd been in her house, in her arms, in her bed. She'd fallen in love with a man who'd fed her rich cheesy omelets and her very first Big Mac, a man who'd licked butter from her lips and salt from her fingers. She'd fallen in love with a man whose eyes and smile mesmerized her, devoured her.

She hadn't fallen in love with the man on the screen. She'd idolized a myth—nothing more.

A tear fell from her eye and dropped just below Trevor Montgomery's eye. She wiped it away and closed the book. She hadn't dreamed about Trevor Montgomery the movie star in over a week. She hadn't seen him swinging from a yardarm or floating in a pool. Instead, she'd seen a man in white boxers and a ribbed undershirt, eyes red and rimmed with dark circles. A man who needed a shave. A man who'd bruised her wrists, who drank too much, who'd promised to stop and had, as far as she could tell.

A man who was very, very real, who had too many faults and too much passion.

And she loved him.

Where had he gone? Would he come back? She shouldn't care about either, but she did.

She loved him. It didn't matter if he was a fraud or not.

The ringing doorbell startled her from her thoughts, and she ran to answer it.

Maybe he'd come back.

Disappointment filled her when Hannah, the manager of her Hollywood store, burst inside.

"Wait till you see what came into the shop today."

"What is it, Hannah?"

"The gold doubloon Jack Warner gave Trevor Montgomery."

Adriana gripped the edge of the door. She'd been looking for that piece for years, and all she could determine was that it had disappeared right along with Trevor Montgomery.

"Take a look at it," Hannah said, holding the gold piece out for Adriana to inspect.

Adriana closed the door, took the doubloon from Hannah, and went to her desk. She flipped on the light, pulled out a magnifying glass, and scrutinized the front, the back, the edges. She'd seen many fakes over the years, but not this time. It didn't take a jeweler to know the value of the piece.

"Did you buy it already?" she asked.

Hannah shook her head. "I gave the owner a deposit. It looked like the real thing, I just wasn't sure."

"It's real all right. My guess is we could purchase it for fifteen . . . no, closer to eighteen thousand." She ran her fingers over the piece, noting the slight wear in the engraving, as if it had been carried in a pocket for quite some time. That's how she'd always known the fakes. According to Harrison, Trevor had always carried that coin in his pocket. It was bound to get worn over the years, and the fakes had been much too perfect.

"Is there any way we can get in touch with the owner now?" Adriana asked, anxious to make the purchase.

"It's the oddest thing," Hannah told her. "A man

claiming to be Trevor Montgomery's son brought it in."

Adriana's heart skipped a beat. Was it her Trevor who had taken the coin into the shop?

"Did he tell you where he got the coin?" Adriana asked, trying not to show her excitement.

"In a pair of tuxedo trousers."

He'd been wearing a tux the night he came into her life. A tux that was wrinkled and sodden. The same tux he'd been wearing sixty years before when he stepped into the pool at Sparta and tried to end his life.

Could everything he told her have been the truth? She'd believed it once, so why was it so difficult to believe it now? Maybe if she saw him again she'd believe.

"Did he leave a phone number or address?"

Hannah laughed. "The bus depot. Locker 372."

"That's it? That's all he told you?"

"No. He said he'd be back in two days to get the rest of his money."

Hannah seemed hesitant, as if there was more to the story.

"What else did he tell you?" Adriana asked.

"He was a very strange man. He asked me to give you a message."

"Which was?" Adriana prodded.

"That you should watch *Captain Caribe* very closely, especially the scene where he's taking off his boots. He said you should look at Trevor Montgomery's ankles." Hannah frowned. "Is this all some kind of joke?"

Adriana remembered that first morning Trevor came to her home. She remembered the way he'd walked around her bedroom while she lay in bed trying to stay calm. He'd picked up the video of *Captain Caribe* and told her about spraining his ankle and wrapping it himself. Had he been telling the truth all along?

Or was all of this just another lie to confuse her?

"I've got some work to do in the shop, Hannah. Why don't I come down day after tomorrow and spend the day. I'd like to meet the man who brought in the doubloon."

"Would you like me to take it to a jeweler, see if I can have it authenticated?"

Adriana shook her head. "I don't think that's necessary. If he's a fraud, he'll be happy with the five hundred dollars. I doubt he'll want or need anything else."

✍ Twenty-one

Adriana prayed that Trevor would come. She'd even plucked a red rosebud from one of the bushes in her garden before driving to her shop in Hollywood, kissed it, and made a wish. "Come to me, Trevor. Please."

Long before business hours she'd busied herself around the store, sorting through merchandise to determine what should go in the next catalog. It was a month before it had to be done, but she needed to stay occupied while she waited for the man who'd brought in the gold doubloon.

Her stomach churned while she waited. Her palms were damp. Swallowing was difficult. And she jumped every time a customer walked into the shop.

At ten she sat alone in her office sipping at a cup of Earl Grey with a dollop of thick cream, like Trevor would have made it. Closing her eyes, she relived the moments when she'd danced in his arms, the way he'd masterfully maneuvered around the dance floor in spite of the times she'd stepped on his toes, and the way he'd whispered that she was born to dance. No, he'd told her that she was born to be in his arms—and she longed to be in them now.

She thought of his gentleness when they'd made love. She thought of his passion for all the good things in life.

And she thought of the way he'd looked over sixty years ago when he'd filmed *Captain Caribe*. He'd worn gray buccaneer breeches, a patch over one smoldering brown eye, a leather vest, and a white cotton shirt with voluminous sleeves that billowed in the wind as his galleon sailed the seas. He'd grown his ebony hair long for the role, and he'd had it pulled back into a queue, except for that lock that refused to stay in control and waved over his forehead.

Breathtaking. There was no other way to describe him—on the screen or in real life.

Captain Caribe. She'd watched it last night, laughing, crying, wishing she was the captive princess the Captain teased unmercifully, the woman the Captain saved from the churning ocean and kissed passionately as the screen darkened and the credits began to roll.

Captain Caribe. The privateer who'd laughingly made a slave of a princess. "Fetch my wine," he'd demanded, then pulled her onto his lap while he drank, stealing kisses from the protesting miss. She fought him in the beginning, hating his miserable, sea dog's hide, and halfway through the movie she had hidden in the darkened corner of his quarters and admired his form as he'd pulled on his boots.

Adriana watched every second of that part as if she'd been the one hiding in the dark. The Captain hoisted one long leg on the edge of a chair and struggled into a boot. The other leg was next.

That's when she saw it for the very first time. Under the tight-fitting breeches he wore she could see the swollen outline of a thick, protective bandage around his ankle.

Never before had she heard stories about a

sprained or broken ankle. Harrison had never mentioned it. None of Trevor's biographers had mentioned it. There was nothing in the studio notes.

But there on the screen was Trevor Montgomery, obviously suffering from an injury.

Just as he'd told her.

She thought about the swollen ankle, and the fact that some man claiming to be Trevor Montgomery had brought it to her attention. How could he possibly have known unless . . . unless he was really Trevor Montgomery.

Oh, Trevor. I should have believed you.

"Would you like more tea?" Hannah asked, jerking Adriana back to the present.

"No, thank you. This was delicious, but I need to get back to work."

She took the teacup to the small kitchenette in the back room, then went back to work, trying, unsuccessfully, not to think about Trevor.

He'd pledged his love, he'd begged her to trust him, and she'd slammed the door in his face. She wouldn't blame him if he no longer wanted anything to do with her.

Sighing heavily, she tried to get her mind back on her work. She unlocked the glass doors in a display case and removed the Roman helmet Fredric March had worn in *The Sign of the Cross*, thinking how striking it would look photographed on a background of purple velvet.

From one of her hanging files she pulled a movie poster of the Clark Gable and Jean Harlow film *Saratoga*, with the banner at the top reading, *To an expectant public we announce the presentation of Jean Harlow's last screen production!* Hollywood and the moviegoing public had lost a wonderful actress in 1937. In 1938 they'd lost Trevor Montgomery.

In 1998, Adriana had lost him again.

But maybe there was a chance to get him back—if he'd return to her.

She attempted to concentrate. She tried not to think of Trevor, but it was useless. She'd barely slept in the four nights he'd been gone. The house had been too quiet, her bed and arms too empty.

It didn't matter any longer if he'd lied, if he was an impostor, or if he really was Trevor Montgomery. She wanted *him*. That's all.

At noon Hannah brought in salads for lunch and at three-thirty she went out for coffee. At five o'clock Adriana decided that Hannah had given away five hundred dollars of her money to a cheat, a man who didn't really love her, and she decided she should have the gold doubloon verified for authenticity. It had looked legitimate, but the man hadn't returned for more money or to claim his coin—both those things pointed to fraud.

Once again he'd made her look the fool. Once again he'd made her heart think before her head.

Hannah closed and locked the doors at 6:00 P.M., urging Adriana to go home.

"I'll be out of here in half an hour. I promise," Adriana said, as she thumbed through more black-and-white stills, looking for just the perfect thing for the catalog.

"Would you like me to stay?"

"No, no. I'm fine here by myself."

"I'm sorry about the five hundred dollars."

Adriana looked up from her work and smiled. "I probably would have given him a thousand on deposit. Don't worry about it."

Hannah shrugged, grabbed her purse, and headed for the door.

Adriana heard the keys in the lock, heard the tinkling bell of the opening door, then heard Hannah's voice again.

"We have company, Adriana. The Trevor Montgomery look-alike has finally shown up."

Trevor's familiar laugh rang through the shop, and Adriana fought the urge to cry. He had returned. Her wish had come true—again.

Pushing up from the floor where she'd been sitting as she sorted through boxes, she brushed nonexistent dust from her navy trousers while trying to look calm and completely at ease. Slowly she gazed upward, to the man standing just inside the doorway, one hand tucked in his pants pocket, his suit coat hanging unbuttoned from broad shoulders, a lock of ebony hair hanging over his forehead.

Trevor Montgomery, the most devastatingly handsome man she'd ever seen, smiled warmly, the dimple beside his lips deepening, just as it had in so many movies.

How could she ever have doubted him?

She kept her composure, trying to think of all the reasons he might have come to her shop. He needed money. He wanted his doubloon back. He wanted to give her hell for kicking him out. Surely it couldn't have anything to do with wanting to see her again, not after what she'd done.

Act the role of a businesswoman, she told herself. Tucking one hand in her pants pocket, just as Trevor was doing, she assumed a casual, relaxed stance, and forced herself to speak. "I understand you'd like to sell your gold doubloon."

"I've changed my mind."

Hannah peered around Trevor's back. "Do you need me to stay?"

"No, thank you, Hannah. Just lock the door on your way out, and thanks for all your help today."

Adriana leaned against a wall for support as Trevor moved toward her, the light from the back room illuminating the cleft in his chin, the hint of an early-morning shave just breaking through his skin.

Again she heard the bell on the door, Hannah's

keys in the lock, and finally the clip of her shoes as she walked past the front window and out of sight.

Trevor stood beside the cabinet that held all his cherished belongings, and his devouring gaze settled on her lips. "Did you watch *Captain Caribe*?" he asked quite casually, as if they were two friends discussing an old film.

Adriana nodded slowly, and struggled to speak. "I should have believed you."

"Yes . . . you should have."

She could see the pronounced movement of his Adam's apple as he swallowed. She could see the heavy rise and fall of his chest. Was he in nearly as much turmoil as she was? Did he love her nearly as much as she loved him?

"May I have the doubloon back?" he asked, holding out his hand.

She reached into her pocket for the small purple velvet bag she'd stored the coin in, drew it out, and dumped the doubloon into her palm. Her gaze flickered from the coin to Trevor's eyes. The gold was cold, but his eyes were hot, burning deep into her soul.

Stay calm, she told herself. *Stay businesslike.* She had to do it to protect herself, just in case he didn't want her.

"The coin's worth a small fortune," she said. "Why don't you want to sell it?"

"I don't give up the things that mean the most to me."

He took the doubloon from her palm and she felt the instant shock of his touch.

"I won't give *you* up, Adriana. Not today. Not ever."

She wanted to step into his arms, but she felt foolish for not having believed in him.

"How could you possibly want me after the things I said, after I kicked you out of your house?"

"You cried when you kicked me out," he said, moving close and wiping an escaped tear from her cheek. "No one else ever cried for me. No one else ever cared. I'd be a fool not to want you."

"I'm the fool. I never should have . . ."

"Just kiss me, Adriana," he interrupted. "Don't apologize. Please."

In less than a heartbeat she stepped into his embrace, stood on tiptoes, and kissed him. Slow and easy became hard, hot and passionate when Trevor took over. In the middle of his searing kiss, she felt him push the suspenders off of her shoulders, felt him nimbly release the button at the side of her trousers, and felt them float to the floor.

She was lost in a whirlpool of sensations, drowning in the excitement of his touch as his fingers feathered over her belly.

"I need you," he growled, as his mouth slanted over hers.

And she needed him.

Her mind whirled as she pulled away his tie, unbuttoned his shirt, and helped him shed his slacks. She was caught up in the erotic sensations of his lips on her neck and her chest, while her hands pressed against the heat of his back and pulled him ever closer. His teeth and tongue teased her breasts, and his fingers deftly explored her legs, her thighs, and the warm, moist center of her being.

He laid her gently down on the carpet, his smoldering brown eyes never leaving hers when he covered her body with his, when he whispered "I love you," and when he entered her slowly and smoothly—and loved her—giving her a feeling of pleasure and fulfillment that she wanted to last forever.

The small, mid-twenties Spanish-style house sat just off Sunset in West Hollywood. In the bright light of the streetlamps Adriana could see fresh grass clippings littering the sidewalk and orange and yellow marigolds planted in neat beds along the sloping wall that edged the steep driveway to a single-car garage.

The place was lovely, but Adriana had no idea why Trevor had brought her here straight from her shop. He insisted it had nothing to do with the role he'd won, starring as himself in *Shattered Dreams*. As they'd lain together on the carpet in the back room of her shop, he'd told her all about his trip to the studio, how he'd impressed the producer. He'd told her about the agent he'd hired, about his excitement at acting again. And he'd told her how much he'd missed her while they were apart.

But he hadn't told her why they had to make a detour on their way home to Santa Barbara. "It's a surprise," was all he'd say. "A special treat."

He was back in her life. That was the most wonderful treat she could ever want.

When they reached the door, he rapped on the screen and waited.

"I hate secrets, Trevor. Please, tell me."

He shook his head and knocked again.

Behind the door she heard the sickeningly familiar voice of a man calling to someone else in the house. The door creaked open, and Bill Paxton's face peered through the screen.

Adriana's fingers tightened around Trevor's hand. She attempted to pull away, not wanting to be anywhere near the vile photographer, but Trevor held her close, refusing to let her run.

"Well, what a surprise," Paxton said in his normal, cocky tone. "I didn't expect to see you here, Ms. Howard." He took a quick drag on his cigarette and blew out a puff of smoke. "I didn't expect you, either," he said, his brow furrowing as he looked at Trevor.

"Just checking out a little rumor I heard," Trevor said casually.

"And what might that rumor be?" Mr. Paxton asked, beginning to look a touch uncomfortable with their presence.

From deep inside the house Adriana heard another man's voice, unfamiliar this time, call out, "Is that the production company people?"

Paxton's face reddened, and Adriana noticed the quick rise and fall of his Adam's apple. He was terribly nervous now, but Trevor stood tall and calm, his eyes twinkling with some hidden merriment as he stared down at Paxton.

The photographer twisted around and answered the man hidden in another room. "It's someone else. No need for you to come to the door."

His words were too late, though. Adriana heard footsteps and saw a near mirror image of Trevor peer around Paxton's shoulder.

"Well, I'll be," the man drawled in a thick Southern accent. "What did you do, Bill, find someone to take my place?"

Paxton shook his head and leaned against the doorjamb. "Just shut up," he muttered, before inhaling deeply on his cigarette.

"I see the rumor's true. I do have a double," Trevor said, his gaze sweeping over his twin, who was dressed in gray sweat shorts and nothing else. "You must be Paul Dean."

"Yeah. The one and only," the model quipped.

Adriana studied him quickly. The cleft in his chin wasn't as deep, and he didn't have a dimple. His ebony hair didn't shine as brightly, and his skin was paler—it didn't have the sheen of Trevor's sun-bronzed body. He wasn't nearly as tall, and his physique was much too slight. His hands weren't strong, and he was much too pretty. There was nothing rugged in his face, nothing masculine or heroic.

She'd been right that first time she'd seen Paul Dean at Sparta. She'd been so very wrong to have ever questioned Trevor's identity.

"I've seen enough," she said, tugging on Trevor's arm. "Can we go now?"

"Not until I get a few things straightened out with Mr. Paxton."

"Like what?" Paxton asked, regaining a hint of composure. "You can't keep me from taking photos. I've checked you out, and I know who you are. Don't think that just because you claim to be Trevor Montgomery's son you can intimidate me."

"I don't make empty threats, Mr. Paxton."

Paxton laughed, but Adriana saw the iciness in Trevor's eyes.

"My attorney's in the process of filing a restraining order against you. Trust me, if you come within half a mile of Adriana, we'll make sure you're thrown in jail. There's a lot of power in money, Mr. Paxton, and we're going to back up this threat with every penny we've got."

"We've done nothing illegal. No judge is going to give you a restraining order."

Trevor shrugged. "If that doesn't work, I'll use my backup plan."

"Which is?" Paxton asked.

"I took some very interesting photographs of my own this afternoon."

Adriana watched Paul Dean's brow furrow as he listened to Trevor's words.

"Pictures?" Paxton questioned. "Of what?"

"Nothing of much concern, I'm sure. A kiss or two while you and Mr. Dean were working in the yard. An affectionate hug."

Perspiration beaded on Paxton's brow, and Paul Dean gripped the edge of the door.

Trevor tucked a hand into his pants pocket, and continued casually. "I was thinking about selling them to the tabloids. I know you're trying to get a start in the movies, Mr. Dean, and I thought a little exposure might be good for you. Your friend Mr. Paxton seems to think that the public is intrigued by pictures of this sort."

"Don't listen to him, Paul. He's bluffing."

"I don't like the sound of this," Dean stated.

"There's nothing to worry about," Trevor said with a grin. "Just give me the pictures you've taken recently, and the problem's solved."

"That's enough, Montgomery," Paxton bellowed. "You can't intimidate me."

Paul Dean put a hand on Paxton's shoulder. "Look, Bill. I'm not coming out over this. My folks don't even know."

"No one has to know a thing," Trevor interrupted, directing his words to Paxton. "I want the negatives, and I want you to stay away from Adriana."

"I want your negatives, too," Paxton said. "Turnabout's fair play."

"I don't think so. They're my insurance policy against any future encounters Adriana might accidentally have with you."

Paxton laughed. "No photos from you. None from us."

"Give them to him," Dean stated through clenched teeth, "or I'm history."

"Don't be an idiot, he's just bluffing."

"Well, I'm not willing to take that chance."

Paxton looked at Dean, and, shaking his head, he stormed into the house.

"Sorry this little problem came up," Dean said to Trevor and Adriana. "Money's not always easy to come by."

Paxton pushed around Dean and shoved a large envelope in Trevor's hands. "That's everything. Now get out of here."

Trevor smiled. "Thanks for being so accommodating."

"Get out," Paxton bellowed.

"Right," Trevor stated, tossing Paxton a two-fingered salute before grabbing Adriana's hand and sauntering down the stairs.

Adriana looked back when she heard the slamming door and raised, but garbled, voices coming from inside the house.

"Do you really have pictures?" she asked Trevor as they neared the Duesenberg.

"I might stoop to threats, but never to blackmail."

"Then how did you know about the two of them?"

"I saw them together, just as I said. I honestly didn't pay much attention to their relationship, but Stewart made a wisecrack, and it made me start thinking."

"Stewart was with you?" Adriana asked, surprised at this newest revelation.

"Last night, too. He and Maggie, both. We had dinner together, so I could tell him how I want my finances handled."

"I don't understand," Adriana said, when Trevor opened the car door and she slid inside.

Trevor leaned over the passenger door, smiling easily as he stroked a finger over the pencil-thin mustache he'd just started to regrow. "Movie stars make a lot of money—if the negotiations are handled correctly. Fortunately, I found a damn fine agent. I figured I'd need a business manager who's just as good."

"But Stewart despises you."

"We'll work through that." Trevor circled the car and climbed behind the wheel. "It took him a while to warm to the idea that I was really Trevor Montgomery—Junior, that is. It didn't take long for him to warm up to my money. I'm sure he'll come around in time."

Always so positive, she thought. *Always so sure of himself.*

"I missed you," she said. "I've never felt so lonely. So lost."

He leaned across the seat, wove his fingers through her hair, and pulled her close. "I'm not going anywhere ever again."

His lips touched hers tentatively, then she felt the pressure of his fingers on her neck as he held her close, as if deep inside he was just as afraid of what the future might hold for them as she was. He'd never show it though. Never. The Trevor Montgomery she'd fallen in love with was determined to laugh and make her happy—for whatever time they had together.

Adriana smoothed her fingers over his cheek, smiling softly as she kissed him, and silently prayed that he'd never again disappear.

Twenty-two

"I can't remember another thing," Trevor moaned, massaging his temples in the hopes of driving away the pain of too many bad memories. He leaned back in the ornate wrought-iron patio chair and gazed out at the ocean and the cloudless blue sky. He was tired of sitting at the table, tired of looking at stories about his life, tired of rehashing events best left forgotten.

"We've been over this three times, Adriana. Why don't we give it up?"

"You told me you don't give up," Adriana threw at him, "and I'm not going to let you run away from this. The only way we can prove your innocence is to document every single thing and make sure we have some evidence when we confront Janet Julian."

Trevor got up from the chair and walked behind Adriana. He put his hands on her shoulders and gently kneaded the tightening muscles. "I don't want to confront her. What good's it going to do?"

"Maybe she'll confess."

"You want too much. She's old. She's not in the best of health. Even if she confesses to the crime I still doubt she's guilty of, no one's going to prosecute her. Besides, she's been living in her own kind

290

of prison for sixty years. Isn't that enough punishment?"

Adriana twisted around in her chair and looked up at him. "What about the punishment you've suffered?"

He laughed, thinking of all that he'd gained by leaving the thirties. "I'm not suffering."

"You are," she interrupted. "You thought the nightmares had ended, but they haven't. Last night and the night before you tossed and turned. They're not going to go away until you know the truth."

She turned away from him and flipped over another page in the book she'd been perusing. "You're innocent, Trevor," she said softly. "But if we don't bring out the truth, history will always point to you as the guilty one. You can't live that way. I don't want you to have to."

She was right, of course. If they could prove his innocence, the movie script he'd been reading could be changed. Trevor Montgomery wouldn't be branded a murderer. His image wouldn't be tarnished, his dreams shattered. The film could reveal to the world what had really happened that horrid night sixty years ago.

"All right," he said on a sigh. "Where were we?"

Adriana tapped her pen on the paper filled with scribbled notes. "The shiny thing that slipped off your body."

Trevor tried to remember what he'd seen when he'd rolled out of Carole's bed, but all he could remember was a flash of light off something shiny. "It must have been one of Carole's bracelets. I didn't stop to look."

"But nothing was ever found," Adriana stressed. "It wasn't mentioned in the police report or in any of the newspaper accounts."

"Maybe I imagined it, then."

"Did you imagine anything else?" Adriana asked,

obviously annoyed that he'd suggested such a thing. "Did you imagine the blood or the slash across her throat."

"No. I didn't imagine any of that. Everything I saw, everything I did after I woke up is perfectly clear, and I've relived it every day since it happened."

"Then," she said adamantly, "you didn't imagine something shiny falling off the bed, either."

Adriana pushed back in her chair. "We need more information. I'm going to the library to check out the microfiche of the newspaper accounts. There's got to be something we're missing."

He couldn't bear the thought of her leaving and reached for her hand.

"Don't go, Adriana. Stay here with me."

"I won't be gone for long."

One minute away from her seemed an eternity. He couldn't let her go. "What if I disappear while you're gone?"

The laughter and joy he'd seen in her eyes for the past two days dimmed, and worry filled her face. "Has something happened? Do you know something you're not telling me?"

Trevor pulled her down into his lap. "I'm afraid if we're torn apart, for any reason at all, that I'm going to go back."

"I don't want to talk about that. Besides," Adriana reminded him, "you can't go unless I wish you back."

"That's only a guess. We don't know for sure."

Adriana rested her cheek against his, and he could feel the heaviness of her sigh. "I won't let you go," she whispered.

They'd been on edge since they'd returned from Hollywood, both worried that life was too good, that something awful was going to rip them apart. For two days he hadn't let her out of his sight. He showered with her, sat by her side when she worked. They ran errands together, and made love each time as if for the very last time.

If he was going to be pulled back to his own decade, he planned to grab on to her hand and pull her there with him—if he could. If he couldn't, he wanted to make sure she'd remember him.

"Promise you won't forget me if I do go back," he said.

Adriana laughed lightly, cupping his cheek in the palm of her hand. "How could I ever forget you?"

"You may not have a choice, any more than I have a choice about leaving you."

She pushed up from his lap, turning her back on him. "I don't want to talk about the possibility of your leaving."

"I do."

He shoved himself out of the chair and grabbed her hand. "Come here. I want to show you something."

He drew her through the house and into her bedroom. Opening the closet door, he got down on his knees, pulling Adriana down beside him, and rummaged behind shoe boxes and other odds and ends crammed in the corner.

"Remember the secret stash of money I told you about?" he asked, looking at her in the closet lit only by the sunlight beaming through the bedroom windows.

"Of course I do."

"Well, this is where I kept it."

Adriana peeked her head around his shoulder as he tugged at the baseboard.

"Once you pull the strip of wood off, you'll find a sliding door."

"I have no intention of hiding my money in there. Banks are perfectly fine with me."

"I'm not saying I want you to hide money here, it's just that . . ."

"It's just what?"

"If I go back in time . . ." He hesitated again, plowing his fingers through his hair. "If anything happens, I'll try to leave you a message, something to let you know what's happened to me."

"You're not going to go. I told you that already."

She didn't want to think about it any more than he did, but it had to be discussed.

"If I go back," he continued, "I think it will happen after we learn the truth about that night."

"Then I don't want to find out," she said adamantly. "We won't even think about it any longer. Let's just put the books away and do something else. We can go back to Sparta. We can go to Hollywood and visit cemeteries. I don't care what we do, but I'd rather have you here than—"

Trevor gripped her arms and held her close. "You told me we had to learn the truth, and you were right. No matter what happens, you have to help me find out what occurred that night."

She rested her forehead on his chest. "If you leave me, I promise never to forget you," she said. When she looked up, he could see a faint sparkle in her eyes. "I won't forgive you, either."

"Empty threats don't scare me," he teased, trying to lighten the moment.

"Of course they don't. You're the hero. You always find a way to get out of trouble."

They huddled together in the small confines of the closet. It was warm. The light scent of her perfume wafted around him, and he kissed her slow and deep and long.

God, he never wanted to leave her.

"Marry me, Adriana," he whispered, right there in the middle of her gowns, her trousers, her blouses, and shoes. "Marry me so I know you'll never leave me again."

"I won't leave you, Trevor," she said. "You don't have to marry me to make me stick around."

"Then marry me because you love me."

He pulled the ring off the end of the string attached to the overhead bulb.

"I've got something here to bind us together—forever."

He felt Adriana tremble when he took hold of her left hand and slid the plastic ring on her finger.

"Someday I'll give you diamonds the size of walnuts."

"I've had diamonds, Trevor. I'd rather have you—and this little plastic ring—any day."

A tear slid down her cheek.

"Marry me," he pleaded as he kissed the hand that wore the ring. "Marry me *now*, Adriana."

The private plane Stewart had chartered landed in Las Vegas at 8:22 in the evening. A long white limousine was waiting at the airport, as was the florist.

"Oh, you're just going to be *the* most beautiful bride," Maggie quipped, as the florist placed a bouquet of two dozen red and white roses and baby's breath in Adriana's arms.

"They're lovely, Maggie," Adriana said, kissing her friend's cheek. "How did you ever manage to do all this in just a few hours?"

"Money talks, darlin'. Fortunately, Stewart has lots of it. Isn't it wonderful!"

Maggie buzzed around, confirming all the last-minute details, looking the perfect—but extravagant—matron of honor in shocking pink feathers. She stuck a white rose in the lapel of Stewart's somber navy blue coat, picked up her own bouquet of white roses, and shuffled off to give the chauffeur directions.

Adriana smiled at her husband-to-be and nervously pinned a red rosebud on the lapel of his white dinner jacket.

"This is the happiest day of my life," she whispered. "I never knew I could love someone so much."

Trevor kissed her forehead, and curled a lock of hair behind her ear. "Thank you for marrying me." He took a deep breath, and for just one instant Adriana thought he was going to cry. Then, he smiled that wonderful movie-idol smile. "I love you, Adriana. God, how I love you."

Adriana turned at the sound of Stewart clearing his throat. "Are you sure you want to go through with this, Adriana?" he asked.

"Mind your own business, sweetie," Maggie drawled, breezing up behind him. "They're in love, and they're going to get married. We were asked here as guests, not as advisors."

Adriana caught the wink in Trevor's eye as he grinned at Maggie, then he turned to Stewart and patted his shoulder.

"We really have to work on this relationship of ours, Stew," Trevor declared. "We're going to have a lot of years together, as business associates and, hopefully, as friends."

Adriana kissed her attorney on the cheek, hoping to remove the scowl he'd worn throughout the plane ride. "I want you to be happy about giving me away. Please."

A slow grin tilted Stewart's lips. "I skipped a round of golf to get this show organized. Guess I might as well be happy about something."

"See why I love him so much?" Maggie said, pecking her husband's lips. "And, oh, I just love a pretty wedding."

They rode rather quietly to the courthouse to get a license, then even more quietly down a street of a million glittering lights on their way to the Little Church of the West.

Trevor took hold of her hand after he stepped out of the car. She put one white-satin shoe on the pavement, then the next. He slipped an arm around her waist as they walked toward the quaint wooden wedding chapel, and just before they reached the door, a man rushed to Adriana's side.

"Smile!"

The bright light flashed in front of Adriana's eyes, and she jumped, her hands flying in front of her face.

"Stop it! Please," she begged.

"There's nothing to fear, Adriana." Trevor's low, soothing words comforted her. He gathered her hands in his and tucked them close to his chest. "No one's going to hurt you and no one's going to gossip."

"But—"

He stilled her words with a kiss. "It's our wedding day, and this is the photographer Maggie hired. I want to look at these pictures when we're old and gray and we have fourteen grandchildren running around our house."

Grandchildren? They hadn't even talked of a family. "I didn't know you wanted any children."

"I want everything life has to offer. But first I want you. Just you."

He kissed her again as the camera flashed. She couldn't help but smile. It was her wedding day, and she was marrying the man of her dreams.

No woman could ever wish for more.

She felt she might smile forever.

They stood before the altar, Trevor radiant in his tux, she in a shimmering white-silk sheath studded with seed pearls across the shoulders and bodice. It was long and flowing, as was the lacy veil that trailed lightly down her back. A masterpiece from the thirties, it was something she'd bought at an auction the year before but had never had the heart to sell. Instead, she'd hid it away in her closet, thinking she might be able to wear it someday.

And tonight was perfect, in every respect.

From a corner of the room, Adriana could hear the violinist playing a beautiful rendition of "The Way You Look Tonight," the song they'd waltzed to the first time Trevor held her in his arms. Bouquets of red and white roses were clustered about the altar, and Trevor stood at her side, smiling softly as he held her hand tightly in his.

"Do you take . . ."

She barely heard the minister's words, but she heard the love in Trevor's voice when he said, "I do."

She repeated the words herself, then laughed as Trevor slipped the plastic ring onto her finger once more. There hadn't been time to pick out wedding rings, but that didn't matter. They didn't need gold or platinum or diamonds to bind them together, they didn't even need the pastor's words. But, all the same, she melted into Trevor's embrace when the minister pronounced them "husband and wife."

"I love you, Adriana," Trevor whispered. "Forever."

"Forever," she whispered back.

Nothing could ever pull them apart.

Nothing.

✑ *Twenty-three*

Trevor lay beside his wife, wondering how he'd gotten so lucky. Sixty years ago he had no idea what happiness was all about, but Adriana had taught him. Of course, she'd also taught him about perseverance, and sticking with something even though it drove him insane.

Even now, on the third day of their marriage, she was lying on her side, flipping through books about his past, determined to learn something new. She'd promised not to leave his side, and she hadn't. Still, she continued her search for Carole Sinclair's murderer.

Why couldn't they continue the honeymoon, thinking of nothing but each other? They'd shared two days of absolute bliss, laughing as they read old scripts together in the comfort and privacy of her suite at Sparta. They'd danced under glimmering crystal chandeliers and made love behind a mummy case.

He couldn't get enough of her, and even on the short trip home, he'd taken a detour, pulling off the highway onto a deserted road, and made love to his wife in the backseat of the Duesenberg.

Each moment together was precious, and he savored every second. Deep inside, he feared their days together were numbered. It was a feeling he refused to talk about or share. He kept his worries to himself. There was no need for Adriana to live with the fear that was haunting him more than his fear of being a murderer ever had.

They were together. Forever.

That's all she needed to think.

It wasn't true, though. He knew he was going to be torn from her—soon. His dreams last night and the night before had been filled with visions of that last party he'd attended. He'd dreamed of arguing with Carole, of Janet asking him to stay with her, of having mixed emotions about what to do. He wondered if his dreams were a premonition of things to come. A premonition of reliving those moments all over again, and of living a life without Adriana.

Lying beside her in the middle of their bed, he wrapped her hair around his finger, memorizing its silkiness and capturing the mere scent of strawberry that wafted toward him. He had to remember everything—tomorrow it might all be gone.

Adriana closed one book and opened another, looking toward Trevor through long, pale lashes. "Your thoughts are a million miles away, aren't they?"

"No," he said, shaking his head as he drew his fingers across her cheek and over her lips. "They're here with you, right where they belong."

"Do you feel like sending your thoughts back sixty years?"

"Do I have a choice?"

"Not today."

She sat up, pulling one of the books with her as she settled her bikini-clad bottom against his stomach. If she wasn't careful, he'd push the book away and make love to her, storing one more memory away.

"I know you don't want to look at these photos again, but something doesn't seem right to me."

She opened the book to a black-and-white of Carole's body and that morning rushed through him—very vivid, very real. He turned away from the picture, but Adriana was studying it intently.

"I never noticed it before, but Carole wasn't wearing any jewelry. None at all. Look at her wrists, her neck. No rings, no bracelets, no necklace."

Trevor glanced at the photo, but all he saw was the blood, and the horror in her wide-open eyes.

"Did she usually wear jewelry?" Adriana asked.

"I suppose. I didn't pay attention."

"Then you don't know if she was wearing any at the party?"

"Dammit, Adriana. I told you. I don't remember."

He shoved up from the bed and went to the window. Adriana followed, touching his arm gently.

"I'm sorry. I'm pushing too hard."

"You want to learn the truth. That's all."

She wrapped her arms around him and rested her cool cheek against his back. "I want *you* to know the truth. I want your nightmares to stop. That's what matters the most to me."

He sighed, releasing some of the frustration that had been building within him all morning, and tried to remember that night at the Trocadero. "She was wearing white, something long and slinky," he related. Closing his eyes, he tried to picture the dress, her long, bare arms, the curve of her neck. He remembered putting on his top hat and taking her arm as they walked out of the club. He remembered the fans standing around, cheering, calling out Carole's name and his. He remembered signing autographs while the attendant brought the Duesenberg. He remembered the photographers snapping pictures.

He remembered the photo he'd seen in one of Adriana's books, a photo taken that night.

Going back to the bed, he sat on the edge, grabbed one of the books, and began to search.

"What are you looking for?" Adriana asked.

"A picture taken of Carole and me when we were leaving the Troc. I saw it that first night I was here."

Adriana sat beside him and joined the search.

"Here it is," he said, tapping the black-and-white photo.

"She's not wearing any jewelry," Adriana said, leaning close. She tilted her head to look at him and frowned.

"What about Janet? Are there any photos of her that night?"

More than likely, although he hoped she wasn't wearing anything that might sparkle. He didn't want to find proof that Janet was guilty. With all his heart, he wanted to find out that the murderer had been someone else, even if it took years of searching.

Flipping through even more photos, he stopped when he saw one of Janet Julian taken the night of the premiere.

"She's wearing what looks like a diamond necklace," Adriana said.

"A lot of women were wearing diamond necklaces."

"But a lot of women didn't hate Carole Sinclair. They disliked her—but that's as far as it went."

Maybe someone else had hated her. Maybe someone else had killed Carole, but it seemed as if everything pointed toward Janet.

Trevor watched Adriana wedge a scrap of paper into the binding of the book, and pull another biography from the stack on top of the bed.

"Why are you marking that picture?" he asked.

"I'm not sure yet, but see if you can find any more photos of Janet taken before that night."

Trevor laughed at her determination, but he humored her, tagging numerous pages in his book while she did the same in hers.

Finally she stopped, and drew her finger over a caption. "Listen to this. It's about a party that Janet attended with several other people. It gives their names, and next to Janet it says 'Janet Julian, wearing the diamond choker she claims she wears twenty-four hours a day.' "

"What's so odd about that?"

"Look." Adriana flipped through the pages, stopping here and there to comment. "She's wearing that same necklace at a picnic in Palm Springs. Here she's wearing it at the beach. In this one she's at a party." Adriana stopped turning pages and looked at Trevor. "She never took it off. It's in every photo, including the one taken the night Carole was murdered."

"I still don't understand."

Adriana flipped to another page and tapped her finger on the photo of Janet. "She's not wearing it in this photo. It was taken at the Fourth of July party at Sparta—the night you disappeared. Why wasn't she wearing it that night if she says she never took it off?"

"Maybe the clasp broke? Maybe it was stolen?"

"Or maybe it fell off when she murdered Carole."

Twenty-four

Hand in hand Trevor and Adriana walked along the fragrant, rose-lined path at Magnolia Acres. A year before—back in 1937—Trevor had been one of Janet's regular visitors. He'd brought her roses each time he came, while Charlie Beck, the young photographer who'd been smitten by her, brought her rosebushes.

Charlie Beck was in love. Things might have been different if Janet had loved him in return.

Trevor halfway wished he could return to 1938, to right all his wrongs and to change the course of his future, Janet's future, and Carole Sinclair's.

But, if he was somehow tossed back into his own decade—alone—was there any way he could change the past, and still come back to his wife?

He didn't want to think about it. The thought of going back and never holding Adriana again frightened him more than living with the horror of his memories.

He plucked a red rosebud and handed it to Adriana. "You know," he said, "a few short weeks ago—when I saw Janet last—she was twenty-two. She's eighty-two now. I wonder if she'll recognize me."

"She lives in the past, not the present. I'm sure she'll know who you are."

"And Charlie Beck? If he shows up while we're here, do you think he might guess at the truth?"

Adriana shook her head. "People might travel through time in the movies, but no one would ever believe it could actually happen."

"You believed it."

"I wanted to believe it. You're all I'd ever wanted."

He couldn't help but smile at her words. God, how he loved her.

A nurse met them at the back door and led them up the stairs to the second-floor room where Janet lay in bed. "She's had a bad bout with the flu, and I'm afraid she's not very strong. Don't stay long, please."

The nurse left the room, and Trevor crossed the floor to the bed and sat in a chair at one side while Adriana sat on the other.

For the longest time he studied Janet's features, but he saw nothing familiar. She was an old lady now and very frail. Her face had turned the palest of gray instead of being ivory tinged with pink, as he remembered it. Her skin hung in wrinkles from pronounced cheekbones, and her white hair was sparse.

Trevor looked across to Adriana, shaking his head. "We shouldn't be here. There's nothing she can tell us."

Adriana put a quieting finger to her lips and smiled at Trevor, then leaned closer to the lady in bed and whispered. "Hello, Janet."

Nearly translucent eyelids raised and a quiet, feeble voice asked, "Do I know you?"

"I'm an old friend. Adriana Howard. Remember?"

"Are you an actress?" Janet asked, and Trevor caught the familiar sparkle of excitement in her eyes.

It lasted only an instant, but he remembered it just the same. "Are you working on *Break the Night*?"

"That was filmed a long time ago, Janet. And, no, I'm not an actress . . . just a friend. I've brought you a rose."

Janet looked at the deep red bud. "You're so sweet," she said. "Would you mind putting it in my vase. Charlie brings me flowers every day. Aren't they beautiful?"

"They're lovely," Adriana said, tucking the rose into the already overfilled vase next to Janet's bed. "I've brought another friend with me, too.

Janet slowly rolled her head to the left and a soft smile crossed her lips. "Hello, Trevor. I haven't seen you in a while. Why haven't you come to visit?"

Trevor easily slipped back to the past, to a time more than sixty years ago when he'd sat next to Janet in this very same room, and talked to her about the studio, about the day's events.

"I've been working a lot of hours," he said. "You know how it is with production schedules."

"Jack keeps you too busy. You should tell him you need a rest."

"I suppose I should. But I like making movies."

"I do, too, but Jack told me yesterday that my contract was up. He doesn't want me at the studio any longer. He wants Carole, but not me. Can you believe that? I'm as good an actress as she is." Janet sniffed back tears. "Oh, Trevor, I don't know what I'll do."

He put a calming hand on her cheek, and she clutched it with fingers gnarled with age. "I'll help you find another job," he whispered, wishing he had helped her all those years ago. But he didn't know she'd lost her job, he didn't know how badly she'd needed him that night.

"I'll help you Janet. Whatever you need."

"No. You won't help me," Janet sobbed, her eyes

reddening with tears. "You'll leave me—for Carole—just like you always do."

"I never meant to leave you."

"You wanted Carole, not me. Charlie's the only one who ever wanted me."

A tear fell down her cheek. Slowly she whispered, "Charlie loved me. He said he'd do anything for me."

"Of course I'd do anything for you."

Trevor spun around, startled by the intrusion.

Charlie Beck. Older. Stooped and walking with the aid of a cane. Heavier than he'd been as a very young man, but beneath the wrinkled skin Trevor could see the same warm, loving eyes he'd seen smiling at Janet all those years ago.

"I have visitors, Charlie," Janet said, her eyes narrowing as if suddenly confused. "I don't know who they are. Do you?"

"It's our friend, Adriana. You remember her, dearest. She's the one who brings you the chocolates you like so much."

"Oh, yes." Janet turned her head to Adriana and smiled. "I remember you, now. You're the one who asked so many questions about Trevor Montgomery." She laughed lightly. "He was such a wicked man. Not at all like my Charlie."

Trevor stood up, shaking Charlie's hand. The old man studied his face, and Trevor could feel a slight tremble in Charlie's fingers. Had he recognized him, or had age taken the strength from his hands as well as his body?

"You must be Charlie Beck," Trevor said. "Adriana's told me about you, and my father mentioned you a time or two. I'm Trevor Montgomery—Junior. Adriana's husband."

Charlie pulled his hand from Trevor's as if he'd been shocked, and gripped his cane with both hands.

"Why don't you sit down?" Trevor moved away from the chair where he'd been sitting, and Charlie lowered his body to the seat.

"I didn't know Trevor had had a son," Charlie said. He looked down at his unsteady hands, then slowly looked into Trevor's eyes. "I didn't know."

"No one knew," Adriana interrupted. "Not even me, and I thought I knew everything there was to know about Trevor Montgomery."

Charlie was quiet a moment, deep in thought, or so it appeared. "Is your father still . . . " Charlie's words faded away, but Trevor knew the question. It was the same one he'd asked Adriana about so many of his old friends.

"He died about ten years ago," Trevor said, repeating the story he'd told Stewart.

"I'm sorry. I wish I could have seen him again. I wish . . . " He shook his head, sighing deeply. "It was all so long ago."

Charlie stood again, leaned over Janet's bed and smoothed wrinkled fingers over her cheek. "Would you mind if I take your visitors outside and show them the gardens?" he asked Janet. "I can point out all the beautiful roses you've planted."

"You won't be gone long, will you?"

"No, dearest. I'll be back as soon as I can."

He kissed her brow, his lips lingering a long moment before he pulled the covers closer to Janet's chin.

"Why don't you sleep a while. I'll be back shortly, and we'll talk."

"Be sure to show them the Ingrid Bergman. That was always my favorite."

Trevor saw the love in Charlie's face as Janet closed her eyes. Again Charlie kissed her, then holding on to his cane, walked toward the door.

"She needs her rest," he said, turning back to Trevor and Adriana. "I hope you won't mind going outside. It's rather beautiful today, and the roses are at their loveliest."

He didn't wait for an answer, just walked out the door, and Trevor could hear the thump of the cane and the sound of Charlie's slow, awkward step on the hardwood floors.

Trevor took one more look at the woman lying so helpless in bed. It seemed difficult to believe she'd once been the young woman who'd acted the part of his wife, the pretty young thing who'd giggled and smiled and wanted so much for him to love her.

And it was even harder to believe she could have murdered anyone, unless she'd done it in a moment of total madness. Human nature was often mysterious. He should know. Who would have ever dreamed that Trevor Montgomery, the man whose bravado made him look strong and heroic to millions of people around the world, could have attempted suicide?

Adriana caught his attention as she circled the bed and took his hand. "I wish we hadn't come," she whispered. "I want so much to prove your innocence, but I don't think we're going to learn anything from Janet. I don't even want to try."

"You want to give up the search?"

Adriana nodded slowly. "I know you're innocent. There's no doubt at all in my mind. But what about you? Can you stand not knowing the truth?"

"I don't know." Trevor led her from the room, taking one last look at the shell of a woman he'd known a long time ago. He didn't want to cause Janet any pain. Whether she was a murderer or not, she'd already lived through enough grief in her life.

"Why don't we talk to Charlie," Trevor said. "He's been with Janet for sixty years. If she did murder Carole, maybe she's confessed it to him."

"He'd never tell us if she had," Adriana noted. "He loves her too much."

"Charlie's our only hope of learning what happened. If he can't help us, we'll go home and put it all behind us."

"Can you do that?"

"I want a life with you, Adriana. I want to forget the past and move on. As long as you're by my side, I think I can do anything."

Twenty-five

"I'm so glad you've joined me. You'll enjoy Janet's roses. She's responsible for most every plant here. Of course, she's been here a long time," Charlie reflected. "Come, walk along the path with me. There's a gazebo at the far corner of the property. We can sit there and talk."

Trevor wrapped his arm around his wife's waist, and they followed Charlie slowly along the flower lined path.

"I'd never paid much attention to roses until I met Janet," Charlie said. "I was just barely nineteen the first time I saw her. I don't think I ever looked at another woman after that. She was so pretty, all that thick, wavy brown hair and those big blue eyes. I asked her out over and over, but she was in love with your dad. She had no interest in me at all."

They stopped beside a rosebush, abundant with long-stemmed red flowers, and Charlie leaned down slowly to sniff one of the wide-open blossoms. "She planted this Mr. Lincoln the first time she stayed here at Magnolia Acres. She had two breakdowns, you know. She recovered from the first. The second, well, that was a long time ago."

He reached into his coat pocket, took out a pair of

clippers, and snipped off a rose. "This was just a scrawny, ugly plant in 1937. I didn't have much money, but I remembered the way her eyes always lit up when someone gave her a rose. I figured giving her an entire plant was better than one little bud. She kissed me when I gave it to her. Of course, she had no idea who I was. She thought I was the college boy she'd had a crush on in her very first movie. She still mistakes me for others at times, but I don't mind."

Charlie wiped a tear from his eye and started to walk again.

Trevor glanced at Adriana and saw the redness in her eyes and the pools of tears at their corners. It took all his power to keep from having to wipe tears from his eyes, too. He didn't think anyone could love a woman the way he loved Adriana. He'd never known love like that existed. But Charlie Beck knew how to love. He hoped Janet knew how fortunate— how blessed—she was.

"Your dad used to visit her here," Charlie continued. "No one else from the studios ever came, and she felt abandoned. Jack Warner sent her flowers once, but no one else, just Trevor, me, and her parents. She didn't deserve that."

Charlie stopped at another rosebush, picked off a few dead flowers, and tucked them into his coat pocket. "Did you know that she'd been asked to star alongside your dad in *One More Tomorrow?*" he asked, looking directly at Trevor.

"No." Trevor shook his head. "I . . . my father never thought Carole Sinclair was right for the part of the wife," he said, not seeing even a flicker of concern in Charlie's eyes over the instant correction of his mistake. "My father thought they should have cast a sweeter woman."

"They did—originally. When Carole got wind of it she went screaming to Jack Warner. I have no idea what happened, but one of Jack's assistants told Janet she was out of the picture. Shortly after that, she came here. She used to recite the lines to me. She would have been perfect for the part. She might have even gotten an Oscar—like your father did."

If he had only known, Trevor thought, maybe he could have done something. He hadn't wanted Carole to play his wife. God, if he'd just made his feelings known, maybe things would have been different. Maybe Janet wouldn't have had that first breakdown, or the second, which had left her a permanent guest at Magnolia Acres.

Trevor looked at Charlie. The old man was studying his eyes, looking deep down, as if he could read his mind, as if he knew the truth of who Trevor really was. Then he frowned, turned away, and walked farther along the path.

"I never talk about those things with Janet. It's all in the past. We try to remember only the good things—like the gardens."

He stopped again. "Ah, here we are. This is Janet's favorite. The Ingrid Bergman. She planted it twenty, maybe thirty years ago. Gardening and remembering her past—those are her favorite pastimes. She never was cut out for the stress of Hollywood. She should have been a housewife with half a dozen children. That would have made her happier."

"What about you, Charlie?" Adriana asked. "What would have made you happier?"

"I try not to think of what could have been. All I've ever wanted since I was nineteen years old was to be with Janet and make her happy." He sighed deeply. "All my efforts haven't been successful, but I've tried."

They reached the gazebo, and Charlie labored up the two steps and sat inside on one of the benches circling the white wooden structure woven with vines of pink and yellow roses.

"I built this gazebo right after the war. I was away from Janet for a few years. She didn't remember me at all when I came home from Europe, but one day I brought her a climber and she said she thought it would be nice to have a gazebo covered with vines. She helped me hammer and nail when she was able to, but mostly she just sat and talked to me about the roses she wanted to plant." Charlie looked at Adriana and smiled. "We've planted at least one rosebush a year ever since."

Charlie leaned over and rubbed his knees with knotted fingers, then looked across the gazebo at Trevor, who was leaning against one of the uprights, holding Adriana close.

"I suppose you've been told quite often that you look just like your father."

"It's been mentioned a time or two," Trevor quipped. "Did you know him well?"

"I was a cub reporter with the desire to be a photographer, and hanging out at the studios and at the parties was one of my favorite pastimes. I took a lot of photos of your dad. I didn't know him well, but he always had a friendly word for me. Some of the others snubbed me, but not Trevor Montgomery. Everyone liked him. It was hard not to."

"The press didn't say much of anything good about him after Carole Sinclair was killed," Adriana said. "They said he was a murderer, even though the police never found any evidence."

Trevor watched Charlie's brow furrow while Adriana spoke, he listened to the depth of his sigh, and watched him hang his head and stare down at the wood plank floor.

"I always felt bad about that," Charlie said. "Trevor didn't deserve it."

"You don't think he was guilty, then?" Adriana asked.

"No, I never thought he was guilty."

Holding on to his cane, Charlie pushed himself up from the bench and walked to the edge of the gazebo. He cupped a rose in his palm, inhaled the fragrance, then stared off toward the magnolias and deodora pines lining the property.

"I wrote several books about Trevor Montgomery," Charlie said. "I included the best photos I had, ones that would show his charm and friendliness. I wanted people to know what he was really like."

"I have every one of your books," Adriana told him. "They're some of my favorites. It's nice that you've included so many photos of Janet and Mr. Montgomery's other friends."

"I wanted to do a book just about Janet, but the publishers weren't interested in her story," Charlie related sadly. "I wanted people to remember her, though. She was so beautiful. So sweet." He turned, balancing himself on his cane. "I made sure there were no pictures of Carole Sinclair in my books. I could never forgive her for the things she'd done to Janet, and I wanted people to remember the good things about Trevor. There were enough books written about him that glamorized Carole and sensationalized Trevor's part in her death."

"My father's been dead for a long time," Trevor said, noting the sadness in Charlie's eyes when Trevor said the words. "All the rumors, all the books claiming that my father killed Carole can't hurt him any longer, but they still hurt me. He was a good man. I don't think he killed Carole, and now I'd like to prove that he didn't."

"I don't know if that's possible. No prints were ever found. No one saw him there. No one saw anyone else there, either. The only evidence the police had against your father was that he was the one who'd taken Carole home. Your father's guilt was mere speculation by the police and the newsmen."

"Pretty flimsy evidence," Trevor said sarcastically.

"If he hadn't disappeared . . ." Charlie began, then stopped. He looked into Trevor's face. "If he hadn't disappeared, maybe someone would have come forth and confessed."

"My father's disappearance was the perfect cover for the real murderer," Trevor said. "Do you honestly think Carole's killer would have told the truth to protect my father?"

Trevor watched Charlie's hands squeezing the knob at the top of his cane until his knuckles were nearly white. What was troubling him?

"Yes. I honestly believe the real killer would have done something to save your father—if it hadn't been too late."

"Why do you feel that way?" Adriana asked.

"Because Trevor Montgomery was a good man. He cared for people, like Janet. He helped her rehearse her lines and gave her the confidence she needed to be a good actress. He made sure there was an acting job for her when she got out of the hospital. She got to play his wife in *Break the Night*." Charlie looked up, and Trevor saw the tears in his eyes. "She'd always wanted to play the part of Trevor's wife. She might have been through in Hollywood if it hadn't been for your father."

"Most people have forgotten how generous he was," Adriana said, "how much joy he brought into peoples lives—on-screen and off. He tried to live a normal life after Carole's death, but he couldn't. He loved being an actor, he loved being with his friends—but he lost the things that meant most to him after Carole died."

"I'm so sorry your father had to suffer. He didn't deserve it," Charlie whispered, glancing at Trevor. "I wish there was something I could do to make things better for you."

"We've read the police accounts and studied the photos," Trevor said. "I doubt that you could help, unless you have a clue who might have killed Carole. Of course, if you knew anything at all about the truth, I'm sure you would have helped my father sixty years ago."

"I wish I could help him now," Charlie said. "But it's too late. He's dead."

"If you know anything at all, Charlie," Adriana pleaded, "you could help my husband; that would be almost the same thing as helping his father. Please. Help us. My husband doesn't believe his father was a murderer, but he has no proof."

"I wish I could help," Charlie repeated. "But I can't."

"It happened a long time ago, Charlie. I don't want the public to know the truth. I just want to know for my own peace of mind. My father and I were very close. If you know anything at all, anything that might help me, it will be almost the same as helping him."

"Yes, I can understand the need to protect the one you love." Charlie walked slowly back to the bench and sat down. His fingers trembled as he rubbed his knees, his voice was barely a whisper when he spoke. "If I tell you . . ." His words trailed off, and then he began again. "It's not fair of me to ask for forgiveness."

"The only thing I want is to know in my heart that my father didn't murder Carole. Nothing else matters to me anymore," Trevor said. "Please, Charlie. Tell us what happened."

Charlie stared at the floor for what seemed like an eternity. Finally, he spoke. "You have to know everything, right from the beginning."

Adriana sat at Charlie's side, and Trevor leaned against one of the uprights, waiting to hear what he hoped would be the truth.

"We were at the Trocadero," Charlie began. "Janet looked beautiful. She was smiling and laughing with everyone, no one ever would have known that Jack had fired her that morning. I knew, of course. I'd run into her shortly after she left Jack Warner's office, and she told me everything. 'It's not fair,' she'd cried. 'Carole told him she'd quit if he didn't get rid of me. She hates me, Charlie. She's always hated me.' "

Charlie looked up at Trevor, all his concern, all his love for Janet showing in his eyes.

"She was so upset. That night, I knew she was close to another breakdown. She kept slipping in and out of her old roles. I don't know if anyone else realized it, but I'd seen each of her movies so many times that I knew her parts by heart.

"I wanted to take Janet home," Charlie continued, "but she told me that Trevor was going home with her. She had it all planned, she told me. 'I've got champagne chilling, some caviar. We're going to have a party. Just the two of us. Carole might have stolen one of my roles. She might have made Jack Warner get rid of me, but she's not going to have Trevor Montgomery tonight.' God, I was such a fool. She wanted Trevor, not me, but I kept hanging on in the background, waiting for my chance. I knew Trevor wasn't interested in her as anything other than a friend, but she couldn't see that as clearly as everyone else.

"Later on, I found her sitting all by herself, crying. She told me that Trevor didn't want her. He wanted Carole instead. 'I hate her,' she said. 'I wish she were dead.' Again, I begged her to let me take her home, but she said she didn't want to spoil my evening the way hers had been spoiled—and then she left. I thought about following her, but I had a job to do. Pictures to take. I waited until the last of the stars had left the Troc, and then I drove to Janet's. I was going to ask her to marry me. I knew she'd laugh, but I didn't care. I wanted her to know how much I loved her, and that it didn't matter to me if she was a star or not.

"Her car was gone when I got to her house. It must have been close to four in the morning. I waited for a long time, hoping she'd come back. When she didn't, I started to worry. She was so upset when she left the party, I was afraid she might have tried to kill herself. And then I thought about what she'd said—that she wished Carole was dead. I didn't think she could do it, but I got worried.

"I sped to Santa Monica. Trevor's Duesenberg was in front of Carole's house. I could see Janet's car parked about a block away. I remember running up to the house, knocking, then just letting myself in when no one came to the door. There was blood everywhere. I gagged on the smell, willing myself not to get sick."

Charlie's lips trembled as he turned toward Trevor.

"I went into the bedroom. Janet was kneeling beside the bed, holding Trevor's hand and crying. The knife was lying on his chest and there was blood everywhere. Oh, God. It was awful. I knew he was dead. He had to be. And Carole was lying there with her eyes wide open—just staring at the ceiling."

Charlie hung his head and took several deep breaths.

"She was dead." He looked at Trevor, at Adriana. "You've seen the pictures. She couldn't possibly have been alive. I had to get Janet out of there. I knew what she'd done. She'd gone crazy, she'd done something horrible, and I didn't want the police or the press to find out. She'd suffered enough already."

Charlie took another deep breath. "I was sure that Trevor was dead, so I put the knife in his hands, making sure my fingerprints weren't on it, then I picked up Janet and got out of the place."

Charlie leaned against the wooden slats of the gazebo and closed his eyes.

For one short moment, Trevor thought about comforting him. Charlie loved Janet. It was easy to feel the pain he had gone through then and was going through now. But Charlie had let Trevor—a man who he'd thought was dead—take the blame for a murder. He felt no sympathy for that.

He looked at Adriana, at the tears streaming down her cheeks. She was trying to smile at him, but in spite of the revelation, happiness wouldn't come.

"What did you do then?" Trevor asked, needing to know everything.

"I took her to my house. I carried her into the shower with me and got the blood off of both of us, and then I put her to bed. She didn't know why she was in my house. I told her she'd gone home with me after the party, and she seemed to believe it. When she fell asleep, I called a cab and paid a fortune to be driven to Santa Monica. I got Janet's car and took it back to my house. She was still asleep, and I just sat there on the edge of the bed praying that she'd never remember what happened."

Charlie swept a hand through his hair. "It all seemed like the right thing to do at the time. Carole was dead. Trevor was dead. It didn't matter to me that he'd be blamed for the murder. He couldn't be hurt anymore."

"But he was hurt," Adriana blurted out. "He spent the rest of his life wondering if he'd killed a woman."

"I didn't know he was alive," Charlie stressed, his anguish clear in the redness of his eyes, the deep creases between his brows. "I didn't know until I went back to Carole's later that day.

"It must have been close to noon when I got a call that Carole Sinclair's body had been found. Janet was sleeping soundly, so I grabbed my camera, jumped in my car, and sped to Santa Monica. There were no other photographers there, and I pretended I was with the police and sneaked inside. It was my chance to make sure I hadn't left anything behind that might implicate Janet.

"Carole was on the bed, but Trevor was gone. I didn't see a knife anywhere. I didn't see any signs that Trevor had been there, either. I was beginning to think I'd lost my mind. I knew Trevor was dead when I put the knife in his hands. He wasn't moving. He wasn't breathing. I didn't know what had happened, but I tried to stay calm, tried to pretend that this was just another murder case. No one seemed to care that I was snapping pictures of Carole. I was popping out flashbulbs right and left, and one rolled under the bed. I got down on my knees to get it, and I saw something sparkle just under the bedspread. I grabbed the bulb and pulled at the shiny thing. It was a diamond choker, and I knew immediately it was Janet's. I'd seen her in it dozens of times.

"I put the choker in my pocket and got out of there. Janet's car was gone when I got home. She hadn't left a note. Nothing. I went to her place, but she was gone from there, too. It was the Fourth of July, and I remembered Janet saying something about going to one of Harrison Stafford's parties at Sparta. I hoped she'd be there, that she wouldn't do anything crazy. I was afraid, too, that Trevor would be there, that he'd know what Janet had done and confront her, or turn her in to the police.

"It took so long to drive to Sparta. God, I hated those winding roads along the ocean. I got there as fast as I could. I ran out to the terraces where people were gathered. I heard a woman scream, and I ran toward the pool. Janet was on one of the upper terraces by then, yelling something about Trevor Montgomery floating in the water. I ran down to the pool, but no one was there. A crowd was forming. Janet was telling everyone that she'd seen Trevor floating facedown in the pool. They were laughing at her. They knew she'd had a breakdown before, that she was unstable.

"She was sobbing. 'Don't let them laugh at me, Charlie. Please. Tell them I'm not crazy,' she begged. I took her into the house and got her a drink, but she kept on crying, saying it was all her fault, that she hadn't meant to hurt Trevor. I didn't know what was going on by that time. People were running around the place looking for Trevor. Someone said he'd been acting strange. Someone said he was drunker than normal. People were talking about Carole's murder, about Trevor being with her the night before, and one assumption led to another. Harrison Stafford was worried sick about his friend. 'Trevor's not involved. That's impossible,' he was shouting. He told everyone to leave—so Janet and I got out of there."

Charlie looked at Trevor, at Adriana. His eyes were red, filled with unshed tears. "I know what I did was wrong. But once I'd put the wheels in motion, it was too late to turn back. I'd hidden the only piece of evidence that would prove Janet's guilt. If the police found out what I'd done, I would have been arrested as an accessory.

"Janet cried all the way back to L.A. 'I remember it all, Charlie. Oh, God, what did I do?' she sobbed over and over again. 'I didn't want Carole to have Trevor,' she kept saying, and then she told me everything. She'd gone home to get the champagne she'd planned to have with Trevor, and then she drove to Carole's. She was tired of Carole getting everything. Tired of Carole taunting her and telling her she was mad.

"She got to the beach house before Carole and Trevor arrived. She crumbled sleeping pills into the champagne, hoping they'd drink it and fall to sleep. She wanted Carole to die, but she didn't want her to feel any pain."

A vacant stare filled Charlie's eyes as he looked across the gardens. "Janet was hiding in the living room when Carole and Trevor arrived. Carole was mad about something and stormed off to the bedroom. Trevor took the bottle and went outside."

Trevor wanted to shut out the rest of Charlie's words. He didn't want to hear any more about the nightmare, but he needed to fill in those missing hours of his life.

"What happened then?" he asked.

Charlie tilted his head, looking away from the wall of roses he'd been staring at.

"Are you going to tell the police?"

"We're not going to tell anyone a thing," Adriana said. "We just want to know the truth, so Trevor can put it behind him. Please, Charlie. Go on."

"Carole was asleep when Janet went into her room. She'd gotten a butcher knife from the kitchen." Charlie closed his eyes for a moment, took a deep breath, then continued. "She thought if she stabbed Carole in the chest, she'd die instantly and not feel a thing. 'It didn't work,' she told me. 'Her eyes popped open, and she stared at me until blood came out of her mouth.' She tried to struggle, Janet told me. She was screaming, and Janet kept hitting her with the knife, wanting to put her out of her pain. But Carole wouldn't die, so Janet put the knife to Carole's throat. Carole tried to grab it, but her strength was gone, and Janet wanted it all to end." Charlie shook his head. "She sliced her throat."

Charlie's head sank into his hands. "I've lived through those moments every day for sixty years. Better that I should remember them than Janet. She didn't know what she was doing. She doesn't remember any of it now, either. It's as if telling me erased it all from her mind. She's never repeated a word of this to anyone—not to her parents, not to the doctors. No one. She doesn't remember a thing about that night. Please, don't ask her about it."

"There's no reason to," Trevor said. "You've told us all we need to know."

"I'm sorry," Charlie said. "I'm sorry for what I did to your father. I'm sorry for you, for Carole, for . . ." His words trailed off, and he stared at his trembling hands, which clutched the top of his cane.

"I tried to care for her for a while, but I couldn't. She wasn't violent. She just sat and stared straight ahead, looking at nothing. I talked to her parents, and they had her committed. She's been here ever since."

He wiped a tear from his cheek. "She's been my life, you know. She's dying, and I'm not going to have her much longer." He drew in a shaky breath. "When she's gone, you can tell the police. I'll even go with you. But please, wait till she's gone."

"We're not going to the police," Trevor said, fighting back tears. "You've served enough time already."

Trevor heard footsteps on the brick pathway and turned around.

"Excuse me, Mr. Beck," a nurse interrupted. "Miss Julian's calling for Mr. Montgomery. I didn't know what to do."

"I'll be right there," Charlie said, then turned to Trevor.

"Do you mind going up?" Charlie asked. "I know you don't owe her anything, but she's old and dying. I know she loves me. She's told me that in so many ways over the years, but she still calls your father's name."

"Of course I'll go," Trevor said, holding his hand out to Adriana. "Then we'll leave the two of you alone. I promise."

They went to Janet's room and Charlie neared the bed. "How are you feeling, dearest."

"Tired." Her word came out amidst a raspy breath. "Is Trevor with you? I need to see him again."

Charlie turned to Trevor and Adriana. "I'll wait outside. Don't stay for more than a few minutes. Please."

Trevor closed the door behind Charlie and went toward the bed. He had no reason to comfort Janet. She'd killed a woman. She'd been responsible for ruining his life. But when he remembered the sweet young woman who'd been his friend, who'd loved him so desperately, he felt a strong sense of compassion. He should despise her, but he couldn't.

Slowly he reached out and touched Janet's cold, wrinkled cheek.

Cloudy eyes looked up at him.

"I'm so sorry for what happened. You must hate me terribly," she said.

Charlie said she didn't remember. Had the memory of that night suddenly come back to her? Could he give her absolution for what she'd done?

He looked at Adriana, at the gentle smile on her face, and he knew the answer. Janet had set in motion unbelievable events that changed the lives of so many people—especially his. If she hadn't, he never would have met the only woman he had ever loved, the only woman he ever would love.

"I don't hate you, Janet."

She smiled sweetly, and a trace of the young woman he'd known long ago shone on her face. "I knew you'd come back someday. I knew it."

She gasped for breath, clutching the edge of her blankets. She was dying, and Trevor wanted to forget and forgive her for the horror that had happened. He tried to remember the good times they'd had together, and the fact that he'd enjoyed working with her.

"I'm sorry I wasn't always there for you, Janet," he said. "You were my friend, and you know what else? You were the prettiest, sweetest lady on the set."

He smiled when he saw that old familiar twinkle in her eye.

"You told me that once," she said, "but I didn't believe you. I thought you said that to all the girls."

"I always mean what I say, Janet."

"You were always such a nice man. My Charlie's a nice man, too. Did you see my roses?" Janet asked. "They're beautiful, aren't they?

"The prettiest I've ever seen."

"Let me give you one," Janet said. "Here. Take it. Please." She opened her hand and inside Trevor saw a crushed and withered red rosebud.

He'd seen prettier things, like the woman standing across from him, but he reached out to take the bud from Janet's hand.

"I always prayed you'd return to me," Janet said, grasping his fingers as he took the rose. "Always. Every night I'd wish for it. Come back to me. Please. Come to me. That's what I wished."

An instant of panic ripped through Trevor's body as he heard Janet's words. They were the same words Adriana had whispered when she stood over the Poseidon Pool.

But they weren't beside a pool now. Nothing could happen.

Nothing.

He tried to pull his fingers away from Janet's but couldn't. He was too weak.

Oh, God. No!

His head felt light. Dizzy. A great roaring sound filled his head.

"Come back to me," Janet continued to beg. "Please. Come to me."

Adriana screamed. "Don't go, Trevor. Please. Don't leave me."

But all he heard were whispers, the faint sound of a woman's scream, and . . .

🌣 *Twenty-six*

"Please, Trevor! Don't leave me!"

Adriana reached out for him, to fingers and hands that stretched toward her, but there was no substance, no skin or bones or warmth. Only a fading vision.

"Please," she begged, but just as suddenly as he'd come into her life, he was gone.

Tears streamed down her cheeks. Her lips trembled while she stared at the emptiness across from her, at the spot where just a moment before the only man she'd ever loved—the only man she would ever love—had stood.

Closing her eyes, she prayed. "Come back to me, Trevor. Please. Come back to me."

When she opened her eyes, the place where he'd stood was just as empty.

He was gone.

She slumped into the chair beside Janet's bed, wrapped her arms around her stomach, and wept.

"I love you, Trevor," she whispered, hoping he'd hear her words, no matter where he was. "I love you."

Loneliness engulfed her. Then she remembered his smoldering eyes, his movie-idol smile, his tender kisses, and his passion. And, from deep in her heart, she heard his voice. "I love you, Adriana. Forever."

Suddenly she was filled with hope. "Come back to me, Trevor," she prayed. "Soon."

Wiping the tears from her cheeks and eyes, she thought about Janet, lying so helpless in her bed. Had she seen what had happened? Did she understand? Did she feel the horror and loss?

Adriana reached out to comfort her, but the bed was vacant, the pillows fluffed, and a crumbled red rose was scattered over the perfectly smooth covers.

Adriana spun around. Where had Janet gone?

"Charlie," she cried, but the door didn't open. She heard no human sound, only a deafening roar. Pain pulsed through her head. A wave of nausea clutched at her stomach. The room twisted and turned about her, as if she was on an out of control merry-go-round. She wanted to get off, but her legs wouldn't move.

The lights dimmed, brightened, and dimmed again, then suddenly everything went black.

July 3, 1938

The Trocadero reeked of elegance. Champagne flowed. Gold lamé shimmered on the sleek bodies of a dozen stars and starlets. Diamonds glistened, and men and women swayed gracefully to the melodic strains of Cole Porter, Irving Berlin, and George Gershwin.

The dreaded night had finally arrived.

"Dear God," Trevor silently prayed. "Help me to make it all end differently."

He stood in a far corner of the ballroom, his hands casually tucked into the pockets of his black tuxedo trousers, and observed the familiar scene unfolding before him.

Jack Warner strolled amongst his guests, patting backs, shaking hands, and kissing the women. Carole Sinclair—still alive, still a ravishing, platinum beauty—swept from man to man, laughing off the crude comments of her ex-husband, who'd just been escorted out of the nightclub by two burly doormen.

Janet Julian—no longer wrinkled, no longer scarred by the murder she'd committed—stood in a crowd of people but didn't appear to be listening to a word anyone spoke. Instead, the pretty brunette, a picture of sweetness in a froth of pale pink ruffles, searched the room until her eyes lit on Trevor, and she smiled.

Feeling an overwhelming compassion for his friend, he smiled back. A bright light flashed, and Trevor turned his attention to the man who'd just snapped Janet's picture.

Charlie Beck—no longer stooped, no longer walking with a cane—whispered something into Janet's ear. She giggled lightly, and fondly touched Charlie's cheek before he walked away, moving almost invisibly through the throng, shooting photos of luminaries who set the screen ablaze. Bette Davis was there. Olivia de Havilland, and Carole Lombard. Gable, Bogart, and Grant. Errol Flynn, too—his old friend, his drinking buddy.

Trevor soaked up their magnetic presence, trying to remember each unique movement, each distinctive facial gesture, bits and pieces of his past to carry with him to another lifetime if, God willing, he were given the chance to go back.

Oh, Adriana. If only you could be here with me.

For one entire year he'd wished for her to come to him. He'd kissed roses and tossed them into the Poseidon Pool at Sparta, he'd walked down to the beach and prayed that she'd magically appear, and he'd lain in bed at night and touched the pillow where her head should be resting, her pale blond hair feathered about her like a halo. But still she didn't come.

Did she have any memory of their time together? he wondered. Or had she forgotten him, like he'd forgotten her—in the beginning?

He remembered that first moment back in his own time. He'd felt dizzy, numb. Nausea had weakened him, and a woman's screams pounded through his head. He'd stumbled across the hardwood floor and sat down on the edge of an empty bed, pressing his fingers to his temples while he tried to get his bearings. Slowly it all came back to him. He was in Janet's room at Magnolia Acres. She'd had a breakdown, but she was going home in a day or two, and he wanted to tell her that he'd gotten her a part in his next movie—as his wife in *Break the Night*.

He'd remembered everything about his past—but he had no memories of his future.

He remembered Janet breezing into the room, a pretty young thing who looked as if she hadn't a care in the world. A year of rest had been the perfect antidote for her worried mind. She'd smiled sweetly at him, and then a slow, questioning frown furrowed her brow. "Is something wrong, Trevor," she'd asked. "You look so odd, as if . . . oh, I don't know. You look different somehow. Happier, I think."

Happier? He was. The pain of a lonely childhood no longer haunted him. The devastating rejection by his parents seemed nothing more than a vague memory of a time best forgotten. The urge for a drink was gone—and he had no idea why.

It took a few days, but slowly the memories began to return with just a few subtle reminders: a tall, slender woman with corn-silk hair wisping across her face seemed oddly familiar, yet they'd never met; a storefront mannequin dressed in a flowing white gown with ropes of pearls around its neck brought back a hazy memory of a beautiful woman adjusting his tie; dancing with an uninhibited friend under a crystal chandelier at the Biltmore made him yearn for someone timid and shy.

He couldn't understand any of it. All of those things were only vague reminders of an indistinct memory.

But the wonder of his future—the life he'd once lived—came back to him with an unexpected jolt when he said "I do" before a make-believe minister on the set of *Break the Night*. Suddenly the face of his costar, Janet Julian, became the face of an angel—a beautiful woman who'd comforted him when he was distressed, who'd cried for him when he'd told her of his childhood—who'd loved him, without question.

Adriana.

He'd prayed continually for the moment he'd return to her, prayed to the God he finally believed in, and he had no doubt at all that he'd shortly be back in the arms of the woman he loved.

The light touch of a woman's hand on his shoulder snapped him out of his musing. "Trevor?"

He blinked away his memories of happier times, and smiled at Janet—the woman who'd called him back to her solitary hospital room, to his lonely existence, to a time one year before the horror began.

"You had that odd look in your eyes again, Trevor," Janet said. "You seemed to be off in another world. Were you thinking about . . . that woman again?"

He'd told her months ago that there was someone else in his life, someone he'd love forever. She hadn't wanted to believe it, but was slowly, regretfully accepting the truth. Janet could have his friendship—but not his heart. That was already taken.

"I think of her always," he said softly. "You know that, Janet."

"I suppose. Of course, I occasionally wish you'd forget all about her. She's such a mystery, I often wonder if she really exists, or if she's just a convenient excuse to keep me at bay."

Trevor lightly brushed his knuckles over Janet's cheek, and avoided her comment. Adriana was real. No dream could be so wonderful.

"Care to dance with me?" he asked, and Janet floated into his arms. He swirled her about the room, leading her with the slight press of his hand against hers. When the music calmed, he slowed their pace, and looked into Janet's pretty and innocent face.

"I heard what happened this morning. I'm sorry, Janet."

He could sense her fighting back a tear, and her eyes clouded over in a faraway stare. "Carole told Jack she'd quit if he didn't get rid of me. I don't know why she hates me so much."

"She doesn't hate you," he lied, wishing that his words were true.

"She does." Janet rested her head against Trevor's shoulder. "I hate her, too," she whispered. "Sometimes I wish . . . I wish she'd go away and never bother me again."

"Carole's not going anywhere, but neither are you. I told Jack I'd quit if he got rid of you."

Janet tilted her head, her perfect brows raised in question. "You did?"

"Of course I did. He didn't care much for the position I'd put him in, so he informed me that if I didn't fulfill my contractual obligations I'd never work in this town again. Then I reminded *him* that you can't force someone to be a good actor if they don't want to be." Trevor winked. "It didn't take long for him to see my point."

"You shouldn't have done that, Trevor. Your career's too important to you."

"You're important, too, and I want you to be happy."

"Then come home with me tonight. I've got champagne chilling. I was hoping we might celebrate our success together."

Trevor shook his head, realizing too late that turning Janet down was a mistake.

"Why?" she asked abruptly. "Are you spending the evening with Carole? She told me you're lovers. She told me you're thinking of moving into the beach house with her."

Trevor silenced her words with an index finger to her lips. "I have no interest at all in Carole. Don't let her get to you. She's just a selfish, lonely woman. I know she's vindictive, but she can't hurt you unless you let her."

"Then you don't love her?"

"No, I don't."

"Do you love me?"

"As a friend. The best of friends. I know you want more, but . . ."

"But there's another woman," Janet interrupted. She sighed, and a faint, acquiescent smile slowly touched her lips. "As long as I know it's not Carole, I suppose I can accept it."

Trevor swirled Janet twice around the floor, hoping to soften his rejection. He swayed with her, leading her toward one end of the ballroom, close to where Charlie Beck was snapping photos.

Dancing nearly cheek to cheek, he whispered, "It's hard to be in love with someone and not have the feeling returned, isn't it?"

"Very hard," Janet acknowledged. "You must think I'm silly."

"No. You're a sweet lady, and you deserve someone just as special."

She laughed lightly. "Most men aren't looking for a sweet lady."

"That's not true. Charlie Beck's in love with you. You do know that, don't you?"

Janet leaned back, and Trevor could see the familiar twinkle in her eyes. "He doesn't hide it very well, does he?"

"He'd do anything for you if you gave him half a chance."

"He's still a boy."

"He loves you," Trevor stated, stressing the fact once more. "I hear he's a good dancer, he's got a promising career ahead of him as a photographer, and he—"

"He likes roses," Janet said wistfully. "He was always so nice when he visited me in the hospital. I'd somehow forgotten that."

"He's a good man, Janet."

"He's not you, though." Resting her cheek against his, Janet remained silent for several moments, obviously deep in thought. Finally, she said, "I suppose I've been holding on, hoping you'd forget that other woman and want me."

Trevor shook his head. "I can't forget her."

He saw the sadness in Janet's eyes, the hint of a tremble on her lips as she moved out of his arms. "Maybe I should ask Charlie to dance with me."

"He'd like that." Trevor stroked away a tear from the corner of her eye, and smiled. "He might enjoy that champagne you have chilling at home, too."

"Possibly. Maybe he'll even accompany me to Sparta tomorrow."

"I hope so." He winked, as Janet backed away. "I want to see you happy."

Trevor watched Janet's gaze flicker from his eyes, to his lips, then back again. A hint of a smile tilted the corners of her mouth. She blew him a kiss, then spun around and glided across the floor to Charlie.

She whispered something into Charlie's ear, and

his eyes beamed with joy as he pushed his camera to his side and took her into his arms.

"Consorting with lunatics, I see," Carole breathed in that deep, resonant voice that had long been her signature, along with pouting lips and curves shaped by the gods. "I just don't understand you, Trev."

"What don't you understand?" he asked, standing casually, his hands once again tucked into the pockets of his trousers, while Carole fingered the buttons of his coat.

"I don't understand why you'd want to spend time with a girl like her. Why you've changed so drastically."

"Changed?"

"A year ago you were climbing into my bed every week or so. You'd treat me like a queen, even though you'd leave before morning. You used to take me dancing, buy me drinks. But you stopped—just like that," she said, snapping her fingers in front of his face. "You're just no fun anymore. No drinking. No smoking, and as far as I can determine, no sex, either. Has something gone wrong?" she asked, glancing slowly down his jacket and pausing briefly at a spot just below his stomach, before her gaze crawled up him again. "It's such a pity, Trev."

"If you're trying to find a way to determine if my manhood's still intact, you're failing miserably."

"Oh, Trev, darling. I'm only teasing." She snaked a finger up his shirt and seductively stroked his ear and jaw. "I have no one to go home with tonight. How about you?" she cooed. "Wouldn't you like to help me forget all those nasty things my ex said to me? Wouldn't you like me to help you forget whatever it is that's been troubling you all these months?"

"Sorry, Carole, but I have other plans."

Her neck stiffened, and she drew her hand from

his face. "With who? Not with Janet, I hope."

"Actually—"

"That little bitch," Carole spit out before Trevor could tell her he was going home to write a letter to the woman he loved.

"She's so damn sweet," Carole continued to rave. "God, but she grates on my nerves. How could you possibly want a crazy woman like that?"

"She's a friend, Carole. A good friend. You should try to like her."

"You have such a bleeding heart. When will you ever learn that being nice gets you nothing in this world?"

"And when will you ever learn that you can't hide your fears behind an overblown ego?"

"How dare you!" Carole snapped, swinging a hand toward Trevor's face.

He caught it just before it connected, and held on tight. "I dare because I did the same damn thing. If I'd kept on hiding, God only knows what would have happened. I drank too much. I thought it could mask all the hurt I was feeling inside, but it didn't. It just made me drunk. So damn drunk that at times I didn't know what I was doing."

"I don't really care about your troubles," Carole stated flatly, as she tried to pull away.

"Well I care about yours."

"Like hell! No one cares. No one in this whole goddamned world cares about me. Not you, not my ex, not Jack Warner. No one. Now let go of my arm, so I can get out of this hole."

She jerked away and ran through the crowd, all eyes on her.

Trevor plowed his fingers through his hair. What had he done? He'd made her angry. She'd even had tears in her eyes when she pulled away from him. *Tears.* Something he'd never seen on Carole Sinclair's face—except when she was acting.

But these tears weren't part of a script. He had to go to her. He had to tell her he was sorry.

A narrow path cleared as he stalked through the once merry-making partygoers. He breezed past his friends in his rush to catch up with Carole, to apologize for his insensitive comments, but Janet caught his arm.

There were tears in her eyes. "Please. Don't go with her."

"She's upset. She needs someone."

"Does she need you more than I did? Did you lie to me so you could go with her?

Trevor shook his head. "No, I didn't lie."

"Then don't go."

"I need to apologize to her, that's all."

"That's never all there is where Carole's concerned. She'll dig her claws in you and never let you go." A tear trickled down Janet's cheek. "Please, Trevor. You told me to ignore her. You should do the same thing."

Trevor knew Janet was right, but he couldn't let Carole leave angry. He'd apologize, and then he'd return to the party.

Charlie sauntered out of the crowd and slid an arm around Janet's waist. "Come dance with me, Janet."

She wiped the tear from her face and looked at Charlie, offering him a trembling smile. "Did you ask the band to play my favorite song?"

"Of course I did. I asked them to play a few others, too. I thought we could dance all night—if you're willing."

"I'd like that," she said, and turned to Trevor once more.

"Let her go, Trevor. Be good to yourself for a change. You don't have to help everyone."

She swept long fingernails gently over his cheek,

smiled weakly, and headed for the dance floor with Charlie.

Trevor took a deep breath. All he planned to do was apologize for his heartless words, then he'd come back inside and watch Charlie persuade Janet to love him.

He caught up with Carole as she stepped into her chauffeur-driven Lincoln. He climbed in after her, hoping she'd accept his apology, then listen to reason and keep away from the beach house. Logic told him he should stay as far away as possible from Carole tonight. Yet, even though he was trying to change the future, he had a horrid fear that something might happen to Carole if he left her alone.

"Don't go," he said softly, repeating Janet's steady refrain as he took a seat on the cold black leather and wrapped his fingers lightly around Carole's arm.

Once more she jerked away and anger flashed in her eyes. "Get your hands off of me. I don't want you or anyone else telling me what to do or what's wrong with my life."

"I'm sorry."

"Save your sorries for simpering bitches like Janet. I don't need to hear them."

"Stay here, Carole. We'll get coffee and talk."

"Coffee? Talk?" she laughed. "You think I still want to give you another chance to prove you're a man?"

"I think you don't want to be alone, that's all."

"Go to hell."

"I've been there already. I have no intention of going back."

She laughed again. "You're just as demented as your little friend."

She knocked on the glass that separated her from the driver. "You'd better get out, Trev. I plan on

getting the hell out of here, and the sooner the better."

He touched her arm one more time, and she jerked
away. "Get out."

Tears streamed down her face as she screamed the
words. She was lonely, tortured, and she needed
someone desperately.

He should stay with her.

No, he should climb out of the car right now, and
stay the hell away from her.

The Lincoln's engine started, and he took a deep
breath, rehashing his options, then closed his eyes
and prayed that he'd made the right decision.

July 4, 1938

Trevor gazed at the fireworks exploding over the
swaying palms and the magnificent columns of
Sparta, lighting the midnight sky with a profusion
of sparkling colors. Off in the distance he could hear
laughter and loud voices ringing out as partygoers
celebrated Independence Day.

But Trevor couldn't bring himself to celebrate.

Carole Sinclair was dead.

History *had* repeated itself. In spite of his efforts
in the past year to change the course of events, Carole Sinclair still was dead.

He'd failed.

He stood on one of the terraces which was fragrant with roses and honeysuckle, and looked down
at the Grecian temple that stood solemnly beside the
Poseidon Pool. Once he'd tried to end his life there,
now he wanted to go back to the life that held his
fondest memories. He prayed he would not fail
again.

With one hand tucked in the pocket of his crisply
pleated trousers, he ignored the rain of firelight in

the sky and cast his eyes downward to study the reflection of a million sparkles on the calm surface of the water.

From the corner of his eye he saw movement on the stairs leading to the pool. It was the shadow of a woman dressed in flowing white, and for one heart-wrenching moment, he thought—he hoped—it was Adriana. And then he realized—it was only Janet Julian.

He watched her walk slowly and gracefully past the temple and stop at the edge of the pool. Her long gown was pale pink, not white, and it swirled at her feet. She looked sweet and innocent, like a girl at her first cotillion. But instead of laughing and acting carefree, she looked just as troubled and tortured as he. Carole would still be alive if . . .

What good did it do to dwell on it. Carole was dead. If he tried a thousand times, he doubted he could change the tragic circumstances of the night before. Maybe he wasn't supposed to. Maybe some things just couldn't be changed.

From where he stood, he could hear Janet's sobs. Her head had bent in sorrow, and she'd covered her face with her hands. He wished that he, too, could cry, but no amount of tears would bring Carole back.

The sudden crash, crackle, and bang of the fireworks exploding in the sky caught his attention, and he ran his fingers through thick ebony hair, combing back the lock that insisted on falling over his forehead when caught in the cool night breeze. He wished that he could celebrate. He wished that Carole was alive and that Janet was happy. But those things weren't meant to be. When . . . *if* he could return to Adriana, he'd just have to forget. He could do nothing else.

Taking a deep breath, he sucked in the scents of star jasmine, closely clipped grass, the obtrusive smoke and gunpowder from the Fourth of July festivities, and, from a distance, the salt air of the Pacific Ocean that he loved. He'd done the same things before. He'd given up hope the last time. This time, hope was all he had to hang on to. As soon as Janet left the Poseidon Pool, he'd walk into the water, float facedown, and hope when he woke, he'd be in Adriana's arms once again.

Janet was gone when he turned toward the temple. The fireworks had stopped exploding, and only dim light brightened the pool—and the silky pink fabric that floated on the surface.

Oh, God!

He ran across the terrace, leaped over a hedge, and raced down the stairs, two and three at a time.

Please, Lord. Let her be alive. Please.

He rounded the temple and dived into the water. He was at Janet's side in less than a moment, pulling her limp body close as he made his way back to the marble steps leading out of the water.

Charlie was waiting at poolside, his face filled with fear, and Trevor placed Janet into Charlie's outstretched arms.

Trevor took a few deep breaths, then felt like a helpless bystander as Charlie knelt on the marble and cradled Janet in his arms. Slowly her eyes opened, and even through the pool water streaming down her face, he could see the flow of tears.

"It's my fault. It's all my fault," she sobbed. "She'd still be alive if it wasn't for me."

"Don't say that, Janet," Charlie whispered. "Please. She's dead. There's nothing you or anyone else can do now. Just try to forget everything."

"I wish I could. Oh, I wish I could."

Janet buried her head into Charlie's shoulder, and she continued to weep as he stood with her cradled in his arms.

"I'm going to take her inside," Charlie said to Trevor. "See if I can find someplace quiet and let her rest."

"I'll go with you," Trevor said.

Water dripped from his tuxedo and Janet's gown as they walked in silence up stairs that led them across deserted terraces rather than the crowded ones, and entered the mansion through one of the back doors.

There was a small reading room just off the library that Trevor led Charlie to, and Janet curled up on the black-leather sofa where Charlie had laid her.

Trevor poured a snifter of brandy, and held it out to Janet.

"Drink this," he said, not knowing what else to do or say. "It might warm you up a bit."

She took the glass with trembling fingers. "I wanted to die," she cried. "It's all my fault that Carole's dead. It's all my fault."

Charlie helped her to sit up, and she took a sip of the brandy. The eyes that had smiled at him last night were vacant now, glazed over in a look Trevor remembered so well. It was the same empty stare she'd worn the first time he'd seen her at Magnolia Acres.

She drank the rest of the brandy and held the empty glass out to Charlie. "Thank you, dearest," she said, as he took it from her fingers "You're so good to me. So very, very good."

She tilted her head to look at Trevor and smiled. "You really shouldn't be here, you know. You should be with your mystery woman. She must miss you."

She said the words as if she knew he was going away, as if she knew the future.

"I wanted to make sure you were okay, first," he said.

"Charlie's with me. He's always with me. Go now, Trevor. Everything's going to be fine. You'll see."

He hoped she was right. He prayed everything would be fine, and that he'd soon be back in Adriana's arms.

Leaning over, he placed a gentle kiss on Janet's forehead. "I'll see you soon."

She touched his cheek. "Of course you will."

Trevor shook Charlie's hand. "You'll take care of her?" he asked.

"Always."

Knowing the truth of Charlie's statement, Trevor crossed the room and opened the door, long past ready to attempt a journey back to Adriana.

"It's gone," he heard, turning back at the sound of Janet's faint, tear-filled whimper.

"My necklace," Janet cried, clutching her neck. "Oh, Charlie. I must have lost it in the pool. Please find it."

"I'll go right now. You just stay here and relax."

Trevor shook his head at Charlie. "I'll go. You take care of Janet."

He started out the door, then tilted his head to look over his shoulder at Janet. "I'll bring it back to you. Don't worry."

Trevor ignored the stares and laughter of his friends as he walked soggily across the terraces. He patted backs, shook the hands of age-old friends, and hugged his dearest friend, Harrison, as he headed for the pool. *They must think I'm a fool*, he laughed to himself, not really caring any longer what anyone thought.

The only person who mattered to him was Adriana, and he'd give anything to hear her laugh—with him or at him.

The surface of the water was calm when he stood before the Poseidon Pool. At the bottom, resting on top of an emerald green tile, he saw the sparkle of a diamond choker.

He'd picked a red rosebud on his trek down to

the pool. Now, he held it close to his face, inhaling the sweet fragrance, and thought of Adriana's own unique scent wafting about him. The memory made him smile.

"Soon, Adriana," he whispered, half-hoping, half-praying that his words were true. Once he returned the necklace to Janet, he'd try and return to the arms of his wife—and he'd keep on trying, even if it took a lifetime.

He'd failed Carole. He refused to fail Adriana.

He kissed the rose and tossed it onto the water, took a deep breath, and dived to the bottom of the pool. With his eyes open, he could see the shimmer of diamonds, and he followed their glow.

The necklace was just inches from his fingers when he heard thunder roaring through his ears and felt a turbulent whirlpool surrounding him. Reaching out, he clutched the choker, turned, and attempted to push off the bottom and head for the surface.

But the strong, swirling water pulled him down. It felt as if icy fingers had wrapped around his ankles, his knees, his waist, halting his escape. The water choked his lungs. He couldn't breathe.

Fear wrapped around him. He thought he was going to die without having a chance to get back to Adriana.

All of his instincts fought for life. He scratched at the water, wanting to reach the surface, wanting a gasp of air.

But he couldn't move. He couldn't swim. He could just barely think as the water pressed against him like a vise.

Adriana! he attempted to scream, but his words were drowned out by water rushing into his mouth.

Dizziness engulfed him, as his thoughts drifted

from his fear of dying, to once again being with the woman he loved, to lying in her arms.

I love you, Adriana.

A dark void filled him then, he felt tired, he wanted to sleep, and . . .

✒ *Twenty-seven*

"Miss Howard."

The woman's voice was hazy. Faint and indistinct. A nurse maybe?

Adriana felt cool fingers on her forehead, then the voice again.

"Miss Howard? Are you all right?"

"Just a little dizzy." Adriana struggled to sit up, then doubled over, wrapping her arms around her stomach to fight the nagging nausea. "I'll be fine in a moment," she said, choking out the words.

"I'm going to get something cool for you to drink. Try not to move until I get back."

Adriana pressed her fingers to her temples, hoping to rid herself of the headache and the persistent ringing in her ears. Her fingers were numb, and an icy chill fluttered through her arms.

Opening her eyes, she looked around the unfamiliar room. Sun streamed through an open window where white eyelet curtains fluttered in the breeze. Floral paintings hung on the walls in pristine white frames, and a yellow-and-white chenille spread draped over the side of the narrow twin bed. A white, lacy doily sat on a nightstand, and one simple long-stemmed red rose occupied a tall crystal bud vase on top.

Where could she possibly be?

The room seemed oddly familiar, but the decorations were different. Soft and feminine rather than sterile and plain.

She rose from the floor and hesitantly walked to the window to look out. She was at Magnolia Acres, but it seemed so different. Happier.

Downstairs, on the vast expanse of green lawn bordered by rows of multicolored rosebushes, an old man was lighting a barbecue, and the fumes of lighter fluid and charcoal wafted up to her. A child was laughing as he ran around waving a sparkler, and gray- and white-haired men and women with crocheted lap robes over their legs sat about in wheelchairs listening to Sousa marches on the stereo.

The Fourth of July? No, that couldn't be right. That holiday was several weeks ago. She had planned to spend it with Elliott and Juanita but something had kept her from celebrating the Fourth at Sparta, so she'd gone there on the fifth, instead.

Oh, why can't I remember anything else?

She pressed her burning forehead against a cool yellow wall and tried to remember something, anything that might remind her why she was here. She didn't remember the drive, but her green Mercedes was parked downstairs in the gravel circle. She didn't remember coming to this room, but her purse sat on the nightstand.

Am I losing my mind?

She turned when she heard footsteps on the hardwood floor, and the woman's voice once again. "Are you feeling better, Miss Howard? I was worried about you."

Adriana studied the frail but still pretty woman with curly white hair wisping about her head, trying to remember who she was. She had blue eyes that twinkled when she smiled. Pink lace gloves covered her hands and an exquisite pink-and-white cameo had been pinned at the neck of her frilly, pale pink dress. She was lovely.

Of course. Janet Julian. Adriana laughed inwardly. How could she have forgotten the sweet movie star of the thirties whom she'd visited several times?

Adriana began to smile, and white light flashed before her eyes. She clutched the windowsill as a vivid image of a dying woman flashed through her mind. There were no pretty pictures on the stark, sanitary white walls. The smells of alcohol and pine cleaner assaulted her.

In an instant, the vision was gone. But the dizziness remained.

"I'm sorry," Adriana apologized, massaging her temples. "I seem to have developed a horrible headache."

Janet set a tray containing two frosty glasses on the bedside table, then moved slowly toward her.

"Just sit a moment, dear. I'll call one of our doctors."

Adriana shook her head. "No. I'll be fine. Please, just stay with me for a while."

"Of course I will. Come. Sit down and have some lemonade."

Adriana took hold of the woman's arm and allowed her to lead her to a chair next to the bed. She slumped into the pretty floral cushion that softened the wooden seat. Taking the glass that was offered to her, she took a slow, tentative sip, then set the glass back on the tray and closed her eyes.

Why am I here? she asked herself. *Why do I feel so confused?*

She could hear Janet moving about the bedroom, her sweet voice humming a tune as she opened and closed a drawer, then walked toward Adriana and sat on the edge of the bed.

Adriana opened her eyes, and watched Janet flip open a photo album. "I so enjoy looking at these old photos," she said, turning the pages slowly. "They bring back many fond memories." She glanced at Adriana and smiled. "I'm glad you've asked Charlie and me to help with the movie you're producing."

Movie? What movie was Janet talking about?

"No one today knows the thirties better than Charlie," Janet continued, "and what he can't remember, well, perhaps I can help fill in the blanks. It's about time someone made a movie about Trevor Montgomery."

A movie about Trevor?

Adriana closed her eyes again and tried to think, willed herself to remember what was going on.

Bits and pieces came to her. A call from William Castle asking if she'd be interested in coproducing a film about Trevor Montgomery. Consulting with screenwriters. Sitting in on auditions with nearly a dozen actors who weren't half as wonderful as Trevor. The minute flashes of memory churned in her brain and made her head ache. Again she pressed her fingers to her temples and hoped the haziness in her mind would clear.

Taking the glass of lemonade, she sipped on the cool, tangy drink, and watched Janet as she studied the pictures.

"Charlie took these photos in the thirties. Actually, they were taken in thirty-eight, when I was filming *Break the Night* with Trevor."

Adriana sat up, looking closely at the photos Janet was flipping through. At least one thing was clear in her mind. Her passion for Trevor Montgomery. Her friends had laughed at her obsession, but she didn't care. No one understood how precious he'd always seemed to her, how real, especially in her dreams and in the visions that came to her without warning—visions that warmed her heart and soul.

"Trevor was different before we started filming that movie," Janet said.

"In what way?"

"It's common knowledge that he drank—a lot—and that there were many women in his life." Janet's eyes flickered toward Adriana. "He was a very wicked man, and I suppose I shouldn't have been in love with him, but I couldn't help myself. When I came out of the hospital that first time, he'd changed. He seemed happier. He said there was a special woman in his life, although none of us ever met her."

Adriana found it difficult to believe Janet's words. She considered herself an expert on the life of Trevor Montgomery, and she'd never heard a story about him having just one special woman. Perhaps that was something Janet had dreamed up to soothe her feelings after Trevor rejected her. Janet had a history of slipping into a fantasy world. Still, Adriana didn't want to discourage Janet's words.

"I don't know much about that year of his life," Adriana told her. "All I've ever read said he stayed in Santa Barbara when he wasn't filming or attending special functions. Is there more you can tell me?"

"I'll tell you everything I possibly can. The only reason I agreed to talk with you about this is because I know you want his story to be completely factual," she stressed. "No innuendo."

"You mean about Trevor possibly murdering Carole Sinclair?" Adriana asked.

"Why, no. I'd never heard that story," Janet declared. "Everyone knows that Carole committed suicide. You *are* aware of that, aren't you, Miss Howard? Carole Sinclair swallowed a bottle of sleeping pills along with too much champagne."

Suicide?

Nausea suddenly overwhelmed her, and she gripped her stomach as another image flashed through her mind. A battered and slashed body. Platinum hair, and Carole Sinclair's frightened—but dead—eyes. A bloodstained knife. And Trevor Montgomery lying at Carole's side. Just as fast as the memory came, it was gone, but the horror remained in Adriana's mind.

Murder? No, it was impossible. She'd never read anything about a murder. Why, then, had that image come to her so vividly?

Janet's cool fingers touched her arm. "Are you sure you wouldn't like me to call the doctor?"

"No, please. I'm fine." Adriana said, closing her eyes for a moment as she took a deep breath.

When she looked at Janet again, she smiled faintly, not wanting to worry the lady. "I'm feeling a little better, Miss Julian."

"Mrs. Beck, please," Janet corrected. "I haven't used the name Julian in nearly sixty years. Charlie and I were married not too long after Trevor disappeared. But, I'm talking far too much about myself. I know you have an appointment to rush off to, so please, tell me again what it is you'd like me to help you with."

Appointment? Again she couldn't remember. It was the Fourth of July and she always spent the day at Sparta, but today was different. Why?

Suddenly she remembered the phone call from London. The collector wanted to look at Valentino costumes, and he was going to be in California for just one day. Of course. It was all coming back now. She'd had to make the trip in to her shop in Hollywood, and she'd decided to visit Janet at the same time, to try and learn more about what happened the night Trevor Montgomery disappeared.

A flood of relief washed through her as her remembrances collided with each other. The pain in her temples and behind her eyes was subsiding.

"Miss Howard?"

Adriana looked into Janet's worried eyes.

"Would you like some aspirin?" Janet asked.

"No. No thank you. I'm tired, that's all. I should have stuck with running my memorabilia business instead of coproducing this film, too. It's been one headache after another, especially the star."

"I've read so much gossip about that Mr. Dean," Janet said, shaking her head. "I'm sorry, Miss Howard, but he's not at all like Mr. Montgomery. I honestly can't see why he was hired for the part. He's much too pretty."

"Yes, I always felt that way, too. The Trevor Montgomery I knew was taller. His shoulders were broader . . ."

Adriana's words trailed off when she saw the frown on Janet's face.

"You couldn't possibly have known him, Miss Howard."

Adriana laughed nervously. "Of course not," she said, covering her mistake. "I just imagine that he was taller."

Another vision swept through her mind. Dark circles under bloodshot eyes. A harsh—but sensuous, whiskey-tasting—kiss in the pounding ocean waves. Bronzed skin that felt warm and wonderful to the touch.

A tear slid down her cheek, and Adriana hastily wiped it away.

Maybe she was losing her mind. She'd seen visions of Trevor before, but they'd never seemed so real.

A light tap on the doorjamb made Adriana instantly turn her head. Charlie Beck was walking toward her with the aid of a cane.

"Janet told me you'd come by," he said, shaking Adriana's hand. He once again gripped his ivory-handled cane as he looked deeply into Adriana's eyes. "She said you weren't feeling well. Is there anything I can do?"

"I think it's just a mild case of exhaustion. Your lovely wife's been kind enough to keep me company until my headache goes away."

"Then I won't be imposing if I join you for a bit, at least till the charcoal's hot?"

"No, dearest," Janet said. "We'd love your company. We were talking about that actor—Paul Dean. You remember, the one who's going to play Trevor Montgomery in Adriana's new movie."

"Yes, I know the one."

Charlie pulled a low wooden chair close to the bed and sat down slowly, leaned forward and rubbed his knees.

"I had the radio playing earlier," he said, glancing from his wife to Adriana. "I heard the oddest story about Mr. Dean being arrested for fraud and embezzlement. Is it true?"

"Every word of it," Adriana remarked, suddenly realizing how easy it had been to answer Charlie's question. The memory was clear. All of the haziness had seemed to clear just as her headache was going away. "Actually, he *and* his agent, Bill Paxton, were arrested. It's going to slow production down, but I'd been looking for an excuse to find another person to play the Trevor Montgomery role."

"Why?" Charlie asked.

"Mr. Dean just didn't fit the part. His Southern accent was too strong, and we were considering doing a voice-over. It took several weeks to find Mr. Dean, but I'd rather double that time rather than hire someone who isn't close to perfect. It's a shame Trevor didn't have a son who'd followed in his acting footsteps."

"He might," Janet threw in. "We don't know what happened to him after he disappeared. He could have gone to another country, fallen in love, and had several children."

"I suppose we'll never know, though. I wish there was some way we could give the movie a happy ending, but I want to tell the truth—nothing else."

"Then end it by telling the world that he was a hero," Charlie said.

"A hero?" Adriana had always imagined Trevor playing that role, she'd dreamed of him doing heroic things, but all she'd ever read about was his drinking, his womanizing, and his very wicked ways. "I'd love to end the movie that way. But I have nothing to base it on."

"Tell the world that he saved my life," Janet said, then hesitantly continued. "I tried to kill myself once. It was a long time ago, and I didn't want anyone to know—except Charlie."

Adriana watched Janet reach a hand out to her husband, and saw the tenderness in both their faces as Charlie squeezed her fingers.

"I realize your movie isn't about me," Janet said, "but I'd like to tell the truth, so people will see that special side of Trevor that Charlie and I got to see that last year."

"If you feel like sharing, I'd love to hear the story, and I'll make sure you have the opportunity to read the screenplay before we start to film. I told you I needed your help."

"I don't honestly know where to begin," Janet said. "Of course, I'm sure you've read all the stories about the party the night before Carole died."

Adriana nodded, and Janet continued, her eyes glazing over as she stared out the open window.

"Carole left the Trocadero early, but most everyone else stayed until nearly dawn. Charlie was going to take me home, but he got a phone call and had to leave, so Trevor took me home." Janet frowned. "No, that's not quite right. We went to my house and I packed a few things to take to Sparta for the Fourth of July weekend, then we drove to Trevor's place in Santa Barbara. He said he had a letter to write to a friend."

"A letter?" Adriana asked. As far as she knew, Trevor Montgomery had never written letters. She'd never found any in the house—to or from anyone.

"I don't know who it was to," Janet continued. "It must have taken him an hour or so to write, and then we left for Sparta. When we got there, Trevor seemed terribly preoccupied. He spent a lot of time with Harrison, reminiscing about old times. He seemed happier that night than he'd been in a year, as if he knew something good was about to happen."

"But you don't know what?"

"I just assumed it had something to do with the woman he said he was in love with," Janet said. "Of course, the happiness disappeared the moment Charlie showed up at Sparta."

"I'm the one who told them about Carole," Charlie said. "The phone call I'd gotten at the Trocadero was a tip that the police had found a movie star dead in Santa Monica. I didn't say a word to Janet about it—I figured I should check it out first."

Instantly, the stark photos in Charlie's books of Carole's silk-clad body lying lifelessly on white-satin sheets filled Adriana's mind. Her hair and makeup were perfect. Her eyes were closed as if in sleep. Her hands were folded over her chest, as if she'd done nothing more than lie down to rest.

"Trevor and I were out on one of the terraces watching the fireworks when Charlie showed up," Janet related. "He told us that Carole had committed suicide sometime during the night."

"I'll never forget the horror in Trevor's eyes," Charlie said. "I remember his words, too, although they didn't make any sense. 'I've failed,' he said. I expected him to go off and get a drink, but instead he just walked away. He wanted to be by himself, and I didn't bother stopping him. Janet was crying, and I couldn't leave her. Not then."

"I felt like Carole's death was all my fault," Janet said. "If I hadn't begged Trevor not to go with her, things would have been different. I was so sure of that."

"It's not true, though," Charlie insisted. "We learned later that Carole had attempted suicide several other times—and failed. None of us realized how depressed she was."

"If she hadn't hidden the fact, maybe we could have helped her," Janet said. "Maybe I wouldn't have been so selfish in wanting to keep Trevor away from her. At the time, though, all I could think of was that she had died, and I was responsible."

"She asked me to get her something to drink," Charlie said, gazing reflectively at his wife. "I needed something strong, too, so I went inside to the bar. I wasn't gone long, but I couldn't find her when I got back."

"I'd decided I wanted to die," Janet said. "It seemed like the easiest thing to do. I didn't want to think about what had happened to Carole. I didn't want to deal with any of my problems any longer, so I walked down to the Poseidon Pool, stood at the edge for the longest time, and then I walked into the water. I don't remember anything else until Charlie was holding me in his arms."

"I was frantic," Charlie said. "I'd searched everywhere, and then I heard the splash in the water and saw Trevor swimming toward Janet. I ran down the stairs and down to the pool."

Charlie hesitated, and cleared his throat. He reached up and wiped his eyes, then continued. "I thought she was dead. I can't tell you how happy I was when she started talking. Trevor and I took her inside, got her something to drink. She was feeling better then, until she realized her diamond necklace was gone."

"My parents had given it to me," Janet added. "I thought I must have lost it in the pool, and Trevor said he'd find it for me. But he never came back."

Adriana saw the trembling in Janet's lips, heard the quiver of sorrow in her voice.

"I had another breakdown after that," Janet said. "I felt responsible not only for Carole, but for Trevor's disappearance. If he hadn't gone searching for that necklace . . ." Her words trailed off. "I came here to Magnolia Acres. It was the best place for me at the time, at least until the doctors found the right medication to treat my depression. Charlie stuck by my side until I was well. We were married not too long after that."

"I tried searching for Trevor when Janet was well, but I wasn't successful," Charlie said. "Finally I wrote a few books on what I knew of Trevor's life. I left out the parts about Janet's attempted suicide, and Trevor going back to the pool for her necklace. I was afraid of what people might think. It's so easy to find fault with someone if they can't defend themselves."

"I didn't care about the necklace after that," Janet said. "I wanted Trevor to come back, that's all. I wanted him to see how happy I was, to let him know that if he hadn't pushed me away—pushed me in Charlie's direction—I might have spent my life wanting someone I couldn't have."

"We owe everything to him," Charlie said. "We always wished he'd return."

"I've wished that, too," Adriana said. "Many times."

"I'd like to show him what we did to Magnolia Acres. We bought this place when Charlie returned from the war. I didn't want to act anymore, and it seemed like it would be the perfect place to raise children. Of course, we weren't blessed with any. We wanted to share it with others, though. It's such a beautiful place. Most of the people living here were actors at one time, and we try to make it nice for all of them."

Charlie got up and walked slowly to the window. "And they're all going to be expecting hamburgers and fireworks soon."

Janet reached out and took Adriana's hands. "I hope we've told you something that will help, Miss Howard. I don't mind if people know about my suicide attempt. It's past history. I just want the truth to be told about Trevor. Some of the books don't paint a pretty picture of him. He did drink a lot. He loved women. But he was the best friend I ever had—until Charlie. He saved my life in more ways than one. I don't know what happened to him, but I've always hoped that he found a new life with the mystery woman he'd fallen in love with."

Adriana hoped the same thing.

And she wished that her dreams of being Trevor's mystery woman would come true.

✍ *Twenty-eight*

Adriana swept her fingers over the green-and-yellow body of the Duesenberg, remembering photos taken in the thirties of Trevor and his favorite car. Whenever she touched it, she sensed his closeness, although she knew that couldn't be. Trevor Montgomery had disappeared in 1938. He was probably dead. Yet, she could almost smell the faint scent of tobacco on the seats. Chesterfields, maybe. The brand Trevor had always smoked.

That was impossible, though. A cigarette hadn't been smoked in that car for six long decades.

She touched the pale green leather of the driver's seat and the slight indentation where his back had always rested. She opened the door and climbed inside, smoothing her hands over the steering wheel. The fragrance of musky cologne wafted around her, so strong, so real, that she could see Trevor sitting in the seat, one hand on the wheel, one arm extended over the back, his fingers playing with a woman's hair—her hair—which blew gently in the breeze as they navigated the winding turns of Highway 1.

Only a memory, she told herself.

No, not a memory. A dream.

And dreams like that don't come true.

That's enough folly for tonight, she told herself, as she left the car and walked toward the house. It was late, well past midnight, yet she wasn't tired. Instead of going inside to bed, she strolled to the edge of the grass and stood at the top of the stairs, looking down at the beach.

For one instant she thought she saw a man standing in the moonlit waves, his white jacket swirling about him. But there was no man, only a gathering of foam on the water.

Taking off her shoes, she walked down to the sand and put her toes in the outgoing surf. She shivered in the cold night air, and curled her arms around herself, wishing someone else was there to keep her warm. She didn't want someone else, though. She wanted Trevor Montgomery—but the man she'd long been in love with, the dashing, daring movie idol, no longer existed. He would never hold her. He would never love her.

Except in her dreams.

She walked back up the stairs, across the terracotta patio, and into the house that she loved because it held so many memories of Trevor. He felt so close, so real when she moved through the rooms where he once had walked, when she touched little things that he once had touched. For nearly eight years the small adobe had eased her loneliness and brought her comfort at night. Tonight, though, she felt empty, as if her heart had been torn away. She felt lost, as if she was destined to wander forever in search of the one she loved.

She turned on the lights in the living room, and for just one moment she thought she saw a desolate-looking man sitting on the sofa skimming through her books. She thought she saw tortured eyes looking up at her. There was no man, though. Only books about the life of Trevor Montgomery.

In the kitchen, she made a cup of Earl Grey and searched the refrigerator for something sinfully rich to stir into the tea. But there was nothing sinful inside. Nothing fat, or sweet, or salty. Her father wouldn't have approved.

Suddenly, that didn't matter. Suddenly she wanted to go shopping and fill the icebox and cupboards with chocolate chip cookies, black walnut and chocolate macadamia nut ice cream. She wanted to go to McDonald's for a Big Mac and fries—but she didn't know why.

Her impulsive thoughts made no sense at all.

Taking the cup of tea, she walked back through the living room and down the hallway. When she passed the bathroom, she thought she glimpsed an ebony-haired man shaving in front of the mirror. She stopped, turned on the light, and realized the room was empty, but the musky smell of aftershave drifted about her again. She gripped the edge of the door as a blinding vision flashed in front of her eyes.

A man stood at the mirror in tight black Levi's and nothing more. With straight razor in hand, he shaved away the hint of a mustache, and smoldering brown eyes gazed into the crystal-clear glass and smiled—not at his reflection, but at her.

"Trevor," she whispered.

The hallucination shimmered like a summer-day mirage, then vanished.

She forced herself not to cry. Not over a dream. Tears should be saved for real happiness, real sorrow, not for illusions of how she'd like life to be.

Taking another sip of her tea, she watched the mirror, hoping the vision would return. One minute went by. Two. And then she gave up, turned off the light, and went to her room.

She put *Captain Caribe* in the VCR, and lay back on her bed to watch Trevor swinging from the yardarm and teasing his lady. It was impossible not to

love him. He was everything a woman could want—
and more. Dashing. Daring. Tender and warm. He
was a hero in every sense of the word.

But he'd disappeared a long time ago. He couldn't
step out of a movie to love her any more than he
could walk through her door and tell her he'd been
suspended sixty years in time—waiting to become
part of her life.

*Oh, Trevor. You're just a celluloid dream, and I'm a
crazy woman.*

At two in the morning, she climbed from the bed,
pulled a white-satin gown from a drawer, and began
to dress for the night.

She peeled off her pale blue silk blouse, her navy
pin-striped slacks, a lacy camisole, and slid the negligee over her head. Her fingers brushed the mi-
nuscule hairs on her legs as she removed her panties,
and a jolt of desire whipped through her limbs, her
stomach, her heart, leaving her weak and gasping
for breath.

She grabbed hold of the bedpost as other sensations breezed over her skin.

For one moment she felt a strong pair of hands
smoothing over her legs and lightly caressing her
thighs. She felt warm lips teasing her belly and powerful arms pulling her into their embrace as intense
brown eyes gazed deeply into hers. She tasted salt
water and whiskey on her tongue, and felt a sensual
mouth slanting expertly over hers as it coaxed her
to fully enjoy the kiss.

She heard a deep, refined voice with a touch of
bad-boy charm whispering "One step at a time, Adriana. I'm in no hurry. No hurry at all."

A tear trickled down her cheek and she wiped it
away. Where could those feelings have come from?
she wondered. Where was the man who'd held her
and loved her and made her envision all those erotic
and impassioned sensations?

He doesn't exist, she told herself. *He's just a powerful dream taking over the mind of a gullible, love-starved woman.*

She didn't want to think of the dream and visions any longer. They'd come on too strong, and they frightened her. She needed to forget them, and go back to her lonely, stable existence.

Crawling into bed, she pulled the covers close to her chin, turned out the light, and tried to sleep. But the bed felt too big, too empty. As much as she wanted to forget all the things she'd imagined, they were already too much a part of her life, and pretending that someone loved her was so much better than being alone.

She rolled over and touched the pillow beside her, picturing a lock of ebony hair hanging over a sleeping man's brow. *Trevor's brow.* She imagined the lightness of his breathing, warm hands reaching for her in his sleep, and snuggling close to each other in the center of the bed.

"Good night," she whispered, as she kissed her finger and touched it to the pillow.

The musky fragrance of aftershave clinging to the lace-edged case wrapped around her. Not imagined this time, but real.

She smiled, then pulled the pillow close, and went to sleep holding a dream in her arms.

The scent of strong French roast and frying bacon swirled through the bedroom, waking Adriana from her deep, dream-filled slumber.

"Mmmm, smells good," she whispered.

Pushing back the covers, she climbed out of bed and stood in the middle of her bedroom, waiting for her eyes to clear. Rubbing the morning chill from her arms, she followed the heavenly scent down the hall and into the kitchen.

"Good morning," she sang, but the joy left her

voice when she confronted an empty kitchen. No skillets sat on the stove. No bacon had been fried or coffee perked.

It was only a dream—but a pleasant one.

Her stomach growled, and she felt the overwhelming craving for a rich, cheesy omelet fried in real butter. She wanted thick slices of crispy bacon and croissants slathered with raspberry preserves.

She wanted to share them with the hallucination she'd seen in the bathroom last night, the man in tight black Levi's with shaving cream covering his cheeks.

He was only a dream—but she needed him.

Going back to her bedroom, she turned the radio on and the strains of "The Way You Look Tonight" from *Swing Time* echoed around the room. She hummed as she made her bed, grabbing hold of the bedpost, pretending it was Fred Astaire and she was Ginger Rogers as she swayed back and forth, then let go of her partner and waltzed—all alone— around her bedroom.

When the music stopped, she realized what she'd done. She'd danced. She'd never done it before—not by herself, not with Harrison, not with anyone. She'd felt too awkward, too inhibited. But it felt so right this time, as if she'd been taught by an expert, someone who'd held her close, and didn't mind when she stepped on his toes.

Folly, Adriana. Pure folly.

Still, it made her smile as she went into the bathroom, showered, brushed her teeth, and, with a lightheartedness she hadn't experienced in a long time, readied herself for the day.

She took a tuxedo-style jumper from the closet and laid it on her bed, then went in search of a pair of black-velvet sandals—something from the forties— that she'd bought years ago and had never worn.

It was dark at the back of the closet. She reached

for the string on the overhead bulb, and ripped the ring off the end when she turned on the light.

The old plastic ring slipped through her fingers and fell to the floor, rolling somewhere to the back of the closet.

Getting down on her knees, she pulled the shoe box she was looking for from the very back, and saw the ring wedged in a crack in the baseboard.

She reached for it, and the baseboard slid sideways.

Pushing the plastic ring on her finger to keep from losing it while she tried to repair the baseboard, she shoved aside clothes to get closer to the wall, and heard a sudden, faint voice.

Marry me, Adriana. Marry me.

She shivered at the sound, at the feel of lips brushing lightly across her mouth.

Breathing became difficult. Her heart began to pound. The voice wasn't real. It wasn't.

"Marry me, Adriana. Marry me—now."

The fragrance of roses wafted around her, and in her hands she saw a huge bouquet of long-stemmed red and white roses. She closed her eyes to rid herself of the vision, but sounds came to her instead. A violinist played the song she'd been dancing to, a minister spoke words she'd heard only in movies: "I pronounce you husband and wife."

She touched the plastic ring on her finger, and saw another hand touching hers, strong, bronzed fingers sliding the ring on her hand. She heard other tenderly spoken words. "I'll give you diamonds the size of walnuts next time."

She looked up through tear-soaked lashes and instead of seeing the clothes, she saw a wavery vision of Trevor Montgomery.

"I love you, Adriana," he whispered. "Forever."

The words rang out loud and clear, stronger than any words she'd ever heard.

Other things came to her, too. Stomping grapes on the beach. Skinny-dipping in the ocean. Making love behind a mummy case. Those weren't dreams—they were memories.

Had it really happened? Had she married Trevor Montgomery and forgotten?

He'd disappeared sixty years ago, though. He'd disappeared after Carole Sinclair committed suicide, after he'd gone to his home— this home—and written a letter.

Janet Julian's words came back to her.

Trevor's words came to her, too. "If anything happens, I'll leave you a message."

A message. She tried to smile through her tears. He *had* been here. He'd proposed to her here in the closet.

She wasn't crazy.

She pushed aside the baseboard and peered into the darkened hole.

A yellowed envelope rested inside. She took it from its hiding place, and staring up at her were the words: *For Adriana.*

Her fingers trembled as she opened the envelope and began to read:

Adriana,

I love you. That's the one thought that has kept me going these past twelve months—that, and the thought of being with you again.

You're my life, Adriana. Without you, I feel I'm but half of a man. With you, I'm whole.

I live on the memories of our days together. Quiet walks on the beach, a drive along the ocean. Teaching you to dance and loving the feel of you floating in my arms. Our wedding, and our wedding night, when we made love and promised we'd never be apart.

We couldn't stop that from happening, though. We are apart—for now—but I won't rest until we're together again.

It's July 4, 1938. I've done all I could to change history. I hope I haven't done too much—or too little. Maybe I'll never know, but tonight I'll try to come to you again.

I pray that you'll remember our time together. I pray you haven't forgotten—as I did at first. The memories, though, were too precious to stay forgotten. I hope that you, too, will remember me again.

I love you, Adriana. I'll be waiting for you at the Poseidon Pool.

Wish me back, Adriana. Please, wish me back.

> *I love you,*
> *Trevor*

Adriana clasped the letter to her breast, and tears streaked her cheeks. Everything she'd imagined was real. Trevor had come into her life. He'd loved her.

It was all so real.

And she wanted him back again.

The drive from Santa Barbara to Sparta was nothing but a blur of asphalt and memories: Trevor smiling at her as he stood in a doorway, one hand tucked in the pockets of his trousers while his coat hung loose from broad shoulders; Trevor wiping pinkish hamburger sauce from her lips and licking his fingers; Trevor lying in the grass, his arms folded behind his head, talking of nothing more than dancing the night away, and making her happy.

He did make her happy, and she wondered how she could possibly have forgotten so many cherished moments.

She prayed that he'd come back to her. Prayed that they could make more memories together; the children they had talked of; the grandchildren he wanted to bounce on his knee when he grew old; the second Oscar he still wanted to win.

He had a chance at all those things—if only she could bring him back.

Elliott, standing tall and serene, was waiting for her in the circular drive when she reached the mansion.

"We missed you last night," he said, backing a discreet distance away after she affectionately brushed her cheek against his. *So very proper*, Adriana thought. *Once a butler, always a butler*—and she laughingly remembered having those same exact thoughts once before.

History *was* repeating itself. She prayed it would repeat itself at least once more.

"Our Fourth of July celebration wasn't quite the same without you," Elliott said in his decidedly British tone. "We hope this won't become a common occurrence."

"Of course not. You know I'd rather be here than anywhere else on the Fourth, but I just couldn't get away." She pulled the black-silk scarf from her head and dropped it on the passenger seat in the Duesenberg, then removed her sunglasses. She looked over Elliott's shoulder toward the rose gardens, the flower-laden terraces, and the Poseidon Pool, where her adventure with Trevor had begun.

"You seem terribly preoccupied, Miss Adriana. Is something amiss?"

"A restless night, that's all," she said, knowing she could hide little from the man who'd helped to raise her. "I thought I'd walk through the gardens a bit, maybe stick my toes in the Poseidon Pool."

"I could bring iced tea out for you."

"Thank you, Elliott, but that won't be necessary."

She looked around for visitors, for strangers—for Trevor, hoping he might have miraculously shown up without her help. But she saw no one. "Are there tour groups here today?" she asked.

"One in the east wing of the mansion, one on the grounds. Would you like me to ask the guides to make a slight detour so you won't be bothered?"

Adriana smiled, fondly remembering the way he'd always anticipated her needs. "Thank you, Elliot. I feel like being alone."

"You're alone too much, if you ask me. That's probably the reason for sleepless nights."

"I imagine you're right."

She tucked her sunglasses into her purse and held it out to Elliott. "Would you mind taking these in for me? I should be up in an hour or so."

He took the purse from her hands, and tucked it under his arm. "I'll ask Juanita to prepare a light lunch for you."

"Could you ask her to prepare something for two? And something not so light?" she asked, delighted at the questioning frown on Elliott's face. "I remember tasting her chocolate chip cookies once."

"You don't like chocolate chip cookies."

"My *father* didn't like chocolate chip cookies, Elliott. I loved them, and I'd like to try them again if Juanita has time."

A smile tilted Elliott's lips, and she saw a twinkle in his wise old eyes. "And the second person, Miss Adriana? Are you expecting a guest, or are you especially hungry today?"

"A guest—I hope. I'm expecting him, but I'm not sure if he can make it."

"Someone I know?"

Adriana winked. "It's a surprise."

She brushed a kiss across Elliott's cheek, and decided to give him one more surprise. "I'll be staying in my suite for a few days. My guest might be staying also. I don't want anyone to know we're here."

Elliott winked back, and turned toward the house. "As you wish, Miss Adriana."

She heard the rumble of laughter in his words as he walked up the stairs.

The scents of honeysuckle, star jasmine, and roses surrounded her as she walked along the meandering path. She remembered the gardens at Magnolia Acres and the story Charlie had told her and Trevor about Carole Sinclair's death—originally murder, now suicide. Trevor *had* changed history—in a way. Maybe some things, like Carole's sad, unfortunate death, couldn't be changed, but Janet's life had taken a much happier course. As Trevor had always said, Janet was sweet. It seemed impossible that she could be a murderer.

Pushing the thought away, she snapped a red rosebud from one of the bushes and ran toward the Poseidon Pool.

Wrapping her arms around one of the marble columns, she stared at the sun's sparkling rays bouncing off the water. So peaceful. So serene.

Please, bring him back to me, she silently prayed, then moved to the edge of the pool, trying to remember exactly what she'd done before.

She kissed the rosebud, thinking of Trevor's kisses, wanting to taste them again, and tossed the rose into the pool.

"Come back to me. Please, Trevor. Come to me."

The flower floated on the surface, slowly gliding to the center of the pool. Adriana followed its movements, hoping and praying that something would happen.

Suddenly the water percolated, it churned. The rose bobbed up and down, then the water calmed.

A tear slid down her cheek.

It wasn't going to work this time.

"Please, Trevor," she begged. "Come back to me. I love you. I need you with me."

Still, nothing happened. The rose just rested on the water.

She had to do something more. She slipped out of her shoes and walked into the water, hoping her nearness would make the miracle occur. She'd stand there for a week—for a lifetime—if that's what it took.

"Please, Trevor," she urged, hoping he could hear her across sixty years in time. "Please, come to me."

The water gurgled and sputtered. A whirlpool swirled around her, building momentum as it sucked at her legs and pulled her under the water. She fought the torrent, fought her fear of drowning. She gasped for breath and swallowed the chlorinated water. It burned her throat, her eyes, her sinuses, and she struggled, trying to reach the surface.

I'm going to die, she thought, then wondered if this was all part of the plan. Was she going to join Trevor in limbo? Oh, what did it matter, as long as she was with him?

Suddenly, the whirlpool spit her out of its grasp. All around her, the water waved and crashed, then it exploded, shooting high into the air like a geyser.

She pushed hair and water from her face and her eyes. A vision appeared before her. Ebony hair. A white jacket, a black tie, and she prayed the man who'd just burst forth from the water was Trevor, and not another hallucination.

Her lips trembled as she reached out to touch the face she thought she'd only dreamed. She felt the roughness of a cheek that hadn't been shaved since early morning. Felt a dimple at the right side of his mouth, the deep cleft in his chin.

He was real. So very, very real.

Tears flowed from her eyes and mixed with the pool water cascading over her face.

And then she saw the slightest hint of the movie-idol smile she loved.

He held out his arms, and she floated into them.

There were tears in his eyes. Tears that she'd never seen before, not even in the movies.

"I love you," he whispered. "Oh, God, how I love you."

The mouth she remembered so well covered hers, not gently, but passionately, full of need and want and desire. He kissed away her fears, and kissed back all her memories of the days they'd spent together.

Her fingers tightened around his back as his hands swept down her sides, over her hips.

"You are real, aren't you?" he asked. "You're not a dream?"

"I'm just as real as you are." Her lips trembled as she hugged him tight.

"Don't leave me again, Trevor. Please."

"I'm not going anywhere," he said. "You don't have to hold me tightly to know that I'll always be by your side."

"I lost you once."

He shook his head. "You never lost me. I was in your heart, just as you were in mine. We'll always be together, Adriana—wherever we are."

She rested her head on his chest, listening once more to the familiar beat of his heart.

She felt his fingers slip beneath her knees, his hand slide around her back, as he lifted her into his arms and walked from the pool.

"It's been a long year, Adriana."

"It's been just a day for me, but it seems an eternity."

"We have a lot of catching up to do," he said, and she could feel the warmth of his lips against her brow.

"There's so much I need to tell you," she said. "About Carole. About Charlie and Janet getting married. You need to know about the movie I'm making, and how you changed history—"

"Not now, Adriana." He kissed away her words as he entered the mansion and headed up a long marble-tiled hallway. "We'll talk about all those things tomorrow."

"But you said we have a lot to catch up on."

"It's not current events I'm interested in." A wicked smile tilted his lips, and she could see fireworks—so much brighter than those on the Fourth of July—sparkling in his eyes. "What I *am* interested in is you, and making up for all the days and nights we've been apart."

She fought back the tears of happiness swelling behind her eyes, and held on tight as he raced up the sweeping staircase and shouldered through the tall, heavy doors leading into the suite that had once been Harrison's, but now indelibly belonged to them. Just like the hero in so many movies—but so much better—he carried her across the ancient carpets, giving little thought to the water dripping from their hair and clothes, concentrating only on her lips, her eyes, the tip of her nose.

Pressing one foot against the door at the far end of the room, he shoved it open and took her to the bed where they'd first made love, and laid her down in its downy softness.

"God, how I missed you." His words were little more than a whisper, spoken tenderly as he sat at her side and curled a lock of hair behind her ear. "Every night and every day, I prayed that you'd come to me, or that I could somehow find my way back to you. I kissed a lot of roses and made a lot of wishes. I hoped they'd come true—and now they have."

She smiled softly at the man who'd shown her that life, with all its trials, was better than what she'd seen on a movie screen. "You were a dream to me, but now you're real. There's nothing more I could ever wish for."

"Nothing at all?"

She cupped his beard-roughened cheek in her palm. "You're all I need."

He drew his fingers away from her hair, and reached toward the bedside table. From a tall crystal vase he plucked a long red rose, and held it between them. He lightly brushed the velvety petals across her lips, then kissed it himself, just as she'd done while standing by the Poseidon Pool. Then he set it on the pillow alongside her hair.

Slowly, ever so slowly, he kissed her. "I love you, Adriana. You wished me into your life, and I came to you. Now . . . there's just one more wish I want to make."

He held her near and gazed lovingly into her eyes, just like the closing scene in so many of his movies. But this embrace wasn't scripted, it wasn't rehearsed. And *The End* would never flash before them.

"Tell me what you'd wish for, Trevor."

He smiled, and whispered softly against her lips. "A million more tomorrows with you."

Dear Reader,

Coming next month from Avon Romance are terrific stories—historical and contemporary—beginning with *Perfect in My Sight*, the latest from bestselling author Tanya Anne Crosby. Sarah Woodard and her cousin Mary had vowed never to wed, but Mary breaks that vow. Now, she has died under mysterious circumstances, and Sarah travels to meet her dear cousin's husband for the first time. Sarah has no reason to trust Peter, but she begins to find it impossible to resist his charms . . .

If you like western settings, then don't miss Karen Kay's *White Eagle's Touch*, the next installment of the Blackfoot Warriors series. Katrina is a wealthy English socialite travelling west; White Eagle is the proud and powerful Blackfoot warrior who once saved her life. Together they find an unforgettable love that spans their two worlds.

For fans of Regency settings, don't miss Marlene Suson's *Kiss Me Goodnight*. The devilishly charming Marquess of Sherbourne never expected to be so entranced by radiant redhead Katherine McNamara, but her fiery kisses quickly ignite passion's flame in this seductive, sensuous love story.

And if you prefer a more modern setting, don't miss *Baby, I'm Yours* by Susan Andersen. The last place Catherine MacPherson ever expected to find herself was sitting on a bus, handcuffed to a sexy bounty hunter, with only a suitcase of her twin sister's shrink-wrap clothing to wear. Sam MacKade doesn't care how irresistible Catherine is, he doesn't believe for a minute that Catherine *isn't* her showgirl sister. Will Sam solve this case of mistaken identity and lose his heart at the same time?

Look to Avon for romance at its best! Until next month, enjoy.

Lucia Macro

Lucia Macro
Senior Editor

AEL 0498